EQUILIBRIUM

JAMES LUTHI

To my family, wife and children for your love and support and for being shining lights in an otherwise dark world. Thank you for daring me to reach.

Dark Wing
PRESS

CHAPTER 1

Nick strained to blink away the fading black from his eyes as the room slowly blurred into shape. His crawling skin caused him to shudder as sensation began to flow through his body again. His hands trembled slightly as his nerves seemed to be calming down from being, what, electrified, maybe? Being electrocuted could have explained what he was feeling. His senses were on fire but somehow numb at the same time. The simple act of opening his eyes felt like trying to hoist theater curtains.

Another shudder ran through him, a feeling of violation, of trespass. He tried to put the scene together in his mind and realized he didn't remember what day it was. He imagined that this listless feeling of sluggish rapport with his senses must be how a statue, being animated for the first time, may have felt. He tried to sit up but had the impression of a weight pressing down on his chest. He strained his mind to animate his limbs.

Nick continued to lay on his bed, mentally assessing his condition. His muscles twitched and ached as they responded to his mental commands as if being driven by a remote. He became aware of a pounding sensation at the back of his head that thrummed like a slow breathing squid.

Nick's self-analysis was interrupted by a fog of some memory fragment trying to push its way to the forefront of his mind. His thoughts seized on an idea. He was supposed to be somewhere else. He wasn't sure where but not here in this room.

Nick strained against the thump in the back of his head as it seemed to gain slightly more vigor before it eased again. *I'm on vacation,* he thought. *Tikal? Am I? Why is my mind so damned disengaged?*

Nick strained to sit up again. His second attempt yielded him only slightly more success than his first. Nick made a slow scan of the room then realized where he was. *No, not Tikal. Home.*

God. What the hell did I get into? Did I get blackout drunk last night? As soon as the thought cleared his mind, he immediately thought that getting hammered and then wishing yourself home in a drunken haze didn't seem right either. Nick had not been a heavy drinker since college.

So okay, not some epic college-style drunk fest, he decided. The closest thing to what Nick was currently feeling, of which he could almost think to compare it, was the time when he had gotten his tonsils removed.

Nick, Little Nicky was his most used moniker at that age, had awakened in a recovery room at eight years old in a post-surgical haze. A nurse stood over him, telling him he needed to try and wake up and drink something. Nick's strength had been surgically and pharmacologically removed. His body wanted to function, but just the act of standing up was labor. The drugs still in his small system caused his arms and legs to respond like alien appendages. What he felt now was the same, like someone had drugged him, pulled part of him out, then left him to deal with the aftermath.

Nick questioned whether he should go to the hospital then quickly decided against this idea. He had no idea how to *begin* to explain what was going on with him, much less how he had arrived in this particular form.

Nick tried again to sit up. Moving his head maybe ten inches up from his pillow, then falling back down with an exhaling breath. Pausing, then trying again, Nick groaned his way up to a sitting position. As he looked around the room, he began the seemingly arduous task of moving the dead weight of his body to the side of the bed. He eventually maneuvered himself to the edge of the bed and slogged his legs over the edge as if he were a sloth having a bad day. Sitting with his legs dangling from the bed, he felt more fragile than when he had been lying down as he struggled to steady his shaky spine. He sat for about five minutes, measuring whether his strength was returning or still on pause. Nick looked down at his legs and questioned whether they were trustworthy.

Just as Nick decided to give his legs a bit more time to build up some steam, he had an unsettling thought. Nick's childhood memories were images of a drug-addicted mother out of tune with reality. Day after day, year after year, growing up in that destruction made Nick far too familiar with mental illness. Then there was his grandmother, who had shot her first husband's head off with a shotgun. You name it, from depression to schizophrenia to violent tendencies, Nick, unfortunately, was familiar with all of it.

Even though Nick's family history supported a complete mental illness record, he had not worried much about it over the years. The thought now loomed in his mind as he awakened with no remembrance of how he had gotten home. Nick was beginning to think he was taking a significant first step toward spending the rest of his days in a fuzzy bathrobe and slippers.

Is that what this is? Nick asked himself. He quickly decided that he was not going crazy, insane, getting ready for the wacko shack. This just didn't seem like a mental type of thing to him. Neurological, maybe, but not mental. He sighed as his thoughts seemed to shift again, wavering in and out of some strange unreality.

Something's wrong here, but it can't be, he gave his head a mind-clearing rattle and refused to finish the thought, lacking the courage to draw his sanity into question as a possible explanation.

Having now made his way to a seated position on the edge of the bed, Nick tried to stand, slowly testing his alien legs. He didn't have full confidence in his ability to walk, but he thought they seemed to be getting stronger.

As Nick stood, he focused on balance and stability while more of his senses continued to rouse. He noticed a faint whiff of a familiar odor filling the room. Nick knew the smell but did not recognize its source immediately. He smelled the air again then he remembered the aroma floating through his room. Ozone. The charged smell of stale, battle-scarred atmosphere. Nick knew the smell of ozone was typically only produced by a supercharged thunderstorm, a banger, as his mom used to say. Nick could still hear its distant thunder exploding like iron bombs on a battlefield.

That was one hell of a banger, he thought.

He listened a moment more to the far-off rumbles of God working at his anvil. Nick thought the storm that had just passed over his house must have indeed been a banger to leave the air smelling fried.

A gentle breeze caused Nick to turn. The gentle stroke on his cheek was the calm reassurance you often feel after a late summer storm has passed. The breeze gently stroked Nick's face as it wafted in from an open window to tell him the chaos of the angry atmosphere had gone. Nick noticed the breeze coming from an open window, resulting in the rain pouring into the room and soaking his bedroom floor. The puddle left covered nearly a third of the room.

Nick always awakened during thunderstorms, having persistent anxiety about tornados. Why then had he not awakened during this storm, which must have sounded like a marching band rehearsal? With enough energy to fry the air in its wake, Nick should have awakened after the first few strikes, much less during the heart of the storm's passing. Even small boomers caused Nick to get up, check the weather app on his phone and watch for signs of the ninja stroke of an attacking torrent. Nick took a breath to clear his thoughts as the numbness continued to fade from his limbs. He questioned again how he had gotten home safely.

Just as his last thought was fading into the mud of this waking moment, Nick became aware he was standing relatively stable. Most of the wobbling had subsided. Just as he was beginning to trust them, a sudden shudder shot down his legs that threatened to fold his knees.

Nick swung his arms like a balancing pendulum. He drew in a deep breath that caused his ribs to burn with dull fire. He held it for about three seconds then exhaled. There was a flash of unexpected intensity on the left side of Nick's ribcage, as well as in his left shoulder. After the moment of uncertainty passed, he lowered his arms and caressed his burning ribs.

Nick's thoughts slogged again, firing in slow motion. It was like everything around him was running at double time, but his thoughts were moving like a snail traversing a twig.

Man, my ass is dragging, and what the hell did I do to myself? Nick questioned, then made a slow plod toward his bathroom.

Nick stood over his toilet, relieving himself when he noticed the air in his condo was a thick, steamy encasement wrapping around his body like a blanket. The air conditioning was not running. Nick knew the air would have to be switched off, not broken. The condo's management staff monitored the air units and temps in every tenant's condo. The heating and air system had been upgraded about eighteen months ago to allow twenty-four-hour diagnostics and reporting on unit performance and servicing intervals. Maintenance would know if the control unit for his condo was not working and would have repaired it, so it must have been switched off for some reason.

Why would the air be off? It's August, for shit's sake. The fog of confusion thickened in Nick's mind again. He walked from the toilet over to the AC controller and stared at it, questioning why the AC was off in mid-August. It just didn't make sense.

From July to around mid-September, Georgia's climate transformed into a balmy tropical soup. If you lived in Georgia during a regular summer season, you knew how every day would feel outside the confines of your comfortable, artificially adjusted indoor climate. You are hit in that face with a furnace blast of wearable air each time you opened your front door. The atmosphere becomes an on-demand, open-air sauna.

Nick decided he was tired of puzzling over the climate control unit's switch position. He flicked the controller to auto, verified the temperature setting, then began to move back toward the bathroom.

About halfway across the room, he stopped. When Nick had

moved his stiff arm up to flick the AC control unit to on, he noticed, although it took a moment for his brain to register what he was seeing, that he had awakened from this surreal sleep still wearing the clothes he had been wearing on the second day of his vacation. He looked down and saw he was still wearing his hiking boots as well. Not only was he wearing the same clothes he had put on the second day of his trip, but he also noticed they were now tattered rags. He examined his shirt and noted a covering seemingly held together now by stains, dirt, and just general unknown filth. He saw his pants and boots were just as filthy. Nick took another breath, and his eyes began to water. God, did he stink. Now that his nose was working again, Nick thought his shirt smelled like it must have been used to wipe a dead man's ass. Nick started to put a hand over his nose and then stopped after seeing how dirty they were. He started again toward the bathroom.

As Nick approached the bathroom door, he paused, straining for a glimpse of clarity. He looked around the room for his phone, hoping to check the time and date.

"Great, I hope I didn't lose another phone," he thought, "That phone was only two months old."

Nick sauntered toward the bathroom, pulling his shirt up over his head and dropping it on the bathroom floor as he walked through the door. He sat down on the edge of the tub, pulled his shoes off, then finished disrobing. After a few careless groping moments, Nick found the shower control and turned the knob. The showerhead burst into life as it poured out fresh cleansing rain. Nick stepped into the shower and began to lather himself. The water, which closely resembled sewer sludge running down his body, puddled around his feet on its way down the drain.

CHAPTER 2

Gerald walked over to hover beside Ethan's desk and stood silently waiting with his hands in his pockets. Ethan stopped typing and looked up.

"Hey, Ethan," Gerald said. "I am getting throughput complaints from the Weatherly, Hawkins, and Winder Law firm."

"What kind of complaints?"

"You know," Gerald replied, "the usual list of suspects. It takes forever to open a document. My email seems slow. It took four seconds for a YouTube video to start. You know, the usual list. Probably nothing, but we need to check it so the monthly will show the activity on the request."

Ethan was very aware as to which monthly Gerald was referring. Any of Core Tech's clientele could at any time request a report of work order status and history. Most of the company's customers could care less about the information. The anally visceral clients would expect their statement to show up on command or at scheduled intervals so the report could be scoured for any hint of misdealing or sluffery for which they could argue for discounts and refunds for services. The Weatherly, Hawkins, and Winder Law firm was an especially tight-fisted case. Ethan often mused how surprisingly ironic it was that a law firm would hold such a vice-like grip on their own wallets while expending so much energy trying to find pennies to recover in every report, which they demanded to be delivered weekly when their whole existence was based on chasing ambulances. They would sue other companies into oblivion over things like a squashed grape on a grocery store floor or a patch of ice on a city sidewalk in front of an accountant's office, which would cause some hungover drunk to take a slip and break his tailbone. The Weatherly, Hawkins, and Winder Law firm had single-handedly caused six sales team members to quit rather than handle their account.

Gerald continued, "I don't think you'll find anything. We just upgraded that router two weeks ago, so it's still on the enhanced watch list in the NOC for another two days. So far, the NOC hasn't alerted any new codebase issues. No throughput, route flap, or any other issues."

Ethan leaned back in his chair and rolled his eyes, to which Gerald replied, "Look, just take a quick look. Remember what I always say about the people you should never piss off."

Ethan delivered Gerald an unenthusiastic sidelong glance. One of Gerald's favorite pieces of wisdom to share was the two people you should never piss off are your accountant or your attorney.

"Yeah, I get it," Ethan replied, "but lawyers are by far the whiniest bunch to deal with. They complain the most, have the most imaginary issues and are ever only *adequately* satisfied with any work you do for them. Then they bitch about their bills every month and try to throw shade at the techs. It's like it can never be easy or straightforward with them."

Gerald held up his hand then calmly said, "And they pay *your* check and mine. Look, I get it. I hate dealing with them most times, but they are our best customers, right behind the doctors' offices. We need to keep them happy. Just take a quick look so we can show the activity on the work order, then I'll make them go away as soon as you see it's all good," he paused a moment, then added, "I mean, unless you find a real issue."

"You know I'm going to look. I just need to vent sometimes. Those guys are especially aggravating, and my job load has more than doubled since we lost Nick. I'm already buried today, dude."

Gerald nodded and said, "I know. Nick being gone has put us all in a bind. He's also proven to be not so easy to replace. The guys I've been interviewing for his replacement should apply for internships. I mean, what the hell exactly are they teaching at these schools nowadays. These poor kids aren't learning anything, well, nothing job applicable anyway. But hey look," Gerald motioned to Ethan and himself, "we still have a job to do."

Ethan swiveled his chair toward Gerald, palmed his cheeks, and made a surprised face, making himself resemble the man in Edvard Munch's The Scream, and said with a gasp, "Wow, what philosophical insight Socrates. Please pour your wisdoms into my brain."

"Alright, fine, you don't have to be an ass."

"Ah, you know I'm joking," Ethan replied. "I don't have anyone to bitch at anymore. Nick was my sour shoulder when I needed to shit on someone. Nick being gone has still got me a little off rocker. I can't get it off my mind." Ethan picked up his cell phone and opened the Notes app, then said, "Whatever. I know there's nothing I can do about it—"

Gerald interrupted in a melodic tone, "And you're a little controlling."

Ethan cocked his head to the side and started to say something, then Gerald added, "Well, you are about some things."

"Fine. Agree to disagree. What router do I need to check?"

"It's rack thirteen router six. It's on the service order."

"Okay," Ethan acknowledged as he typed the number into his Notes app, "13 06. Got it."

Gerald spun and began a brisk walk toward his office to catch the phone ringing on his desk. Ethan pulled up the company documentation for router 13 06 and tried to access it. When the session timed out, he tried again. After four more attempts, he closed his eyes and sighed as he muttered, "Ah shit."

The router was online, but he couldn't connect to it. *Someone must have disabled the remote server,* Ethan thought. *Great, now I'll have to drive to the datacenter and stand around there with my thumb in my ass while the center validates my card again.*

It had been over a month since Ethan had needed to drive over to the data center. Six months earlier, the data center had implemented new security protocols that stated any access card not used in over thirty days would have to be re-cleared for access before it could be used. Ethan had heard the other techs in the office bitching about the new protocols, so he knew the entire process took between forty-five minutes to an hour and a half to complete.

There's a waste of the rest of the afternoon.

Ethan knew his biometric data stayed active until revoked because it's a lot harder to line up people like herds of cattle and run them through two biometric scans a month to keep the system current. Yet, that little plastic card will shit on the whole process every time.

The check-in process for data center access was simple, if not a bit aggravating at times. When you walked into the data center, you were met by a security guard. You were assigned a plastic RFID proximity reader card that let you into the facility's first floor and granted you elevator access after checking in with the guard at the desk. Once in the elevator, your fingerprint activated the floors for which the elevator is authorized to deposit you. When you arrived at one of your authorized floors, you had to submit to a retina scan to access the actual data equipment room.

Ethan packed his computer and other supplies into this bag then walked across the open office to Gerald's door. Ethan stopped in the entrance, then reached up and softly knocked softly on the open door.

Gerald was looking out his office window, still on the phone, easing the anxious nerves of some client on the other end of the line. He spun his chair around and held up one.

"I can guarantee that I will have my top engineer on this in the next 3 minutes," Gerald reassured the client. "I understand. Believe me. I am as concerned about this as you. Well, I would say that I am more concerned about this because it's our responsibility to make sure you don't have to worry about these things." He paused to listen to the caller, then replied, "Believe me. We're on it. Absolutely. Absolutely. Expect an update within the hour. Absolutely. No ma'am, thank you. Bye-bye now."

Gerald hung up the phone and fell back into his office chair to exaggerate his exhaustion. He let out an exaggerated, "Wooooo!" then sat up in his chair and looked at Ethan.

"Who was that?" Ethan asked.

"That, my good man, was Ms. Iris Ildabar of the SFP."

"Who?"

"You know. The lady who runs the SFP. The Society for Fauna Preservation. It's that group up in Cobb who runs the preservation group that raises money for protecting all the poor defenseless animals in the southeast."

"I wasn't aware that there were any endangered species in the southeast."

"Yeah, apparently, we have some water boogers and a couple of fish that are classified as at-risk."

"Okay," Ethan said slowly, "So, what's up with them?"

"Nothing really. She has this guy who keeps forgetting his password."

Ethan raised his eyebrows, "So you told her you were going to put your 'best tech' on a forgotten password?"

Gerald gave Ethan a sly grin. "Yes, Ethan, I told her my 'best tech' would be assigned to it immediately to verify that there was no egregious breach of security."

Ethan stared at Gerald for about 5 seconds, then said, "Since we lost Nick, *I'm* the best tech you have, and I am leaving for the day."

Gerald laughed softly. "Yes, you *are* the best engineer we have now. I am going to assign this one to the new guy. You know…", then he trailed off, paused briefly, and seemed to be checking his office ceiling for the answer as he snapped his fingers, "What's the new guy's name? You know the guy we brought on a couple of weeks ago. The one we both think won't cut it." Then Gerald's eyes shot wide, and he threw his arms out in front of him as he half yelled, "Don! The new guy is Don."

Ethan liked Gerald, but sometimes he thought it would be fun to tie Gerald's hands behind his back, then watch him try to talk. To say Gerald was animated be a vast understatement.

"Gerald," Ethan said, "I'm surprised that dude can find his way to the office most days."

"Yep, but he can reset this guy's password then call Ms. Ildabar in 45 minutes to reassure her that there was no evidence of a security breach. We'll say the password must have been corrupted due to a system error. We'll tell her it was corruption in the encoding hash algorithm in the password database—"

"An encoding hash algorithm error? That's horseshit."

"Yeah, but at the end of the day, we need to make our customers feel safe, secure, well-kept, and most of all, not stupid. And *stupid* is precisely how they will feel if I tell them they should quit hiring people who have never seen a computer or were born when the printing press was new.

Ethan stared at Gerald, "Seems a bit exhausting to me."

"Yes. It is exhausting." Gerald replied, leaning back in his chair. "But, it's the politics of the job. It's the relationship management aspect. Never make the customer feel like they have made a bad decision or like their problems are not real or unimportant. Spoon feed them." He fed himself with an imaginary spoon to stress the point, then smiled, "After all, you care. And I really do care. It's just that this guy forgets his password every week."

"I don't know him. I haven't dealt with them."

"Oh well. Anyway, what's up? Did you check the router?"

Ethan took a couple of steps into Gerald's office, "Yeah, that's the bad news. It's one-thirty, and I have to go to the datacenter."

Gerald stopped creating the new work order for the SFP and looked up, "Why do you have to go to the datacenter for an imaginary throughput issue?"

"Well, that is the issue. It may not be imaginary."

"What does that mean?"

"Well, we thought it was another imaginary issue, and the root of it probably is, but the overnight techs may have done something to the router. I was logged into that router yesterday, but I couldn't get a console session when I tried to access it today. It's online and functioning, but something may be misconfigured. So, I need to go on-site to access the local console to figure out what's going on with it. The bigger issue is that I have not been there in over 30 days, and you know the new datacenter rules."

Gerald groaned, "Yeah, the new policies. You'll have to go through re-validation." He shook his head. "That place is harder to get into than virgin asshole."

"Well, it's kind of supposed to be," Ethan said.

"I know, but you had a full plate today. With it being a Friday afternoon, you're pretty much screwed. You won't be home until 7 or 8 tonight now."

"Yep. That's about what I figure."

"Well, I guess it is what it is. Be careful on the drive and just get it done, I guess." To that, Ethan gave a two-finger salute and turned to make his way to the parking garage.

CHAPTER 3

Kiera was sitting at the table holding a large Caramel Macchiato with the lid off, blowing softly across the surface of her drink to cool down the molten rage the barista had given her. She put the cup to her lips to test the temperature, then quickly pulled it away as she licked her upper lip and sat it back down. By this time, Tabetha had collected her order from the counter and was pulling a chair out from under the table so she could sit to be an ear for Kiera's woes.

Tabby reached across the table and offered Kiera's hand a squeeze. Kiera looked up from the steaming Macchiato she had been studying.

"What's up?" asked Tabby. "I can tell you were having an off morning when you called. Was it another dream?"

Keira started to speak, then closed her mouth, unsure how to begin. She breathed as if a weight had been slung around her shoulders. Tabby could see a slight tremor in Kiera's hands and movement in Kiera's shoulders from her hitching breath. Tabby could also see shiny diamonds forming in Kiera's eyes. She was biting her lower lip almost to the point of blood. Kiera sat, breathing in small, uneven breaths. Tabby sat back.

"Just sit for a minute," Tabby suggested. "I have no place to be. I cleared my day."

The two ladies sat in silence for a few moments until Kiera shuffled in her seat, picked up a napkin, and blotted the corner of both eyes. She took in another deep, chuffing breath, picked up her Macchiato, and took a small sip. After sitting the drink down, she looked at Tabby.

"I had that dream again last night," Kiera began, "only this time it felt real. I woke up around three-thirty again. Terrified. I was shaking and couldn't catch my breath." Her voice broke on the word 'breath,' and she began to cry softly. After a moment, she continued, "It's never been that intense before. My clothes were soaked. It felt like waking up from a fever dream. I was so scared I went through the entire house and turned on every light. I've never needed to do anything like that before. I've never been afraid in my own home." Her face warped into an expression of angry violation, then she continued, "It was like I just needed to have light. I just had to be out of the dark. Ten minutes after I got up, I was still shaking."

"It was just a dream," Tabby said as she reached out and gently squeezed Kiera's hand again. "Look, you've had a lot of emotional turbulence the past couple of months. Everyone knows how serious you and Nick had gotten, and I understand the strain you are under right now."

Keira winced and thought, *There it is again, 'had gotten,' in the past tense.*

"I know, but this time the dream was different," Kiera replied. "It was darker. More twisted. In the dream, I felt like reality itself was warping, shifting, and beginning to, I don't know, melt."

"Melt. How does reality melt?"

"I don't know. In the dream, I just knew everything was ending. I felt like I was being sucked out of myself somehow. Like some force was," then she paused, "Like something was pulling me away from myself. I could see it, whatever it was, but I couldn't really make it out. There was nothing there, but there was something."

Tabby sat, patiently listening to Kiera's recounting of the dread and fear over the dreams that had been plaguing her over the past two months. Tabby knew that a person's mind could cause them to blend reality and fantasy into scenes every bit as real as the drink she was holding if given the proper setup and environment. While Kiera's environment was supportive and present, having one's soon-to-be fiancé vanish from the world like a morning fog fits nicely into providing the proper setup for intense reality blending.

Kiera continued, "I don't know how I knew, in the dream, I mean, that Nick was the source of the decay somehow. Nick was there, but it wasn't Nick. It was like I knew it was Nick, but it was really someone, something else."

Suddenly Keira snapped back in her chair and scowled at Tabby. "Don't look at me like that. I'm not crazy, and you're the only one I can talk to about this." Keira's eyes filled with tears, the uncontrollable ones this time. She kept her head down, holding her hand over her mouth, and tried to keep her sobs quiet so she would not bring unwanted attention to their conversation.

Tabby placed a hand on her shoulder and said, "Kiera, look at me." Kiera wiped her eyes with the napkin again and slowly looked up. "It was a dream. I have had vivid dreams before too. Terrifying ones. You have been under enormous emotional strain for two months, which has caused these images to intensify. It is your mind's way of trying to cope, to get you past the stress, but they are just dreams."

"That's what I thought," Keira snapped.

Tabby waited for Kiera's next statement, giving her time to frame what she wanted to say next.

Kiera straightened in the chair, pulled her hands away from Tabby, then began wringing them together in her lap. She continued looking down at her Macchiato, then said in a whisper, "He's back," When Tabby said nothing, Kiera looked up so there could be no misunderstanding and said again, "He's back Tabby."

"What? Honey, there's not been a…." Tabby, remembering that hers was a position to listening, not advisement, stopped and started again by asking, "What are you talking about, sweetie? Tell me. What's happened?"

Kiera was no longer crying but had begun biting her lip again.

"Honey," Tabby said, "please tell me what is going on."

"After I woke up, I knew that there was no going back to sleep. So, after I calmed down, I took a shower. I was changing the sheets when I got another one of those yearnings. You know, I've told you about them before. I had to see Nick's place. It was like an ache in my gut."

"I remember. You said it helped you feel close to him again."

"Yes. It's stupid, I know, but it does help. I've gone to that condo twenty times since his disappearance. I just couldn't shake wanting to see it. I just wanted to hear his voice again, and I don't know, to remember the smell of his cologne. This morning I had that feeling stronger than ever, so I drove to the condo again.

As Tabby studied Kiera's expressions, her body language, the strain of her voice, she began to understand that she may not have realized the depth of Kiera's pain and the bleakness of her longing for answers.

Tabby softly started, "It was—"

"A dream. Yeah, I know." Keira shot back through clenched teeth, "That's what I thought too until I saw him in his fucking bedroom this morning."

After a stunned moment, she asked, "What? Did you talk to him? What was he doing?"

Keira continued, "I am sure it was him. I wanted to go beat the door down. I didn't. But I know it was Nick. Something just began to roll in my stomach, and I couldn't go up. It was like something held me there. I couldn't move."

"But, Kiera, if it was Nick—"

Kiera saw that all color had drained from Tabby's face.

"I am one hundred percent certain that it was Nick, Tabby. He was wearing the same clothes he had been wearing in his last Instagram post on the second day of his trip, the shirt anyway. That's all I could see through the window. Another thing was that a huge thunderstorm had just passed. Nick's window was open through the entire storm. He never got up and closed it. That was odd too. Nick never leaves his windows open. He got up a few minutes after the storm passed. I thought I had lost my mind at first. Then he got up from his bed and started moving away from the window. He looked terrible. I'm telling you it was Nick. I was too scared to go talk to him." Kiera stopped speaking and began to weep again.

Scanning the café, Tabby noticed that the room had begun to watch the pair of them as if they were a new reality show. Several patrons were staring and murmuring behind menus to one another. *Oh crap!* Tabby thought. *She doesn't need this.* Tabby snatched her purse from the table and stood up as she said, "Let's go down the block to the park and finish this conversation. Too many assholes in here with too much free time." Kiera quickly did a passive scan of the café and noted several pairs of eyes enjoying the show that was neither their business nor their concern.

"Yeah," she said. "Let's go."

A couple of blocks down the street, they found an unoccupied park bench and sat down. Kiera turned to Tabby, "I can't understand why I couldn't go to him. I mean, it was like getting a second chance at life, but I just froze. Every fiber of me wanted to run across the street and beat the door off its hinges. It's like my feet just wouldn't move. The only way I could get unfrozen was to move away. To get away from him and away from the window."

"Kiera, I am going to ask again. Are you sure it was him? His bedroom *is* on the second floor."

"Yes," Keira replied with a sigh. "Nick and I had such instant chemistry that we have spent as many waking and sleeping minutes with each other as we could since we started dating. I would know it was him from a hundred yards away."

Kiera looked out over the park and asked, "What are we supposed to do now? He didn't even call any of us, Tabby."

Tabby thought for a moment, seeming to be formulating a plan, then said, "Here's what I think. First of all, you shouldn't be around him until we know what happened. I mean, we can't begin to understand his mental state, so I think it would be a risk for you to try to meet him without others around. Secondly, Ethan. Ethan will know what to do and how to handle this. He's spent more time with Nick than anyone. They've been working together for six years now. He should be able to figure this out."

Kiera looked out across the park. A young man dressed in red and white joggers and a Georgia Bulldogs shirt walked a Beagle named

Rusty. Keira knew the dog's name was Rusty because the man was close enough that she heard him use the dog's name a couple of times while trying to teach the little hound how to sit and stay. The young dog began to argumentatively mule and howl at his owner. Rusty bellowed whoup, whoup, in his hound dog moan to express his displeasure with his owner's instructions.

"No, Rusty. Stay. This is good for you to learn. Stop arguing with me," the young man begged.

Then again. Another outburst from the aggravated puppy, "Yop yop. Yoooooooup," the beagle exclaimed in another bellow of hound dog drawl, this time a blend of howl and yelp.

"Okay, Rusty. One treat. No more until you sit." The man held out a treat to Rusty, who quickly gobbled it from his owner's hands.

"Ohohyop," Rusty yelped this time, half howling and half barking.

The man gave Rusty another treat then the beagle began to tug on his leash, wanting to walk further down the park's lawn as he buried his sniffer in the grass, hunting his next trail.

"Rusty, please. Stop." The man called as he followed after the pup.

Two middle-aged women jogged past, drawing Kiera's attention away for Rusty and his trainer. A small distance away from the bench, Kiera saw two young mothers policing the playground area with two children who looked to be three or four years old. The park was bright, clean, with still green grass even though it should have turned that dirty yellowish-brown color as lawns do when fall approaches. The sun was warm but not hot. A cool breeze blew across the park from the cold front that passed through with the morning storms. Keira soaked in the activity and thought, *How can such a gorgeous day be so unquestioningly sour?* It just didn't seem fair.

Suddenly Tabby broke in on Keira's thoughts. "Okay. Let's do this step by step and see if we can make sense of any of it. Let's slow down and go over everything again. I'm here, just you and me, so let's start from the dream and go over everything slowly and calmly to see if we can make any sense of what he was doing."

"Okay."

"Later, we can talk to Ethan about this tonight. We also need to go to your place so you can pack an overnight bag."

"Why do I need an—"

"I don't want to stay up all night worrying about you. I want you to stay with Ethan and me tonight. Please." Kiera didn't argue. She just nodded in agreement and began to sob again, but this time Tabby thought she saw what looked like relief on Kiera's face.

Tabby placed her hand on Kiera's shoulder and began to rub, "Hey, stop that. Come on. Calm down. We're going to figure this out. There has got to be something we are not seeing yet. Come on. Let's go over it again."

Then slowly, and much calmer, Keira began her story again, starting with the dream.

CHAPTER 4

Kiera and Tabby had spent the better part of an hour at the park going over the details of Kiera's seeing Nick and of her dream. After a while, they decided nothing was any clearer than when they began rehashing the morning's events. The two ladies collected their purses and their now empty cups, which they deposited in the nearest refuse bin, and began to make their way back over to their cars.

As they approached their parking spaces, Kiera asked, "So, to my house first, then to yours?"

"Yes." Tabby replied, "I want to follow you over there. Since you last saw Nick, it's been four or five hours, so I want to make sure he hasn't tried to come over to your house, at least not until we know what's going on. When we get there, I want you to get enough stuff to last at least a week."

"A week? Why a week?"

"Because we don't know how long it will take to get this sorted out, and I don't want you to be by yourself. Sweetie, I'm not leaving you hanging after the last two months of riding an emotional shit tornado to work this all out on your own."

"Okay," Kiera agreed as Tabby got into her car.

"Hey," Kiera called while knocking on Tabby's passenger side window. Tabby lowered the window, and Kiera leaned in and asked, "What if he went to *your* house?"

Tabby considered for a moment, then shook her head, "I wouldn't think he'd go there first."

"He and Ethan are best friends, Tabby. If he's going through something or gotten *into* something, he may want a friend too. Ethan is his closest friend."

"Maybe. If so, my security cameras will catch any activity at our house and alert me. Look, it'll probably be like an hour or two before we even get there. It's," Tabby looked at the time on her dashboard display, "four-thirty. We probably won't get to my house before six-thirty, and we can push that time even later if you want to stop and grab a bite before we go home."

"Okay. Let's do that." Kiera agreed, "By then, maybe Ethan should be home from work."

"Alright. Let's get going then."

On arriving at Kiera's house, they pulled into the paved drive and parked alongside one another. After exiting their vehicles, both ladies stood for a moment scanning the house and surrounding area, looking for any sign there had been, or were still, any visitors. Kiera held up her house keys, jiggled them nervously, and motioned for Tabby to follow her into the house.

They walked cautiously up the walkway toward the front door. Kiera continued scanning the front of her house, remembering how she felt when she awakened from her nightmare. She now thought the two large windows in front of the house looked more like two prying eyes and the giant red door, a monstrous mouth stretching open to devour her. Kiera made a mental note to change the door color as soon as she had time. Kiera's hands trembled, and the pulse. The pulse in her surging heart sounded like the deepening thuds of hammer blows in her ears.

Once they reached the door, Kiera slid the key into the lock then stopped. She stayed locked in a momentary haze as thoughts about the dream, remembering again the way Nick had looked through the window along with all the surreal foolishness of Nick showing back up. As she held, vanishing deeper into her thoughts, something touched her shoulder. She jumped, let out a yelp, and spun around only to find that in her hesitation, Tabby had reached up to put a reassuring hand on her shoulder.

"Holy shit," Keira said with wide eyes. "I seriously forgot that you were even behind me. Ah! I'm way too wound up right now. You scared the shit out of me."

Kiera stood with the back of her right hand pressed against her forehead, her chest heaving. She could feel the stickiness from the sweat that had begun to bead on her forehead.

Tabby grabbed Keira's shoulders, gave her a single, reassuring pat with both hands, then said, "Hey. It's Okay." She spoke slowly, trying to convey confidence by using a calm, measured tone. "Look, if he were here, he probably would have shown up by now. It's going to take you a month to open that damn door at the rate you're going." Keira smiled and began to laugh as a sensation of relief ran down her back and through her tensed shoulders.

"Yeah, you're right. You're right. I have myself completely freaked out."

"Yeah. So, calm down before you get me freaked two. There is nothing in the world worse than two hysterical women with no assess around to kick. Now, let's open that door, get your stuff, and get on the road."

"Alright. Yeah."

As they walked to their cars after collecting a week's worth of Kiera's things, Kiera said, "Okay, see you at your house."

"Hey, we have to make a stop on the way," Tabby replied.

"Where?"

"The liquor store."

"Ah, okay, I guess."

"Yeah, tonight we are going to sit up, talk, unwind, and just be the girls until we decide the day is over. No rules tonight."

Kiera started to protest, but Tabby interrupted by holding up her hands and saying, "I know it's not your *thing*, but you need to unwind and get some real rest, so it's screwdrivers all night." Kiera looked at Tabby, uncertain. "Yep, we're getting shitfaced, baby."

"I don't know about—"

"No. No. No," Tabby cut in, "No arguments tonight. You need to unwind, and you will be with your two best friends. Safe, secure, and as worry-free as you're going to get right now, so, yes, shitfaced." Tabby had a huge grin on her face as she waited for Keira's response.

"Okay," Kiera said, giving up and shaking her head, "I guess you're the captain tonight then. Let's get going, mom." Kiera smiled for the first time that day as she thought, *Tabby always knows how to pull me out of a funk.*

CHAPTER 5

Traffic, Ethan thought as he maneuvered his black Chevy Tahoe into the far-right lane of I285, *must be God's way of reminding us humans that at the end of the day, we really are just ants.* He had crept closer to the head of the clog and could now see this was no usual pileup. The interstate tussle was an eight-car pileup, with one of those cars being an overturned tractor-trailer. Ethan could see raw animal bits and pieces strewn across the roadway. It looked as if the top of the load hauler's roof had burst open and spilled the trailer's contents as it came to an abrupt stop, lying flat on its side across three lanes of traffic.

"It's gonna suck to be the guy who has to clean up that mess," Ethan said softly to himself as he watched a department of transportation front-end loader roar to life. It spewed a thick, acrid diesel cloud from its stack as it started a slow crawl toward the spilled contents of the big rig's cargo trailer.

I'm glad it's not rush hour, he told himself. *This would've been a three-hour traffic jam for a mess like this.*

After Ethan had gotten into his car to leave the data center, he reached for his charging cable and had grabbed air. "Ah crap," he groaned, leaning back in his seat. Ethan owned three or four charging cables at one time, but over the course of time and inconsiderate use, he was now down to only one non-defective charging cable, which was still lying atop his desk back at the office. He put his hands on the steering wheel and hung his head.

Well, Ethan, that's what you get for procrastinating, he chastised, *You knew you needed to buy another cable for weeks now, and you just didn't take the time. Why do you always do crap like this? Just take five minutes to stop and get a damn cable.* He sighed, then changed his internal tone. *It's okay. Nothing you can do about it now. Don't beat yourself up.* Now that his service ticket had been closed out, Ethan's mind was spent. He breathed deep, let out a slow, controlled exhale, and then started his car and headed for home.

Now that he was clear of the traffic jam, Ethan eased down on the accelerator as he steered the heavy SUV along the interstate. Now that he was moving again, he relaxed a bit.

Should be a quick trip from here unless some dipshit decides to smack one of the interstate barriers again, he decided. He scanned his rear-view mirror and then both side mirrors to ensure no police were anywhere around him. Seeing none, he pressed down a little harder on the accelerator to increase his speed to a respectable eighty miles per hour. Ethan leaned back against his headrest and let the broken lines of the highway clip by in an endless parade.

A sound echoed through his commute's quiet, which caused him to look down at the dashboard panel where he discovered he was running on fumes because of the amount of time spent sitting idle trying to clear the wreck. *Well, that's another ten or twelve minutes. Guess it's more like get home closer to nine-fifteen now.*

After fueling his car and picking up an energy drink, he continued home. No other surprises or delays plagued him for the remainder of his drive. Ethan guided his car along Irvine Street until he reached his subdivision located on Mossy Ridge Drive.

He pulled into the drive then made a mental note that the lawn would need to be cut one last time over the weekend. Most people would say that the yard didn't look overgrown. Even though the weather was warmer than usual, it was still late September, so the growing season had crawled to a slow end.

As he pulled up to the garage door, he reached up and pressed the door opener. As the door slowly made its noisy ascent, he cocked his head, furrowed his brow, and investigated the garage in bewildered amusement. There were two cars in the garage already. There was Tabby's car, then another car in *his* spot. He didn't know whose car it was at first until he spotted a sticker on the back window that read, "Artists are creative lovers." A switch flipped in his mind, and he spoke out loud to no one in particular, "Oh, that's Kiera." Ethan put his car in park, set the brake, and closed the garage door. He reached over to the front passenger seat, grabbed his laptop bag, and stepped out of his car.

Ethan knew Tabby would have the door locked since it was dark, even though virtually no crime ever occurred in their neighborhood or the surrounding neighborhoods. Tabby said she always felt safer when the house was secured. He paused on the top landing by the front door and fumbled in his bag for his keys.

Just as he was about to put the key into the lock, he heard Tabby's voice from the other side of the door, "Hold on!" she yelled. Then he heard the security panel keypad's tones as Tabby entered the disarm code into the alarm panel. The front door swung open, and Ethan saw Tabby wearing her favorite pajamas, the red silk jammies with Chinese writing, and embroidered bamboo forest.

Ethan always teased her about the Chinese writing on the pajama top since no one they knew could read Mandarin. Sometimes he would tease her by saying the letters spelled "Fried Rice," and at other times, he would say the letters spelled "Crab Rangoon." Regardless, Tabby would respond by telling him she didn't care because they were the most comfortable pajamas she had ever worn. When she wanted to be swaddled and relax, these were her go-to evening wear.

Ethan stepped inside the entryway and kicked off his shoes as Tabby greeted him with a kiss. She tasted of oranges and alcohol. Ethan squinted his eyes and licked his lips as he offered Tabby a questioning glance, "Screwdrivers?" he asked.

"Yep," she replied.

"Rough day?"

"Nope. It's a celebration. Well, kind of. There's a mystery afoot, my good man." Her speech was moderately slurred, and the words came out in a slow, clumsy rhythm between her giggles.

"Okay, what kind of mystery?"

"Go get your shower, and I'll tell you everything. I don't want to get into it until you're refreshed and ready to relax with us."

She used her index finger to wander up his right cheek and around his ear. She ended with a light tap on his nose, then kissed it and said with her glassy eyes trained on him, "I need you to have open ears and an attentive mind." This was a phrase that Tabby used when she wanted to have a serious talk.

"Yeah, I saw Kiera's car in the garage. She staying the night?"

"Yes. Maybe the week." She said, giving him a tight hug as she pressed the side of her head against his chest.

"The week? Is something wrong?"

"Just go get your shower," Tabby said, moving around behind Ethan and beginning to push him out of the foyer toward the stairs.

"Why did you have her pull into my spot in the garage?"

"Just go shower. Did you eat anything on the way home?"

"No. I didn't want to stop. I was just ready to get home."

"You want me to get you something ready while you shower?"

"Really? A late meal that *I* don't have to cook. That would be great."

"Okay. Kiera and I will get you a bite to eat and get you a drink ready. Hey, why didn't you call or text to let me know you were going to be late?"

"I had to go to the data center today and figure out some goob's configuration hackery. He had killed the remote access to one of the routers and set up a policing policy to throttle down the throughput, which was the opposite of what he was supposed to have done. I had to undo everything, fix the remote access then complete the config the other guys were trying to get done. When I left to go to the data center, I left my charging cable on my desk at the office," Ethan was saying as he and Tabby strolled into the living area. He gave a casual glance to Kiera, "Hey Kiera. How goes life?"

"Complicated suddenly," she said, then took a bird sip from her drink. She grimaced and sat the glass on the end table beside Ethan's oversized recliner where she was sitting.

Ethan stood for a moment, switching his gaze from Kiera to Tabby before he shook his head and threw up his hands, "Okay, whatever. Be cryptic. I'm hitting the shower. Don't drink so much you can't unveil this giant mystery you are building up the suspense over."

"So," inquired Tabby looking at Ethan and giving a slight shrug, "did you stop and get another power cable for the car."

"Nope."

Tabby slumped her shoulders and exclaimed, "You dufus! You passed like twenty stores on your way home. Why didn't you stop and pick one up?"

"Because I was tired, it was already getting late, and I wanted to get home," Ethan answered.

Tabby turned Ethan around playfully and gave him a gentle kick in the rear, and said, "Ah poop, that was goofy, you Dufus McGee. You gotta go get a cable first thing in the morning. Now get your shower. We ladies gots a story for you."

"I'll go shower if you have a couple of glasses of water and maybe some bread."

"Fine. Just go." Tabby said.

Ethan walked up the stairs toward the master bath while Kiera and Tabby shuffled into the kitchen to whip up something to fill Ethan's empty belly.

CHAPTER 6

Ethan sat on the living room sofa in a silent disbelieving trance. His eyes fixed on the half-eaten turkey and bacon sandwich, trying to process the story he was hearing. As Kiera and Tabby delved deeper into their tale of Kiera's dream and then of Nick's return, Ethan began to feel like the room shifted around him. His mind became a flood of emotions and thoughts that were now bordering on delusion.

"Ethan," he heard a voice calling. The voice called again, "Ethan," more forcefully. He felt a light thump on his right arm. While it didn't hurt, the impact did wake him from his trance. He turned to Tabby, who was seated beside him.

"Well, what do you think?" Tabby asked.

Ethan shook his head again and held up a finger in a 'give me a moment' gesture. He took a sip of his beer and sat it back down beside the half-eaten turkey sandwich.

"Okay. Hold on a minute," Ethan finally said.

Tabby sat staring at the floor in front of the sofa in a half-drunken haze, sipping her drink, while Kiera followed Ethan's movements into the open kitchen. He reached into a cabinet and brought out a shot glass along with a bottle of whiskey or maybe scotch. After three shots, Ethan stood at the kitchen island, exhaling the fire from his throat.

"Alright," he said, making his way back to the sofa. "Let's think this through. Keira, I do not doubt that you *think* you saw Nick this morning, but how can you be sure? His room is on the second floor, and—"

"It was Nick," Kiera cut in on Ethan's dismissal, "I know him. There is no way I could have mistaken someone else for Nick."

Ethan looked at Kiera and saw the brut certainty in her face.

"I want to believe too, but let's look at the facts we have to work with." Ethan tried to sound cautiously comforting as if he were walking across a floor full of mousetraps.

"Nick disappeared from his hotel room on August 5th. That's when everyone thinks, at least, because, on the 6th, the cleaning service found all his stuff in his room and no Nick. No one in Nick's tour group had seen him since the morning of the 5th. Not to mention there was blood in his room."

"All that gives us is a bunch of questions," Keira argued.

"I know, but hold up, let me finish. There were bloody handprints on the walls, and one of his shirts was lying on the hotel room floor soaked with blood. His luggage and computer, still in its backpack, were left in his room. That's the worst part of all. Nick and I treat our computers like a third arm because we are always on call, even on vacation. Nick doesn't go anywhere without it, yet it was left behind still in its pack. I have it in my desk at the office. There was nothing on it out of the ordinary. I checked it myself when I was cloning the drive for the feds. No pictures, documents, odd browsing history, nothing that would give anyone any clues, just work stuff. We also know that he never got on his flight back home. And now we sit here on September 29th, two months later, and no Nick. It was a one-week vacation, and he's been gone for two months. Besides all that, how could Nick have gotten into the condo? Wouldn't his landlord have rented out his condo by now, or at least changed the locks?"

"No," Keira said as she shook her head and wiped a tear. "Nick has his rent set up on auto-pay. The complex's management wouldn't care if Nick was gone, not until the money dried up anyway. Nick managed his money well, so his account would hold his condo for six, or eight months, at least. So, he *could* feasibly come home and walk right into his condo."

"Keira, but what about the blood everywhere in his room. There was blood smeared on the clothes in the closet, the bathroom, the bed. One of his shirts was soaked in blood. I know. I saw the photos when the Feds showed up asking questions at the office. It looked like someone was murdered in his room, then the killer just rummaged around in Nick's things. That's what it looked like in the photos the feds showed us."

"No one said it was Nick's blood."

"But then that leaves an even more terrifying possibility, that Nick was the murderer. He was not only the murderer but then had enough presence of mind to just dematerialized into the jungle carrying a body. Does that sound like Nick? Dude hates butchering a chicken from the grocery store, much less a person."

The room fell silent as the trio sat exchanging glances. Ethan *wanted* to find a sliver of hope in Kiera's story to which he could grab onto, but to him, the thought that Nick was home again was thin at best.

Kiera was overly desperate to hold onto any hope that Nick was still alive and could make it home. Ethan sank back into the sofa. Any chance that Kiera was right left him speechless. In all his years working alongside Nick, there was just nothing that he had ever seen that would explain Nick pulling off a stunt like this.

Tabby broke the silence, "Look; we can sit here all night asking each other questions and trying to figure out what happened until the sun comes up. God knows we've done enough of that since Nick disappeared. But guess what, when the sun *does* come up, we'll still be sitting here with the same answers that we've come up with over the past two months. Bubkes. Zilch. Nada." Tabby seized Ethan by the arm. "There is only one way we can know for sure."

Ethan replied, "Okay. I am just not sure what to expect if it's true. We have no way of knowing what happened down there or who he is anymore if he is home. You have to admit; the prospect seems unlikely."

"I know, but we have to go see ourselves tomorrow, even if it's just to put this all behind us for Kiera." Tabby's alcohol-glazed eyes seemed to beg Ethan. "What if it is Nick? We may be able to finally find out what happened down there."

"Fine. Okay then," Ethan replied, "I guess we really have no choice if we want answers. We'll go over tomorrow and see if he's at home. I don't want anyone to get their hopes up yet. If this is Nick, why hasn't he called any of us, especially you, Kiera? I mean, how long has he been back in town. How the hell did he get from a fucking jungle in Guatemala to Georgia without using a plane. That's one hell of a trek."

"Migrant workers do it every year," Kiera offered, "and then back home at the end of the year. No plane, ever. Most are illegal, so they can't make it through customs or get a ticket. They just hop rides and walk. Whole families."

"Ah… Yeah, fair point," Tabby agreed.

"Yeah, but Nick? I know he's a resourceful guy, but he's a city boy through and through. He's lived in Atlanta his entire life. Do you think he knows how to survive in a jungle? Not to mention the hundreds of miles of desert he would need to traverse with no money for travel. Then there's the issue of food and water. If he survived the jungle by some miracle, the desert would definitely kill him."

Ethan caught Tabby's scowl, so he said, "Look, I'm just trying to be realistic. If this is Nick, and he made the whole trip on foot, not only is he a supreme badass, he has to be some kind of deep-cover special ops guy. Really, just look at the scope of it."

Kiera sat looking at the coffee table in front of her and repeated, "Whole migrant families do it twice every year."

Again, near palpable silence fell across the room until Ethan said, "Well, how do we do this?" Ethan looked back and forth between the two women's gazes. "I mean, I know what we need to do, but how do we do it? Do we call the cops and meet them there? Do we go over to his condo and try to get some answers ourselves? I just don't know how we should play it."

"No cops," Kiera suggested. "He has been gone for two months. I want a chance to talk to him before he gets locked in an interrogation room."

"Are you—" Tabby began.

"Yes. Yes, I am. I want some answers. This whole incident has made life a shit show for months. Now the whole situation has gone from horrible to insane, like some kind of messed-up dream. I want to know what happened. We are owed an explanation. All of us."

"Alright," Ethan concurred, "how do we want to do it?"

The group studied one another, not daring to speak what needed to be said until Ethan spoke up, "Okay. Tomorrow morning, we go to his condo. Just show up." It sounded more like a question than a statement, but the two women got the meaning. Tabby and Keira nodded in agreement.

"This whole thing is screwed up," Ethan said, shaking his head.

"Yep," replied Tabby lazily.

Tabby leaned forward and gave Keira's leg a light-handed pop, "Come on. Let's get you settled in the guest bedroom, honey."

Upstairs, Tabby and Kiera found themselves facing one another, tossing clean sheets in the air as they dressed the guest bed. There was an uneasy silence between them as they worked. From among the rustling and tugging of mattress corners, Kiera spoke up from her crouched position where she was carefully tucking in corners at the foot of the bed, "I don't think I will sleep much anyway. Those dreams are starting to get to me."

Tabby stopped and said, "Hey, honey, listen. If you need anything, you come down the hall and wake me up."

"Yeah, like a little kid, huh, mom?" she said, offering her best innocent little girl smile.

Tabby responded, emphasizing every syllable, "Anything."

Tabby stepped around the foot of the bed and walked over to where Kiera stood. "Look, it will be okay. We're going to figure this out. Either there is a reasonable explanation, and we'll recover, or Nick's lost his mind and is now a cartel hitman. And hey, if he's a hitman or a secret agent, you won't ever have to worry about being robbed. That'd make him a badass, okay, slightly nuts, but a badass. Either way, the sun will rise, the birds will sing, and we'll all make life good again."

"Make life good again, huh. Thanks, auntie Trump." This comment brought both women into a fit of girlish giggles.

Hearing the unexpected nonsense from the bedroom, Ethan popped his head in the doorway and asked, "What the hell are you two hens clucking about? Ya'll sound like two high schoolers on your first bender at the quarterback's party."

Tabby made a wobbly whirl and said, "You need to vacate my doorway, Mr. Hot Sauce." Kiera covered her mouth to attempt to contain her giggles. "This," Tabby paused and motioned around the room, "This is girly stuff. You go wait in our room. I'll deal with you in a minute." Then she turned back to the still giggling Kiera and bent over in another fit of laughing.

After Tabby had gotten her giggles mostly under control, she said, "Well, okay then," and turned to leave the room. There was a slight meander to Tabby's walk, which caused Kiera to giggle more. As Tabby wobbled to the doorway, Kiera thought, *I guess those screwdrivers drilled a little deeper than she thought.*

"Don't worry, sweetie," Tabby reassured her as she stepped into the doorway and spun around. Reaching to grab the door frame as a brace, she missed. She looked at the door frame as if it had moved out of the way, then made a second, more determined attempt to use it to prop herself up.

Looking at Kiera, Tabby said through heavy lips, "I promise, this is all going to work out." Then, she paused a moment and continued, "Oh," again with half-numb lips, "one other thing. You need to just ignore the screaming from the end of the hall. I promise you no one will be getting murdered."

"Oh, God!" Kiera exclaimed, letting out a not entirely disgusted groan. "Are you two going to tear the house down tonight?"

Tabby put her outstretched fingers together in front of her, thrummed them together, and said, "I'm going to go with a probable yes. Vodka has that effect on me." Then she covered her mouth and lifted one leg as she bent over in more laughter.

"I should've brought my earmuffs," Kiera moaned.

"Nighty night," Tabby said, letting go of the door frame. She turned to face down the hall toward the master bedroom. She backed one step out of the doorway, then suddenly did a little leap into the air, twisting her rear to face Kiera. She then proceeded to poke out her rump into the open doorway, swing her left arm around in an exaggerated circle, slapping her butt then squeezed. She then repeated the action with her other hand, uttering first, "Oh," then, "Ah," respectively with each slap, using her best airy, seductive tone. Tabby then twisted her upper torso around, giving Kiera a look back. With buttocks still grasped, she gave her best stripper shake. Then she turned back around and danced backward down the short hallway, giggling the entire time. As she walked into her bedroom with an out-of-control smile, she saw Ethan had already turned the bed down and lay waiting for her. He looked up from his book and returned her smile.

Tabby closed the door of the master bath until there was only a thin crack of light illuminating the darkened bedroom.

"Guess I'm done reading for the night," he said, marking his place in the book and laying it on the table beside the bed.

"You already know what happens." Tabby said, motioning to the book, "We watched the whole series twice."

"Yeah, but the TV people never stick to the original story."

"I know. Have you got to the part where they killed that little brat king yet?"

"Yep."

"That was my favorite part of the entire series. Watching that little shit choke was awesome."

"Geez. Little dark, don't you think?"

"Not for him. Kid or not, he deserved it."

Tabby removed her pajamas and slid under the crisp, clean sheets of their bed. Ethan immediately rolled over and slipped an arm around her. He could feel her heat radiating. Ethan also did not fail to note that his lovely, athletic brunette had gotten into bed without her usual panties-only sleeping attire. He noted this primarily because his now growing cock was pressed up to her smooth, naked butt.

"Oh my," he said, moving his hand up to her left breast and beginning to delicately rub the sensitive dark skin around her nipple, "apparently, someone is a little randy tonight. I like it."

"Randy, who are you, Austin Powers?" she asked, then had another giggling fit.

Giggles or not, Ethan felt her nipples rise in anticipation. He rolled her onto her back and kissed her.

"Hey," she said suddenly, "what do you think happened to Nick all this time?"

He pushed himself up and looked at Tabby, "Can we not worry about this right now. I thought we had other issues to deal with," giving a downward glance toward his now fully erect penis.

Down the hallway, lying alone in a moonlit room, Kiera stared into a black ceiling. If she were to have guessed, she would have thought it had been about thirty minutes since she had lain down to try to go to sleep. A sudden sound came beating through the night air. First, she heard what sounded like someone knocking at her door, but no one should have been at the door. Tabby and Ethan were down the hall, and no one else was in the house. She sat up on her elbows and listened intently to the darkness. *What is that?* she questioned as her gut began to harden.

She listened, focusing her senses on the sound. Then knock, knock, knock again, but this time, a ghostly moan followed the sound. Kiera held her breath as if whoever was on the other side of the door could hear her breathing. The knock came again, but this time the knocking was followed by Tabby's muffled voice as she cried from down the hall, confirming that Ethan was, in Tabby's words, "right there," and that he could "give it to me."

Kiera relaxed and collapsed back onto her pillow with a palpable sigh of relief. *Oh good God,* she thought, *I didn't know they were filming a porno down the hall.*

Kiera lay in her darkened room listening to sounds of what was apparently exquisite ecstasy and continued to try and usher herself off to sleep. However, sleep had proven to be far more elusive than first expected, and now she had this commotion going on down the hall with which to contend.

The X-rated movie playing out, more loudly now, did unexpectedly quicken a yearning deep in her that she did not anticipate, which seemed to be growing more resonant with each gasp of Tabby's enthralled voicings. She considered ushering away her own growing female need, then said aloud, "No. No. No. Just go to sleep." She grabbed the pillow from the other side of the bed and covered her face, hoping to muffle the noisy amorous sounds emanating from the end of the hallway. It didn't work because the knock, knock, knock only got louder now as Tabby and Ethan were both bellowing in what Kiera could only assume was erotic torture.

Kiera removed the pillow from her face dropping it back to the other side of the bed, and let out an exaggerated, "Jesus. Is he trying to break her in half?" to the empty room. Then the sound changed. Now Ethan was the louder of the battling duo. He was now letting Kiera know that "it feels so good," to which Tabby loudly encouraged him to "Fuck it!"

Ethan again, "Oh baby, yes," which was followed up with a "feels so good" from Tabby. Kiera thought there might have also been a, "You like that baby?" thrown in, to which Tabby replied a lengthy, "Ooooo-hhhhhh, so damn good," The, "Oh," having been drawn out, the volume rising then falling with each knock, knock, knock. And the "so damn good" matching the timing of the knocking each time with that last, "good," being stretched out as it rose then fell in volume with each of the knocks from what Kiera had now figured out was the master bed's headboard banging against the wall.

Then Tabby again, reassuring Ethan that he could, also in Tabby's words, "fuck that ass all night," if he wanted it.

Kiera's eyes shot wide, and she covered her mouth with both hands to contain the laughter that now had her curled up in the bed, rolling back and forth in hysterics. She gathered herself, wiped the tears from her eyes, took a deep breath, and considered, "I don't know why I'm laughing. At least she's getting some."

"Those two are going to be dead tomorrow morning," she thought, "Hell, at this rate, they may need to stop for a snack," Kiera noted the aching in her belly had been elevated to maximum by the goings-on down the hallway. She considered again self-pleasuring her ache away but decided to roll over and shortly found sleep.

CHAPTER 7

Kiera looked up into the cloudless day as she stood in the parking lot of Big D's Bar-B-Que, the autumn sun lending a cozy comfort to the day. Now that autumn was beginning to arrive, the stifling Georgia humidity no longer choked the atmosphere, so Kiera breathed in the cooling air. She stood facing the neighborhood bar and grill, asking herself if she was ready. Big D's was one of Kiera and Nick's favorite bar-b-que joints where with nearly ritualistic certainty, Nick always chose the brisket and Kiera the pulled pork plate.

We haven't been here since before Nick did his disappearing act.

She struggled for a moment to recall the events of the past month since Nick's return, only to draw a blank where her memories should have been. Big D's, she thought, looking across the crowded parking lot at the sign on the building. *This should be nice. The four of us having a regular—* but then her thoughts trailed away as she was drawn to a leaf that had just let go of its last breath of summer and began its journey down to return to its place in the earth.

The foliage on the pear trees along the verge rustled in the brisk October breeze. The orange and yellow leaves danced from side to side at the ends of their branches, making the trees look as if they were covered in dancing flames. As the breeze continued to prod the vibrant colors of the autumn leaves, more of them leaped into the air, surrendering their brilliant colors to the quickening fall winds in a listless aerial ballet. Kiera's eyes followed another leaf until it came to a stop among a covey of its brightly colored siblings on the cool fall ground. Forcing her focus away from the seasonal dance of the leaves, Kiera took a moment to scan the parking lot to see if Nick, Tabby, or Ethan's cars we parked among the sprawl.

Typical, Not an on-time bone in the bunch. She decided to go inside and get a table for the four of them, knowing that the rest of the group was rarely on time for anything, Tabby and Ethan especially.

As Kiera stepped into the doorway, Bobby greeted her in a deep Georgia drawl. "Hey, Kiera. I haven't seen you for a while. How ya been?" Bobby Ray Nevel, the host at Big D's, had an uncanny ability of remembering most of the regulars' names on sight.

"Hey, Bobby Ray. Oh, hey, I like the new design," she replied, motioning to Bobby Ray's shirt. He was wearing a tee-shirt that read, "Big D's. Come hangry, leave happy!"

"Yeah, Big D just got these in. I like the redesigned logo. Thought it looked pretty spiffy."

"It does look nice. Let me see whatcha wearing today." Kiera asked as she looked at Bobby Ray's cap.

Bobby Ray was an avid collector of hats, so he had a seemingly endless supply with every logo and brand imaginable. Since Bobby Ray seemed to have a never-ending supply, Kiera had never seen the same hat worn twice.

Bobby Ray tilted his head and pointed, "Well, this one here is one of my favorites. It has a logo showing America's favorite pass time."

Kiera smiled as she read the logo, "Yep, I think you may be right about that. Drinking beer does seem to be a common activity among all walks of life in this country."

"So," Bobby Ray asked, "How you guys been?"

"Okay," Kiera replied with a smile. "We've just been so busy. I am looking so forward to some of that house-made sauce you guys whip up."

"Well, you're in luck. We've got buckets of it ready to go."

"What I really want is the recipe."

Bobby Ray raised his right eyebrow, "Well, I can give you the recipe. Doug told me I could next time you come in."

"Really?" Kiera exclaimed, adding a little hop and clap.

"Y'all's little group have asked me so many times that you just wore him down, so I talked to Doug, and he told me I could give it to you. Only you," he added. "But there's a catch."

"Okay." Keira looked at Bobby Ray suspiciously.

"Well, Big Doug said that you could have the recipe. You'll just can't ever leave the restaurant or talk to anyone ever again."

Kiera gave Bobby Ray a playful pop on his arm and smiled, "That's not a valid offer," she said, rolling her eyes. "I tell you what, just show me a table for four, and I'll keep my freedom."

"Not into servitude for life, huh," Bobby Ray said with a chuckle.

"No. No one is."

"Well, I guess right this way then, madam."

Kiera sat for about five minutes, repeatedly checking her watch before Nick, Tabby, and Ethan made their way into the front door of Big D's. She stood partially from her chair and waved to get their attention. As she caught their eye, Tabby gave a frantic wave in return. The late trio made their way across the restaurant to the table, where Nick leaned down and kissed Kiera on her cheek as he pulled out a chair beside her.

"Hey babe, what did you get into today," Nick asked.

"Ugh… I had to do staging for a panty commercial."

"A panty commercial?" Tabby asked as she was shuffling out of her jacket. "What type of setup could you possibly need to shoot a panty commercial?"

"You'd be surprised," Kiera replied, "All these male directors think that if they show women in their underwear with angel wings beside fountains, staged in these perfect glamour shots with glitter and full makeup, they'll sell more bras. It's so dumb."

"Oh God, tell me about it. It's gross." Tabby said, bobbing her head in enthusiastic agreement. "A better marketing campaign would be to have a woman stand there, look into the camera, and say, 'Buy this bra, and your back won't hurt, your tits won't sag, and it won't slice into your ribs all day. I'd buy stock in that company."

Ethan turned to Tabby with a raised eyebrow, "So you're pitching the 'No Saggy Tits' campaign?"

"Exactly. If the twins are happy, I'm happy. That's all I'm saying."

Kiera waved her hands frantically at Tabby as she laughed, "Oh, oh, oh, you know what the worst part was?"

They all turned to Kiera.

"This jackass director asked if I would model for him too."

Kiera fell back into her seat, laughing.

"Wow, what an ass," Ethan said.

"You're kidding?" Nick asked.

"Nope. Not at all."

"Man, that's not sleazy at all," Tabby said.

After they got their chuckling under control, Ethan asked, "What are in for tonight, Nick? Usual? Brisket?"

"I think I want to go for the ribs tonight."

"Ribs? Man, you are truly a changed man. You never order ribs."

"Yeah. I think so. I haven't had ribs in a while so let's change it up. What do you want, babe?" Nick asked, turning to Kiera.

Kiera looked up from her menu, "It's been a while since we've been here, so I just want my usual. I've got a craving for it."

"Pulled pork plate, heavy on the sauce, extra crispy fries with slaw on the side," Nick said with a proud smile.

"Yeah," Kiera said, slowly closing her menu. A small gathering of butterflies in her belly increased their fluttering. She could see something different about him since his miraculous resurfacing into life a month ago, but Kiera had so far not been able to pin down what had changed. She tried again to remember the last four weeks and only succeeded in causing the flurry in her stomach to increase as the memories failed.

"What can I say. I know, my lady." Nick said, then leaned over and kissed her cheek.

As Nick returned to his menu, Keira reached up and touched the spot where Nick had kissed her. His lips felt cold, not at all like the warm fullness she remembered. She looked around the room. Everything seemed normal, but Kiera could not get the thought out of her head that something did not feel exactly right about this whole scene for some reason.

Kiera was pulled back to reality when someone approached the table. Their waitress, Jennifer, walked up and stood with order pad in hand, rummaging in her apron for a pen.

"Okay, folks. What'll it be tonight?" Jennifer asked.

"Hey Jenn, are there any specials tonight?" Tabby asked.

"Well, we have shrimp skewers for nine ninety-nine," the waitress replied with more pep than required for the question.

"Shrimp at a bar-b-que joint?"

"Yep, Doug came up with this Southwestern Cajun fusion deal that he sprinkles on them. They're so good."

"Oh, okay. That does sound good. What comes with an order?"

"You get three skewers with six shrimp each, chipotle garlic aioli with a side of red beans and rice. Then you can pick either one, or two, other sides of your choice." Jennifer replied, then added, "I suggest the cheese grits."

"Okay," Tabby said, looking back down at her menu, "Where are the sides, again?"

As Jennifer pointed out the side dishes to Tabby, Kiera scanned the restaurant again. Nothing seemed out of place. Everything was normal, so why did nerves feel so raw? Somehow the room just didn't seem right. Was it the light? The room seemed darker. Maybe the shadow of a cloud had fallen across the windows in the front of the dining area. If so, Kiera had not noticed it.

It's just nerves, Kiera reassured herself. *This is the first time we've been out as a group since he got back home.* She caught a glimpse of the waitress's smile as Jennifer glanced over at her briefly. Jennifer's smile felt off. What was it? It was the eyes. They seemed darker, too, like the room. Were they darker than they were a minute ago? Yes, and her smile seemed to be uncomfortably wide, bordering on unnatural.

Of course, Kiera reasoned, It's fake. She's working for tips, so in her mind, the bigger the teeth, the better the tip.

"Kiera." She turned toward Nick. The room seemed normal again, as did Jennifer's eyes.

"Sorry, what?"

"Baby, what do you want, the pulled pork plate you said, right?" Kiera looked over to Jennifer, poised, ready to write Kiera's order on her pad.

"Oh, sorry. I just want my usual. I'll just have the pulled pork plate with house fries and toast."

"What side?"

"Just the slaw is fine."

"What to drink?"

"Coke is fine."

"Alrighty. I'll get this to the kitchen, and it'll be out in just a few," Jennifer said as she gathered their menus. "I'll get your drinks right out."

Kiera scooted her chair out from the table and stood up, "I'll be right back. I've gotta go to the restroom."

"Do I need to come with you," Tabby was looking at Kiera as if she were oddly suspicious of why Kiera needed to leave the table?

"No. It's okay. I'll just be a minute."

Kiera finished using the toilet then walked to the sink. Her feeling of unease had subsided. She stood looking into the mirror, noting that the portrait staring back at her wore a numb, almost expressionless mask. *What is wrong with you?* She asked the reflection. As Kiera washed her hands, she saw in the mirror that the room behind her seemed to be slipping into shadow, growing dimmer as she watched the reflection. Formless darkness grew from the walls and descended from the ceiling, spreading slowly toward her like a black cloud. She spun to see the shadow continue to spread toward her, seeming almost to be reaching. She tried to blink it away, but nothing changed with each attempt. The shadow continued to move and swell toward her as if it were a living mass of formless determination.

As it continued, Kiera felt its sickness, its darkness, pulling at her like a thick, pulsating river of hatred. The room continued to disappear into the dark decay. The sounds of decay began to fill Kiera's ears as the crumbling walls and ceiling deteriorated and hit the tile on the bathroom floor. The splashing of flowing water filled the decaying room as a now exposed pipe corroded, burst, and rained down onto the floor. The resulting pool of water spread toward her from under the disintegrating bathroom stalls until it reached across the floor to lick at Kiera's shoes. Pain began to radiate from the muscles in Kiera's forearm as she tightened her hold on the bathroom sink to stop the uncontrollable shaking in her hands and to help steady her failing legs. Her heartbeat was as if someone with a hammer was trying to beat their way out from within. She turned back to the mirror and tried again to blink away the dark. Her reflection glared back at her from within the mirror with black, empty eyes and a smile that offered no sympathy. Kiera screamed to break herself out of what she thought must be a delusion. Her legs refused to move. Kiera knew she needed to get her legs working as she struggled to force air into her lungs through her closing throat. She closed her eyes, telling herself, "This is not real. It's some kind of hallucination," as if willing the sickness in the room to obey.

The shadow will be almost on top of me now. The hair on the back of her neck bristled. She could almost feel the cold grasp of the corruption, reaching for her like a massive, slow-moving avalanche. The sounds of withering walls and ceiling continued to fill her ears as they cracked and swayed under the rot of the shadow's presence. "No." she cried, then opened her eyes to face the black force.

She saw no shadow, no crumbling walls or flaking paint. The blackened rot that spread out from the darkness like wisping tendrils was gone. She turned back to see her reflection and gazed into the pale face of fear staring back at her. There were no cold black eyes, no insane smile, or unsympathetic eyes. Kiera's ears heard only the sound of water rushing from the tiny spigot on the bathroom sink and the drain gurgling it away. Her reflection was her own again.

Kiera shut off the water and left the bathroom. When she arrived back, the food was already on the table. Kiera saw Nick was holding a portion of ribs and seemed to be thoroughly enthralled. He bit and tore at them as if he were eating corn on the cob. Kiera could see a smear of sauce across his right cheek.

She sat down and picked up her fork, then turned to Nick. She tried to act as if there was no tremble in her voice as she asked, "Hungry tonight?"

Nick did not acknowledge her as he continued to tear another large chunk of flesh from the ribs.

"Nick," Kiera said, then waited. "Nick," she called again, more forcefully.

Having almost caught her breath from her bathroom delusion, she felt her respirations begin to shorten and accelerate again, her chest growing tighter. The room started to look as if it were wavering, taking on the appearance of someone viewing it from across a hot surface. It began to swoon around her, and she began to feel unhinged again. She felt the slipping from her reality into the reality of the black corruption. Kiera scanned the room as the taste of bile rose to the back of her throat. She turned to Tabby.

Tabby was frozen, staring at her plate of food, the look on her face more closely resembling an animal. She held her fists clenched in rage. The veins alongside her neck bulged to bursting. Kiera could see them as they stood out, running from under Tabby's blouse until disappearing into her hair as thick blackened lines. Her smile was larger than should have been humanly possible, and her eyes looked near to rupturing their sockets, past insanity or fear.

Ethan sat seemingly motionless as well, a brainsick expression on his face. Blood had begun to run from his eyes. Kiera clutched her chest, her lungs struggling to fill. Her mind began to unravel like the delicate knot at the center of a spider's silken web. When Kiera tried to stand, to flee, she felt only statuesque appendages below her waist. She felt the paralysis that had held her in place in the bathroom begin to retake her legs. The cold of numbness moved from her feet slowly up to her thighs.

The light in the dining room continued to dim. Kiera saw that all the restaurant's guests were frozen just as Kiera's companions appeared. Everyone was locked in tableaus of agony.

The shadow is here! Keira thought. She tried to swallow as fear closed its hand around her throat.

The room began to melt away, being pulled apart by something she could not see. The faces in the dining room began to distort, slowly writhing from unseen tortures. Some faces began to melt and wither as others seemed to rot from their skulls.

Kiera looked back to her friends and saw Tabby's smile had smeared across her face pulling her lips back in a tight, unnatural grimace; Her parting lips revealing rows of sharp, narrow teeth. Kiera's grasp on reality slipped further as Tabby began to slowly open her mouth. Her smile parted, growing wider until Tabby's jaw cracked and unhinged like a serpent. Her bulging eyes rolled back into their sockets like a great white shark at feeding time. Kiera's legs surged with life again. She jumped up from her seat, knocking her chair back and stumbling over it, nearly losing her footing. Tabby's head began to turn toward her.

Kiera reached for Nick. She grabbed his shoulder and pulled with enough force to spin him around in his chair. When she saw his face, her last fragmenting shared of reason broke. Nick continued to eat in his trancelike gorging. His cheeks stuffed to swollen. Yet he bit and tore at the meat on the ribs. Half chewed bits were falling from his mouth as he tried to force more into his gnawing teeth. Sauce smeared over the lower part of his face, rolled down his chin, and glopped onto his shirt.

Kiera screamed, released Nick, and stepped back. Kiera could now see the body of a charred infant smothered in Big D's house-made sauce. One-half of the charred infant's ribcage was missing and in Nick's hands. Nick continued growling and grunting as he gnawed at the meat. More bits of flesh fell from his overstuffed mouth, rolling down and collecting on his pants and the floor around him. His shirt was now a smear of sauce and half-chewed bits of charred flesh. His throat began to swell as he forced more of the flesh into his mouth. The swelling continued, the skin around his throat thinning until it looked as if it would burst.

Kiera slapped the remains from Nick's hands which seemed to disturb his trance. He looked up at her with eyes devoid of light except for faintly glowing, silver pupils. He grunted and spun back around to his plate. He began to open his mouth like a slow-moving bear trap, just as Tabby had done. His lips stretched so thin that Kiera expected them to rip open, exposing black gums. Kiera could see the line of narrow teeth filling his mouth. The upper portion of Nick's head fell back as if a hinge attached it as his lower jaw opened until it almost touched his chest. His open throat seemed to gag at the air around him. He lurched forward and slammed his face down onto the plate, and began to devour the infant carcass like a starving dog.

Kiera screamed until all she could produce was a near-silent rasp. She swayed as the ground shifted beneath her. Above the roar of the wind, there came the crack of timber followed by the ghostly moan of twisting metal. Nick continued to tear at the infant corpse.

Kiera covered her ears as the restaurant continued to quake and tear itself apart as if being nestled within the bowels of a tornado. Kiera turned and put her head down as debris whipped around her and clawed at her face. Air was a privilege at this point, as Kiera's lungs heaved as if being sucked from her chest. The diners were also ripping apart as they sat frozen, time-locked. Their faces twisted into murals of decay and agony. The macabre statues silhouetted the darkened room as the violent winds ripped off limbs and robbed them of their internal organs.

Keira's head pivoted like a funhouse clown as she frantically looked around for safety. Remembering the bathroom's decay, Kiera buried herself in the oncoming wind. She clawed toward the sturdy bar at the front of what remained of the room, intending to lie down on the floor behind it when Nick abruptly appeared, blocking her path. He caught her in his black gaze, opened his distorted mouth, and cried with a voice like a demonic chorus that shook what remained of the walls and floor of the restaurant, "Lemesu fa slovate dashkwel!"

His figure swelled as he rushed toward her with the river of wind and debris. In the dim light, his face rippled, began to change. Kiera could see that the form before her was Nick but corrupted. He grabbed her by the shoulders and opened his mouth. Kiera tried to scream, but her ragged throat would not allow it. Nick pulled her forward and fell upon her with his dog-like teeth.

Kiera sprung from her pillow, gasping in a breath that pushed her lungs to the point of rupture. Her body shook as the thumping of her heart drowned all other sounds. Kiera saw shadow after shadow in the room until she realized she was not home. *Just a dream,* she tried to reassure herself. Then again, still trying to catch her breath, *Just a dream.*

After a moment, the room faded into clarity as the ghostly white aura of the objects in the room took form, illuminated by the moonlight through the window. When Kiera remembered she was in Ethan and Tabby's guest bedroom, she fell back onto the pillow, her chest still heaving the nightmare away.

I won't be getting any more sleep tonight. She reached up and placed the back of her right hand on her moistened forehead.

Goosebumps rose on her arms as a breath rushed over her elbow from the empty side of her bed. She turned, first noticing the press of the sheet on the mattress. Nick lay beside her, his pale skin almost matching the pallor of the moonlight. She moved her arm down to her side and felt the wet decay of moist earth. The wet of the black fluid seeping from his bruised lips discoloring the pillow. Keira saw white smoke wisping from faint, silver dots of his pupils through the lifeless gaze of his eyes. Nick's thin skin seemed to weep putrefaction from every pore. As he opened his mouth, the smell of moldy soil and corrupted flesh filled Kiera's nostrils. He tried to speak, which caused more black, putrefied fluid to ooze out along with blackened earth that choked his words. Kiera managed to make out the words, "The Guard."

Kiera awoke, flung the sheets back, and jumped from the bed, a constant thump in her ears from her exploding heart. She groped around the edge of the bed, feeling for the other side of the room. Kiera's lungs ached as she grabbed at the dark until she found the bedroom door. She slid a sweaty palm along the wall by the doorframe until she found the light switch. Once the lights flooded the room, she spun to see an empty bed. Sliding her back down the wall, she sat hugging her knees until she could breathe again.

Kiera reached over and felt the moist sweat on the back of her left arm, testing to see if there was black dirt stuck to her. When she found none, she sighed. What was Nick trying to say to her in the dream? *The Guard? What does that mean?*

Kiera slowly got up and walked back over to the bed to examine the place where Nick had lain in her dream. She sat down on the bed and ran a hand over the sheets, trying to remember the feel of Nick's arms around her. She picked up her cell phone from the nightstand to check the time. Five thirty-nine. It didn't matter. Convinced the dream was over, she arose, gathered some clothing, and walked into the adjoining bathroom to shower.

CHAPTER 8

Around eight-thirty, Tabby came downstairs looking like Medusa with a hangover. A skidding sound accompanying her every step as if her shoes were filled with lead. Kiera sat at the dining table, quietly sipping a cup of coffee. Tabby looked at her through squinted eyes as Kiera returned her straining gaze with a bright morning smile.

"Morning," Tabby said as she plodded toward the safe harbor of morning coffee.

"Morning," Kiera replied, then began to giggle.

"What are you already chuckling about?"

"Oh, nothing," Kiera replied. "I was just sitting here watching you come down the stairs and get your coffee and realized that you simply amaze me."

"Amaze you?" Tabby asked as she switched on the coffee maker and turned to lean on the counter. The coffee maker started emitting a series of gurgles and hisses. "What's so amazing?" Even though Tabby felt as if someone was driving a spike through the side of her head, Kiera's glowing childlike grin was infectious.

"I'm just surprised. That's all." Kiera replied, taking a sip from her coffee. "I'm just surprised that you can walk this morning." Kiera held up her coffee cup to hide her giggling.

Tabby slumped to her elbow on the countertop and laughed as well. After a moment, she stood up and said with an unapologetic tone, "Yeah, sorry about that. Total accident, but Ethan was in rare form. I couldn't just let it pass." Tabby picked up her cup and walked over to the table, "Good god. He was in very rare form. If he was like that every time, I'm not sure we would ever leave the bedroom." Then she laughed again, almost spitting out her coffee.

"No, too much," Kiera said, shaking her head but still laughing.

"Oh girl, it was so good I started to come down the hall and invite you to join."

"No. Yuck," Kiera exclaimed with a gasp giving a slap to Tabby's forearm, "You guys don't do that, do you?"

"Three ways, oh hell no. Well, one time in college."

"What? You did not."

"Yeah, but just the one time."

"Does Ethan know?"

"Good lord no," Tabby said, almost spitting her coffee out with another burst of laughter, "You know how guys are. My man only has eyes for me, but he's still a guy. If he thought I was open to that, ah, type of situation, he'd be begging at least once a month for some new snatch to play with."

"Tabby! No, he would not. Not Ethan."

"Look, I love him, and he loves me. But at the end of the day, he's a guy, and," Tabby gave Kiera a wink, "he's got the appetites. Between you and me, he may be getting older, but his drive hasn't aged past twenty yet if you know what I mean."

Kiera started to laugh again before saying, "Oh yeah, I'm surprised you can do that too."

"Do what?"

"Sit."

Tabby gasped, "You heard that, too?"

"Honey, I think the neighbors heard you."

"Oh god," Tabby moaned. "Oh well, sometimes you just gotta go for it."

"Hey, I'm not judging."

"Life's short. You know how it is. You gotta get all the fun in early." Tabby said.

Just then, Ethan came into the kitchen. He looked over at the two giggling women and asked, "How did you ladies sleep?"

"Awesome, baby," Tabby responded. "Whew. I was so tired by the time I got to sleep."

"Yeah, me too," Kiera agreed, then added, "But, I guess I'd sleep well too after a forty-five-minute cardio circuit before bed." She leaned back in her chair and acted exhausted. "God, I'd be so beat."

Tabby stopped hiding her laughter behind her coffee cup and sat back in her chair, laughing harder after seeing Ethan's cheeks turn a beautiful shade of fever red.

"Yeah," Tabby said between breaths, "according to Kiera, apparently even the neighbors could hear our little antics last night."

Ethan opened his mouth, then closed it, not really having an acceptable response. He tried again, "Well, you know," but trailed off, which caused both ladies to laugh even more.

Tabby looked at Ethan and saw his face had turned from fever-red to a bulb in a red-light district. She thought she could physically feel the heat radiating from it. This thought, coupled with Ethan's expression, which made him look a lot like a child peeing his pants in public, made her laugh so hard she grabbed her sides. Ethan turned away, forgetting to grab his coffee, and briskly walked back to the stairs.

"Oh no, Ethan," Kiera called, "Please. No. Don't be embarrassed. Forty-five minutes. Really, I was very impressed."

Ethan gave an utterance that Kiera *thought* may have been, "Okay," as he vanished up the stairs.

"No, really," she continued. "And Tabby said I could join you guys next time." This remark earned Kiera a gasp from Tabby and a reciprocal pop on the back of her hand. The tap caused some of Kiera's coffee to slosh out of her cup and onto the kitchen table. Kiera had sat her cup down and was now leaning to one side of her chair with tears coming from her eyes, trying to catch her breath.

"Don't tell him that!" Tabby exclaimed between breaths.

"Hey, it was your idea. I'm just passing along the news."

After another minute of much-needed laughter, Tabby asked, "Did you see the look on his face when he realized what we were talking about? He looked like he'd just pissed himself." Then she slapped the table as she struggled through another gale of laughter.

After they had gotten some moniker of control over their laughing, Tabby thought that Kiera *actually* looked tired, not at all rested, so she asked, "Hey, did you sleep? What time did you get up?"

"Five thirty."

"Five thirty? Why did you get up that early?"

"Another dream. It feels like it's a nightly thing now. This was the worst one yet."

"Wanna talk about it?"

"No. I just want to try and forget it."

"I still think it's stress, sweetie."

"I know. Maybe they'll go away when we get this whole Nick thing figured out."

"Well, if they don't get better, I have a friend you can talk to."

"Why can't I just talk to you? You're a psychiatrist."

"If you want a *professional* session, you shouldn't talk to your best friend. You get better results when you talk to an *unbiased* observer. I've already formed an opinion and have concluded that it is stress. Since I've already formed an opinion, I may miss something important because I'm predisposed to my own pronounced bias."

"So now I'm a nut case?"

"Okay. Well, firstly, 'nut case' is not an approved or smiled upon diagnosis, and no, I told you already that I think it's just stress-related. But, *if,* and that is a big if, there's something more to it, I would want you to get help from someone unbiased. I have colleagues who treat their friends and family members, but I've never agreed with the practice. It just seems loaded with potential issues."

"I guess that makes sense. Maybe they'll stop once we have some clarity on this whole mess."

Picking up her coffee, Tabby got up from the table and said, "I have got to go take a shower."

Kiera smiled back at her. "Oh, I one hundred percent believe that. Maybe two."

As Tabby walked into the upstairs master bathroom, she heard the shower transition from heavy rain to a drip as Ethan finished his bath. She called, "Hey, babe."

"Hey," Ethan called back. "I'm getting out. Be out of your way in a minute."

"I brought you a surprise."

Ethan peered out from around the bathroom door as Tabby handed him his abandoned cup of coffee.

"Yeah, I remembered when I got to the top of the stairs. It's okay. Kiera's little comment woke me up."

"I wish you could have seen your face. It was so red that I thought you were going to burst into flames."

"I wasn't embarrassed as much as caught off guard by her saying anything. She usually doesn't joke about stuff like that. Then come to find out you two are treating our kitchen like a locker room."

Tabby was laughing again. "Well, you gotta admit, it got pretty primal last night."

"Primal? Sexy as hell would be my description. We need to find out how to recreate that every night. It would seem vodka is the key," he said, holding his hands in front of his face and tapping his fingers together. "So, I've already started looking up drink recipes."

"Nice, we could maybe break the bed next time," she said, stepping into the doorway and kissing his cheek.

Tabby walked back over to their bed, untied her bathrobe, and let it fall across the foot of the bed. She didn't take anything else off because the robe was the only item of clothing she had put on to go down to the kitchen. She gathered some clothing then walked past Ethan into the bathroom. Tabby was wrestling a towel from the bathroom linen closet as Ethan finished toweling off. He stepped into the bathroom doorway, wearing his towel around his waist like a kilt.

"So," he paused and looked at Tabby with an expression that one could only describe as indulgent. Tabby turned to see him standing with a sly grin on his face. "So, you, me, and *Kiera* next time?"

Tabby threw her towel at him as he ducked to dodge it. He hadn't needed to duck since Tabby's aim was wide right, causing the towel to strike the doorframe. He picked up the towel and handed it to Tabby with a laugh.

Tabby stepped through the bathroom door and turned to show her side profile. She used her hand to give an inviting trace around the curvature of her exposed right buttock. "Well, I *was* thinking me, you, and Kiera."

"What?" His face was awash with disbelief, and was that anticipation he was shielding?

"Oh yeah. Kiera will start on the bottom and me on top. You have to watch first until she's comfortable."

Kiera spanked her butt, closed the bathroom door, and thought, "Let him think about that fantasy all day. He'll go nuts."

CHAPTER 9

It was around eleven o'clock before Ethan, Tabby, and Kiera made their way out of the house. As they turned off Daniel's Drive into Arrington Condos, the silence in the car seemed to become an almost tangible presence. Nick's condo was at the front of the complex, his small yard backing up to the sidewalk along Daniel's Drive. On the opposite side of Daniel's Drive was a small row of independent shops lining the side-walk. One of these shops was Kevin's Meats, from whose awning Kiera had been sheltering from the storm the morning she had seen Nick's return from the dead.

Ethan did not see Nick's car in his parking space, so he pulled into Nick's spot. Ethan put the Tahoe in park, shut the engine off, and sat staring at Nick's front door.

Ethan spoke, seemingly to himself, "I don't think he's home. His car is gone, and there's no movement from the windows." After a brief pause, he continued, "Well, I guess I'm gonna go check it out anyway."

Ethan got out of the car and walked to the front door. He reached an unsteady finger toward the doorbell and pressed the button, waited, and listened but heard no movement from the other side of the door. He pushed the doorbell again. Still nothing. He rang the bell a third time and waited. After thirty seconds, he started to turn away when he heard a faint "Hello," come from behind the closed door.

"Nick! Oh my god! Is that you?" Ethan nearly yelled. "Nick!"

"Yes, hold on a minute," came the reply. The voice sounded weak, but Ethan recognized it.

Ethan turned to look back at Tabby and Kiera, his ordinarily pale complexion seeming somehow paler as he mouthed to them, pointing almost franticly at the front door, "It's Nick. It's Nick." He turned back to the door listening for any sign that would signal the door's opening.

Kiera opened the rear passenger door and got out of the car. Ethan heard the car door close and turned to see Tabby and Kiera walking toward Nick's house. Ethan shook his head and held up his hand, motioning for them to stop. The women stopped. Tabby reached an arm around Kiera, who was shaking. Whether from fear or the tears she was fighting back, Tabby was unsure.

"It's okay." Tabby offered in a tone that she thought didn't sound entirely confident or reassuring, "He really is back now. Stay together." Kiera nodded but said nothing.

Ethan called again after he didn't hear the door unlock, "Nick! Come on, man, open the door! Please!"

The door rattled as Nick unbolted the lock. He opened it about six inches, then stopped, having left the safety chain in place.

"Nick?" Ethan asked in a small voice.

"Yeah, Ethan. It's me."

"Dude, what the hell? We thought, hell, everyone thought, you were dead. We thought we lost you, man."

"Yeah, I know. I figured that out."

"What do you mean you figured it out? Where have you been?" Ethan was moving past his shock and began to note the unsettled tone in Nick's voice as he said, "I figured that out," then began to question him again, "Nick, did you get hurt or something? Can we come in?"

"No." Nick quickly responded, almost interrupting Ethan. "You can't come in right now."

Nick refused to make eye contact. Nick's usually confident voice was now dry and shaky. Ethan had seen Nick come to work sick, powering through the flu, bronchitis, and a couple of other respiratory ailments, but he had never heard Nick sound so frail.

What Ethan wanted to do was to scream about being owed an explanation, but what came out was a delicate, "Okay, dude. It's alright." Ethan held his hand up to show that he was not there to push, "Can we talk anytime *soon*, I mean?"

Nick didn't answer at first and seemed to be considering.

"Nick?"

"Yeah. Let's meet later at the food court. In the mall."

"Food court? Alright. When? Today?"

"Yeah. Give me three hours."

"Okay. But hey, where's your car? I mean, how are you going to get there?"

"If it's not impounded, it should still be at the park and fly lot out by the airport. I was planning to take a cab over to pick it up."

"Well, hey, we're here. You want us to—"

"No! No, I've got it covered."

"Alright, look, it's eleven fifty-five now," Ethan said, checking the time on his phone, "We'll meet you over at the mall in three hours.

Let's call it an even three o'clock so you have plenty of time to pick up your car and get there."

"Yeah. Okay. Good." Seeing Nick look so frail and hearing the weakness in his voice made Ethan feel sick.

"Nick, are you okay?"

"See you at three," Nick replied, then closed the door and locked it.

The door closed so suddenly Ethan took an involuntary step back and stared at it. He turned and started back toward the car. As he approached, Tabby began, "Is he—"

"Get in the car," Ethan said, pointing. "Come on, get in."

As the three got back into the car, no one spoke. Ethan started the engine and backed out of Nick's parking space. As he cleared the space, the car's tires gave one short bark as Ethan navigated out of Nick's complex.

"Ethan, honey, slow down." Tabby cautioned. Ethan didn't reply, so Tabby repeated, "Ethan, slow down."

Ethan turned. His eyes were wide with the shock and confusion having just spoken with the dead. In truth, the pale face, wide eyes, and bloodless hands told Tabby that Ethan was again in rare form. Afraid.

"Ethan, what happened?" Tabby asked.

Ethan slowed the car. "It was Nick, but he wasn't himself."

"What do you mean?" Kiera asked, drying her eyes again with a tissue. "Was he hurt?"

"I don't know. He sounded different."

"Different how?" Tabby asked.

"I don't know. I can't explain. Something is just different."

"Well, what do we do now if he won't let us in?" Kiera asked.

"He said he would meet us later," Ethan replied.

"Ethan, he just shut the door in your face," Tabby reminded.

"He said he didn't want us to come in, but he would meet us in three hours at the food court in the mall."

"Why the mall?"

"I don't know, but after seeing him, it may be better that way. Look, maybe we didn't think this through. We don't know where he's been, what happened to him, *why* it happened, or what *it* actually is. We don't know why or how he made it back. At least at the mall, there will be other people around. It may be a better place to try and figure out what is going on with him."

Ethan looked in the rear-view mirror to see Kiera staring back at him, with blank eyes, red nose, and trembling lips.

"Look," he said, looking at Kiera in the mirror, "I mean, what if…" then Ethan stopped.

"What if what?" Tabby asked.

"What if it's not safe to be around him right now?"

"Nick wouldn't hurt anyone—"

"The old Nick, Tabby. We don't know what is going on with this Nick until we get the story from him. Believe me, that did not seem like the old Nick. I'm telling you something felt off. And I don't think it was just nerves. I can't put my finger on it, but it just felt weird. Hopefully, we'll know more in few hours," then he added, "If he shows."

"And if he doesn't?" Kiera asked.

Ethan looked at Kiera in the rear-view mirror again, "I don't know. Let's solve one mystery at a time. Right now, meeting at the mall is plan A."

"What's plan B?" asked Tabby.

"I have no idea at this point."

CHAPTER 10

Marcus Garvey sat in the car staring a block down the street at the target's house with his phone pasted to his ear, growing more annoyed with each word from the caller's mouth. He had been skulking around with the field team for almost a week now, hating every minute of the job. Though the field assignment was not Marcus's first, he didn't care for the work. He was, after all, the data guy. After his previous field experience, he still couldn't get the taste out of his mouth or the images out of his mind. At hunting obscure data and making the seemingly random connections to otherwise unremarkable bits of collected data, Marcus was a regular Sherlock Holmes. He saw the things that most others missed or dismissed, some would say. The field team felt that Marcus, being the most knowledgeable regarding the target subject matter, should serve as an on-site guide to the operation. They felt that if this target were what they all believed it to be, Marcus would need to be there to help the team navigate this new paradigm. So, Marcus sat, spied, took photos, made notes, and took annoying phone calls asking for updates on an otherwise mundane stakeout.

"Yes, Amanda. I said yes, didn't I?" Marcus responded to the caller. He wiped a hand down his face trying to drag away his annoyance. Was he being doubted by Amanda? Top of the food chain or not, Amanda came to him any time she needed data assessed, some rare piece of archive searched, or placement of the seemingly non-connected dots.

First, she throws me out here in the wind with a bunch of psychos and then has the gall to double-check my work. Marcus thought as the voice on the other end of the call droned.

"Amanda, look, I know how important this is. I'm the one who found the patterns and the trail. I assure you that the farthermost idea from your mind should be of missing something. I have already identified the candidate and traced the path to where you guys have placed the teams," Marcus paused as Amanda said something on the other end of the line, then replied, "Yes, I know that. How many times must I have to tell you I know? I have already connected the most likely candidates for personal connections, and I have another team on the girl as we speak."

As Marcus continued to watch the target's house, a car pulled into the drive. A man got out and began walking up to the target's house.

"Amanda, I need to go. I have something at the target's residence." Marcus said, "Not right now, let me see if there is anything of note. I'll call back with a report as soon as I have something appreciable or at the next check-in window. Okay, I understand. Bye," he said, then disconnected from the still chattering call.

Marcus picked up a case from the back seat and put it on his lap. He opened the case, took out a camera with a long-range lens, and began to snap pictures of a mid to late-twenties-something male ringing the doorbell and shuffling side to side in front of the target's door. The guy in Marcus's viewfinder rang the bell again. Nothing. After the guy on the other end of Marcus's lens rang a third time, there still appeared to be no activity.

"Geez," Marcus uttered to himself, "this guy's pushy. Nobody's home, fella. There hasn't been any movement at that place all week." Suddenly the guy at the door started doing a bouncy little dance instead of the slow side-to-side shuffle. "What in the world is he," then Marcus stopped.

"Holy shit, he's talking to someone," Marcus said to no one. "To whom is he talking?"

Marcus raised his camera again and peered through the viewfinder. Zooming in the full one-thousand-millimeter range of its lens to get the shot as tight as he could, he pressed the shutter release button repeatedly. The camera's mechanical eye clicked like a combat rifle.

"He cannot be there. Jordon and I cleared that place two days ago. We watched it for three days before that," Marcus told himself. But, the mid to late-twenties-something guy was talking to someone on the other side of the target's door.

"To whom is he speaking?" Marcus swallowed to get his heart back down into his chest. He licked his lips as he recounted the teams' handoff exchanges. How could all his meticulousness lead him here? Sitting, taking pictures of some guy talking to the door of the target's house when his whole team thought no one was at home. Yet, here this guy was at the front door of a supposedly empty house, having a conversation with someone.

"I need to reposition. To get a better shot." Marcus opened the car door and then stopped realizing this was his inexperience trying to take over. He took a couple of breaths then thought, "No, do not move. I will have a chance to get the shot later. Now, we know he is home."

He watched as the guy backed slowly away from the target's door, then briskly walked back to his car. Marcus calmed and began to recount details of the teams' surveillance, replaying logs, check-ins, shift handoffs, and procedural protocols. How could the target be at home? How had he gotten past the teams? The shifts were lined up back to back, with shift changes overlapping to make sure no one missed anything. Had this guy been able to walk right into his house without anyone seeing him?

Someone had gotten lax or neglected to report a timeframe where someone had left their post and taken an unscheduled piss or gone for a snack. That had to be it, Marcus decided. Someone went for a snack or a piss, and the target must have come home during that narrow window of time.

He paused again, his eyes darting around in their sockets as he rolled the thoughts around in his internal analytical cycles. *Wait that is too cozy a timing.*

An unsettling thought came to Marcus that he wished had not. Have the teams been watching the target, or has the target been watching the teams? Marcus shivered. He reached over to his phone in the passenger's seat, started to dial, then paused. This call would not be pleasant. Looking at the phone in his hand, he sighed, then dialed Amanda's number. After two rings, someone answered.

"Hello, this is Carly."

"Carly, this is Marcus. I must speak to Amanda immediately."

"Ms. Dalling is currently in a—"

"I do not care what she is currently doing! This is team Red lead. Get her to the phone now!"

CHAPTER 11

Ethan, Tabby, and Keira sat exchanging silent glances at the herd hurrying from store to store, busily gathering their goods while bleating non-stop to one another. The food court's conversations rose into a blend of constant indiscernible noise as shoppers darted in and out of the area. Ethan checked the time on his watch.

"He's not coming," Ethan said, looking over at Tabby.

Keira, who was seated to Tabby's left, leaned forward and suggested, "Maybe he got stuck picking up his car. It could've taken him longer to get it at the park and ride."

"Maybe," Ethan replied, "But how long are we going to sit here? He's thirty-five minutes late. And really, would you come here knowing that you were essentially sitting down for a grilling?"

No one answered. Again, the trio exchanged glares, each feeling like this was becoming more a watch of dwindling hope rather than one of waiting. Suddenly Ethan nudged Tabby in the arm, then said in a low tone, "Hey, hey, hey. Check it out. Over by the Shoe Depot."

Tabby and Kiera looked at Ethan as he looked out over the food court to a figure standing just outside the trough of restaurants ringing the food court. Nick stood with his hands in his pockets, scanning the tables in the area.

Nick surveyed the atrium a second time, then suddenly turned and began to walk away. After about four steps, he stopped and lowered his head.

"Wait, he's leaving," Ethan said, rising from his chair.

Tabby grabbed Ethan's arm, "Ethan, hold on. Just give him a minute."

Ethan looked down at her, and she repeated, "Just give him a minute."

Ethan slowly sat back down. The three of them watched as Nick lingered with his back to the food court. Nick shook his head, slowly turned around, walked over to Greek Explosion, and purchased a drink. After taking a sip, he walked over to the group.

Nick reached a shaking hand out to pull a chair from the opposite side of the table. He sat down but did not say anything as the three opposing figures sat like gothic statues, their unblinking eyes drinking in Nick's every move.

Just as Nick thought the knot in his stomach would choke him, Ethan spoke, "Hey, Nick."

Nick stopped biting his lower lip long enough to reply, "Hey, Ethan. How have you been?"

"What? How have I been? In mourning for my best friend," he wanted to add, "asshole," but instead took a breath and said, "All three of us have been pretty upset, man."

Nick studied the lid of his cup, running his finger across its surface. He shuffled in his seat, refusing to make eye contact.

"Nick," Ethan was straining to keep his tone calm. "How are you? Are you okay? If so, where the hell have you been, man?"

Nick didn't answer. He continued to trace the designs on the lid of his cup.

Ethan continued, "Did you get hurt or sick down there? We gotta know cause I gotta tell you that we've been more than a little messed up since you disappeared on us."

"I seem to be fine," Nick answered, still not looking at any of them. "As far as I can tell, nothing's wrong."

Ethan started to say something else, but before he could, Kiera asked, "What do you mean 'seem to be'? Where have you been? What happened, Nick?"

Nick turned to Kiera. "Hey, Kiera."

"What's going on, Nick?"

"Nothing, as far as I know."

"What do you mean 'as far as I know?" asked Ethan, "Are you saying that you aren't going to tell us why you vanished and then popped back up like a damn jack in the box?"

"I can't give you what you're looking for, Ethan."

Ethan scowled. "What's that supposed to mean?"

"I can't tell you anything."

"Why is someone after you? Did you get into some kind of trouble?"

Nick didn't answer.

"What happened that is so bad you can't tell us? Nick, look, man, we just want to know where you've been and if you're okay."

Without looking up, Nick said, "I can't tell you because I don't know." He wiped his right eye with the palm of his hand.

"Nick, can you expand on that statement?" Tabby asked, her clinical training kicking in as she observed Nick's behavior.

"I mean that I don't remember anything, okay. I don't know what happened to me. I don't know where I've been. I don't even know how I got back home."

"Are you saying that you have *no* memories from the past two months? *Nothing?*"

Nick did not answer.

"You have no flashes at all? Nick, what *is* the last thing you remember?"

Nick sniffed and pulled a napkin from the dispenser on the table.

"Nick. If something's wrong, let us help," Ethan offered.

"The only thing I remember clearly was that I had breakfast on the second day of my trip and joined a guided tour. I remember seeing what I thought was a partially uncovered cave or another temple entrance, so I left the tour group to check it out. I remember going in, turning on my flashlight, then I woke up on my bed yesterday morning."

As Tabby sat listening, the conversations and activities around their table seemed to fade into the background as she focused on Nick.

"That's it. When I opened my eyes yesterday, I was in my room. I was confused, weak, dirty. I didn't even know that two months had passed until I got another phone from the wireless outlet. After the guy at the store handed me my new phone, my first thought was to call Kiera. When I swiped the screen, I saw the date," Nick let out a nervous chuckle, "I thought the guy behind the counter had somehow messed up the activation or the phone was defective. I walked back into the store and asked the guy what the date was. When he told me, I didn't know what to say. I just stood at the counter in a daze. It felt like I was in some kind of dream. I heard the guy behind the counter saying something that took me a moment to understand. He was asking me if I was okay. I told him yes then walked out. The guy stood there staring at me like I had three eyes. I couldn't blame him after I thought about it later."

"Why didn't you call one of us anyway?" Kiera asked.

"Yeah, okay, Kiera. How would that have worked? What was I supposed to say? Hey guys, it's Nick. Haven't seen you guys in a couple of months. Let's get together. How would you have answered that one?"

No one argued, so Nick added, "Exactly. That would have gone over like a lead balloon. Think about it."

"I saw you."

"What? When?"

"Why do you think we came over this morning? I saw you yesterday. Through your bedroom window. I was across the street."

"Why?"

"I've been by there a few times since you…." Kiera shook her head. "Sometimes, it just helps. Going there has been my way of getting by, of easing the…." She trailed off then started again. "I saw you through the window. It was a shock," then she added, "A little scary, really."

"Scary?"

"Yes. Wouldn't you be? No one has seen you for two months, then all of a sudden, you show up, looking beat to death. I didn't know what was going on, and now you're telling us you don't know where you were or what you were doing. So yes, it is a little scary."

Nick didn't say anything as he returned to studying his drink. "That's the reason I wanted to meet here. I mean, *I* don't know if I'm dangerous, in danger, or just losing my fucking mind." Nick bit his lower lip again as a tear fell from the tip of his nose onto the table.

"Okay. So, how can we help? What do we need to do?" Nick looked up, then Ethan asked again, "How can we help?"

"I don't know," Nick replied.

"The first thing we do is get you checked out." Tabby offered. "You need a full medical workup to make sure nothing is wrong physically."

"And if everything is fine?" Nick asked.

"Then we move on to something else."

"You mean we start checking my brain. Check if I'm crazy or not."

"Crazy is not a medical diagnosis."

"Yeah, tell that to my mom."

"Nick, not all mental—"

"It doesn't matter, Tabby." He interrupted, slamming his fist down on the table. "If I can't tell you where I've been or what I've been doing for two months, then something is seriously wrong, and a tumor wouldn't explain it. I know that much. You can label it however you want; it won't change what it means. An official diagnosis is just a way to label whatever fucking flavor of crazy your genetics have saddled you with."

"Nick, it will be alright. Regardless of whatever is happening to you, we are going to be there to help you through."

"What if there is no through? What then? Are you guys just gonna stay around and help change my diapers?"

"Look, I understand the feelings that you are experiencing right now but lashing out will not help. We need to get to the root. Together. I'll make some calls, and we'll start working this out tomorrow."

"Tomorrow is Sunday," Ethan said.

Tabby turned to him and smiled, "Yeah, but I have some favors owed to me that I am going to cash in." She turned back to Nick, "Nick, will you let me set up an appointment with a friend of mine for first thing tomorrow morning?"

After a moment, Nick agreed.

"Alright," Ethan said, "at least we have a game plan. Look, dude, I don't know what has been going on since you left, but you are around people who can support you now. We've got you covered."

After a moment passed, Ethan said, "Look, we'll start getting this sorted. For now, ah, you wanna cruise the mall a bit. Get back into life for a few minutes? It may help you to be around other people you know."

"Not really up to it right now."

"Alright, man. It's okay. We'll start catching up tomorrow."

"Yeah, okay," Nick replied weakly.

"I'm still pretty tired. I think that I'll just go home."

"Yeah, okay. Listen, if you need anything, please call."

"Sure. Will do. See you tomorrow."

They watched as Nick turned and began to walk away from the food court, then disappeared into the mall. Tabby was on her phone calling in her favors before Nick vanished around a corner.

CHAPTER 12

On the way home, Nick decided sitting around in isolation may not be such a great idea and regretted not taking Ethan up on spending some more time with the group. Around seven-thirty, he decided that a drink might soothe his nerves.

When Nick opened the door to Sullivan's Bar and Grill, the sound of laughter, sports playing from the mounted TVs, and the clink of glasses slipped out onto the sidewalk. He had driven around looking for a spot where hopefully no one he knew would find him. Sullivan's had three different locations in the area, which meant he could go to a familiar environment but perhaps not see anyone he knew. Nick squeezed his way through the door of the bar, in between trays with waitresses attached and tightly packed tables. Once seated at a spot at the bar, he turned to look back over the room. As he scanned the area, a voice suddenly drew his attention.

"What can I get you?"

"Scotch. On the rocks," he said without looking.

The bartender nodded and walked away. When she returned and sat the drink down, she said, "You like you're carrying a particularly weighty cross on your back tonight. I haven't seen a face that long since my last horseback ride. I used the top-shelf stuff, but there's no top-shelf charge for it."

Nick raised the glass and tipped his head in thanks, "You have no idea," he said.

"Well, you just yell if you need anything else," the bartender replied with a wide smile.

"Thanks, I will."

Nick took a sip of his drink then took a moment to skim to the room again, hoping no one he knew was in the bar. If anyone he knew was in the bar, Nick decided he would dart for the exit. Talk was not the reason he was here. Instead, he wanted to be around the normalcy of noise and people. Most of all, to drink until he felt just numb enough for his mind to allow him some sleep. As Nick moved his gaze from the other side of the bar to where he was seated, he, unfortunately, caught some unwanted attention. Sitting about mid-way down the front of the bar, a desperate housewife-looking woman was hungrily giving him a look that he recognized all too well and wanted no part of tonight. He quickly averted his eyes, looking back down at his drink. The woman apparently read into his millisecond of eye contact some invitation because a smooth hand with brightly polished nails appeared in between Nick's face and his drink.

"Hey, I'm Rhonda." She leaned in, putting her mouth close to nick's ear to be heard over the live band that had started up with a boisterous opening round of The Boys are Back by the Dropkick Murphys.

"I'm Nick," he said, ignoring her outstretched hand.

Another bar patron came up alongside Rhonda and climbed onto the stool beside Nick, leaving him feeling like fate was trying to lend him a hand by sending a message to Rhonda. The message was to leave. Without looking, Rhonda raised her rear and backed it onto the stool. Her bottom met the guy's left hip that had taken the seat, so he turned to look at her.

The man looked down at her intruding ass. "I like it, but may I help you?" the man asked.

"Yes. Move your ass. You're in my seat."

"I didn't see you sitting here."

"You saw me standing here talking to my friend, so let's go."

Rhonda put her left hand on Nick's arm and used him as a bracing wall to drive her ass into the man's hip until she had nearly pushed both the man and Nick out of their seats.

"Alright. Alright. Damn lady," the man said. "Here. You can have the damn stool." The man said as he hopped down and followed with a, "And fuck you very much," as he turned and walked away.

Rhonda called after him, "Not right now, but maybe later. Let's see how the night goes," then she turned back to Ethan and smiled.

"Speaking of…. You here alone, or are you meeting someone later?"

Trying to remain pleasant, Nick replied, "No, not meeting anyone. Just trying to get an elixir before heading home," He held up his glass and took a drink, hoping Rhonda would take the hint.

Seemingly fueled by the hint, Rhonda motioned for the bartender to make her a fresh sangria. When the bartender sat the drink down, Rhonda grabbed an orange wedge that was bobbing at the top of the glass and turned to Nick, "So, your whole plan is just to go home? Alone? Why that doesn't sound fun even a little." Then Rhonda promptly put the orange wedge in her mouth and slowly drew it out, sucking its entire length until she ended with an exaggerated smack from her lips.

Desperate, Nick thought, then replied, "Been a long day. That's the plan. Just home."

"You sure? There's nothing you may want to do that's more interesting than watching the eleven o'clock news?"

"I appreciate your taking the time to come over and introduce yourself, Rhonda. I'm just not firing on all cylinders tonight. So, the eleven o'clock news is all I plan on getting involved in."

"Well, okay," she said, offering him a pouty lower lip. Nick thought the conversation was over until she continued, "I haven't seen you before. You come here a lot?"

"Pretty often, well not to this one," he corrected, motioning around the room, "I usually go to the place off Dixon Road."

"Ah. Okay, well, maybe we'll meet up another night," she placed her hand on the inner portion of Nick's upper thigh and gave a longing squeeze, "one night when all those cylinders of yours are running on turbo, maybe."

Rhonda smiled, hopped down from the barstool, and weaved her way through the room until she found an open spot at the front of the room near the stage, where she sat down and started casting her line at the band members to see which one would bite.

"I don't think I have ever seen *anyone*, male *or* female, turn that woman down," Nick heard a voice say.

Nick whipped his head around to see the red-headed bartender leaning on the bar in front of his seat. "Oh yeah, she's pretty," Nick said, looking back across the room. "I'm just not really into any excitement tonight. I've had enough of that for today."

"Be glad you passed, honey," she leaned in closer and lowered her voice, "She's what I would call a professional fisherman."

"You mean she's a hooker?" Nick asked, nearly spitting his drink out.

"Oh, hell no, at least I don't think so," the bartender distorted her face as she thought for a moment, then said, "Let's just say, anytime she comes in, if she *wants* to leave with a catch, I have never seen her leave without a fish, that's all. Come to think about it, I've never seen her leave with the same fish more than once."

Not knowing exactly how to respond to that statement, Nick just held up his drink and said, "Nice. Well, guess I dodged a bullet then."

"I'm Jenn," the bartender said, holding out an outstretched hand.

"Nick," he said, returning the gesture.

"I've only been here about three months, but I've never seen you in here. You new to the area or just passing through?"

"Neither," Nick replied, "I've been out of town the past couple months and was pretty busy the month before that, so I'm actually a regular at Sullivan's," Then he added, "Not this one. I usually go to the place off Dixon."

"Nice."

Nick smiled, relieved that this conversation felt a lot less desperate than his talk had been with Rhonda. He found himself starting to enjoy the interaction. The tension in his shoulders began to ease as he thought maybe Ethan had been right. All he needed was some facetime with other people.

Nick continued conversing with the bartender until a vice seized his shoulder in mid-drink and spun him around, nearly pulling him off his stool. As the sudden whirl came to a stop, Nick saw that the vice was attached to a roid-raged mountain of flesh. Nick also saw, regrettably, that half his drink was now covering the man's shirt.

"Brad, what the hell?" Jenn exclaimed.

"You stay out of this," Brad said, thrusting an angry finger in Jenn's face.

The mass of flesh then turned from Jenn back to Nick and asked, "You think it's okay to talk to my woman, you little fucknut?"

"I'm not your woman. We haven't been together for a month because you're a whoring asshole. Now get out, or I'm gonna get Ronny to *put* your ass out."

"Let Ronny try." Brad chuckled. "And on top of everything," Brad looked back at Nick, "this asshole dumps his drink all over me."

"In my defense," the words spilled out of Nick's mouth before he knew he had even spoken them, "you dumped it on my behalf there, Brad." Nick's breath caught for a moment. He could not believe what he had just said. Was he really taunting this guy?

Brad's eyes tightened as the muscles of his jaws worked in and out, "You shit sucking little," the mass of flesh that was Brad grabbed Nick's shirt with one fist while his other fist was already on a collision course toward Nick's face. Nick felt the room shift around him as he watched Brad's fist hurtle toward his face in slow motion. He could see each knuckle protruding from under bloodless skin. He could see the pulsing blood in Brad's veins along the top of the hand. Before Nick's actions could register, he snapped his hand up to block the attacker's offensive like a Kung Fu god. To his and Brad's, astonishment Nick caught Brad's fist, stopping it as if it had hit a wall. Brad's face contorted again, but this time instead of rage, it showed shock.

Brad began to jerk and heave at his fist to free it from Nick's grip with no success. The light in the room slowly started to morph into a shrinking orb of light as darkness closed in on Nick's sight from all directions. He felt the muscles in his arm contact as his grip on Brad's clenched fist tightened.

"What am I doing?" Nick thought as he felt his mouth spread into a baleful grin. He tried to let go of the fist, but his hand would not respond. He felt his grip tighten more than he would have ever believed possible. His eyes narrowed as he continued to bear down on Brad's fist until the bones began to give way, snapping and cracking like dry twigs between Nick's fingers. Brad screamed. His pleadings turned to cries of ragged pain as he fell to his knees, tears flowing uncontrollably. He tried to beg Nick to stop but what came from his mouth between flying spats of spittle was a high-pitched whine of indecipherable dribble.

Nick dropped Brad's hand, placed his now empty hand under Brad's chin, and gently nudged him to his feet. Brad continued to sob, holding his crushed hand to his chest. Nick looked at him with cold curiosity, calmly examining the agony on Brad's face like a child studying a bug. Taking in the features of Brad's face and his hand's condition while he slowly moved his head from side to side, observing Brad in emotionless silence, seeming to drink in his suffering. With Nick's nudging, Brad looked from his mangled hand to Nick. On seeing Nick's black eyes, a dark spot appeared on the front of Brad's jeans and grew until the darkening pattern in the fabric ran down his leg and a puddle formed around his feet. Brad started chattering something unintelligible again, then to franticly whimper, making him sound like an abused dog. Nick lifted his left hand and placed it gently on Brad's chest. Nick felt a sensation begin in his chest then radiate down his arm until a pulse of invisible energy exploded from his hand. The whole sensation taking less than a half-second. The pulse seemed to radiate outward, through Brad, once it left his hand, then spread across the room. As the pulse ripped through the bar, the entire room erupted into violence.

The sound of the music in the bar was replaced with electronic feedback, mixed with smashing guitars that rang out from the still active amplifiers. Screams of both men and women pierced the air as glass broke over people's heads and bottles smashed against tables. The mirror behind the bar was shattered, along with all the display beverages, as two men hurled a third man across the bar into the back wall. People threw chairs and overturned tables in a riot of rage that had driven everyone mad with the need to kill everyone else around them. Nick smiled and began to hum as he casually made his way through the melee toward the door. His vision, nearly clothed in black, was still functioning enough so he could see a man slamming another man's face into a table, causing his nose to bloom like a springtime rose, just as another man was breaking Rhonda's arm over the back of a chair. The tiny orb of light that was Nick's sight vanished completely into darkness as he walked out the door of the bar.

CHAPTER 13

Kiera blinked against the blackness in the room, allowing a moment for the shapes in the shadows to form. She walked over to the bathroom door, opened it, and froze as she stared out across a vast open nothingness. There was no ghostly glow of the toilet beside the sink's white and silver form. The space beyond the door seemed an infinite black. She reached for the door, wanting to slam it closed, then stopped.

Turn on the lights. Run back to the bed, fear screamed in her mind.

Instead, she found herself moving forward, almost as if being pulled, not caring where her feet fell as she walked.

As she stepped through the expansive black, cold embraced her. She looked down to see she was standing in water. She wiggled her toes from inside her wet socks and studied the shimmering black beneath her feet. Except for the ripples from her movements, the wet surface ran as far as she could see in a shallow glass sea of silence. The water rippled out again as Kiera found herself taking another step away from the comfort of the bathroom door, the water rippling out like a heartbeat. As she continued forward, the bathroom door remained, standing out of place in this unbroken night like a beacon against the dark, casting the moon's pale glow into the space. Kiera turned, then decided that to call this place dark was not exactly right either. She noted that while everything around her seemed to be shrouded in night, she could see herself clearly, and in full color as if being lit by a noonday sun. Kiera squinted at the distance as something caught her attention. She saw a faint glow emanating from a small, distant spot directly in front of her. She looked back toward the open bathroom door and shuddered again, this time, not from the cold. She saw herself, her body anyway, through the doorway lying peacefully in the bed. Seeing herself lying sound asleep, she told herself that this was another stress nightmare.

"At least this time," she thought, "I know it's a dream."

Armed with the knowledge that this was a dream made her feel a little more at ease, so she continued, feeling drawn toward the spec of light in the distance. As she moved toward the dimly lit area, the pounding in her chest seemed to rattle her ribcage with each successive beat. As she drew closer, she could see an object in the middle of the lighted area, floating above the watery surface.

The object became clearer as she moved closer. Another step and the shape more closely resembled a human body, hanging suspended as if it were a balloon on a tether. The body's head was laid back, arms out to its sides with its legs dangling as if the body were floating on an invisible surface, and the legs were dangling just below the top of the pool. The face smiled at Kiera as the body's dry, dead skin pulled back around the mouth in a grey smile. Realization hit her like a club. The suspended body floating before her like a disembodied ghost was Nick.

A stream of gray-black dust rose from the suspended body's right hand and trailed away seemingly into nothingness. Kiera reached for the stream, then drew her hand back to cover her mouth. At first, Kiera thought the dust appeared to be suspended, unmoving. As she watched, she noticed it was moving up, away from the floating apparition. Her eyes followed the stream of dust back down to his hand. Stepping closer, she could see as the particles pulled away from Nick. The edges of his fingers seemed ragged. What she was seeing was not dust at all, but instead, it was the apparition's essence. Nick's essence was streaming out to vanish into the blackness. The particles continued to lift away as if he were slowly dissolving, one cell at a time. Already half of one finger on his right hand had dissolved. The finger beside it had begun to fade into the stream as well.

"Kiera," a voice echoed from the darkness. The reverberating echo boomed at her from all directions. The voice slipped and shimmered as if coming from underwater. Kiera franticly searched the expanse for the source, although it seemed to come from all directions at once.

"Kiera," came the voice again.

"Nick? Is this Nick?" No answer. "Who is this? What is this place?"

"This is the black," the voice returned like a ghost on the wind. "The space between places."

"What does that *mean*?" Again, the voice gave no reply.

"Why are you here? Nick, what's happening?"

"It is the Ehus Salmu Duranki."

"What?"

"Ehus Salmu Duranki," the voice repeated.

"Why are you here, like this? What does it mean?" she motioned to the body as she continued to search the darkness.

"For enu?"

"What is enu?"

"For enu," the voice echoed again. "For change."

"Nick, I don't understand. Tell me what you mean?" Kiera closed her eyes and slapped herself, "Wake up, damn you. Just wake up," she demanded. She opened her eyes only to see the images did not change as Nick's floating body remained suspended before her. Only now, his eyes were open. He was looking directly at her with the milky eyes of a long-dead corpse. Kiera's bare feet were starting to grow numb from the exposure to the frigid water. She closed her eyes and slapped herself again, demanding that she wake up.

"Kiera, find Nasaru," the voice chorused.

"What is a Nasaru?"

"Find the Nasaru."

"Nick!" she screamed into the expanse, "What is the Nasaru?"

She felt a tug from behind her, and Nick began to shrink away.

Kiera clawed for purchase at the nothingness in front of her as she screamed, "No! Nick!" The tug from behind her became a blast from in front of her, forcing her backward toward her body. She turned to see the doorway through which she had entered the black. She didn't understand why the door was now just a distant speck. As she approached the opening, she saw her body through the doorway, still lying asleep. She tensed, thinking she would almost certainly smash into the bathroom doorway. She raised her arms to shield her face.

"It's just a dream," she heard herself, over and over through quivering lips.

She passed through the doorway and slammed into her body, jolting awake. She bolted up and threw the covers off her as she gasped for a desperate gulp for air. Her stomach churned. She covered her mouth with her hand and ran to the bathroom.

Seeing that the bathroom was as expected, she plunged through the doorway, reaching for the toilet as she fell to her knees and heaved what she thought may have been her soul into the bowl. Vomit hit the water and splashed back up onto her face from the soupy surface, causing her to vomit more. She had nothing left to offer the bowl after two more convulsive heaves. Her body tried to wretch twice more, producing only greenish froth. She caught her breath, wiped the spittle from her mouth with some tissue paper, and flushed.

After sitting on the floor for a few moments, making sure her nausea had passed, Kiera grabbed the sink and pulled herself up from the floor. Turning on the faucet, she took a moment to rinse her mouth and face with some cool water, then followed up by brushing her teeth. Afterward, she grabbed some tissue paper and wiped the toilet's rim clean before leaving the bathroom. As she walked toward the bed, Kiera jumped at the sound of a knock on her door.

"Hey." It was Tabby's voice. "Are you decent?"

"Yes, come in."

"Hey girl, you okay?" Tabby asked, opening the door. "It sounded like you were puking your guts up."

"I did."

"You feel alright?"

"I feel fine now."

Kiera looked down at the bed. She reached a trembling hand down to where her feet had been as she slept and felt the sheets. There was a dark spot on the bed linen, where the sheets were now soiled.

Noticing Kiera's expression, Tabby asked, "Kiera, what is it?"

"Tabby come here; I need you to see something."

Tabby walked over and looked at the area where Kiera was staring.

"So, you spilled water on the bed. It's not the end of the world." Kiera looked to the still half-full glass of water on her bedside nightstand.

"I didn't *spill* anything. But you see that spot, right?"

"Well yeah. The bed's wet." Tabby gave Keira a puzzled smile.

"I didn't spill anything on the bed, Tabby, but I *did* dream that I was walking through water last night."

The two women stood, silently looking at one another, waiting to see who would speak the next, hopefully sane, explanation for the soiled linens.

"No," Tabby said with a dismissive tone, "honey, that's ridiculous."

"Then how did the water get there?"

"Well, I don't know but come on." Tabby studied the spot some more, then added, "I don't know, but Kiera, come on. Dream water?"

"Nothing else in the room is wet, and I dreamed that I was standing in water. When I woke up, the sheets were wet around my feet. How do you explain it?"

"Okay. Okay. Okay." Tabby said, shaking her head and waving her hands. "Before we go for a stroll through paranormal corner, let's just get our showers and some coffee, then we can remake your bed and talk."

Kiera dressed and made it down to the kitchen before Tabby had gotten out of the shower. She grabbed her laptop and powered it on. She pulled up a search engine and began to type in the words and phrases Nick had told her in her dream.

After attempting several spellings of the words, struggling to recall how the voice in her dream pronounced each one, the search engine returned a successful result, although not very helpful. ENU came back from the search engine as a mutagenic agent used to create genetic change in lab mice. After finding no other useful results, she found an online ancient language database and tried several guesses of the spellings, again turning up nothing. With her frustration on maximum, she sighed and closed the laptop. She sat sipping her coffee in silence until Tabby came downstairs.

"Morning again," Tabby said, making her way to the coffee maker, "You get calmed down from earlier?"

"Yes," Kiera answered, biting her thumbnail.

Tabby made a cup of coffee and sat down at the table with Kiera, "Okay, so let's go over this dream. You were freaked. I get it. So, tell me about it."

Kiera recounted the details as Tabby sat with her mouth agape during most of the telling. She would sip her coffee periodically and listen as Kiera rehashed the details. Kiera looked up to see a look on Tabby's face she recognized. She stopped speaking and leered at Tabby.

"What?" Tabby asked.

"Don't psychoanalyze me?"

"I'm not."

"I have seen that look before, Tabby. I know when you're working."

"I'm not, honest. This is just my face. I am just trying to make sense out of all these dreams you keep having. They seem to be a nightly event now. I'm concerned, that's all."

"Concerned that I'm going crazy?"

"No," Tabby cut in, ignoring Kiera's use of crazy as a descriptor for mental illness, "I am just concerned how Nick's returning is wearing on you. I mean, you can't tell me that him coming back to life, so to speak, is any easier to deal with than his disappearance. I mean, it's one thing to vanish that unfortunately happens to people often, but then to pop back up with no memory of where you have been or what has happened for two months, that's a lot to take in. These nightmares, every night, were never an issue before Nick magically reappeared." She reached across the table and took Kiera's hand, "Kiera, I just care about you, and I want you to be okay."

"No, it's not normal." Keira acknowledged, "I know part of this has to be stress," then Kiera paused, trying to direct her thoughts before she continued, "but this time, I can't get past having a dream about standing in water and waking up with wet sheets, Tabby."

"I don't have an answer for that," Tabby quickly responded. "Look, we're going to figure this out. In the meantime, let's just try to stay as calm as we can. You sit. I'll get some breakfast whipped up before we go pick up Nick."

CHAPTER 14

Josh sat staring out the second-floor window of Our Lady of Peace, considering his place in life. It felt like a kick in the nuts to be alone. No relative had ever come looking for him, but now to be alone and losing what felt like the better part of his mind seemed to be the icing on a four-tier shit cake. He had learned years ago that feeling sorry for yourself didn't help anyone, so he had decided he would stop. Stop all the pity parties and woe-is-me sessions and focus forward. He was young, healthy, and could always look to making a future for himself since the past didn't leave a lot to look back on and remember. But still, now, sitting here looking out this window, he began to ask himself something he had never asked before. He started to reason that maybe, losing it, losing yourself, may perhaps be the last straw. If the world found no value in him, should he continue to take up space in it? He had never been adopted, only served time in a foster home twice, and the world ran on around him. Without him. It was as if he were a spare cog instead of an essential spoke in the wheel. He told himself there would always be a tomorrow but was that true. Did there need to be a tomorrow for a kid who sits, taking up space, watching his bunkmates all cycle out around him as he remained, a lone soldier, manning his post by this window until the bitter end?

Stop it. You promised that you would not have pity parties anymore, much less whatever this is that you are thinking about.

He dragged his hand down his face and felt an odd thing as he closed his fist. His palm was wet. He reached his other hand up and touched his cheek. Realizing that he had been so deep in thoughts of being in a world that he was not a part of, he had started to cry. Yeah, a *really* odd thing and out of character for Mr. No Pity Party. He had managed to do a pretty good job of not letting himself mope around and sulk like the lame emo kids did all the time. Thinking about making a last decision while crying unawares pushed it a bit too much. He wiped his eyes and looked around the room to make sure none of the other house members had been watching him baby it up. Seeing no one, he wiped his hands on a shirt that had been lying beside him and said, "No, I *have* to go. I know it's stupid. I have to know, so I have to go." He sighed and thought, *I'm going to be on shit duty with the sisters for a year if they catch me.*

Josh stood up, took a moment to make sure his bed dressings were wrinkle-free, then bent and pulled his backpack from under the bunk. He let the pack plunk onto his bed, unzipped it, and emptied it of its content. Walking over to the storage locker at the foot of his bed, he knelt and removed the belongings from the locker, then stuffed everything into his pack. Then another thought hit him, an idea for striking a blow for justice. He looked across the shared dormitory toward the trunk at the foot of Jeff Turner's bed.

He walked over to Jeff's trunk and opened it. He knew Jeff always had extra money stashed away in the bottom of his trunk, not only because Josh had seen Jeff pull out his hidden funds several times, but because Jeff was the biggest asshole to come through the home in a long time. Jeff usually filled his time by busying himself with finding new ways to extort, exploit, bully, and otherwise harass all the other kids, hence the striking a blow for justice angle. Josh hoped the extortion and exploitation portion of Jeff's industrious nature was about to pay. Josh opened the trunk and dug to the bottom, trying not to disrupt the trunk's contents. Stuffed into a back corner of the trunk, Josh felt a wad of money. *Good grief, Jeff's been a busy boy.* He pulled out the wad and stuffed it into his pack, thinking he would count it later, which, when he did calculate his haul, amounted to a total of one hundred fifty-one dollars. Josh nestled it into his wallet beside the three hundred forty dollars he was still holding on to he had earned cutting neighborhood yards within biking distance all summer long. He had earned just over a thousand dollars during the whole season but, since Josh was an old-timer in this home, the sisters at times allowed him a bit more freedom to go, do and spend, so the three hundred forty dollars was all that was left.

You've got it coming anyway, you jackass, Josh thought as he slung his pack over his shoulder and quickly stepped through the bunk room door. Just as he reached the floor at the bottom of the main stairs, Sister Nestor was there to greet him.

"Hello Josh," she said in what sounded like a song. Sister Nestor was always unnecessarily cheery, sometimes to the point of Josh questioning her state of mind. "Are we skipping lunch again, Josh?" Sister Nestor tilted her head and pooched out her bottom lip in disapproval.

"Yes, ma'am, Sister Nestor. I want to go out and get a few errands done."

Shit, Josh thought, *that was the wrong answer. Now she will ask me a million questions about the errands.*

"Chasing more yards to mow at the end of the season, Josh?"

Josh sighed in relief, "Yes. Yes, ma'am. Yards will only need cutting a couple more weeks, and I wanted to see if I could pick up a few extra. It's good money, especially this late in the season."

Since Josh had not thought up a plan any more complicated than going downstairs and walking out, a plan which had already gone off the rails, he decided to try to sell it a little harder.

He leaned in as if he were about to share a secret with Sister Nestor and lowered his voice, "I also want to put out some feelers in the area for fall work." Sister Nestor gave Josh a questioning look, so Josh clarified, "You know. The grass cutting is starting to fall off, and that always leaves me dry in fall and winter unless I want to work fast food, so I was thinking I would ask around about doing fall work." He held up an open hand, then counted off the options as he said, "You've got leaves, fall flowers, pine straw, you know, fall stuff. Hey, some of the houses within my work area even have firewood, and I bet someone would love to trade a little help for a little scratch."

After Sister Nestor understood, she gave an approving, "Ah, well thought out, Josh." Josh liked Sister Nestor, she was always kind, and he had never heard her say a cross word to anyone in the home, but he couldn't stop himself from wondering why she had to sing everything. Sister Nestor may have been cheerful to a fault, but Josh knew she was street smart, shrewd, in a nice way, and could smell bullshit from across the yard. Just as Josh thought she was about to call him out, Sister Nestor asked, "Josh, when you get your wages do you pay the church's required tithe?"

Josh's heart started beating again as he answered, "Oh, yes ma'am, you know that I believe in the levy, Sister. I mean, I always pay according to canon law."

Well, maybe lying to nun is not as bad a sin as it seems, Josh assured himself.

"After all, I am grateful to have a warm bed and food in my belly every day." He almost cringed as the words came out of his mouth. He thought it must have sounded like a used car salesman trying to spit-shine a rusty tug. Josh was shining this lie to the point where you would be able to see its reflection from space.

Having not sniffed the bullshit this time, Sister Nestor gave Josh a gracious smile and nodded her head, giving him her most pious approval right before she hit him with another question. "Josh, are you feeling alright?" This time there was no melody, just a flat, sincere question.

"Joshua, do you feel okay this morning?" she asked again.

"What do you mean, ma'am? I feel fine."

"Well, it's just," she made a circle in the air, motioning to his eyes, "your eyes are very red. Are you certain everything is okay?"

Josh thought since he had already lied to a nun once today and was still alive, he may as well heap coals onto the fire and answered, "Oh that. You know the nice lady I told you about, the one that always gives me the fresh lemonade? Mrs. Wiggins." The name didn't seem to register with Sister Nestor, so Josh continued, "Anyway, I cut her yard yesterday, and she had a couple of like bare spots. When the mower went over them, I got completely dusted. My eyes are just irritated."

Sister Nestor did not look convinced but said, "Okay. But Josh, they were not red at breakfast this morning."

Oh, here it comes. Her bullshit detector is starting to light up, Josh thought but responded, "Yeah, I've been rubbing them all day. The redness is probably from the rubbing."

This excuse seemed to convince Sister Nestor. "Okay, as long as nothing is bothering you, you may go."

Josh walked past Sister Nestor. He had made three paces when she called his name, causing him to stop and turn around. He saw Sister Nestor looking at him with a look he seldom saw on her face, concern mixed with what he assumed was seriousness. "Mister Roland," she said, "I think one day you are going to find yourself very surprised at what you will be able to accomplish despite your humble beginnings. I can see it in you, Josh. You just need to see it for yourself."

Josh nodded, then thought he needed to get moving before he started crying again. He wanted to believe what Sister Nestor was saying, but deep down, where no one could see no matter how big the smile on his face was, Josh still could not shake the growing feeling that he almost certainly was just a useless cog. One that didn't seem to fit into any other machinery in life. So the cog was left to lay as a spare. Rusting. Wasting. If Sister Nestor saw something that made her believe he would accomplish big things one day, then let her believe it. Lately, Josh had difficulty seeing anything in the mirror other than missed opportunities, *his* missed opportunities.

Opportunities like when couples came seeking to adopt, he and the other boys were paraded around like livestock, then seated for the crucial meet and greet. Afterward, none ever returned to tell Josh he now would have a home and a family. As days passed, the repeated rejections left Josh lying alone in the dark with the covers pulled over his head, asking what was wrong with him. What was his defect that caused first his mother to abandon him, then all the other couples seeming to approve of her decision by doing the same? Josh often questioned what caused families to pick all the other boys instead of him in the early years. He would lie in his bed day after day, month after month, then finally year after year, growing older. As expected, as time moved on, requests to interview him slowed. Around twelve years old, no one ever wanted to see him. Who wanted a boy who would be a teenager next year when all the shoppers came to pick out the shiny, new boys, not the angst-filled, abandoned, pimply-faced loaner that must, it was usually assumed, be damaged goods? What else could explain why he would still be in the orphanage.

When the requests for boys Josh's age stopped, Josh barely noticed because hope had left him about four years earlier. In truth, when he saw couples coming into the home with their bright smiles, walking arm in arm or hand in hand, he would quietly pray that the sisters did not ask him to meet the couples so he wouldn't have to lay in bed and beat down the murderous lies hope brought in the night when no one was watching. Hope tried to make you think that you would have a home this time. You would have a family. You may even have a brother or sister. He would tell himself that hope was dead, that there was not a chance he would be selected. He had to beat hope down and stuff it into a box in the corner, then cover it every time. Hope made you feel like you may be worth something after all, that you are someone that another wants to love, only to find out that you are not. Hope was a killer. Each time your hope is shattered, you die all over again. So, hope was a companion that Josh had long ago found a way to put out of its misery so the dying could be stopped. He thought he had done a fair job, that is, until the last couple of months.

Josh swallowed as his throat tightened, his true feelings nearly choking him. He nodded in thanks to Sister Nestor and turned to hurry out the door. Once outside, he walked past his bike, deciding to leave it at the home. He couldn't take it with him on a bus anyway. He felt like this was the last time the useless cog would never see this home, his *only* childhood home, ever again. Thinking of what it must be like to say goodbye to an old friend, Josh looked over his shoulder to get one more look at the home. To his surprise, he felt a sense of loss. He thought of how he would miss the sisters, the only mothers he had ever known. He questioned if the things he felt now were similar to normal teens' feelings, the unbroken ones, once they finally leaped from their nests and spread their wings for the first time. Like so many others, he guessed the question was another for which he would never receive an answer. Josh looked away and focused forward.

CHAPTER 15

Nick awoke from what felt like a very restful sleep, which was in direct opposition to how he had awakened two mornings earlier, disoriented, filthy, and in pain. He looked at the time on his new cell phone, gave a long, satisfying stretch, and sat up. He started thinking about the conversations that had taken place with Ethan, Tabby, and Kiera. Only questions persisted. The mounting sense of dread that gnawed at the back of Nick's mind began to eat away at his newfound sense of restful sleep.

Nick got out of bed and walked into the bathroom. As he stood brushing his teeth, he recalled his conversation with Rhonda at Sullivan's the night before. He then drifted to thoughts of talking to Jenn, the bartender. After the discussion with the bartender, he met her amped-up boyfriend. He stopped brushing and stared at himself in the mirror, his face becoming slack. The night's recollections began to get a little fuzzy from that point forward. Wasn't Jenn's ex some meathead who tried to start something with him? Yes. It was Jenn's ex-boyfriend. The reflection in the mirror stared back at Nick with a worried look on its face. How did that turn out? Nick tried to remember but only drew blank spaces where the memories should have been. He assumed it had all worked out since the face in the mirror with the toothpaste-frothed mouth did not show any signs of having been pummeled. Nick spat, resumed brushing his teeth, then realized he didn't recall driving home last night either.

Shit, another blackout.

Realizing he had once again lost time, he rinsed his mouth and walked to his nightstand to check the time and date on his phone again. At least it had only been a few hours this time instead of two months. Yet, the fact that Nick had gone oblivious again and then had awakened in his bed only caused him to sink deeper into his growing depression. At least this latest episode had happened at home and only lasted a few hours. At least this time, he could try to retrace his steps.

He looked through the contacts on his phone until he came to Ethan's name. He tapped the icon beside Ethan's name, and the phone began dialing.

"Hello," came a voice from Nick's phone.

"Hey, Ethan, it's Nick."

"Hey, man. Ah, morning. What's up? You good?"

"Yeah, fine," he lied. "I know that you guys told me last night my appointment is at ten-thirty, but I wanted to run an errand before we go. I will meet you guys there when it's time?"

"Sure, I guess. It's your call," then Ethan added slowly, "but you'll be there?"

"Yes. Definitely. Look, I need to figure this out. I just, I've been gone a while, so there is something I want to do while it's early."

"Okay," Ethan said hesitantly, "I guess we'll see you there."

"Yes." To convince Ethan, he would not blow off the appointment. He added, "Don't forget to text me the address."

"I will. I'll do it as soon as we hang up."

"Okay, bye," without waiting for the reciprocal bye from Ethan, Nick ended the call.

As Nick drove back to Sullivan's, all he could think was how nothing was making sense any longer. He had never had any mental episodes, and now to start losing time was becoming more than he could take. Nick was beginning to hope the doctor would find a tumor or some disease he had contracted while on vacation to explain it. A condition that affected the brain caused by some exotic parasite would feel like a win. Nick chuckled as he realized he was hoping some microbe was eating away at his brain. At least that idea sounded better than merely admitting defective mush underneath your brainpan was the issue.

Nick turned a corner, and Sullivan's Bar and Grill came into view. He pulled into a space across the street from the bar and surveyed the scene. There were yellow ribbons on the front door flapping in the morning breeze. Nick stared at the party ribbons, which caused his "Oh shit" meter to jump. What first appeared to be yellow party remnants from a distance had the words "Police – do not cross" printed on them in a repeating pattern. He also noticed other ribbons that read "Crime Scene" tied across the door. Barriers were set up on the sidewalk to quartan off the area. Nick thought this could only mean that the steaming pile of horseshit his life was becoming was only beginning to ripen in the sun.

The large plate-glass window beside the bar's entrance lay strewn in pieces across the sidewalk. The delicate song of tinkling glass mixed with a workman's broom's rhythmic sweep floated on the air. The glass looked as if it had burst outward, ruling out a robbery. Nick could see two men installing plywood boards in place of the windows, presumably to cover the empty sockets where the windows had been the night before. Nick got out and crossed the street.

"Hey guys, got a minute?" Nick asked, approaching the two men hanging the plywood.

The workmen manning the broom did not look up. The other two men stopped working and abruptly turned to see Nick but said nothing. They turned back to their work.

"Hey guys, can I, please, have just two minutes of your time. I'll pay for the conversation," Nick said, reaching for his wallet. He took out two ten-dollar bills and held them out to the men. Both men looked at each other, then looked at Nick. The older man of the pair reached out, took the money, divided it between himself and the other worker, then stared at Nick as they waited for his questions.

Nick reached out a hand and said, "Hi. Nick Mercer."

The older man shook Nick's hand and replied, "How can we help you, Mr. Mercer? I'm Steve, and this young man is Chris," he motioned to the younger man, then turned back to Nick. The man was an older black man, Nick guessed about mid-forties. He was broad, with shoulders that looked like they had been born of hard labor for most of his life. He also had a grip like a bear trap. "You a little late if you're a reporter. Everybody done come and got this story last night."

Nick looked at the man's dark eyes then at the windows. "No," he said, "I'm not a reporter. It's just that I was here last night. When I left, the place was fine. I was driving by and saw it this morning and wanted to know what happened?"

"Story we get is that some asshole tried to start some shit over another guy talking to this lady bartender. The bartender's ex-boyfriend had a bad case of startshititis and picked the wrong guy to mess with."

"Really? So this was a fight?"

"Yeah, bartender's ex got fucked up too. One punch is what everybody's saying. Hell, they ain't even sure if the dude's gonna make it," the man replied, "The bar owner says dude got knocked across the bar. He got messed up."

Nick swallowed and wiped his sweating palms on his pants, then asked, "What happened to the guy that beat the shit out of the asshole?"

"Nobody knows," the man replied.

"Well, it look like these guys fight charged the whole damn place."

Nick looked at the younger man. "What do you mean, charged it?"

"Everyone said that by the time the asshole's body landed on a table across the room, the whole damn place just lost its mind."

"Lost their mind how?"

"The mystery guy walked out the bar, folks that could remember anything said he was smiling like he thought it was all funny. Everybody else that was there just stayed in the bar and started trying to kill each other. This mess here," the young man motioned to the glass covering the sidewalk, "this was one of the band members. Everybody said the drummer threw the bass player through the window. If it happened like everybody said, this shit was crazy," The young man gave an extra emphasis on the "crazy" and finished with an animated nod that caused his long dreadlocks to swing around his shoulders.

"Yeah, crazy," Nick almost mumbled, then asked, "So, who called the cops?"

"The bartender, the hot little number that the fight started over.

She wasn't fighting none, so she hid behind the bar and called the cops."

"Does anybody know why everyone went berserk?" Nick asked.

"Nah," replied the older man, "shit just seemed to kinda go south when these two dudes got into it. Everybody came to their senses by the time the cops got here."

Nick wiped his hands on his pants again and swallowed with a hard gulp. "What are the cops saying happened?"

This time the younger man answered, "They said it was like mass hysteria or some shit. Blaming it on a new unknown club drug that must be hitting the streets."

"Sullivan's doesn't have a drug scene," Nick interjected.

"Look, man," the younger man said, "not my hangout. That's just what the cops are saying."

"Yeah. Well, thanks, guys, for taking a few minutes to talk."

"Yeah, man, no problem."

The older man asked, "Hey man, you okay? You look white, I mean, whiter than you should be."

Nick looked at the furrowed brow on the man's face, "No, I'm fine," Nick assured, then forced a smile, "It's just I can't believe I barely dodged all this. Kind of shakes me up a little."

"Yeah, man, I get it. Look, take it easy. We gotta get this window closed up before they open back up today."

"They're opening back up? Already?"

"That's what the guy who hired us said. We just gotta get this mess cleaned up and the window patched."

"Sure. Thanks for your time." Nick said as he shook both men's hands. Once Nick was seated in his car, he turned to look at the bar again. The two men had returned to hanging the plywood. He turned away and saw the time on the dash console. If he intended to keep his appointment, he needed to get moving. He started the car and drove away, checking the scene in front of the bar one more time in his rear-view mirror.

CHAPTER 16

Nick sat listening to muffled voices through the thick office door. A few moments after the muted tones ceased, Dr. Scott walked into the office and sat down behind his desk.

"I thought you weren't allowed to talk to anyone about my medical info," Nick said, looking at Dr. Scott with a grim face.

"Normally, I would say you were correct. However, yours is an especially severe case, what with your disappearance coupled with your amnesia." Nick looked up at hearing that word. Dr. Scott, seeing the look on Nick's face, said, "Amnesia is a very generic term for a grouping of symptoms that concern the state of a person's memory, or lack thereof. Unfortunately, the diagnosis does not lead to any origin of the condition. With that being said, you have a group of very concerned individuals who are trying their best to relink you with your life, Nick. I think we would all agree that your friends deserve a little bit of info. The problem is that I haven't any information for them."

"What does that mean?"

"Well," replied Dr. Scott, "the tests were inconclusive."

Nick looked at the bland folder on Dr. Scott's desk. He had walked into the office with it and laid it down on his desk as he sat.

"Why are they inconclusive?"

"Inconclusive," replied Dr. Scott, "Because while there is a presenting set of symptoms, medically speaking, your results say that you're perfectly healthy from a physical standpoint. Most of your tests are clear, so no definitive diagnosis, or root of your condition, is presenting itself neurologically."

Most of the tests?

"The results from one test, your active brain scan, presented an abnormality in electrical activity, but not any activity pattern linked to any known condition."

"Okay." Nick sat with his hands in his lap, clenching his fists to the point his fingers began to ache.

Doctor Scott paused a moment to watch the muscles in Nick's jaw work.

"Well," Dr. Scott began again, "I deemed the activity scan as inadmissible as an acceptable lab result. There was some distortion in the final result."

"What type of distortion?"

"An anomaly?"

Dr. Scott leaned back in his chair, "I can't explain it. The electrical was most prevalent in the cerebrum and the cerebellum. Your EEG showed enhanced activity levels over several regions of your brain."

Nick opened his clenched hands and grabbed the sides of his jeans to keep himself from reaching across the desk, grabbing Dr. Scott by the shirt and screaming at him to get to the point, then asked, "So are these patterns like what I've read about from brain scans of people with schizophrenia?"

"No. Schizophrenia patterns are relatively well defined now. Your brain waves are enigmatic. I've never seen patterns like this in my years of brain analysis. It's more like your brain waves are supercharged. Several independent regions of your neural network, regions that normally do not work in tandem and that do not tend to be active at the same time, all show signs of hyperactivity simultaneously."

"Okay. So, what does that tell us?"

"Look, Nick," Dr. Scott said, then paused to read Nick's reaction before he continued, "It's like I said, regions of your brain are active in sequences that should normally not be active simultaneously. Normally, the aggregate activity is reserved in the brain's primary control region, not in multiple. Your scans show multiple control regions of your brain firing simultaneously. I've never seen results like these. It is more an anomaly in the test than any indicator of a particular condition because the human brain doesn't function this way. It is not how we are wired. That is the reason that I dismissed the result. All other results were nominal."

Nick said nothing but sat glaring at Dr. Scott like a wounded dog.

Dr. Scott continued, "Nick, in some cases, meaning in cases where clear medical science cannot pinpoint the source of a patient's condition, I have explored the use of interventive psychoanalysis."

"You want to send me to a shrink. You think it's all in my head and that the results of the blood tests will show nothing." Nick's said through trembling lips as his image of Dr. Scott blurred.

"No, quite the opposite," Dr. Scott replied. "Please understand, the mind is an incredibly complex organ. The scientific community is just *beginning* to understand a *small* portion of it. Sometimes, we can extend the discovery of a patient's need by utilizing psychoanalysis to better understand a patient's symptoms. The two approaches work in concert, not at odds. It's a method of making sense out of unknown patterns. Suppose your results turn out to be valid after being scrutinized again. In that case, we can use the psychological data to perhaps strike a treatable correlation between these blackouts and your neural activity. Nick, I have seen this approach produce benefits, and I, so far, do not find any physical abnormalities, other than this one outlier in the scan result."

The room began to shrink around Nick, as if he were slowly being stuffed into an invisible cage, as its door was pressed shut, threatening to crush him. He sighed to force open the closing hole of this throat.

"Nick?" Dr. Scott's voice seemed to come to Nick from across a chasm. "Nick." Dr. Scott said again.

Nick slowly turned his lost gaze back to Dr. Scott, "Yes," he answered listlessly.

"Look, Nick, this is not a bad thing. If some psychological disorder does present itself, most of them can be treated nowadays with proper diet, stimuli reduction therapy, and pharmaceutical treatments."

"What exactly would you be treating," Nick asked, his face the sober mask of a fresh cadaver.

"I can't answer that. I can tell you that there is no physical evidence pointing to any known disorder that would cause the issues you have been experiencing. I would say there is nothing, physically anyway, that I have observed that would cause your episodes of lost time."

Nick's attention drifted again as he heard a faint voice in the back of his mind repeating, "Enu. Enu. Ehus Salmu Duranki." Nick did not know the language but somehow knew its meaning. The House of the Black Bond.

"Nick," Nick focused on the sound of Dr. Scott's voice.

"Yes?"

"I asked if you would be willing to talk to a colleague of mine who works in the field of psychiatry?"

"Yes," Nick said, the words tasting like rotten fish, "if you think that is the best next step."

"I do, and Nick, please let me assure you again that this is not a bad thing. Today we have found there are a great many things of which you do not suffer. That, in and of itself, is a positive report. If there are no physiological reasons for these episodes, and tests show that there are not, then these symptoms are most likely treatable and with a great degree of success."

Nick looked soberly again at Dr. Scott, not knowing what to say next if anything at all. After a short pause, he said numbly, "Okay, if you think that's best."

"I do," replied Dr. Scott. He took out his prescription pad, wrote down a number and a name, and then handed it to Nick, saying, "Call this number in the morning. She is very good at what she does. Tabetha can attest to this. I assure you that she is more than qualified to talk with you about this issue."

Nick reached out and took the small slip of paper from Dr. Scott. He stood up and mechanically offered Dr. Scott his thanks for taking the time to come in on a Sunday morning.

"It's not a problem," Dr. Scott said, "Believe me, I am going to continue to follow your case until we have a resolution. You have presented with a unique scenario, and I'm curious to know the outcome of your case."

Nick offered Dr. Scott a forced smile again and turned to walk out of the office feeling like a hollowed-out log instead of a man.

When Nick stepped out the office door, Ethan, Tabby, and Kiera were sitting anxiously waiting. Their eyes fixed on Nick as soon as he appeared. Their wide gazes made him feel like the invisible cage was now a zoo exhibit. They all rose to meet him as he exited the office. The three of them stared at him, the man out of sync with his reality.

"Nick," Kiera said. "What did he say?"

Nick returned her question with silence, choosing to look at the floor instead of Kiera's direction. Kiera's words brushed past him before fading away into the surrounding air.

"I am, ah, going to go," Nick said.

"Where? Dude, maybe you—" Ethan began.

"I'm just going to go home for now."

"What did the doctor say?" Kiera asked again.

"You already know what he said. You guys talked to him before he talked to me."

Tabby stepped forward and gently grabbed Nick's arm, "Yes, but he couldn't give us any details."

"Look, I want to go home for now and get some rest. He gave me a number to call in the morning. A head doctor."

Just then, Dr. Scott stepped out of his office.

"Tony," Tabby called, "what's going on?"

"You know that I can't give you any detailed information, Tabby. Nick is my patient now."

"Tony, tell us what is going on," Tabby persisted.

Nick looked at Dr. Scott and said, "I'm leaving. Tell them whatever they want to know."

Nick then strode briskly toward the lobby door as Tabby called after him, "Nick. Wait. Let's go over…."

Tabby turned from the exit door and said, "You heard him, Tony.

Spill. We need to know what's happening?"

"There's really not much to tell, Tabby." Dr. Scott replied.

"Well, let's talk about the test results, then."

"Except for a hyperactive brain scan, there was nothing out of the ordinary."

"What is a hyperactive brain scan? That doesn't tell us anything?" Kiera asked.

"No. Nothing really. I would rather say that it would speak more to my ability to masquerade as a technician than it does to any appreciable result. In my opinion, Nick's best hope of finding his way back to what he calls normal is with Tabby's field of study. I can't help in that area."

"So, you really couldn't find anything?" Tabby pleaded, "No bump on the head, no parasitic presence, or even a small tumor?"

"No. Tabby, I'm sorry," Dr. Scott, "but I am fully confident that whatever is going on with Nick, it's not physiological, at least nothing that shows up on any tests. At this point, my diagnosis would be one of psychological."

Dr. Scott gave the group a solemn look, then said. "Look, the best thing you could all do is to support Nick, encourage him to meet with Dr. Talmadge, and work through a program with her."

"Thank you, doctor," Kiera said, acknowledging her deflating hope.

"Thanks again, Tony. I can't tell you how much this means to me, us." She stepped over to Dr. Scott and hugged him tight around the neck, and said, "Thank you so much. Thanks for giving him Jean's number too. She is great."

Dr. Scott placed his hands on Tabby's shoulders as their embrace broke and said, "Just support him, Tabby. I don't know what is going on with him, but I can see that he is mentally under an intense amount of strain. Support is something for which he will need an ample supply."

CHAPTER 17

Nick tossed and turned in his bed after an evening of carry-out pizza, Jack Daniels, and solitude until he, at last, found a restless sleep. He dreamt of a new world. One he had never seen before. This world was cold, empty, and he found himself surrounded by a dimly lit, seemingly endless black expanse. He could see his breath with each exhale. He rubbed his hands up and down his exposed arms to warm himself as he spun around in a circle, searching for an end to the black sprawl. As he looked around, he noticed a disturbance. The air directly in front of him seemed to waver like a desert breath rising over blistering sands. He strained his eyes as an image began to form from the meandering air, like a forest emerging out of morning mist.

At first, the image wafted and swirled like lazy smoke until it thickened, becoming a translucent shimmer of shifting scenes. As the images began to solidify, Nick saw scenes were playing as if he were watching a movie from an old video reel, slow, skipping, and grainy.

He saw a ritual being performed around a stone altar surrounded by robed figures. The figures chanted loudly in some unknown tongue as a body laid motionless on the altar. The body had two open mouths, one above the chin and one ragged smile below. One member of the chanting circle lifted a golden chalice to the sky, uttered something in the unknown tongue, then took a drink from the cup that left his grey, coarse beard dripping with dark red liquid.

The images shifted to show a girl lying on the dirt floor of a shack. The wavering shadow on the wall of the small shack told Nick her body was surrounded by dim flickering candles. The exposed parts of her skin were covered in black boils and oozing lesions as her breath rattled in and out with short, sharp gasps. She reached a blackened hand toward Nick as dark blood leaked from her mouth and eyes. She tried to speak but, all her mouth could produce was more thick trickles of blood. She let out a ragged cough that sprayed Nick in the face, causing him to cringe.

The image dissolved again, changing from the dying girl to smoke, then steadying into a primal scene. Nick looked around and found himself surrounded by large, broad-leafed plants packed among towering trees. The smoky air burned Nick's throat with every breath. He followed the smoke in the darkened sky and saw a volcano smoldering in the distance. Its billowing acrid smoke filled the sky with black clouds as bright red lava leaped from its peak then flowed down its conical face. Nick assumed he was about to see a giant volcanic eruption, but what he witnessed was far worse.

A small but brilliant white flash appeared in the distance as a tiny dot emanating from somewhere at the volcano's base. The dimly lit sky quickly vanished as the tiny dot expanded into a white-hot orb of radiant heat. The ball swelled in the blink of his eye, reaching toward the sky and in all directions as if it would never stop growing. The thick, lumbering volcanic clouds darkening the sky separated, racing away from the swelling orb as the blast grew, beating everything in its path to dust. Nick felt the ground begin to vibrate as a stampede of prehistoric monsters, some on two legs and some on four, running, leaping, and crashing into one another as they ran away from the growing flash of light. The increasing cloud of rolling destruction hurtled itself toward the creatures, consuming everything in its path. The scene grew more vivid as the blast wave approached. The destruction hurled itself toward Nick at an ever-quickening pace. Nick coward against its oncoming destruction, raising his arms to shield his face as debris began to pelt his face. A hot wind began whipping the air around him. Nick tried to scream, but the thunderous roar of the approaching wave of energy drowned out his voice as it obliterated the landscape. He closed his eyes, praying to anything that would listen to take the image away. He tried to will himself awake from this nightmare. When nothing seemed to answer, he held his breath and waited for the blast to slam into him.

As the deafening blast neared, to Nick's surprise, everything went silent. There was no crushing pressure, no sulfurous heat from the devil's breath. He slowly opened his eyes and found he was lying in his bed. Realizing it had been a dream, Nick relaxed his muscles and unclenched his fists. He tried to get up from his bed to find his arms and legs would not respond. He was paralyzed. Pressure began to build in his chest. The room around him looked empty, but Nick did not feel alone. He couldn't explain, but he felt like someone was watching him, like a lab rat, or as if someone was occupying the space within his room. His eyes found a darkened corner of the room. The shadows here seemed to be somehow slightly darker than they should be in the bright moonlight spilling in through the window. The shadow seemed to be thicker, more tangible. He strained against the dark as the shadows changed. A shade of darkness pulled away from the corner and slowly moved up the bedroom wall. As it glided up the wall, it seemed almost to slither across the ceiling like a thick black snake. The shifting shadow came to a stop on the ceiling over Nick's bed and began to grow larger. Nick felt sweat run into his right eye as his fear turned into mind-shattering terror. Nick thought the shadow seemed to be growing until he realized it was drifting down, away from the ceiling and toward his motionless body.

The shadow stopped descending and hung suspended just above him, its smoky body resisting solid form. Nick continued to lay locked in his invisible prison, not wanting to look at the shadow but lacking the ability to close his eyes to its ghostly advance. The shadow, smoke and formless, was now only two feet from Nick as a face emerged into solidified form over Nick's face. Nick saw the shadow's face and tried to scream. His mouth was welded shut. All he could produce was a pathetic whimper through closed lips. The corrupted version of his face stared back at him with dead milky eyes with no pupils. Blackened veins, like tendrils, stretched from under the visage's black flowing hair, spreading over the head and pallid face like vines crawling across a forest floor.

Nick still could not look away. The head with the body of smoke opened its mouth, first in a menacing smile filled with sharp rows of pointed teeth. Slowly the mouth began to stretch, doubling its human size as the hallow white eyes narrowed to slits that seemed to bore through him. As the entity's mouth spread open, his own paralyzed mouth opened, as if on command from the being, and was now open so wide that pain within his jaw brought tears to his eyes. Once the entity had its now inhuman mouth agape, thousands of green death flies spewed from it and covered Nick from head to toe.

Nick could feel the flies crawling over his entire body, consuming him. Their tiny legs roved over his exposed skin in sharp darting movements. He felt them under his bed garments, roaming wildly across his legs, under his shirt, and over his chest and stomach. Worst of all, he could see and feel the flies lapping at the moisture in his open eyes as they walked across his face. Their buzzing wings seemed to grow into a thunderous drone in his ears. Nick felt pressure on his chest and looked to see a black tendril had grown from the hovering entity and sunken itself between Nick's ribs. It pressed and burrowed through Nick's body. Nick tried to gasp when he felt his flesh separate. Then, his organs shifted within his body as the tendril drilled through his chest, wrapped itself around his heart, and began to squeeze.

Nick tried to breathe as the flies continued to spew from the apparition's mouth in a black and green wroth of buzzing vomits, filling Nick's lungs. The skin tightened around his neck as his throat began to bulge as the corpse flies filled his lungs, then continued to push into him, cramming his throat. Reason began to fail, being replaced with panic as the world started to fade. His lungs were near bursting. His chest was a burning sear as his frozen body began to spasm. His muscles twisted and cramped from lack of oxygen and the exhaustion of trying to move, trying to defend himself. Each attempt to take in a breath was another lung full of scuttering death. He could taste the corpse flies on his tongue as they scuttered about his mouth and lips. The flies pressed into his engorged throat like honeybees pouring into the hive. Gagging and choking, Nick could neither take a breath nor expel the insects from his lungs. Nick strained and finally let out another pathetic whine. Nick recognized the sound coming from his mouth, then knew the last sound his ears would ever hear would be his fly-infested death rattle.

Nick determined to die quickly so the horde of the flies and image of the dark negative assaulting him would end, then there was silence. There was no longer a hovering face with the black shifting body above him. The apocalypse of corpse flies was gone as well as the crushing tendril that had burrowed into his chest. Nick grabbed at his chest, but there was no wound. Nick looked up to see he was again in the black expanse. Images no longer played in their low-res loop. Nick took deep, chuffing breaths, trying to steady his sanity before his mind completely broke. He sensed a presence behind him and whirled to see a vast, empty nothing.

Wait, he thought. There was a scant shimmer in the blackness in front of him. The only description Nick's fracturing mind could construct was of a shimmering pool of oil. It was square with a wavering surface that reflected the indistinct light of this world. It looked like a square pool of oil standing impossibly vertical. The black pool began to tremble, almost to vibrate. Nick saw the oily substance forming into the shape of a hand with the arm attached to it growing toward him from its center.

Nick turned to run, somehow knowing that he could not allow the hand to touch him. He took three strides before the hand seized him. It closed around his head and shoulders and pulled. Nick's last thought was of cold and pain as he felt the fluid fill his lungs as the oily curtain closed around him.

Nick shot up, breathing so fast he at first thought he must be hyperventilating. He looked around and saw that he was in his room. He tested reality by slapping himself. He blinked and looked around the room. Warm rays of light from the dawning sun filled the room and spilled across the bedroom floor. The songs of fall birds chirping from somewhere outside filled his ears. The apparition was gone. There was no dark negative of his face, no impossibly erect oily pool, nor was there any destructive white-hot blast. He reached and felt his throat and was relieved to feel the corpse files were also gone. Nick's sweat-soaked clothes clung to his skin. He felt a warm caustic fluid around his crotch and looked down to see he had pissed the bed. Sitting in his piss and sweat, struggling to catch his breath, he began weeping uncontrollably. His only thought was that he was lost. He knew, whatever *this* was, it made him feel like he was on his knees at the executioner's feet with the ax poised to free him from this world.

CHAPTER 18

The office door swung open. Dr. Jean Talmadge stepped into the room. She bid Nick a good morning then sat down in a big cozy chair situated directly in front of him, who was seated on, of course, a sofa.

"Hello, Nick," said Dr. Talmadge.

"Hi," Nick replied.

She set her coffee down on a small table beside her chair, took out a legal pad, a pen, and found Nick's nervous eyes.

"Nick, please just try to relax. All we are doing here is having a conversation. That's all. No one is here to put you into a box, make any judgments or seek to define you. I just want to understand your needs and discuss how we can both understand what may have triggered this episode. So, shall we begin?"

Nick did not answer.

"Can we begin by you telling me what has been going on in your life these past few months?"

"Okay," Nick began slowly. He shuffled his hands from his lap, then to his sides, then back to his lap, then said, "I don't know how to begin."

"Okay, well then, may I make a suggestion?" Nick nodded, so she continued, "Let's not start with your missing window. Can we start by you telling me about the week before your vacation? I have already been briefed on your case details from Dr. Scott, as well as from your friend Dr. Hensley, but I want to hear the details from you firsthand."

"Okay," Nick began, "The week before my vacation was pretty normal," Nick shuffled in his seat, "I mean other than preparing for the trip on top of my other responsibilities. There's not a lot to tell. I didn't take any time off, so it was just routine. Get up, go to work, see Kiera, my girlfriend, or at least she was before all of this," he added, "then back home in the evening. Rinse and repeat. The night before my trip, I had some last-minute packing to do, so I went straight home from work to make sure I had everything ready."

"When I left on the trip, everything went just as I had planned. There were no bumps or surprises. We didn't even hit turbulence on the flight down. It was nice." Nick gave Dr. Talmadge an uncertain smile. "From the airport, I caught a shuttle to the hotel. It was a bit of a bumpy ride, but there was plenty to look at along the way, so I didn't mind. The first night the tour company hosts a meet and greet for anyone that wants to attend. I spent maybe an hour mingling around the crowd then just went back to my room to unwind."

Nick paused as if trying to remember something from that night until he was brought back by Dr. Talmadge's gentle prod, "Nick, is there anything else from the first night that you remember?"

"No, I went to my room to get some sleep. The next morning, I met my group for our tour. We had the choice of doing individual tours or guided group tours. The first day I spent exploring the site on my own, you know, taking photos and rubbings. I felt fine. Nothing out of the ordinary happened."

"Yes, I am told your missing time began on your second day, is that correct?"

"Yes, I mean, that is the last day I remember," Nick acknowledged, "It's still fuzzy, but I remember that I was on the group tour. We were rounding the rear of one of the outer structures bordering the jungle when I saw an entrance to another temple. It wasn't on the map. I looked around, but it was like no one else in the group saw it. It was weird. No one asked any questions about it or paid any attention to it. It was like they didn't see it. I was curious, so I went inside. After I got a few steps inside the entrance, I woke up in my bed, two months later."

Dr. Talmadge saw the shake that had appeared in Nick's hands. He had begun to bounce one leg up and down, working his right foot like a piston. He was also biting his lower lip.

"Nick," Dr. Talmadge asked, "why does recalling these events make you so anxious?"

Nick let out an exasperated breath and got up from the couch. He walked over to the office window to watch two squirrels scurrying up and down a small tree. They wound their way up and down the tree as if tracing the lines on a barber's pole.

"Because," Nick said, his voice quivering, "I don't like to think about it." Nick began to chew his thumbnail.

"Why does this memory cause you such discomfort?"

"Because, when I think about how I can't remember two months of my life, I feel like I'm slipping, losing myself. Because then I think I know how Alice felt when she fell into the rabbit hole."

"Do you have any theories as to why you can't remember the

events leading up to your return home?"

"How the hell should I know," Nick said, shrugging and wiping a hand down his face, "I mean, isn't that why I'm here? Aren't you supposed to tell me how and why my brain is out of tilt?"

"That's not what this is, Nick. Given that one of your good friends is also a psychiatrist, you should understand. As I said when we first began talking, I am not here to put a label on you or to put you into a box. My role is not to assign what people call normal or abnormal. Mine is simply a role of helping us understand this event to know better what must be done to prevent another occurrence. We simply discuss behaviors and your reactions to those behaviors to gain a better understanding of ourselves."

Jesus, Nick thought, This bitch must have a whole library full of new age enlightenment bullshit at her house. He realized he was grinding his teeth. His jaw had begun to ache.

"Nick, I just want to help you find the origin of this event and to help you put it into place within the realm of your everyday life." She waited for him to answer, but when he did not, she continued, "Have you not had any flashes of the days leading up to your waking up at home?"

Nick chuckled, "None. Not even a blip." He shook his head and looked down. "It's like I was wiped or something."

"Nick," Dr. Talmadge said cautiously, sensing barriers going up between them, "I would like to try something that I normally never do on a patient's first session. Is that okay?"

"I guess that would depend on what it is."

"I would like to try hypnosis."

"You can try," Nick said, "but I really don't believe in all that carnie show bullshit."

"I understand," she acknowledged, "Not everyone is susceptible to hypnosis, but I have used it successfully with several of my patients. If you are willing, I would like to try."

Nick turned away from the dancing squirrels to look at Dr. Talmadge, "What is hypnosis supposed to accomplish?"

"Sometimes things happen to us that our mind blocks off. It sets up barriers to these events, like a defense mechanism at times."

"So, if it's so helpful, why wouldn't you try to use this treatment first with every patient?"

"The mind is delicate. Using hypnosis to pull memories from our subconscious to our conscious mind can carry risks. It can sometimes be damaging if those memories are traumatic enough. I want to use it now because your case is so extreme. You have only been back to yourself for three days. There is something your mind is locking away from your conscious thoughts. You have not mentioned having any more blackouts since you arrived back home." She gave Nick a probing look the asked, "Have you had any new episodes since you returned home?"

"No. None." Nick lied.

Dr. Talmadge could see by Nick's folded arms and narrowed eyes that he had experienced more episodes since his return, just how many she couldn't say, and he was not ready to share the details with her.

"Okay then," she said and flashed a broad white smile, "so should we get set up for the attempt?" She motioned for him to come back to the sofa.

"Fine, you're welcome to try, but I wouldn't expect a whole lot from me with these parlor shenanigans."

Dr. Talmadge flashed another bright smile and said, "I would call that fair. Just give me a few moments to get ready."

Dr. Talmadge walked to her desk and reached into the bottom

drawer, where she took out a device with a heavy base and a small oval-shaped weight perched atop an upright metal rod. She pulled the table from her chair's side and moved it between where she and Nick sat.

She looked at Nick and asked, "Are you ready to begin?"

"Sure, but what is that thing? It looks like a metronome."

"Music lover, huh? It's very similar to a metronome, but it's slightly different. It does keep a single, constant rhythm, but it doesn't produce the ticking sound a metronome produces. Other than that, I guess they are about the same."

Nick watched as she pulled the inverted pendulum to one side and released it. The oval-shaped hammer swung soundlessly, smoothly shifting from side to side in silent rhythm, seeming to keep perfect rhythm with Nick's heartbeat.

Dr. Talmadge began to speak, "Now Nick, focus on the swaying of the pendulum. Don't speak or try to move. Just follow the rhythm. I want you to concentrate on slowing your breathing. Take in deep, calming breaths and release them just as calmly. Continue to focus on the rhythm of the pendulum as you steady yourself into regular, calm breaths."

Nick focused on slowing his breathing and calming his heart as the pendulum swung silently from side to side. His eyelids began to sink, changing his face into the image of a man on a sleepy high. His head began to droop. It suddenly felt too heavy to hold up.

After another few moments, Nick heard a distant, soft voice, "Don't fight the need to allow your body to relax, Nick. Let its warmth cover you." There was a pause as Dr. Talmadge stopped to assess Nick's state, then she continued, "Do you feel relaxed, Nick? Do you feel at peace?"

"Yes," Nick replied, "I am."

"Good. Now, Nick, I want you to go back in your mind, open the doors and windows of your thoughts and go back to the second day of your vacation." She paused, then asked. "Are you there?"

"Yes," Nick replied.

"Good, now move forward until you see the temple entrance that you described to me." Again, she paused, giving his mind time to process the request. "Do you see the entrance, Nick?"

"Yes."

"Now, I want you to focus on the image you see in your mind. Enhance it so that the image is clear to you. Now move forward toward the entrance and tell me what you see as you step through."

"I see a corridor leading into a larger room. The room is huge. God, how is this thing not sticking out of the top of the trees? It's gigantic."

"Nick," Dr. Talmadge's voice came to him from a long way away.

"Yes?"

"I do not want you to focus on the structure. Can you tell me what you are doing? Tell me what else you see in the room where you are standing."

"I see something half-buried in the dirt floor. It's," his brow furrowed. "It's a piece of pottery. I walk over to it and dig it up with my hands. I'm careful. I don't want to break it. It looks old."

Dr. Talmadge watched as Nick examines the pottery in his hand. He turned his hand over, twisting it around to look at the pottery as he replayed the memory.

"Tell me about this pottery."

"It's a small jar. I, I don't know why but it's mesmerizing. I can't stop looking at it. It's covered in markings I've never seen. They don't look Mayan. There's a bunch of lines and squares with arrows etched all over it. This place must not have been excavated yet for some reason. That must be why the jar is still here. Wait." Nick paused. His respirations seemed to speed up and grow more deeply.

Dr. Talmadge prodded, "What is it, Nick? What else do you see?"

"The markings, they're glowing, and the jar feels like it's vibrating." A bead of sweat ran down Nick's temple. "That can't be right. My hands are tingling. I can see a seal of some kind holding the lid in place. The seal is still moist. This thing must be thousands of years old. The seal should be dried out or cracked, but it's not."

"I want you to move past the jar and tell me what else you see, Nick."

"I. I can't."

"Why is that, Nick? Why can't you move away from the jar?"

"I don't know. I'm supposed to open it. I need to open it. The jar wants me."

Dr. Talmadge could see Nick's face had changed. He looked like an addict in need of a fix as he described this scene. "Nick, I want you to move past the jar and tell me what else you see."

"I'm opening the jar. I break the seal. I smell…" He trailed off. "I see…" he stopped again.

Moving to the edge of her chair, Dr. Talmage demanded in a calm but firm voice, "Nick, tell me what you are seeing."

Nick began to say something that sounded as if crossed between a sob and a witless mumble. Dr. Talmadge thought she made out the words, "No." and "Please."

Nick took a deep breath and said, "I see…. it's all…. I can't see. Everything is black. It's black and, oh my god, the cold."

Nick began shivering as he moaned through sobs. He gagged, then coughed as Dr. Talmadge pressed, "What is black, Nick. What do you see?"

"Oh God," Nick yelled. "They are tearing each other apart."

"Who, Nick? Who are they, and where are they?"

"It looks like… like a bar, somewhere." Nick moaned again. "Oh god, they are ripping each other to pieces with their bare hands. There are two men in the corner…." Then Nick stopped again. Drool dribbled from his lower lip as he moaned again and shivered more.

"Who are the two men? What are they doing, Nick?"

"They are eating another man. They are smearing his blood on their faces. My god, why are they laughing?" Nick sobbed as he tried to continue. "Oh god, now the second man is attacking the other one. Why, why, why?" Nick wailed. "He's biting him."

Nick began screaming as if he felt the pain of teeth biting into his neck. He leaned back on the couch and wrapped his arms around his chest.

Dr. Talmadge stood and moved over to him, "Nick, try to slow your breathing and move away from this memory. Nick!"

Suddenly, as if someone had thrown a switch, Nick stopped writhing and sat up, his head hanging limp. Dr. Talmadge opened her mouth to speak but didn't know what to say. She had never seen a patient so abruptly collapse. She reached a quaking hand toward Nick to wake him. As her hand approached, Nick's head shot up, fixing an icy glare on Dr. Talmadge.

"What are you doing, Jean," asked Nick with a taunt.

Dr. Talmadge wanted to avert her gaze, but she could not. Nick's mismatched eyes seemed to hold her. Jean's knees weakened as she stared back into one hazel eye with flecks of amber and one pale grey eye. The pale grey iris almost blended into the white of that eye, causing it to look like a small dirty snowball. Dr. Talmadge's mouth was open, but she neither breathed nor spoke.

"I said, what are you doing, Jean?" The serenely emotionless voice asked again.

"Wh…. Wh…. Who am I speaking with?" she stuttered as she stumbled back to her chair. She grabbed the arm of the chair with one hand as the other clutched her shirt at her chest.

Nick clicked his tongue three times, then said, "You are toying with matters you cannot comprehend, Jean."

"Who is speaking now. Is this Nick?"

"Sorry, Jean," Nick said in a coldly smooth tone, "Nick can't come to the phone right now. He's busy having a breakdown. All you weak little maggots will soon break under the weight of inevitability." He sat back on the sofa and calmly crossed his legs as he slung one arm over the back of the couch and licked his top lip.

"I demand to know with whom I am speaking!" Jean said.

"I am the remnant," Nick replied. "The revenant. The reaper of divine fruits, and I am famished, Jean. I am the residue of a time you cannot know." A smile spread across Nick's face. He licked his lips again.

"Tell me your name. To whom am I speaking?"

"I am mother's favorite little imp, Jean. You know what it's like to be your parent's favorite, don't you, Jean." He leaned forward and continued to bear down on her with those mismatched eyes. Jean's eyes began to ache. His glare felt like two thumbs pressing into her eyes.

"What are you talking about?" she asked in a tone that blended her fear and shock into one fragile voice.

"You know what I'm talking about, Jean. My goodness, look how you've grown. If step daddy could see you now. Um, yummy," he said, smacking his lips seductively, "Jaryl would be so hot for you."

"Shut up," Jean said through clenched teeth. Her throat felt like a straw as she tried to grab thin spasmatic breaths. She shuddered as the sensation of thousands of ants scurrying around inside her head swept over her.

"Oh no, Jean. Don't tell me you forgot about rodeo night. That intense thump in your belly while dear old mommy just sat in the living room and listened to you scream." Nick chuckled deep in his throat.

His voice changed to that of a little girl, "Please not again. It hurts so bad. Please no. Stop."

His voice shifted again to a man's voice, but not Nick's voice, "When I get done, you little bitch, you'll be in love with me."

Then back to the girl's voice, this time crying, "No stop. Please stop."

His voice shifted again to that of a haggard-sounding woman with slurred speech, "Honey, just let him get done. Damage has already been done. One more time ain't gonna kill ya?"

The voice shifted again to a smooth version of Nick's voice, the mocking thick with every word, "You liked it, didn't you, Jean? Daddy's perfect little slut." His words felt like venom pouring out into the room. He continued, "Please more, daddy, please more," he snarled.

"Wake up, Nick! Wake up!" Jean screamed.

Nick sprung from the couch, leaping over the table and landing in front of Jean's chair. He grabbed the chair by both armrests, pulled his face in close to hers, and growled, "Nick is not here, you stupid, worthless whore! You wanted to take a peek inside! Do you like what you see? Look into my face and know me, you heap of putrid shit! Oh yes, Jean. I see you on the inside. All the black thoughts. All the hatred. All of your shadows that hide in daylight."

Jean felt a wave rush over her face like wind punching her with every word that Nick spew. She strained against him, trying to push the chair away from his iron grip. She tried to turn her face away from the cold, mismatched eyes, but his grip on the chair was like a vice. His eyes held her in place as they seemed to glow with rage. Jean could hear someone pounding on the office door. Someone was calling her name. She could hear the doorknob rattling as someone tried to open it.

Nick continued to hurl hatred into her face with words that she could no longer understand. Then he switched back to English. "Was it fun? Did you love it, Jean? Did it make you wet? Snip, snip, snip. Drip, drip, drip. A little clip and a little boom," he breathed through low maniacal chuckles. Then he pulled her closer, despite her efforts to push him away, until his face was only inches from hers, and snarled, "You useless, murdering fucking bug!" Then he screamed, "Hypocrite!"

"Leave!" she screamed, then with all the strength she could summon, then struck him on his left cheek.

Nick snapped back from the chair and stood frozen, his dazed expression signaling that he had returned to his right mind. He saw Dr. Talmadge huddled in her chair like a broken puppy. She looked frail as she crouched in the chair, trembling, and sobbing.

"What happened?" Nick asked, shaking his head in confusion.

"Leave!" Jean screamed.

"Please, what happened?" Nick asked, his voice starting to tremble.

"Just get out!"

Nick turned and ran out of the office, bursting through the exit door leaving Jean sitting in her chair like a broken child. She reached up and wiped her cheek, then looked to see her palms stained with red.

CHAPTER 19

"I can't get an answer at Jean's office or her house," Tabby told Ethan and Kiera as she placed her phone down on the kitchen table.

"What about your doctor friend? Dr. Scott?" Ethan asked.

"I texted him, and he can't get in touch with her either."

"Well, what do we do now?" Kiera asked, "It's not like she fell off the planet."

Tabby jumped up from the kitchen table, snatching up her cell phone and sliding it into the back pocket of her jeans.

"I'm driving over there," she said.

"Where?" asked Ethan. "To Jean's?"

"Yes, to Jean's house. I have her address."

"I don't think that is a great idea, babe," Ethan said as he rose from his seat, "that seems a bit presumptuous."

"It's not presumptuous," she replied, "she and I have cross consulted on several cases over the past couple of years, and I think it will be fine for me to show up considering the circumstances. Kiera, do you want to come?"

Kiera thought for a moment, "No," she said, "I think you will have a better chance of getting info from her by yourself. You know, one doctor talking to another doctor tends to work out a lot better without a civvy around."

"Yeah, you're probably right anyway. I'll call you as soon as I know something."

"Are you one hundred percent sure this is the right move? To just show up at her house?" Ethan asked.

"Do you have any better ideas? We can't get in touch with Nick. We can't get in touch with Jean. Anthony can't get in touch with Jean. What other options do we have?"

As Tabby reached for the doorknob, Ethan asked, "What are you going to do if she's not there?"

Tabby turned, "My best guess is that she is at home and just avoiding phone calls. I want to know why. She knows we need her input, so it doesn't make sense that she would ignore everyone unless something is wrong. Ethan, I'm concerned."

"Yeah, but what could be wrong?" Kiera asked.

"Yeah, babe, she's a psychiatrist. Not a surgeon." Ethan said in a matter-of-fact tone.

"Anything could have gone wrong," Tabby snapped back in a flash of anger. "Have you ever dealt with mentally unstable patients? No. Dealing with some of them is like handling rattlesnakes. Pissed off rattlesnakes, not in their right mind."

"Tabby, I didn't mean it like that, and you know it," Ethan said, "I just meant, well, it's Nick."

"Yes, it's Nick, Ethan," she offered back coldly, "The same Nick that vanished two months ago and then popped back into the world without warning. And oh yeah, he has blackouts and losses time now. Does that sound, at all, like nothing could go wrong, Ethan? We don't even know what happens during these blackouts of his. For all we know, he could have come back a fucking serial killer."

"Tabby," Ethan said, not harshly, but sternly, "please calm down. I see your point, and I know you are concerned for Jean, but can you really believe that Nick could be a killer? I'm sure we are all overreacting."

"You were the first one to make that accusation, remember? I am going to find out if she's okay. I will call you when I get there and again when I leave."

"Wait, Tabby," Ethan said, walking after her. "Let me go with you. If there is—"

"No. Kiera is right. I need to talk to her alone."

Tabby left Ethan and Kiera with nothing to occupy the air between them except the room's easing tension. Kiera looked at Ethan and said, "Listen, I'm going to go lie down for a while. I don't think I'll go to sleep, but I just want to rest."

"Alright. You feel okay? You look a little pale."

"No, I'm fine. I've just been a little extra tired today and want to stretch out and not move for a bit."

"Alright. Well, I'll be watching TV. If you need anything, just let me know. Tabby would beat my ass if you got sick and I didn't take care of you."

"Oh, I'm sure she would," Kiera replied with a chuckle, "but I'll be fine. I just need some rest."

As Kiera walked up the stairs to the guest bedroom, she felt like every step was an exercise in climbing with bricks tied around her ankles. By the time she reached the top landing, her legs were shaking. She paused for just a moment to catch her breath, then continued toward the bedroom, thinking about what an exhausting day this had been. She walked into the room and laid down on the bed. As she closed her eyes, she thought, *I just need to rest. I'll feel better in a few minutes.*

As soon as Kiera's head touched her pillow, she fell asleep.

CHAPTER 20

Kiera looked around franticly as she walked through a black, cold expanse again, her feet sloshing through its watery surface. She recognized, almost immediately, this was the place she had dreamed about before, the place where she found Nick frozen in his suspended hibernation. She could feel the cold seeping through her socks and creeping up the lower portion of her legs as the hems of her jeans dragged through the bedraggled surface. A shiver ran down her spine. Not a shiver of cold, but of the hopeless emptiness that walking through this place conjured in her.

This is the dream again, she thought. *This time at least, I know.*

Realizing this to be another dream, she focused, determined to control it this time. Kiera felt, more in her heart rather than her head, that she could find Nick again in this place of desolation if she could only focus on the thought of him.

"Nick," she called timidly. There was no reply. "Nick," she called louder. Again, no reply as her voice seemed to get swept away into the silent darkness. "Nick!" she yelled again.

She closed her eyes and thought about him. Then she opened her eyes to see a faint grey speck in the distance. This time she was further away from the ghostly luminance than she had been on her first time seeing it. The dim spec was a faint, nearly undetectable, spot in the distance. Kiera concentrated on the spec. She felt the word rise from her chest and explode in her mind. She spoke the word, "There." Without warning, she rose from the water as her body hurtled through the empty space. The cold wind pressed against her face as if she were free-falling through a frigid sky.

As she sped forward, the luminescent spot grew larger, and her certainty solidified. She could *feel* Nick in her head, heart, and bones. Here in this cold dreamscape, knowing could feel Nick seemed to make perfect sense. There was an intensity in Kiera's feeling, no, a knowing rather, that she would find Nick suspended in the center of that distant light. She continued to think about him, to accelerate. Moving with impossible speed, she rushed faster toward the growing spec, careening toward it like a bolt of lightning. Her amazement began to change to concern as she had the sobering realization that she would crash through the distant beacon if she could not slow her pace.

The wind rushed past her, whipping her hair and biting at her face. She could now see Nick lying in his suspended state as she drew near. She thought, *Stop,* but nothing happened. If anything, she thought she might have sped up. She was positive now that she would crash into Nick with a force that would tear them both apart. Dream or not, this was a terrifying thought. She struggled to breathe against the onrushing wind. Her calm was beginning to break as she felt she was losing control of the dream. *Stop.* She thought, and again nothing. Hurtling like a rifle shot through this surreal world, she saw Nick's body floating helplessly. His increasing size yielding to the certainty that they were both about to be crushed in the collision.

She closed her eyes and focused her mind, then screamed with everything she could summon, "Stop!" The ripping wind suddenly stopped screaming in her ears. The icy blast on her face ceased, and her body came to an immediate stop, like a starship dropping out of hyperdrive. She seemed complete, yet it had taken a blink's worth of time to stream her body back into a solid form. She floated gently back down to the liquid surface, feeling the wet again as water seeped coldly through her already sodden socks.

Nick was just within reach, but his image had slightly changed. The hand that had been dissolving in her previous dream was now gone, along with half the arm to which the hand had been attached. One of his feet had dissolved up to his ankle. His skin was different as well. It seemed paler, thinner.

She reached to touch him, but as her hand met his chest, it was thrown back by a jolt that sent stinging pain up her arm into her shoulder that caused her to yank her hand away. She held it to her chest and tried to rub the pain from her arm.

She spun in all directions and yelled, "Nick! Talk to me!"

"Kiera," an echoing voice, like a song playing in reverse, came back at her from the emptiness.

"Nick," Kiera cried out. "Where are we? What is this place?"

"Did you find the Nasaru?"

"I tried but couldn't find anything about a Nasaru. I think I spelled it wrong. All my searches returned nothing. What can I do?"

"Nasaru." Nick's voice rolled through the air like thunder, but as he spoke this time, his words appeared in the air above his body like pale yellow smoke. Kiera focused on the words, straining to commit their image to her memory.

Nick spoke again in that reverberating spectral sound that seemed to roll in from all directions, "Enu." Similarly, the words materialized over his floating body then faded.

"Ehus salmu duranki. That the world may ina etuti asbu."

"Nick, what does all this mean. What do I do?"

Nick replied, "Naparsudu. Naparsudu. Escape."

Suddenly Kiera felt goosebumps rise on her skin as she felt an icy, malevolent presence behind her. She turned, but as Nick's voice faded, she thought she heard him say, "Kiera, he's here." She stood frozen in front of what she thought looked like a shimmering black oily surface suspended in front of her. It looked like it was liquid but defied gravity by standing upright in near-solid form. Kiera thought the gravity-defying curtain of liquid must be par for the course at his point. After all, this was not a real place. It was a dream. In some way that Kiera could not explain, rage and hate emanated from the quivering black sheen. The shimmer began to ripple and quiver as Kiera saw the center of the oily curtain start to form into what resembled a hand attached to a stretching arm. Instead of fear, Kiera's icy despair changed to anger, and she screamed at the hand, "No!"

It appeared to flatten, contort, and fall to the ground in a gloppy slosh at her shout. The quivering black sheet became the waves of a storm-tossed ocean of anger as Kiera's body shot back from the intensifying waver. She hurtled toward her sleeping body, feeling her fear recede as she lowered her head and focused her eyes. Her essence tore through the expanse, away from Nick, away from the dimly lit body, and away from the monstrous screams raging from whatever creature was within the shimmering black.

As Kiera flew toward her doorway, she had only one thought, *It can be hurt,* and a smile grew on her face.

Kiera tore through the open bathroom door so fast and slammed into her body so quickly that the collision caused her to jump up and gasp for air as her eyes shot open with beginning understanding. Kiera felt as if she had been awakened by falling out of the sky. She sat up on the bed and continued to wrestle with the air in the room to gather breath. Her lungs pumped like billows.

"That was not a dream," she thought. She didn't know what it was, but it was no dream.

She looked down at her socks and the soiled legs of her jeans. Water dripped from her socks. Her jeans were now a dark blue shade from the heavy soaking that had leeched into them. She turned to look at where she had been lying. Just as when the previous dream had come to an end, she saw a soiled spot where her feet had been positioned on the mattress. She turned to see her cell phone was lying on the bed. This was curious since she remembered putting it on the nightstand as she laid down. Picking it up, she noted the time, she had only been asleep for fifteen minutes, but she felt energized.

She swiped her phone to see if she had gotten any messages. Her mouth hung open in disbelief, and she stared at the phone as if it were a newly found treasure map. She had not received any new messages. It took her a moment to know that she was not still dreaming, soul walking, or whatever that had been.

She walked across the room, took her laptop from its bag, and turned it on. Once Kiera made it past the logon screen, she quickly opened a search engine and started typing the phrases Nick had shown her. At first, she turned up no results, but once she began to search the more obscure areas of the internet, her frustration turned to confusion as the results of her searches began to take shape.

149

CHAPTER 21

Tabby pulled into Dr. Talmadge's drive. The first thing she noticed was that all the blinds were closed. She didn't see any signs of life from the house. She reached the front door, rang the doorbell, then listened for footsteps, but she heard nothing. She rang again and waited. Again, no footfalls from the other side of the door. Tabby walked to the nearest window, cupped her hands around her face, and tried to look through the closed blinds.

Tabby walked around the side of the garage, hoping to find a window in which to peer. There were three narrow casement windows along the top of the garage wall, designed to let in light but high enough to prevent peeping eyes. Tabby looked around, hoping there may be something in the area she could use to reach the windows and see inside the garage. She walked around to the back of the garage, where she saw there were two wooden benches.

She carried one of the benches to the side of the garage and set it down in the flattest spot she could find under the window. She climbed up but still could not see inside. Thinking that the next step in this plan was a terrible idea, she retrieved the second bench and stacked it unsteadily on the first bench.

She climbed onto the first bench and tested its stability again. Her privacy intruding step stool seemed steady enough. She then climbed onto the second bench, using the garage's exterior wall as she held the window's lip with one hand. She held onto the second bench's seating surface with the other hand, then cautiously gained the second step of her makeshift ladder.

I look like crouching tiger hidden Lady Liberty with this pose, she mused.

She straightened her legs and stood a moment questioning whether this balance beam, bench edition, was a smart idea. The second bench did the trick to elevate her enough, so she did not have to stretch to see into the window. She did not like what she saw. Jean's car was in the garage.

Tabby yelped as the benches suddenly shifted, causing her footing to slip. The benches leaned away from the garage wall and lurched outward as they crashed to the grass, leaving Tabby lying on top of them staring at an overcast sky. Tabby felt pain surging through the right side of her back as she laid blinking at the shifting clouds. She questioned whether she had broken her back or maybe a couple of ribs.

She slowly moved her hand around behind her back and felt the source of the pain. Fear engulfed her. One of the benches had broken. And the support that reinforced the legs had gouged into her side. Butterflies flew from her stomach to her throat. She wanted to move but was afraid of causing further damage.

There was no way to tell how deeply the plank had dug into her side. It felt like it had penetrated halfway through her back. Panicked thoughts rolled through her head. Surges of air rushed in and out of her lungs. Every breath seemed to drive the spear deeper. Her chest began to heave in short, shallow gulps. She felt consciousness begin to fade as the grey sky above her began to slip into shadow. She jerked, which cause the agony to deepen, as a voice called to her. She watched the sky as the daylight shrank from her eyes, her sobs robbing what remained of her breath. She heard a distant voice as hands began to grip and paw at her. The voice seemed to grow closer as Tabby came back to herself.

"Tabby. Tabetha Hensley. Tabby, do you hear me?" the voice called.

"What?" Tabby replied in a stunned, vacant whisper.

"Tabetha, can you hear me?"

"Yes… who…" she questioned in a dreary voice.

"Tabby, it's me. It's Jean."

Tabby tried to sit up, but the pain in her side caused her to stop. Her respirations began to hitch again.

"Tabby, don't move," Jean said in a calm, firm voice.

"How bad is it?" Tabby asked.

"Well, I've scrapped knees worse than what you have going on here." Jean offered with a smile.

"What?"

"Honey, it's just a poke. No more than a quarter-inch deep. Gonna hurt like a bitch for the next week or so, but you won't meet your maker today."

"Are you sure?" Tabby asked, blinking away tears.

"Yes. Now, I am going to stand over you and take both of your hands. I need you to grab on tight. I'm going to pull you up off this mess you've made in my yard."

"Are you sure I should be moved?"

"Yes, honey. it's gonna hurt, but you're going to live, believe me."

"Okay."

Jean stood in front of Tabby and placed her knees against Tabby's knees. She grabbed each of Tabby's hands and said, "Okay, you ready?"

"I guess. This is going to huuuurrrr…. Oh. Ow, ow, ow." Before Tabby realized it, she had been jerked from her painful perch and up onto her feet.

"There," Jean said, "See, that wasn't so bad." Jean's lips were pulled back over her teeth in a pearly white, besotted smile, "Told you it wouldn't hurt too bad. See," she said, patting Tabby on her shoulders, "That wasn't bad. I didn't feel a thing."

Tabby smiled and would have laughed if her side didn't hurt so badly. Tabby looked at Jean. Her cheeks were rose-colored to match her rose-colored, no red eyes. Tabby didn't know if she had been crying or was plastered. When Jean spoke, Tabby could smell the Pinot on her breath mixed with the smell of something that carried a little more grit.

"You mixin, Jean?" Tabby asked.

"Bah," she replied, waving her hands, "you never mind that, dearie. Come on inside, and let's look at that little boo-boo you've got there."

The words, "little boo-boo," running together just enough to give away the fact that Jean had journeyed well past a single glass of Pinot. Jean patted Tabby lightly on the side of her arm again and said, "Come inside so we can get that cleaned up and put a bandage on your new poky hole."

Tabby turned and took one painful step, then stopped. Wincing and drawing in a full lung of air, she pleaded, "Wait, wait, wait. Give me a minute."

Jean moved to Tabby's side and lifted her shirt to inspect the wound. "Yeah, that's going to leave one hell of a bruise. You were lucky. Why the hell were you skulking around my house like a burglar, anyway?"

"I was concerned," Tabby replied.

"I was watching you on my video cameras," Jean pointed to a camera that hung just below the roof of the garage, "got the whole house covered."

"Then why didn't you come to the door? I had made up my mind that if I saw your car in the garage, I was going to call in a welfare check on you."

"Let's get inside. We'll move slow. You'll feel better once you're moving around."

Once inside, Tabby sat down by the gas fireplace. The lights had been on in the house but were dimmed. Recalling her previous visits to Jean's home, Tabby looked around the room and didn't see anything out of the ordinary. Jean walked back into the room carrying a small first aid kit. She set the box on the table between them and told Tabby to pull her shirt off.

"Off?" Tabby asked.

"Sweetie, I've seen tits before. What I haven't gotten a good look at is that wound on your side."

Tabby did as she asked, then Jean carefully examined her back and side.

"You know," she started, "that fall could have been far worse. I could be calling an ambulance right now instead of pulling out band-aids and Neosporin. What in the world were you thinking?"

"I was thinking, maybe not clearly, that I needed to know if you were okay. I called your office, your cell, left messages, and texted. Anthony couldn't reach you either. We were worried, Jean."

"Oh, I got all your messages," Jean replied, seeming to be uninterested while continuing to gently clean Tabby's wound. Tabby jerked as Jean pressed a large square bandage over the "poky hole," as she called it.

"Then why didn't you answer any of them?"

"I wasn't quite ready to talk to anyone."

"That's obvious now," Tabby said, sounding her disapproval.

Tabby turned to face Jean. Jean Talmadge was about twelve years older than Tabby, but her now frail-looking expression, coupled with her red eyes and flaming cheeks, seemed to add a few years to her normal appearance. Her face seemed to be holding something back. Seeing this, Tabby asked, "Jean, what's wrong?"

Jean sighed and told Tabby to put her shirt back on as she picked up the first aid box and returned it to the kitchen cabinet. Jean returned, carrying a freshly filled glass of dark wine. She stopped and looked down at Tabby. Tabby could now see tears in Jean's eyes. Tabby didn't say anything as Jean slowly walked over and sat in the chair across from her. Jean retrieved a tissue from a box on the coffee table and sighed, but still, she said nothing. Tabby was beginning to believe she was not planning to speak when Jean said, "It's not a mental illness, this thing with Nick. I can't help him." Jean looked distantly into the fire as her eyes reflected the fireplace's flames. "I spent all day replaying the session notes and still refuse to believe my conclusions."

"You can't always draw a conclusion in one session," Tabby argued.

"No, not normally. But in this case, I did." Jean leaned back in her chair and took a sip from her glass.

When Jean seemed to be permanently silent again, Tabby prodded, "So, what is your assessment? Anthony says there are no physiological anomalies?"

Jean continued in silence.

"Jean, what happened during your session?" Tabby asked, her voice growing sterner.

After a moment, Jean turned with tears running down her face like blood diamonds in the firelight and said, "Nick, changed during our appointment."

"You mean he presented something during your session?"

"Oh yes, he presented. That's one way to put it." Jean considered for a moment, then said, "No, Tabby. I mean, *everything* about him changed. His eyes changed. His voice changed. He flew at me in rage. I thought he was going to kill me."

"You're not making sense. Jean, start from—"

"I mean, his eyes physically changed colors! They changed from his normal eye color to white."

Jean glared at Tabby. Her fists clenched so tightly the knuckles on both hands had lost all color. She did not want to discuss the details of her session with Nick because she didn't want to remember them.

"Jean, you're not making sense. Please, just start from the top and tell me what happened."

Jean turned away and stared up at the ceiling as if she were wishing for an angelic intervention. She wiped her cheeks and dabbed at her nose with the tissue, then deposited it into the wastebasket beside the table.

Jean took a couple of steadying breaths and began, "Our session began as you would expect with any new patient. He was nervous, and I reassured him he was not there to be judged or labeled. I had him begin by recounting the week's events leading up to his vacation. We then discussed the details he remembered from his vacation and the moments just before his blackout. We briefly discussed whether he had experienced any flashes or glimpses of lost time, and he, as expected, remembered nothing."

Tabby sat quietly, not daring to interrupt now that Jean had begun to talk.

"I asked if I could hypnotize him."

Seeing Tabby's expression change, Jean waved a hand and offered, "I know a lot of people think that hypnosis is just a parlor trick, but I've had several cases where hypnosis has benefitted my patients."

After a moment of silence, Tabby asked, "Okay, what did he say when he was under?"

"Oh," she replied with a grin, "he had plenty to say."

Jean stopped and began taking in chuffing breaths again. She was squeezing another tissue in her left hand as she rested her arm on her lap. Her other hand was holding onto the chair's arm as if she were on a roller coaster.

"I can't," Jean said, studying the tissue in her fist.

"Jean, you have to tell me what happened. I need to understand." Tabby pleaded.

After a moment, Jean continued, "He snapped awake in mid-session. First, he went off on some tirade about everything going black and cold. Then he started to get hysterical, talking about being in a bar where people were killing each other. When he woke up," Jean snapped up to view Tabby squarely in the eyes and said, "it wasn't Nick."

"Do you mean he showed another personality?"

"No," Jean replied, shaking her head. "I mean, it was no longer Nick sitting in front of me."

Tabby could see that Jean's hand was now trembling, so she leaned over and grasped it, ignoring the sharp pain in her side. "Jean, you know how starkly DID can present itself under hypnosis."

"It wasn't DID," Jean shot back. "DID doesn't cause a subject's eye color change."

"What do you—"

"I mean that his left eye changed. He had one green eye, and his other eye was white or grey when he looked at me. His eye color literally changed, Tabby."

"Jean, that's impossible."

"You think I don't know that? And when he started screaming at me, it felt like every word that came out of his mouth was a punch in the face. He never touched me, but…," Jean whimpered, trailed off, and wiped her nose again.

Still grasping for a thread of reality, Tabby said, "I don't understand any of this. Jean, do you hear what you are saying? This has to be a symptom of—"

Before Tabby could finish her thought, Jean jumped to her feet, wrapped her hands firmly against both sides of Tabby's head, and pulled her face in close so Tabby could see her eyes, "I know what you must be thinking, but look into my eyes. Can DID do this?"

It was then that Tabby saw the reason Jean's eyes appeared red. Jean's eyes were not red from crying or drinking. What Tabby saw was broken blood vessels. Shattered veins filled both Jean's eyes, leaving them a blinking Rorschach collage. Tabby pulled away.

"You're saying he did this just by screaming at you? That's not possible."

"There were other things too, Tabby, not just the screaming. He knew things. Things about me."

"Like what, Jean?" Tabby asked, breathing a sigh of relief as Jean moved back over to her seat.

Jean wiped her eyes again, held up a finger, and went into the kitchen. Tabby heard the clink of wine glasses and the ping of bottles knocking together. Jean brought back another glass and two bottles. One bottle was the pinot she had been drinking. The other was a bottle of brandy. She sat the glass on Tabby's side of the table and filled it halfway with the pinot. When Tabby saw that Jean was reaching for the brandy, Tabby motioned for her to hold off on the harder stuff. She didn't think she would drink the wine either but was certain Jean would make sure it did not go to waste, so she let her pour.

"I am going to tell you some things. Things about me that I have never told anyone. Will you listen?"

"What kinds of things?"

"Will you listen?" Jean asked again, giving each word a sense of weight.

Tabby replied, "Yes, Jean. You know I will."

"Okay," Jean took a sip from her glass, set it down, then sniffed. "Did you know I've lived in Georgia my whole life?"

"No. Other than our working together, I guess," Tabby paused, searching her memory until she seemed to come to a realization, "I guess I don't know much about you, privately, at all."

"Well, I have. Born here and raised here."

"Where?"

"North. I grew up in a shit hole little shack with no running water for most of my life. Until my father died."

Tabby didn't know how to take the weight of the secret she had just been given, so she simply said, "I'm sorry, Jean. How did he die?"

"Don't be. Sorry I mean. As far as I can remember, he was not much of a husband and barely a father. He got into a drunken fistfight with a guy in town one night over some dollar poker game, and the other guy knifed him. The knife nicked an artery. He was dead before the ambulance got there."

"Oh my god. How old were you?"

"It was a month after my eleventh birthday. Mom, of course, handled it like a champ. She thought if she could just drink enough, maybe life wouldn't hurt anymore. About a year after my father was killed, my mom hooked up with a man named Jaryl Tunning. He had been living around the area for a few years, and at least he had a steady job, so my mother moved in with him after giving him a month of breaking her in two or three times a week. After six months of shacking up, they got married. That would make me almost twelve. The first year of their marriage was fine. We all kind of fell into a routine."

"Jean, what does this have to do with Nick?"

Jean looked at Tabby as she choked back tears and said, "Just wait, I'm getting to that. I guess it was about two and a half months after my thirteenth birthday. Jaryl came home drunk, as usual, and decided that mom had gotten too old to fuck."

Tabby clamped a hand over her mouth. She held the other hand over her heaving stomach, which made her look like a woman about to vomit. In truth, Tabby felt as if she *were* about to vomit. Tabby felt her eyes begin to brim, and she reached for a tissue.

Jean continued, "He raped me, over and over. I would lay in my room and scream as he did whatever he wanted."

"Oh god, couldn't your mom do anything?" Tabby asked from behind her hand.

"Oh yes," Jean replied with a misplaced laugh, "See, as long as the bastard was fucking me three times a week, he was too preoccupied to beat on my mother. So yes, she did something. She ignored me."

Jean took another sip from her glass. Tabby didn't know when she had removed her hand from her mouth, but she now found it holding the glass of wine Jean had poured for her. She took a long sip before she set it back down.

"After a year of being raped two or three times a week, I started participating willingly instead of fighting it. There was less pain that way, so, you know, less corrective action was applied to my face. By the time I was sixteen, I had started staying away from home as much as possible. That only worked for so long. The fucking bastard even had a special name for his little rape sessions. He called it 'rodeo night.'. It got to the point where I knew his patterns, so I would be ready for him to come home. To come into my room and do whatever."

"Why in the hell didn't your mom kill the bastard, or at least try to run away."

Jean looked at Tabby with sympathy. "If you've never lived in that situation, with a woman like that...." Jean took in another chuffing breath, then continued, "You can't understand when you look in from the outside. I don't really understand how a mind like that works, but women like that just seem to get, I don't know, locked in place. After almost every rape for the first year, she would apologize to me, but eventually, even that stopped. One night, for my seventeenth birthday, the piece of shit forced my mother to come into the bedroom and watch us. God, he had drunk a brewery that night, so it went on forever. Apparently, he liked being watched. I was so used to living with shame that it didn't even phase me to have her at the foot of the bed as he went at me. At one point during the 'birthday romp,' that's what he called it, he turned to my mom and asked her if she wanted to get in on the fun."

Tabby swallowed as the bile rose in the back of her throat. She didn't know what to say or if she wanted to hear any more of Jean's story, then she started, "Did she..." then let her question drop.

"She just sat and watched. Didn't say a damned thing. I thought he would never stop. He even asked my mom if it was fun to watch. She told him it was nice."

"Jesus, Jean. I am so sorry that you had to live through that."

"It's okay. I *did* live." Jean said her words coming out in as ice, "I lived, and put them all behind me, that is, until Nick."

"How did you get away from them?" Tabby asked.

Jean let one finger wander the rim of her glass, and she sat silently. She sniffed again, wiped her cheek, then said, "The old-fashioned way. I killed them."

"What?" Tabby gasped, nearly dropping her glass.

"I killed them both," Jean replied slowly, her voice almost a whisper.

Being careful to keep a clinical tone to mask her shock, Tabby asked, "How?"

"That night, as mom watched something happened. It wasn't like something broke inside me. That had already happened. It was more like something rose up inside me. It was like a spark just appeared in my mind, and I decided they were already dead. I just needed to figure out how I would inform their walking corpses of the news. I waited a week. Jaryl only wanted rodeo night one other week since he met his marathon goal on my birthday. I waited until they were asleep, got a flashlight from the kitchen drawer, and snuck outside. I used the flashlight to find a box cutter in our toolshed. Once I had it, I cut the driver's side brake line on his truck and plugged the line with a screw so the fluid wouldn't leak out. I knew that the following night they would both go out drinking, and he would want to come home and relax", she said, making air quotes as she said relax. "I overheard him telling my mom that the next rodeo night, she would be *required* to participate. I didn't know if I could take that, and if I couldn't, I would get beaten again. I drilled the screw into the cut in the line just enough to seal the leak, knowing eventually the pressure would blow the plug from the line. When they were on the way to their usual Friday night watering hole, a deer ran out in front of the truck. Jaryl stomped the breaks, but only the passenger side brake locked, so his truck warped off the road and into a ravine. At some point, when the truck was rolling down the hillside, the fuel line ruptured, and the truck caught fire. They burned to death if the crash had not already killed them."

Tabby couldn't speak. Her ears had become windows into horror as Jean told her the story. Jean took another sip from her wine glass as Tabby matched her.

At seeing Tabby's sickened expression, Jean asked, "What would you have done?"

After thinking a moment, wanting to say the correct thing, Tabby answered, "I can't answer that question. There's no way I could *ever* answer that question. I think…" Tabby tiptoed, choosing her words cautiously, "I think only someone who has lived a life like that could ever answer that question. I *can* tell you that I will not judge you. I know who you have become. For me to sit here and say it must have been a nightmare doesn't seem to be adequate. Now that I've heard your story, it certainly explains why you've never married or had children."

"I will *never* lay beneath another man, or woman, ever again," Jean said through clenched teeth.

"Can't say I blame you now," offered Tabby meekly as Jean took another sip of her drink. She still did not see how Jean's story related to Nick. Tabby didn't want Jean to think her childhood horror was insignificant, but she needed to know about the session. She timidly chanced a question, "But how does the nightmare you've just described to me tie into your session with Nick?"

"I'm sorry you had to hear that story. I've never told anyone." Jean said, offering Tabby an apologetic glance.

"So, the entire time, no one ever suspected him of the rapes or you for the crash?"

"It was a rural town, in the mountains, in the seventies. People suspected, I'm sure some knew, but people's private lives were just that back then, private. People didn't meddle. No one cared if you were fucking kids, as long as it wasn't *their* kid. As for the wreck, the truck burned to a piece of scrap. Set the whole hillside on fire. The brake lines melted, so there was no evidence left to accuse anyone of anything. Besides, the whole town knew both of them were alcoholics. Everyone thought the bastard finally just drove drunk one time too many."

"Jesus, and you still managed to get from there to here." Tabby held up her hands and looked around the sitting area of Dr. Talmadge's large home. "I mean, most people would be mentally crippled for life from living through a traumatic period like the one you've experienced, much less make a success of themselves."

"I think," Jean said, then paused, "I think that the bastard was planning to kill my mom and keep me as his personal fuck doll after she was gone."

"He had to have known you would leave when you were eighteen."

"I think he had contingencies. After they died, I found records in his room where he had purchased a two hundred thousand dollar life insurance policy covering my mother only."

"That was a crazy amount of money for back then."

"You bet your sweet ass it was. The insurance company wanted to keep the money since Jaryl was the only named beneficiary. Oh, but I got it." Jean chuckled. "I may have been young, but I was not an idiot.

I had a lawyer within a month, and we sued the ass off the insurance company."

"I bet that dragged on forever."

"It should have, but I had a plan. When I got into the courtroom, I laid it on thick. Should've got a goddamn Oscar for my performance. I told everyone how I had been getting raped since I was thirteen and how he would beat me if I wouldn't let him rape me three times a week. I made them think that mommy was just a dear old country girl, and I didn't want to break her heart by telling her, so I just endured. I told them mommy never found out because he was always sneaky. Even the damn judge had a tissue in his hand by the time I finished with them. I had the money in a trust fund two months before my eighteenth birthday."

She sat back, bared her teeth in a broad, satisfied smile. The look of victory never came close to reaching her swollen eyes.

"So, you got the full two hundred thousand?"

"No," Jean replied. She leaned forward, and Jean's smile broadened, "I countersued for three hundred thousand, and the judge let the extra hundred thousand stand as a penalty because the insurance company had tried to bamboozle a poor, sweet child. The lawyer got his ten percent, and the rest went into the bank. I paid my attorney to help me relocate and change my name to distance myself from the whole damn town. After everything was done, I decided I wanted to know how monsters were born. I wanted to know what twisted peoples' minds so that some could become pedophiles and serial rapists and how others could stand by and watch. So, I went to school to become a psychiatrist. I thought it might help me to understand the human condition."

"Did it?"

"Psychiatry? Hell no." Jean scoffed. "All that psychiatry taught me was that if you're fucked in the head, you're fucked in the head. There's no way to rewire the human brain. If it's defective, it generally stays defective."

"That's pretty damn grim."

"Life is what it is, Tabby. Don't be naive."

"What about Nick. Is he *defective*, as you put it?"

Jean sat back in her chair and sighed, her face turned grave again, "Nick is not defective. He's gone."

"What the hell does that mean? He was in your office. We saw him yesterday. You're not making sense again."

"I'm not a religious woman," Jean said, "Never bought into any of that bullshit, but whatever came back from vacation wearing Nick's face is not what left on that vacation."

"Do you hear yourself right now?" Tabby blurted, hearing the anger rolling over her lips and hating herself for the emotional outburst.

"I hear exactly what I am saying, but why don't you make your mind up for yourself?"

Jean got up, walked over to a small cabinet in her sitting area, and took out a small digital recorder.

"You record your sessions? And your patients agree to this?"

"It's in the paperwork when they sign in," Jean said matter-of-factly, "if they chose not to read it, that's on them. I fully disclose every session."

Tabby looked at her uncertainly.

"Look, it's no different than sitting there like Freud and taking mountains of notes as each patient blathers on about some stupid shit like how upset they were when their eggs were overcooked this morning at breakfast."

Tabby looked at Jean in shock. "You were one of my professors," she said. "Why are you so callous?"

"Just listen to the session notes." Jean waved her hands, ignoring the question, then reached down and hit the play button.

Tabby sat and listened to the entire session. At the end of the recording, she let out a long breath realizing at some point, of which Tabby was uncertain, she had started holding her breath as if the sound of the moving air would interrupt the recording. Once Jean hit stop at the end of the session, there was silence. Tabby found she had no words once the recording ended.

Jean asked, "So, what do you think now? Did you hear his voice change?" There was a pause as Tabby sat in stunned silence. She did not know whether to scream or run. She slowly looked from the recorder to Jean, then slowly stammered out, "Ha… how… how many patients did you have in that room? It sounded like a group session."

Jean looked at her solemnly, "Just, Nick."

"But there were four distinct voices on your recording, not counting yours."

"Now, do you see? I do not know *what* Nick is, but no person can throw their voice like that. Whoever Nick was two months ago is gone. As I said, Tabby, I am not superstitious, but I'd call a goddamn priest. That," Jean said, pointing to the recorder, "is not human."

Tabby's stomach rolled as if she were adrift on a tossing sea in a gathering storm. She looked at Jean and asked, "Where is your bathroom?"

"I have a guest bathroom just behind you."

Tabby quickly got up from her chair and ran to the bathroom. As she reached the room, she dropped down with her face in the toilet bowl and wretched. She felt like she was throwing up her soul, which caused the injury to her back and ribs to burn anew. After the convulsive waves passed, she got up from the floor and rinsed her mouth. Tabby turned to see she had not closed the door before her little episode. Her already heated face flushed even more. She ambled out of the bathroom, brushing her hair out of her face.

"I'm sorry for that," she said to Jean as she sat back down.

"Not a problem. I played that scene out a couple of times today myself."

"Jean, if you have never told anyone your story, there's no way Nick could have known about the rapes and the…" she stopped, then said, "The reason they stopped."

Jean looked solemnly at Tabby and said, "Now you understand." Then, thinking back to the sensation of ants marching across her brain, Jean said, "I think he pulled those memories from my mind." She used her fingers to act out something crawling across her brain. "It's like I could feel him crawling around inside my head."

Tabby didn't have an explanation for this, so she asked, "Can I have a copy of this?"

Already anticipating this request, Jean had already made Tabby a copy. She took out another item from her sitting area cabinet and handed it to Tabby, "This is an uncut recording of the session. Do with it what you will. Just don't bring him back around me."

Tabby got up and collected her purse, "Thank you for your help, Jean," then she turned and said, "And Jean, I'm so sorry for what happened to you."

"It's all in the past now, darling. I'm Dr. Jean Talmadge now. Solid as steel."

"Yeah, but still," Tabby replied, motioning between herself to Jean, "If you need this again, you know, to talk, please call me. I am here for you, Jean."

Jean smiled back at her, a tear hanging just on the corner of her eye reflecting the warm orange from the firelight, "Honey, I've carried this around for nearly thirty years. What you have done for me tonight is more than I could have ever asked anyone to bear."

"I know, but I mean it, let's do this again. No one should carry something like that around alone. You know better than anyone that it's not healthy."

"You will be the first one I call," Jean replied, offering Tabby a reassuring smile.

While compulsory, Tabby thought the smile Jean offered was a good sign. Still, the look Tabby saw in Jean's eyes, a blue, heartsore look, made Tabby stop and ask, "Jean, you'll be okay tonight, won't you?"

"Steel, honey. Pure steel." Jean replied, taking a sip from her glass as she motioned Tabby away. "I've got this under control."

Tabby sat in her car in Jean's driveway for about five minutes before she could calm her racing thoughts enough to start the ignition. How someone could live through what Jean had lived through was beyond anything Tabby could comprehend. Tabby's childhood had basically been a storybook. Tabby questioned whether she would ever have had the strength to live through something like Jean had described. As Tabby placed her hand on the key to start the car, she heard a loud pop from inside Jean's house.

The sound was loud enough that it caused Tabby to jump in her seat. She raced back into Jean's house. As she stepped through the door and into the sitting area, she saw Jean sitting in her chair by the fire, her expression one of emotionless horror as Jean sat staring at the ceiling. Her head was leaning back against the chair, a thick red and grey glob crawling out of the hole that had once been Jean's left temple. As

Tabby stepped forward, she saw one of Jean's eyes was open with a look that seemed to be filled with wild, childlike wonder, while Jean's left eye was hanging half out of its socket and looking off to the side. There was a yellow piece of notepaper on the table under the glass from which Jean had been drinking. It read, "Held off as long as I could. Sin stains forever. Sorry. JEAN."

Tabby felt the strength drain from her legs like the emptying of a grain sack. She couldn't stop her knees from releasing as she collapsed to the floor by Jean's body with a hard thump onto her backside. She reached for her phone but fumbled because her hands were shaking. She tried again and managed to dial 911. The 911 operator came on the line, and Tabby heard the operator say, "911, what is your emergency?"

She responded, "My name is Tabetha Hensley. I need an ambulance. There's been a suicide. I am at 4265 Clancy Drive." She turned to look at the corpse, whose eyes were already beginning to cloud.

Tabby sat, staring at Jean as an odd sound filled the room. It took Tabby a moment to realize the sound was an anguished wail coming from her throat. Her anguish turned to rage at the choice Jean had made, and she said, "Steel doesn't bleed, Jean." Her anger then turned back to mourning as she asked with bottomless hopelessness, "Why wouldn't you just let me help?" She reached and gently touched Jean's hand as the sonic scream of sirens began to drift into the range of her ears.

CHAPTER 22

Tabby sat in a languid daze after she shut off the engine and opened the driver's door. She looked at the front of her house and thought the windows now seemed to glare at her like two dark, accusing eyes. The door on the front of the house now looked like a mouth, decrying the indictment, "You failed. You should have seen the signs, Tabetha. Now, live with your poor masquerade as a doctor. You failed. You failed, Jean."

Tabby thought back to when she was fourteen. Her friend Iesha Reins and she were inseparable. Tabby still remembered how Iesha's feet hung suspended above the floor, her body floating above the living room from her house's upper balcony. It would have been a great magic trick to make yourself levitate if it were not for the bulging eyes and swollen tongue protruding from Iesha's mouth. No one ever found a note, a reason. Iesha's family was destroyed after she had done it. Her mother blamed her father. She accused him of failing to provide a safe home for their daughter. Within two years, they had split, and Iesha's father moved away. Iesha's mom withdrew and seemed to wither from life until she, too, performed a magic trick one night with a bottle of wine and a handful of pills. Iesha had been best friends with Tabby since they were in first grade. No one could fully understand the depth of pain the loss was for Tabby. She silently blamed herself partly for not seeing the loneliness. Thinking back, she always knew the depths of Iesha's depression. It was the eyes. The face may lie, but the eyes have a way of always speaking the truth. Whether proclaiming the shine of discovery, proclaiming new love, or showing the void within, the eyes never lie.

As Tabby grew, matured, and moved on with her life, she often found herself remembering walking into Iesha's house and seeing her hanging from the railing. They were supposed to meet for a biology study session for the upcoming finals. Discovering Iesha's body gave Tabby nightmares for years afterward. She would awake from images of swinging friends, family members, and strangers she had never met. Sometimes she would awaken screaming, sometimes just sweating and shaking. Those nightmares drove her to pursue psychiatry. She hoped a greater understanding of loss and pain would provide deeper healing. In truth, it did not. Here again, Tabby began to blame herself, her fraud, for not seeing Jean's void. The emptiness in her eyes.

She began moving toward the door, ignoring the house's accusing face. As Tabby reached the bottom step leading to her stoop, the front door swung open. Ethan ran down the steps and embraced her. Tabby thought her reservoir of tears had been used up as the ambulance took Jean's body away but discovered she was crying again.

Tabby returned Ethan's embrace like a reflex. A shadow fell across them as something moved in front of the light that spilled from the open doorway. Tabby looked up and saw Kiera standing in the doorway.

The embrace broke off, and Ethan said, putting his arm around Tabby's waist, "Come on, let's go inside before Mrs. Rutherford comes out." Just as Ethan's foot touched the bottom step, a crack split the darkened front of the house across the street just before its portico light blinked on. Ethan looked back over his shoulder to see Mrs. Rutherford was already walking down her steps, calling him. Tabby stopped and turned around. Ethan grabbed Tabby and said, "No, Tabby. Hurry up. Get in the house. I will go talk to her." As Tabby went inside, Ethan spun and marked his angle of attack to intercept Mrs. Rutherford's path like a seasoned linebacker.

"Hello, Mrs. Rutherford. How are you tonight?" Ethan called as he waved to her from across the yard.

"Ethan, what is wrong with that lovely wife of yours? I saw her sitting in her car just staring at the floorboards." Mrs. Rutherford asked in her slow southern drawl.

"Tabby is fine, Mrs. Rutherford," Ethan assured her, "she's just had a difficult day."

"Oh, that sweet baby. Is she sick, honey?"

"No. No ma'am. She had a close friend pass away today, and it sort of caught her off guard. She just needs a few days to come to terms emotionally. She'll be okay."

The corners of Mrs. Rutherford's mouth pulled down as she pooched her lower lip and gave sympathetic eyes. She pulled back slightly and lifted her finger, pointing up as if marking an essential point in the conversation. "Well, you go in there and tell that pretty flower of yours that there will be a hash brown casserole and chocolate pie coming her way tomorrow."

"Mrs. Rutherford, please don't do all of that work on our behalf. You know we appreciate it, but we will be fine."

At this, Mrs. Rutherford reached her spotted but surprisingly steady hand out and patted Ethan's shoulder. "Now you just hush. This is something that I want to do for her, Ethan. I can't do much at my age, but I still know my way around a kitchen just fine. So, you just don't fuss cause supper is on me tomorrow."

Ethan smiled at Mrs. Rutherford, leaned in a little, and held his hand up as if shielding someone from reading his lips. Then he said in a mock whisper as if sharing a secret between friends, "Well, you know, Mrs. Rutherford, I would *never* argue about getting one of your home-cooked meals, but if I don't at least put on a show of refusal, Tabby will have my hide for letting you do all that work."

He gave Mrs. Rutherford a wink, causing her to reach up and pat the back of her white head as if adjusting an out-of-place hair, which she always wore pinned up in a bun. She cackled with enthusiastic delight at Ethan's complement.

She turned to walk back to her house and called out without turning around, "Casserole and pie, tomorrow. If you're not home, I'll put it in your garage."

Ethan and Tabby never locked the side door of their garage. Mrs. Rutherford used to leave her treats on the stoop until a neighborhood dog got into a cabbage casserole one day and devoured most of it before Ethan or Tabby got home. Afterward, they began leaving the garage's side door open. They would often come home to find Mrs. Rutherford's little surprises sitting on the small freezer they kept in the corner of the garage. Ethan smiled, then turned and made a quick dart into the house.

As he walked into the room, he saw Kiera sitting beside Tabby on the sofa, gently rubbing Tabby's back. Tabby was sitting with her head hung down, touching a tissue to her nose.

She looked at Ethan, "Is Mrs. Rutherford back home?"

"Yes," then he attempted a shy smile, "But she promised you a hash brown casserole and a homemade chocolate pie tomorrow for supper."

"Oh God," Tabby moaned, "I don't want her to do that." Her shoulders began to jump. Tears ran down her cheeks again. "I don't deserve that from anyone."

Kiera leaned over and hugged her and continued to rub Tabby's back, "Oh honey, please don't say that."

"Baby, why would you say that?" Ethan disagreed.

"I *don't*," Tabby snapped back. She wanted to be angry but didn't have the strength, so her tone lowered, "I should have seen. I could have stopped it."

Kiera asked, "Tabby, what makes you think you could have done anything about what happened?"

Tabby squeaked out, "It is my job. Twelve years of fucking school and six years of practice, and I couldn't see suicide in *any* conversation I have ever had with her for two years?" Tabby's stomach slipped from a small jumping motion to a firm plateau as she birthed grief out into the room.

Ethan sat down on the table in front of Tabby and laid a hand on her knee, "Tabby." He said softly, but Tabby refused to look at him.

"Tabby, look at me," Ethan said again. "Please look at me."

Tabby slowly raised her head. The brokenness written on her face seemed to run soul deep.

"Tabby, you can't carry this on your shoulders. There was no way you could have known."

"I should have known," she said, continuing to sob, "That's my job," Tabby repeated. She then turned guilt-filled eyes to Kiera and said, "I should have known."

Ethan slid both hands down his face and let them fall to his lap, his head wagging with disagreement, "No. That can't be right. You didn't say much when you called, so please tell us what happened."

Tabby thought for a moment, conflicted in her grief. Did she really want to tell Jean's entire, ugly story? The rape? The murders? Her head swam. She didn't want to defile her friend's memory with the details of her silent suffering. She ended it by murdering her parents to escape their humiliation and then murdered her private pain tonight.

Tabby opened her mouth to protest their comforting efforts, but instead, what began spilling out was Jean's story. Jean's childhood, in all its horror. By the time Tabby finished telling them, she had stopped crying.

Kiera and Ethan sat open-mouthed and silent as the death at the end of Jean's story. As the room remained silent, Tabby began to second think about her choice to share Jean's story. She began to believe that it was a mistake, a clinical breach. But no, it couldn't be a professional taboo when the patient was now dead.

Ethan sniffed and said, "Jesus, Tabby. Were you there when she- Well, you know?"

"No," Tabby said, shaking her head, "I was not in the room when she did it. I was in my car."

"I can't believe after living such a nightmare, then overcoming all the shame and humiliation, that she could just end it. I can't imagine what it must be like to live in that type of torment, and for years." Kiera said.

"I think that's the reason she told me her story. She knew there would be no consequences. For her, I mean. Meeting with Nick broke something. Something she didn't even know was there. Besides," Tabby added in a soft voice, "I see that type of profile nearly every day, but until today I've never had one of my patients kill themselves."

Tabby began to weep again.

"She was *not* your patient." Ethan shot back, straightening his back and shaking his head. "No, Tabby. She was not one of your damn patients. You could have helped her if she had given you a chance. She didn't give you that chance. She just dumped this whole damn mess at your feet before she ended it. It was a pretty shitty thing to do, in my opinion."

"No," Tabby replied, remembering the USB drive. "She had a reason to tell me. She wanted to convince me. She needed me to know that she wasn't crazy."

"Wasn't she? She's gone now, Tabby."

"No. Ethan, will you get me your laptop."

After a brief hesitation, Ethan said, "Sure. Hold on."

Ethan walked into the office and retrieved his laptop. He took the computer from its bag and placed it on the coffee table. Once logged in, he spun it around, so the screen faced Tabby. While Ethan had been powering up his laptop, Tabby had fished the USB drive from her purse. She plugged it into the computer and navigated to the drive contents. There was a single audio file.

"This," Tabby began, "is a recording of Nick's session."

"She recorded it?" Kiera asked.

Tabby looked at her, "Yes. But that is not the surprising part. Remember everything I told you about Jean, about her past. The details of Jean's story are crucial for you to keep in mind as you listen to this file."

"Okay," Kiera replied.

"Absolutely," agreed Ethan.

Tabby pressed the play on the audio player. The expression on their faces shifted from curiosity to horror as the session notes played. Kiera felt the flesh rise on her arms as she listened to Nick taunt Jean about being raped, his voice changing like that of a character actor. When Nick's voice shifted to the voice of a little girl Kiera twitched in her seat, gasped, and covered her mouth as the audio track continued. Ethan sat in stony silence, his mouth agape, focused on every word coming from the speakers.

"Jesus," Ethan said when the audio file ended with Jean squalling like a child while muttering something inaudible, "Tabby, what the hell did we just hear?"

Tabby shook her head, shrugged, and offered no further explanation other than to say, "That was Nick this morning with Jean."

"What the hell did he do with his voice? Why did his voice sound like that? Is this something schizo's do?"

Tabby ignored Ethan's rude term for schizophrenia and replied, "No, schizophrenic's *hear* voices, not produce other voices. However, patients with dissociative identity disorder will shift their voices as different personas present, especially if there is a quantitative shift in mood or temperaments between personas, but nothing like this. Nick spoke in four *distinct* voicings, at least two not within his tonal range."

"So, Tabby, what does this mean?" Kiera asked.

"I can't answer that. All I can say is this is something I've never seen. Jean had never seen it either. No clinical record exists, of which we could compare, with a distinct vocalization like this. It's simply never been encountered as far as I have ever read. But that's not even the disturbing part. It's Jean's story. Nick knew. He *knew* Jean's stepfather had molested her. He knew, in *detail*, about the abuse. He knew her stepfather's name, for God's sake. I didn't even know she had a stepfather. He also knew Jean had sabotaged the family truck. Remember, at one point. He said, 'Snip, snip, snip. Drip, drip, drip.' That's a reference to her cutting the brake lines on her stepdad's truck. There is no way that Nick could have known any of it, but he knew it all."

"Okay, so what does all of this tell us?" Kiera asked.

"I'm not sure."

"You've got to have some theory as to what's going on with him," Ethan said.

"I believe that we are listening to…. Well…." she stopped for a moment. If she said the next thing in her mind, she was certain that her friend, and her husband, would think she was on the shortlist for a padded cell. Ethan and Keira's eyes pressed in on her, so she finally said, "I think whoever, or whatever, came back from Tikal is not Nick. Not the Nick we knew anyway."

"What the hell is that supposed to mean?" Asked Kiera.

"Tabby, that can't be right," Ethan followed. "You can't actually believe that. There has to be some physical and reasonable explanation for that vocal shift."

"What about Jean's story, Ethan? Is there anything else you can think of to cause a vocal shift like what you heard on that recording? I mean, Jesus, Ethan, it sounds like listening to an audio track for a horror movie. It's like one of those scenes where they dub someone else's voice over the actor's voice. How could he know all, hell, *any* details of Jean's life or her parents' deaths? That must be accounted for as well, not just the physical voicings."

Ethan did not have a counteroffer to this thought. Tabby moved her gaze over to Kiera as if begging for a more rational explanation. Kiera sat looking as if she had just been slap, so Tabby looked back at

Ethan.

"Okay, Tabby. So, let's say Nick is the devil—"

"Don't do that," Tabby pleaded, closing her eyes and shaking her head.

"Do what, Tabby?"

"You're using your sarcastic tone and being an asshole. We don't have time for that right now. We need real answers here, not agitations."

Ethan sighed. "Okay, I'm sorry. It's just; I can't buy into all that celestial crap. You know that."

Tabby nodded. "You know neither do I, but what else remains if there are no more answers? Look, I'm not saying that this is a God versus Satan thing. I'm just saying there are a lot of things in this universe we, as humans, don't understand. There's a lot of universe out there, Ethan. Our galaxy is a spec of sand on a nonstop beach. I am telling you I agree with Jean. That person, the one on that recording, is not our Nick."

Ethan looked at Tabby as if to say, "You can't possibly mean what you're saying," then asked, "So we're at aliens now?"

"No," Tabby shot back in exasperation, "I just can't explain any of this in any other way than to say it is something that we, or our science, does not yet understand."

Kiera found her voice, and asked "Okay, Tabby. Then what do we do?"

"I don't know. We would need to find Nick before we would have any hope of knowing more, and it looks like he's off-grid again."

"Do any of us have a clue about how to go about finding him?"

After a moment, Ethan stood and looked at Tabby and Kiera, his exhaustion getting the upper hand over his sanity, and said, "Look, guys, I'm tired. I can't think about this anymore. One thing is certain. Between the three of us, we have nothing but this recording. I can't even think anymore. We're all dead. Let's try to get some rest."

Ethan was right. They were all drained. Kiera felt as if she could drop at any moment. She thought back, trying to remember the last time she had eaten. Was it breakfast? Yes, that was why she was so tapped out. She had not eaten since breakfast. The group went to bed and, thankfully, slept a dreamless sleep.

CHAPTER 23

The following day Tabby and Ethan were in the kitchen whipping up what looked like a mushroom and spinach frittata as Kiera came down the stairs. Hearing the commotion of a mixer coming from the kitchen's vicinity, Kiera turned her sleep-filled eyes toward the general area of the sound. She saw, to her amazement, that Tabby and Ethan were fully dressed and looking ready for their workday. She looked at the clock hanging on the wall and saw it was five thirty-six. She had never seen either of these two up at such an early hour.

Kiera took a couple of quiet steps forward, then sleepily said, "Hey guys. Ya'll look bright-eyed and bushy-tailed this morning."

Ethan shut off the mixer and added some cream to the bowl.

"Kiera," Tabby said as she walked around the kitchen island and gave Kiera a big morning squeeze, "how did you sleep?"

"I slept fine, but I yacked again when I got up. Not as bad as last time, but still. I hate yacking. I guess I have a touch of something."

"Do you feel okay?"

"Yes. I'll be fine. I just need to get showered and get myself together."

"Do you need anything?"

"No, I think that I'll be fine once I have a bit of food in me. I feel like I'm starving to death. What." Kiera asked, looking over Tabby's shoulder, "are you guys cooking up? I smell bacon."

"Ethan is fixing his Saturday special."

Kiera looked at Tabby with a perplexed expression.

Tabby saw her confusion and said, "It's a spinach and mushroom frittata. It's really is good. He thought you might like it."

"Oh. Okay. Look, I'm going to go shower. Tell him thanks and that I can't wait."

"Okay, sweetie."

Kiera went back upstairs. She could not shake the thought that there was no way any of them had a hope of finding where Nick had gone off to this time. None of them had experience tracking, hunting, or locating anything.

After her shower, Kiera walked back down to the kitchen. "I am so sorry that I dragged you guys into this," she said, looking at Tabby and Ethan.

Tabby walked over from setting the table, cupped Kiera's cheek, and said, "Honey. No. You did not drag us into anything. If you can't count on your friends when you need them, then why the hell would you need the hassle of having friends."

Suddenly Kiera looked around as if she had been pricked with a pin. She walked to one of the windows at the front of the house and peered out through the blinds. She looked back to Tabby and Ethan and asked, "Did you hear that?"

Tabby nor Ethan had heard anything.

"There it is again. Who the hell…." Keira asked as she turned back to the window.

"What are you looking for?" Tabby asked as she and Ethan joined Kiera at the window. The only thing out of the ordinary was a homeless guy walking down the sidewalk. This was a bit out of place for the neighborhood but not unheard of for their area.

"Ah, poor guy," Tabby said. Ethan looked at her as she motioned to the figure walking down the sidewalk across the street from their house, "Looks like he's homeless. He's young too. We should call someone?"

"Hell no." Ethan replied curtly, "Absolutely not. We have enough shit to deal with at the moment."

"Kiera, what are you looking for?"

Kiera looked at Tabby and said, "I suppose nothing. I guess I'm hearing things now on top of everything else. That recording of Nick still has me a little freaked. I was surprised I didn't have another nightmare last night."

"Me too," Tabby agreed. "Come on, let's go and try to think this through. The guy is gone now anyway, and I don't see any ghosts on the lawn."

Just as Kiera sat down in Ethan's recliner, the doorbell rang.

"Now who?" Tabby asked, sighing and rolling her eyes.

"I'll get it, babe." Ethan opened the door to see the homeless guy standing on his front stoop, trying a little too hard at looking innocent. Ethan's face momentarily warped with confusion at the sight of the kid.

Once Ethan found his voice, he asked slowly, "Ah, hello. May I help you?"

"Maybe," the homeless kid replied. "But I was hoping I could help you." The kid's goofy grin widened.

"Kid, why do you—" then Tabby's voice floated from around the corner into the foyer as she asked, "Who is it?"

"It's the homeless guy from across the street," he replied.

Tabby and Kiera walked into the narrow foyer, nearly bumping into each other, both looking confused.

When Kiera came into view, the homeless kid said, "Oh, hey, Kiera. I've been looking for you."

Kiera took a step forward and apprehensively asked, "I'm sorry, do we know each other?"

"You probably don't know me, but, well," then he paused a moment before continuing, "I know you, and I was hoping I could be of some help."

"Help, with what?" Kiera asked.

"With the Nick thing."

Kiera's heart jumped in her chest as her blood froze in her veins.

"What are you talking about," she asked.

The kid continued, still sporting the goofy look on his face. "You know, the thing with Nick. He disappeared, right. Now he's back, and you guys want to find him."

"I don't know what you are playing at, you little shit, but the best thing that you can do is leave."

Then Kiera stepped forward and slammed the door closed. She turned to go back into the kitchen when the doorbell rang again.

"I'll get this," Ethan said, holding up a hand. When Ethan opened the door, the kid was no longer grinning at him like an adolescent middle schooler. The kid's face looked older, more challenging, and there was no humor in it. The kid was standing on the stoop with his backpack slung over his right shoulder, both hands hanging onto one strap.

Kiera started to open her mouth, but the kid spoke first, "I know about the black dreams, Kiera," then he paused before adding, "And the kid."

They all took a step backward as if someone had punched them. The kid stepped through the doorway and walked past them. Once he had reached the living room, he called back to them, "Can you guys come in here and let's start over, please?"

The group found themselves sitting on the sofa, glaring at the kid who was now seated on Ethan's recliner. After a moment of looking at the kid like they were waiting for an alien to burst from his face, Ethan spoke up, "Alright, you have our attention. Who are you, why are you here, and how do you know about Kiera's dreams?"

"Okay. Fair. I have one request first. Can I use your shower?" The durppy smile had returned.

"What," asked Ethan. "You burst in here and pull out a magic show act, and you want what? To use my shower?"

"Yes, please."

"Kid, are you retarded?"

"Ethan, that is a hurtful word," Tabby chided, giving Ethan a firm pop on his arm.

"Look, dude—"

"Ethan," Ethan corrected.

"Sorry, Ethan, it's just that I've been on the road for like three days, and I have slept outdoors for the past two nights wearing these same clothes since I left Charleston. I just think—"

"Charleston?" Kiera gasped. "South Carolina?"

"Yes," the kid answered. "Our Lady of Peace in Charleston, South Carolina."

This response only added to the group's confusion.

"It's a boy's home. I live in a boys' home."

"Like a detention center?" Ethan asked.

The kid's expression was nixing as he answered, "No. Well yeah, sometimes, but no. It's an orphanage."

"Look, dude, Ethan, I just feel like I could think a little better if I didn't smell like a hobo's ass, okay. I can pay for the water," he offered, unzipping his bag and beginning to rummage through it.

Ethan narrowed his eyes, "If you think—"

"Yes," Tabby said.

"What?" Ethan exclaimed. His voice cracked like a pubescent teen leaving him feeling less a man and more a neutered pup.

"Oh, Ethan, it's fine," Tabby said, waving a hand at Ethan as if warding off a fly, "He does look like he's had a few rough days. I thought he was homeless, for God's sake, when I saw him across the street. A little soap and water might do him some good. It would do the air in the room some good." Tabby smiled at Josh as she pinched her nose closed.

The kid returned her smile and said, "Thanks, I guess I can't blame you for that."

"No. No one really would. Would they? Do you have clothes?"

"Yes. Yes ma'am. I just need to use some soap and shampoo, please. Some toothpaste would be nice if you have some. I forgot mine."

"Of course. I have a travel tube that I haven't opened yet. I'll get it for you."

"May I talk to you ladies in the kitchen?" Ethan asked. "We'll be right back, ah." Ethan paused, looked at the kid, held his hand out, waiting for the kid to fill in the blank.

"Oh, Josh," the kid said. "Joshua Roland."

"Fine," Ethan said, "You stay here a minute, and we'll be right back, Joshua."

The three of them walked into the kitchen and talked in hushed tones. Josh could hear them speaking but couldn't make out much of the muted conversation. As he sat watching, the whole scene reminded Josh of those old mobster movies where the pigeon sat in the Don's office while he and his henchmen discussed whether to give him a pair of cement shoes or just break his kneecaps.

"Look, we don't know anything about this kid. He just shows up, knowing stuff. Stuff that no one outside of the three of us knows, and you want to let him roam around our house?" Ethan was using his interrogator's voice that Tabby hated.

"Honey, look at him. He can't be older than fifteen. What is a fifteen-year-old kid going to do as long as you're here? You do CrossFit like four times a week, and you have twelve inches and probably sixty pounds on this kid. I'm sure we're fine."

"Okay, I'm just saying, have you ever heard of retard strength?"

Tabby's mouth dropped into a frown. She closed her eyes and moaned. She then relaxed her face and looked at Ethan with her "Don't doubt me on this" expression. Being careful to keep a calm voice, she replied, "Honey, you know that I love you more than anything, but you have said the R word two times in the last five minutes. If you say it again, I am going to wait until you are asleep, then I'm going to punch you, right in the dick."

Ethan's mouth hung slack. Tabby typically did not say things like that, so he was stunned into silence, standing with an open mouth to match the dumb look on his face.

"Babe," Tabby said, "Close your mouth. The position for flycatcher has already been filled."

Ethan closed his mouth then opened it, but Tabby pressed a finger to his lips and said, "Look, I'm just saying try to be nice to the kid.

Clearly, something is up with him, and he is just a kid. It's not going to hurt anything to let him get cleaned up."

"She's right, you know," Kiera agreed. "Look, we didn't even know this kid existed until ten minutes ago. What's another twenty to thirty minutes to allow him to get cleaned up before we talk with him."

Ethan threw his hands up. "Sure. Fine. Whatever. I know when I'm outnumbered."

Josh saw the trio break their huddle and start in his direction. As they approached the chair where he was sitting, Josh smiled and asked with his best old school mobster impression, "So, what's the verdict. Am I swimming wid da fishes, or scrubbing wid da soap?"

Tabby motioned for Josh to follow her. "Come on, Josh. I will show you a bathroom you can use upstairs. Follow me, and I'll get you a towel and the toothpaste."

Josh bounced up from the chair with a child on Christmas morning look and followed Tabby up the stairs. Then Josh stopped, looked at Ethan, put on his most congenial, tooth-filled smile, and said, "Thank you, sir. I really appreciate this."

"Yeah, okay. Just hurry up. This conversation is all buildup with no plot at this point." Then Ethan watched as Josh followed Tabby up the stairs.

"Are you sure you've never met this kid?" Ethan asked Kiera, not removing his gaze from the pair headed up the stairs.

Kiera shook her head. "I have been racking my brain, but I can't place him. He definitely seems to know me."

In a few moments, Ethan heard the shower at the end of the hall burst to life as Tabby came down the stairs. "Kiera, have you really never met this kid anywhere?" Tabby asked.

"No, never."

Tabby seemed to be excited rather than creeped out, "I can't wait to hear this story."

Ethan and Keira both looked at Tabby questioningly.

"I mean, come on. You're not? This kid shows up out of the blue, knows about Nick, knows about your dreams, and you aren't curious?"

"I would say more creeped out. And who was he talking about? He said he knew about my dreams and the kid."

"Well, I guess we'll find out in a few," Ethan said, walking over to check on his frittata.

CHAPTER 24

Josh came bounding down the stairs after nearly an hour in the shower. Fresh shirt, clean jeans but the same dirty shoes. He stopped at the bottom and continued to dry his hair with the towel hanging around his neck. "Oh man, I feel so much better. Thank you, guys, so much. That bathroom is awesome. This place is awesome."

"You've never had a shower in a bathroom?" asked Kiera.

"Oh, no, I've had showers. It's just at my home we have prison showers. You know, the community showers where we all just go in and bathe together. Very Romanesque," he said, making a fist and forcing it up into the air, showing the back of his fist in a salute. "The scene is pretty much a pedo fantasy. I could get used to a shower like that."

"Josh," Josh looked at Tabby. "How long have you been at the boys' home?"

"Let's see, I am fourteen, almost fifteen, so that would make fourteen, almost fifteen, years."

"You have lived your entire life in an orphanage?" Ethan's sounded more sympathetic than hostile now.

"Yeah, but it's not that bad. Most of the other guys at my home are pretty cool. Except for this one kid, he's a total jackass." Josh was thinking of Jackass Jeff now. "The sisters are mostly nice. And hey, I've never been diddled by a priest." He held up his pinky finger and wriggled it.

"Wow. Nice." Ethan said with an approving laugh. "I guess I would call that a plus too."

Tabby elbowed Ethan in the ribs catching him unprepared, so he let out a deep-throated puff of air but continued to laugh.

"Josh, has anyone ever told you how you came to be at the boys' home?" Kiera asked.

"Well, not exactly, but I tend to be curious." He tapped the side of his right temple with two fingers. "I may have allegedly executed some recon, on my own behalf, in the records room."

"Did you find anything?" Kiera thought that he must have based on his cheek-high grin.

"I am what we at the home call a forced deposit."

"What is a forced deposit? Tabby asked.

"A forced deposit is a rape baby."

"Oh, good God," Tabby exclaimed.

Tabby had treated several rape victims over the past few years, and there were always emotional ups and downs that accompanied rape cases. Rapes that produce children often leave a ruined hunk of debris in their wake. Sometimes the waste was the victim's life, but usually, it was the child's. The mother almost always gave the child up for adoption, which left the children feeling discarded. In Tabby's experience, the children often remarked that the alternative way of dealing with an unwanted pregnancy would usually have been *their* choice rather than being discarded like old luggage.

"You seem to be unusually at ease with this knowledge."

"Yeah, don't get me wrong, I'm not special. You always want to know who your parents are, but being raised with a group of twenty other brothers, even if the brothers cycle in and out around you sometimes, is not too bad. Getting warm meals, a roof, and a dry bed beats getting raised in a crack den or by a mother who hates you every time she looks at you because you're a reminder of what happened to her. Again, don't get me wrong. I've had some struggles in the past. I just think things could be a lot worse."

"But if you snooped in your records, you must have seen your mother's name. Did you ever try to find her?"

"Nope. There was no record of her. I was a fire sell." Josh saw that none of them had any reference for his slang, so he clarified, "A fire sell. I was left at the front door of a fire station with no note. So, fire sell. Get it." Josh felt like a teacher trying to explain algebra to first graders. "It's a fire sell," He held up air quotes as he said, "fire sell," and then continued, "because you get—"

"We understand what you mean," Tabby said, signaling that he had given enough explanation.

Seeing a look on Tabby's face that Josh could not decide was disgust or just disapproval, he continued, "I've had enough time to figure some of this out. I've learned that you don't have to like a situation, or circumstance, to understand it. Some girl had something bad happen to her fourteen years ago, something that she did not want a reminder of for the next forty to fifty years. She didn't have the stomach for an abortion, so she did the next best thing, she gave me up. So, like I said, I don't have to agree to understand the reasons."

Tabby wiped her eye with the palm of her hand. Josh saw this and said, "You know, you really shouldn't feel like that. There are a lot of kids with my story. A lot of them lead long, happy lives." This reassurance did not help Tabby. She transitioned from palming her eye into a lawn sprinkler. She got up and walked to the kitchen, pausing only to pull a couple of tissues from the box on the coffee table.

Ethan followed Tabby to the kitchen.

"Whoa," Josh said. He rubbed the side of his face with his hand and sat with an awkward look on his face. "Did I say something wrong?"

Kiera leaned forward and said, "No. She's pretty emotional right now. She had a friend pass away last night. With that happening, and what we're dealing with now, with Nick, well, it has her worn pretty thin emotionally, that's all." Kiera didn't know why she was telling him this. It was almost as if she couldn't stop.

Tabby and Ethan came back to the sofa and sat down.

"Sorry, I didn't mean to upset you," Josh said as Tabby sat back down.

Tabby looked up from torturing her nose with the tissue. "You're fine. It's not you. I am just a little extra sensitive right now. I'll be fine."

"Maybe I can try to help?"

"Okay," Tabby straightened up and gave Josh her attention and asked, "how exactly would you do that?" She regretted her tone sounded more sarcastic than she had intended.

Josh got up from the recliner and stepped over to Tabby. He held out his hands, palms up. Tabby considered for a moment, then said, "Fine, I'll play along," then she reached and took his hands.

"Just close your eyes and relax," Josh told her, then he calmly added, "You feel better now."

Kiera and Ethan were watching this performance like a sideshow curiosity. Josh continued to stand silently, holding Tabby's hands until she opened her eyes. She looked at him with disbelief. Josh smiled then returned to his seat as she followed him with surprised eyes.

"What did you do?" Tabby asked.

"I don't know." He replied as he sat back down, "I just learned when I was younger that I seemed to be able to help people feel better. I try to help all the new kids coming into the home if they're upset. The first few nights, or *weeks*, can be tough sometimes, so I help them when they let me."

"But what did you do?" Tabby asked again.

"I don't know," Josh said. "It's like I just sort of *think* at people, I guess, and they seem to feel better."

"Tabby, what just happened?" Ethan asked.

"I don't know," Tabby answered, turning to him and offering a smile, "I just don't feel sad anymore. I mean, I know what happened to Jean, but I'm not sad about it."

"That's great, but…." Ethan didn't finish his thought. Tabby could see that Ethan was running over possible solutions in his mind as to why holding this kid's hands could make her feel better about Jean's death. To be honest, Tabby was trying to wrap her head around the same issue, yet, in the end, she no longer carried the mournful grief that had been sitting atop her like a stone just a moment earlier.

"Let me see your hands," Ethan said, reaching to examine Tabby's hands. Ethan could see on Tabby's face that her grief was gone. She was smiling and looking like her usual, overly cheery self again for the first time in days.

"What did you do? Did you dose my wife with something, you little shit?" Ethan got up and walked over to Josh.

"Ethan, stop." Tabby urged, "I wasn't dosed with anything."

Ethan grabbed Josh's wrists and pulled them toward him so he could examine his hands, being cautious not to touch Josh's palms.

Ethan let go," Tabby said, "You're being an ass."

Ethan looked at Tabby and saw she was glaring at him with disapproval, but her eyes were not the glassy reflections of someone under the influence of anything.

"Ethan, leave the kid alone." Kiera said, "Look, let's just sit and talk. If Tabby feels better, that's a plus, but let's hear what he has to say."

Ethan released Josh's wrists, walked around to the back of the sofa, and stood, arms folded across his chest like a bodyguard waiting to pounce.

"Okay, so you show up here, with your nose uncomfortably deep in my business, having never met me, so why don't you start from the beginning. Why are you here? How do you know me and the things that you know about Nick and me?"

"Well," Josh began, "I don't know if I can explain everything, but I can tell you how I know you." Josh looked up, made a thinking face, then continued, "I guess it was like five weeks ago. I started having this dream. It was one of those, oh what do you call it, reoccurring dreams. I was standing in the middle of this huge open nothing. Everything around me was black but not dark because I could still see. Whenever I had the dream, I would see this guy about arm's length away from me. Nick, I finally figured out, just floating in the air. He looked like he was frozen or something. You've seen those space movies where people make themselves into popsicles to travel over long distances without aging? That's kind of what he looked like."

"Yeah, I had that thought too," Kiera said, looking at Josh with an intense focus now. "It looked like he was frozen in midair."

"Yeah, exactly. After like two weeks of having the same dream, I noticed that the body, sorry, Nick, started to like, I don't know. He—"

"He started to dissolve." Kiera finished.

"Yes!" Josh exclaimed, snapping his fingers, "that's it. I couldn't think of the right word." He felt his confidence grow as Kiera confirmed the details of the dream and thought, "Thank god. I'm not a nut job after all," then he continued. "At first, there was a couple of floaty little pieces of dust. There seemed to be more each night. Anyway, about two weeks ago, I started seeing you, Kiera."

"That's when I started having my dreams."

"Yeah, you came zooming in from a doorway that appeared out of nowhere like a superhero. I don't know how you didn't see me; I was standing right in front of you." Josh said this as if he had met Kiera at the mall instead of inside a dream. "Nick started talking to you. I mean, his mouth didn't move, but I heard his voice. He sounded really wiggly like he was talking underwater or something."

Kiera nodded slowly in agreement, then asked, "You heard Nick when he talked to me?"

"Yeah, that's when I learned your name. Then, you asked him where you were, and he told you he was in the House of the Black Bond, whatever that is."

"That's not exactly what he said," Tabby interrupted, looking over to Kiera with suspicious eyes. "That is not what Kiera told me. She said it was some language she had never heard."

"It was Samarian." Kiera offered, surprising both Ethan and Tabby. "I know that now." Everyone turned to her as Kiera got up to retrieve her laptop. As she sat back down with her laptop in hand, she said, "Ethan, turn on your TV and switch the input to mirror."

Ethan did as she asked. Kiera pulled up her browser and connected to the TV.

"The last dream I had was different. Tabby, remember all the texts

I sent to you when you were at Jean's house?" Tabby nodded. Because of Jean's suicide the previous evening, Tabby had not even remembered to ask Kiera why she had been texting her a bunch of odd gibberish.

"The thing I have not told you," Kiera paused to see Tabby's expression, then continued, "I was asleep when I sent those texts to you."

"How could you have texted me in your sleep?" Tabby asked, unconvinced.

"I don't know, but I did. I somehow got my phone off the nightstand and sent you texts as a way of writing down what Nick was saying, what he was showing me, in the dream so I wouldn't forget."

Tabby had no response. She and Ethan just stared at her. Kiera shifted in her seat and said defensively, "Look, I know it sounds impossible, but I am telling you, I fell asleep, and when I woke up, I had my phone in my hands."

Josh, seeing that the stunned confusion was not abating, spoke up and said, "So, the last night you showed up, you seemed different from the other times. You didn't seem like you were scared out of your mind that time. Nick even pulled off flashing up these runes to you."

"Okay," Kiera said as if having been slightly violated, "Yeah, that's not creepy." She gave a slight shudder at the thought of having her mind unknowingly probed by Josh as she slept, then continued, "But what appeared over Nick's body was not runes. This is what he showed me."

She began typing until she had pulled up an ancient language website. She typed one of the words she had texted Tabby into the search bar on the site's translator. She typed the word ehus and clicked search. The search returned house. She then typed in salmu, and the search returned the word black. The last word duranki returned the word bond making the whole phrase when spoken together house black bond.

Tabby and Ethan looked at Josh like they had just contacted an alien.

Ethan got up and took a deep, nervous breath, and said, "Ah. No. This is insane. I don't know what's going on here, but there has to be some explanation."

Kiera was beginning to get an idea about the translations, so she asked, "Josh, what did Nick say to me when I asked him why he was in that place?"

"Oh yeah, yeah," Josh said, snapping his fingers and making his thinking face again, "he said he was there for change."

Kiera said nothing. She typed in another word from the text message, enu, hit the search button, and the database returned the word change. Kiera closed her laptop and looked at Tabby and Ethan as she waited for their reaction. They sat numbly, looking at both Kiera and Josh.

"So, in my dream that you apparently shared with me, you heard English when Nick spoke to me in Samarian." Kiera felt like she needed to slap herself to wake from this odd, new reality. The fact that Josh had been inside her head and that he had heard a distinctly different language than what she had heard when Nick spoke made her feel like her weird level may be reaching its peak. This kid, whatever he is, is connected to her and Nick, and she had no way of understanding how.

Kiera had another thought, so she asked slowly, "Josh, do you know what the creature was that was in the dream? Or what that shimmering curtain was supposed to represent?"

"What? I didn't see anyone else."

"So, you didn't see the black curtain when it appeared?"

"Oh that," Josh said as realization spread across his face, "I didn't see it when you were with Nick. I saw it when Nick had *his* dreams."

"Wait, what do you mean, 'when Nick had his dreams'?" Ethan

asked. "Do you mean to tell me that you can see what *Nick* is dreaming as well?"

"Yeah. Seems like I can see both of you guys' dreams." Josh answered.

"Can you see *anyone's* dreams?" Tabby asked. "Can you see mine or Ethan's?"

"No. It doesn't seem to work like that. For some reason, I can only see Kiera and Nick's dreams. I still don't know why. I'm just glad to know I'm not losing my mind. I thought I was going crazy when this all started."

"Why did it start? Did something happen to you that caused this? Some type of triggering event?" Tabby asked, her voice coming out in a clinical tone. After a few years of treating patients with traumatic psychological histories, Tabby was very familiar with the concept of a triggering event.

"No. nothing." Josh replied, "It just started. I went to bed one night, had the first dream, then woke up thinking, whoa, that was a freaky dream. But then, it kept happening, almost every night."

"So, what did you see in Nick's dream," Kiera asked.

"It was the same place, but it was different. Nick was there, but he wasn't frozen like he is when you show up. He was just walking around. He looked a little lost, and he was definitely confused. This series of images just like appeared in front of him.

"Images of what?" Ethan asked, leaning onto the back of the sofa.

"It was super weird," Josh replied. "It was like, well, have you ever seen those really old creepy movies where the film is all grainy and it kind of jumps around? Oh, and you know how the images will distort sometimes?"

"It looked like an old movie reel?" Ethan questioned.

"Exactly. These scenes just started playing like really crappy videos, and Nick watched them. They were all pretty freaky too. First, these old dudes were in robes with big beards doing some type of ritual. I didn't get it. Then it changed to some little girl lying on a dirt floor in some medieval-looking shack. I think she had the plague or something. It was gross. She had all these sores all over her that were leaking some kind of nasty puss. There was some gunk leaking from her mouth every time she tried to say something too. Then the craziest part was when the scene morphed into the last one. It was like Nick got sucked in. He became part of it."

Josh paused, taking a moment to phrase the next part before he spoke, then continued, "Yeah, the last one was the worst. It looked like he was in some prehistoric time. He was just standing there when this huge explosion happened, then everything died."

"What does that mean? How did everything die?" Tabby asked as she, too, was now leaning forward, listening intensely.

Ethan offered, "Well, if it was a prehistoric scene, maybe it was the meteorite that killed off the dinosaurs."

"That's it," Josh said. The aha look on his face made Josh look like he had just remembered the answer to a trivia question. "It was like that, but there was no meteorite. The explosion that I saw started from the ground. Nothing fell from the sky. It was just like," he puffed out his cheeks and made an explosion sound with his mouth as he simulated a growing blast with his hands, then added, "Nick looked like he was about to lose his mind by the end of that one. After that last image disappeared, the door appeared."

"Door?" Kiera asked.

Josh looked at Kiera as if not understanding how she didn't get that it was a door and answered, "The black thing you were talking about. You called it a curtain."

"That was a door?" Kiera said.

"Yeah, door is probably the wrong word. Portal maybe? In Nick's version of the dream, something reached out and grabbed him. Some giant hand. He tried to run, but it grabbed him and yanked him into the portal. That's when the dream ended for me. He had more dreams, none of them good, but that last one."

"Alright, so you're a psychic toddler," Ethan said, making sure the sardonic ring in his tone was unmistakable. "What are we supposed to do with all this info? How are we supposed to use it?"

Josh ignored the frustrating toddler comment, although it did cause him to roll his eyes, and said, "I'm not really sure. I just wanted to come and find you." He looked at Kiera. "I just wanted to know that I wasn't going crazy. I can tell you this. I think that whatever is going on with your boyfriend has an end to it, and that end is like a clock that's counting down to zero."

"Well, it looks like we are sort of a posse now, so we will have to work together to figure this out," Tabby said.

"Okay." Josh agreed.

"So, what now," Ethan asked, still looking at Josh.

"Well," Josh started, reaching into his backpack, "Do you have a microwave and bowl I can use?" He held up an unopened can with ring-shaped pasta splashing around in what appeared to be tomato soup on its label.

"Oh, good lord," Tabby said, shooing the can away like a fly, "Come on, we can do better than that." She got up from the sofa and motioned for Josh to follow her to the kitchen.

"Come on," she said as she offered a smile in Ethan's direction, "After all, we have some of Ethan's special frittata leftover from breakfast."

"Why is it special," asked Josh.

Tabby looked back over her shoulder and gave Ethan a playful, pitying smile, and said, "Because it's the only thing he can cook."

CHAPTER 25

Nick's car came to a slow, sputtering stop along 122 in rural Alabama just outside the town of McCaversville. He climbed out of the car and began to walk. He felt good, considering the talking lady had caused him to show his presence too soon. Her little swinging pendulum and her nonstop chatter. He wished he would have had more time to build his strength, but everything seemed okay for now. He looked around and thought how he had not seen so much green for over seven hundred years, only the cold silence of that damnable black box. Waiting. He couldn't put his finger on it, but he thought the cycle would be his greatest epoch this time. He looked around again, then raised his arms into the air and spun. It was electrifying to have a body again. It was *good* to feel his muscles stretch and move, to feel the blood gushing through this heart as it pumped and thumped in this chest. Life was so good now, but there was a lot to get done. The infestation will be contained.

He continued walking, feeling the pavement beneath the padded sneakers covering his new feet. Strange, the clothing of this period seemed most impractical, but this new foot covering was rather clever. Oh well, he guessed even maggots could have moments of glory if given enough resources and time. Yes, time, that was something that he needed to consider. A limiter had been introduced now. No matter how hard he tried to remain undetected, there was always a damn limiter. Yartrua be damned.

He, though, was smarter than all of them. He has been waiting, watching, looking for his new suit while that fool in the cage searched, never finding his little hidey-hole, his safe space, his pocket. Nick snickered at this thought. They had spent the better part of seven thousand years trying to stop him, but *he* was inevitable. His eternal destiny was unavoidable. And yes, it felt so good.

Their technology was advanced now. These bacteria had infested every part of the mother. Nick heard the ground moan as each of their mechanical demons rolled past him. He questioned whether these creatures would ever conquer their realm's outer limits. Well, that simply could not be allowed. They could not be allowed to grow, to infest further.

Nick couldn't remember why he hated the human things so much, but he knew he had to wipe them from existence like the wiping up of dust with a cloth. Yes, a cleaning of sorts. He smiled and nodded as he imagined putting them all under his foot and pressing them into sweet mush. Not crushing. That was too quick. Nick liked to watch. No, he *needed* to see them getting pressed, slowly, as they did in older times. Ah yes, he *loved* to watch the tiny ants get pressed as each new stone was placed on the board covering their deformed bodies. It was a joyous time when he could see how the little ants' guts would split through their sides sometimes and run out across the wide wooden alters to death they had built. Oh yes, and that smell of death, the shit, and piss is the most pleasing perfume. It made Nick so excited. Again, he felt electrified, causing him to do a little stuttering dance. Sometimes he could go over to the little pressed ants and dab his fingers in that blessed perfume so that he could rub it over his face and chest to carry the aroma for days. If he was lucky, he could smell them for a week or more. After all, sanitary cleansing was not as well known to the bugs at that time. In fact, no one seemed to notice Nick as he walked around smiling, sniffing his fingers, and breathing deeply of the sweet aroma of the bug juice perfume he would apply to his chest underneath his shirt.

Oh yes, he *needed* to press some ants. He breathed deeply. Why shouldn't he start with the next village? No, that was not right. He searched Nick's mind. Then it came to him. Why didn't he start in the next *town*? Yes, *town*, not *village*. He continued to walk. He smelled the air and almost wretched at the foul stench of the vermins' new wagons. They sped along, blowing their waste at him in unattended bouts of caustic flatulence. He felt the trees cry and heard the grass wail as he strode along, all choking on the belch of these new machines. Yes, pressing, the sooner, the better was the best plan for him.

The cry from mother nearly tore his heart as he watched the traffic flowing so smoothly and orderly down the long stone pathways. It was disgusting. He turned to face the traffic from along his path at the edge of the roadway. Little fucking bugs all marching in a row. He thought this precision of movement had to be corrected. Their parade was too orderly. Nick focused on an approaching wagon and sent a thought toward the roadway. A pulse moved out from him toward a Ford Mustang containing two young-looking bugs. Nick smiled. After the car had traveled about one hundred yards, an arm stretched out of the young bugs' window with what Nick thought must have been some sort of weapon. Why else point it at another vehicle. There was a bright flash, followed by a pop issuing from the bug's weapon, then the wagon, no, that wasn't right. Nick searched again, his eyes darting back and forth in rapid succession. The *automobile*, beside the shooting bug's car, swerved and slammed first into the shooter's car, then into the other lane. The two shooting bugs screamed their rage at the other automobile before running up an embankment and rolling back into the flowing traffic where several cars smashed into it. Nick felt like a Christmas child watching the rolling, popping, and crunching of the little automobiles.

CHAPTER 26

Susan Rey was taking her daughter to her first dance recital. She was meeting several of the other mothers from the Princess Dance Academia School at the McCaversville community center, where the troupe was participating in a benefit for the assisted living center in town. Elizabeth, Bella for short, Rey was more excited than she had ever been in her entire six-year-old life. Susan had Bella's favorite playlist blaring from the car speakers. She was playing a Disney's greatest hits playlist. Bella especially loved the one about letting go.

Daddy couldn't come to this recital, but that was okay. Daddy had a very important job that took a lot of his time. Bella understood that sometimes daddy worked a lot because he loved Bella and her mommy so much and wanted to give them everything they asked for or needed. Besides, mommy was here and was about to hit the high notes with Bella.

Just as the high note hit, Bella's mommy's car let out a loud smashing sound from the driver's door side and began to spin. Bella thought the world had toppled over. Mommy was screaming and pulling on the circle she uses to make the car turn. Just as fear started to rise in Bella's little understanding of the crisis, their car immediately stopped, and Bella was flying like in the hero movies, having come loose from her defective car seat. Bella met the car's windshield. The last thing little Bella thought, as she lay in the roadway median, feeling no pain, was that the grass smelled fresh, like just after daddy mowed the yard. The world went dark as Bella thought she heard a lady scream, ending in another loud crash.

John Torbend had been driving big rigs since he was twenty-three years old. God, he loved the open road. John often thought he loved the road more than anything in the world. The sound of the tractor's five hundred horses coursing through the cab under the control of his foot felt, to him, like a drug. It was a feeling that never got old. But now there is a problem. John had met Gena six months ago. Now John's mind seemed to be bent a little off-center. He found himself thinking about her more and more during these long hauls across constant black serpents, thinking about spending more, hell all, of his time with Gena. He had decided that he would make this run to California, then look for a short-haul, or a day truck, job to spend more time with Gena.

John had told Gena about his plan to spend more time with her, and she approved. Hell, she had cried. John smiled, just thinking about it. Gena told him no one had ever cared enough about her to change their life around to accommodate *her* needs. She had cried, he had held her, and they had made the sweetest love the night before John left on this run. It was the hottest sex they have had since their first exploratory encounter with one another. John found his mind was drifting to her now as the roadway sang beneath him, all the raw power of his tractor devouring the asphalt in front of him.

Just as an image of Gena's face appeared in his mind, a minivan crossed in front of him after a pickup truck slammed into its side then smashed into the guardrail. John was no more than one hundred feet away and had no time to react. He jammed the breaks. As the big rig's tires squalled, the truck's frame creaked around him, arguing its resentment at the strain of stopping. The rig started to lurch around into a jackknife like an overweight ballet dancer. As John saw the minivan smash into the guardrail, he saw a small body leap from the van's front windshield and land on the grassy median in a heap. He saw one woman in the driver's seat of the van screaming as he hit it broadside.

The big rig's cab jumped into the air then crashed down on its side. John felt the load in the trailer shift. The rig's cab began to roll over like a lumbering dog. The truck disintegrated around him as thoughts of Gena flooded his mind. John felt other vehicles smashing into his overturned rig as it continued its slide. As the cab rolled to face its deteriorating roof toward the onrushing traffic, John heard the screech of tires and smelled burning rubber. He had no more thoughts as the world vanished like the flipping of a switch when sixteen-year-old Nathan Lane's nineteen ninety-five Dodge Ram hit the roof of John's cab, striking it directly above where the rig's driver still sat belted in his seat.

Melvin Thomas was out for a cruise on his Honda Gold Wing. Yeah, his friends teased him for not buying a real hog, but Melvin had gotten a great deal on his Honda. It was just hard to find a good used Harley. It had a few more years on it now, but damn, it was still freedom. The feel of the wind whipping in from underneath his helmet, cooling his sweat-soaked face, was almost orgasmic. The air blowing up the sleeves of his jacket, and his pants, cooling the blast of heat, the rose off the roadway, all with no cage around you at seventy miles per hour, just made you feel alive. Yeah, this was true freedom. Maggie had bitched about him leaving her a widow along with two fatherless daughters every time he came in from a ride. She hated the bike, and he hated the choking noose that marriage had put around his neck along with two little girls, who he, to his surprise, loved with his whole being. He still resented those same two bundles of joy for putting a bit in his mouth and yanking each time they called him daddy.

Melvin always knew that the open road was his true mistress. That was, until he got the news from Margarette, Maggie to her friends, that he had apparently blown an enterprising load the one night he didn't have a condemn, and she didn't want to wait, so Maggie was going to download another clone. Why the hell did he need to use a condemn anyway? Couldn't that bitch had used birth control or a Plan B pill the next day. Why was it his problem if the bitch got loaded? Still, he held up what he considered was a man's responsibility. He stuck around and made good on taking care of all of them, as he would even after the new kid arrived.

Sicily and Becca were his heart's delight. He had never known *real* love until he looked into the eyes of sweet Sicily Ralina Thomas. Then, when his little Rebecca Jane Thomas came along, he thought his heart would explode. How could another human being love another creature like he loved them? Still, love could not always remove that feeling of having a hangman's noose around a free man's throat. So, this bike that Maggie hated was the one true escape that he felt restored the balance. It allowed him to cope with the suffocation of domestication.

Up ahead, Melvin saw the organized lines of traffic devolve into a crisscrossed battlefield of tossing metal. There were ear-splitting sounds of bending metal, grinding pavement, and faint screams from some of the vehicles on the roadway. Melvin saw the line of traffic careening into a crumpled stop in front of him. He thought he was going to lay the bike down, then the thought of hearing Maggie bitch about it was replaced with the sudden angelic ascent of his body from his motorcycle's seat. He felt like he was flying over the road, over the crumpled heap of twisting, turning automobiles.

Melvin's next thoughts were of his little girls. Maybe they weren't little nooses; they were his salvation, the reason he now knew what it was like to be a man, a father. He couldn't remember if he had hugged his girls when he left for his ride this morning. Then another thought pulled at his attention. He saw the top of his feet in front of his face as a cracking sound from just below his head, as well as from somewhere low in his back, vibrated in his ears. He didn't feel any pain but thought it strange he could see the top of this feet beside the sides of his head. As he fell from his collision with the interstate overpass's support pier, his last thought was that he could have been a better man to the woman who had given him two beautiful treasures with a third on the way.

Jordon Lad was on his way to the gym. He was caught up on all his classes, so he took a skip day to get in some extra reps on the bench. He was living it. He was thinking about the three division one colleges from whom he had offer letters. He hadn't decided, but he had a definite leaning on his preference for which school was *his* choice. His parents wanted him to stay close to home so they could support his college career like they had supported his high school career. After all, it wasn't every day that some kid from a four-A high school from Podunkville, USA, got offers from division one schools.

Jordon's parents wanted him to go to Alabama or Auburn so they could travel to home games and support the local Bama teams, but Jordon thought the full-ride offer to attend Miami seemed more to his liking. Just the thought of four years in a palm-riddled tropical party city like Miami made his head swim, and not in a bad way. It made his head swim in that, has it made, high school all-star quarterback way. Jordon realized that he had made his choice at that moment on this stretch of highway. He was going to Miami. He almost didn't have the heart to tell his folks but decided there was no point in waiting, so he would let them know tonight over dinner. Just the thought of all the Cuban food he could eat, coupled with year-round beach access, seemed like heaven to this small-town Alabama boy. What rural Alabama kid could resist? Not to mention all the tanned college hotties that any horny college boy could ever dream of on those beaches. Yep, it had to be Miami.

Jordon thought his dad would reluctantly understand, although he wouldn't like it. His mom would *eventually* adjust to the fact that her 'little man' was growing up and needed to stretch his legs. Besides, there was Junior to keep mom occupied for the next three years. Little brother was only in ninth grade and just beginning to build his high school brand as a first-rate linebacker for the McCaversville Panthers.

It was as Jordon finished this thought that he saw the traffic up ahead shifting. No, not shifting but colliding. Jordon punched the accelerator of his F150 and swerved to miss a Subaru Sidekick. His truck slid sideways, but he recovered. He saw a big rig that was spilling over on its side up ahead. Jordan scanned the scene, searching for options to avoid the colliding cars. Just as he was trained to check down his receivers before launching the ball for the final touchdown of the game, he scanned for open gaps in the careening monstrosity ahead of him. Then he saw it. A gap. His out.

Jordon saw an opening, just big enough for him to throttle down and rocket his F150 round the carnage at the shoulder of the road.

What Jordon did not see was an independent painting crew in a ragged-out pickup truck. An extension ladder in the pickup's bed had no red flag marking its protrusion over the bed's tailgate. Jordon didn't see the ladder until it rammed through his windshield, striking him on the bridge of his nose, punching through his head on its way through the cab of his pickup and out the back window as Jordon rear-ended the contractor's vehicle at sixty miles per hour. Jordon's last thought was not of Miami with all its palm trees and scantily-clad, tanned bodies. It was of Junior. He regretted that he would never see his little brother play another game and how he would never be able to watch his mom and dad roar their excitement at their second son's achievements as they had done at so many of Jordon's games.

Nick stood at the side of the roadway and watched as the bodies and the cars piled up. The screams of the bugs were like music in his ears. Yes, press the tiny bugs. Kill the fucking bugs. He did another crazy little dance. After all, it must have been a mistake to let these little creatures breed and grow. It must have been a mistake. An error. But Nick would fix it. Oh yes, Nick would fix it for good this time.

Nick continued to walk toward the interstate sign that read, "McCarversville, two miles." He walked along, replaying the screaming of the ants in his mind. What lovely melodies. He thought about how good it will feel to press these tiny little ants into the loving sweetness of oblivion. His one faint grey eye smiled, matching the distorted lips on his face, his white teeth growing sharper with each step.

CHAPTER 27

After a brunch of spinach and mushroom frittata, bacon, and half a two-liter soda, Josh was seated once again in the living room with six staring eyes gazing at him. He thought if one were to put their hands over their mouth, one over their eyes, then the third over their ears, they could be the hear no evil, say no evil, see no evil monkey statue that Sister Dunshaw keeps on the desk in her office. It made him want to laugh, but he held it back. They had done Josh a courtesy and not asked him many questions while he ate, other than how the meal tasted, so Josh felt he should say something to break the tension in the room.

"Thanks again for brunch, Mrs. Hensley. That really was the best frittata I've ever had which is surprising considering I hate spinach."

Tabby smiled, "Well, you are certainly welcome. Ethan does make a mean frittata. Maybe you may be around long enough to sample his pan-seared rosemary and garlic ribeye with the spicy pan sauce."

Josh's eyes brightened at the thought, and he responded, "That would be awesome. I've never had a steak before."

"Are you guys serious right now?" Ethan looked at both Tabby and Josh with mild contempt. "You mean to tell me that we are going to sit here and discuss culinary chops? Really? I think we could use our time more productive like, for instance," Ethan turned to Josh, "How the hell did you find us anyway? If you live in Charleston, none of us have ever met you, yet here you sit? So out with it."

Josh didn't want to say the 'how' of just how he had arrived on their doorstep, but he knew before leaving the boys' home he would eventually be asked. Josh had thought up a couple of decent lies that may answer how a runaway orphan of fourteen could make the pinpoint journey from Charleston to the Hensley's looking for a woman he had never met who, by the way, doesn't even live there. Nope, lying was not the answer. Only the truth would work here.

Josh thought for a moment about how he could phrase what he needed to say, then with uncertainty, he began, "Well, I guess I kind of homed you."

"What in the hell is that supposed to mean?" Ethan asked.

"You know, like a bird. Yeah, a homing pigeon or something. I just knew what direction to go. I knew you were in the Atlanta area. I hoped that as I got closer, I would have a clearer sense of what direction to travel."

Josh saw on their bewildered faces that they were not fully tracking with his explanation, so he tried another approach.

"Okay, well, maybe like how a dog makes a cross-country trek to find his lost family. Like I sniffed you out."

"Oh, come on!" Ethan exclaimed.

"Gross kid, and creepy," Kiera said.

Tabby, however, was laughing at Josh's comment, "So, hey Kiera," she said, "might want to tone down that perfume."

Josh held his hands up in apology and offered, "Ok, so maybe not like a dog. Yeah, bad analogy. Okay, so think of a compass. You know how the compass has a needle that always points north, so you know which direction to go? It's like that, only it's like the needle is in my head, and it always points to Kiera and, to a lesser degree, Nick. I can feel him too, just not as clearly."

Josh thought this mental image should have made perfect sense but what he saw staring back at him were three very skeptical faces. Josh sighed and tried to think of another analogy. He started again, "Okay, I guess like, it's like a—"

"No, we get it," Ethan interjected. "We understand what you are saying. We are just trying to figure how something like that would work."

Josh tried to think of an illustration he could use to convince them when he remembered playing a game with the other boys in the home.

"I think I know something that may help. You see, when me and the other guys in the home were younger, we would play a sort of land-based version of Marco Polo. You know the water game where one person has their eyes closed—"

Ethan interrupted again, "We know what Marco Polo is."

"Right, okay, anyway, Sister Adaline made us stop playing because she said she didn't want someone breaking their leg because they were walking around blindfolded. There was nothing in the yard to trip on anyway."

"Kid. Josh. Do you have a point to make?" Ethan asked.

"Yes, do you have a blindfold?"

After a minute of bemused blinking from the group on the sofa,

Tabby said in a doubtful tone, "I think I can scrounge up something we can use. Let me go check."

Tabby went upstairs and dug around in her closet until she found an old tee shirt. She plucked it off its hanger and hurried back downstairs.

"All I could find is this old band tee."

Knowing he was the only one who bought band merch, Ethan asked, "Which band?"

"Ah, I don't know," she held up the shirt. It read "Wasted Daisies Bliss Tour 2010."

Ethan cocked his head and said, "That is one of my favorites."

"Ethan, he's not going to clean his shoes with it. It's fine." Tabby walked over to Josh and handed him the shirt.

"Thanks," Josh said, taking the shirt from her. He tied the shirt around his head to cover his eyes completely, then looked around to make sure he could see nothing.

"Alright," he said, "I want to try something. Kiera, will you help."

"I guess," Kiera said and sighed.

"I need you to walk around the room. Go in different directions, don't move in the same direction the entire time. When you stop moving, I need someone to tap me so that I know you have stopped moving. Once I feel a tap, I'll tell you where you are standing."

"That won't prove anything," Ethan said, "You will hear her walking."

"No, I won't. I am going to ask her to take off her shoes, and I am also going to put in my earbuds and start a metal playlist." Josh smiled in Ethan's general direction as he fumbled around in his bag, eventually pulling out his earbuds and his cell phone. Kiera slipped her shoes off and waited.

Josh reached up to pull one side of the blindfold up enough to see the screen on his phone. After a couple of taps and one swipe, Josh had his playlist running. He felt along the side of his phone and pressed the volume up button until the group heard a concert of gnats coming from his ears. Josh gave a thumbs up to no one in particular, and Kiera began to walk around to the back of the sofa. Tabby watched as Kiera glided around behind them in a delicate waltz. Once she had stopped, Tabby reached over and gave two quick taps on Josh's left knee.

Josh twitched slightly, then said, very loudly, "She's on my left." Then he added, "About ten o'clock."

Keira began another glide and stopped when she was directly behind Josh, making sure to stay as far away from him as the room size allowed. Tabby gave Josh's leg a tap. Again, Josh got the position correct. Kiera was directly behind him at his six o'clock position. Then again at the three, one, and twelve positions.

After several correct call outs, Tabby looked over to Kiera and instinctively put up her hand to shield her moving lips from Josh, even though he was blindfolded, and told Kiera, "Don't stop. Keep walking," as she made a pair of walking legs in the air with her fingers.

After three paces, Tabby tapped Josh's leg, and he called out her position, "Two o'clock, no wait, three o'clock." He stopped as if in deep concentration as Kiera reversed her course.

"One o'clock," he called out, then he shook his head and grinned. "I get it." He shouted, "She's not stopping now. She's just walking back and forth."

That pronouncement stopped Kiera's pacing as Ethan and Tabby sat with disbelieving faces. They slowly turned to each other and shook their heads, acknowledging that this, while impossible, was happening right in front of their faces. It was not some well-rehearsed stage show.

"Twelve o'clock," Josh called out. Tabby shook her head and rolled her eyes. She got up and removed the blindfold. Josh blinked against the sudden change from dark to light as Kiera sat back down. Josh gave them a confident smile and took out his earbuds.

Kiera fixed her face in a skeptical but emotionless glare and said, "How? How do you know where I am in the room?"

"It's like a magnet. I just like kind of *feel* where you are. It's like I feel you pulling at me," then he added, "In my mind."

"I believe you, but it doesn't make any sense. People can't attract someone with their mind."

"Yet here I sit," Josh said, spreading his hands out in front of him, with a wide childish grin on his face. "Look," he continued, "I don't understand it either, but clearly, I made my way from Charleston, and here we sit with you three looking at me like I'm an escaped lab experiment, so clearly, something *is* going on."

Seeing the group wanted to believe but were having trouble moving past his ability to point his consciousness in Kiera's direction. He noted Tabby had more a look of wonder at his latest demonstration instead of disbelief. He guessed that since he had removed Tabby's sadness over her friend's passing, it must have given her a more susceptible perception of whatever linked Kiera and Josh.

"Kiera," Kiera, who was sitting in thought, turned to the sound of Josh's voice, "You have been upset for a long time now, more so since Nick came back. Not to mention having a baby on the way, let me try to help you like I helped Tabby."

Kiera laughed but then slowly stopped once she saw Josh's confused look. Her breathing deepened, and she asked through quivering lips, "What did you say?"

"Can I try to help you?" Josh replied, looking more nervous.

"No, the other thing."

"What?" Josh thought for a moment, then replied, "Oh, the baby. Yeah, how far along are you?"

Kiera sat biting her lip as tears began to well up. Josh didn't know what he had done, but he now understood if looks truly could kill, he may well have been dead by now.

"Why would you say that? I'm not pregnant."

Josh shuffled around in his seat, shifted his eyes from one group member to another, and thought of how to answer the question. Again, Josh thought that the truth would serve him best here.

"Well, it's just…." He began, then stopped. He rubbed the top of his head and looked down at the floor, thinking, then looked back at Kiera and continued, "I figured you knew. You have two heartbeats. I'm sorry. I thought you knew."

Kiera got up, wiping her eyes, and went up to the guest room with a determined stride.

"Kiera," Tabby called after her, "hang on." Tabby followed Kiera up to her room.

Ethan sat back and looked at Josh. Josh could not tell from Ethan's expression what he was thinking. He could hear muffled talking from upstairs but couldn't make out the words. Josh squirmed around in his seat as he heard Kiera and Tabby coming back down the stairs. Tabby was saying, "Well, let me come with you. Please."

Kiera turned to Tabby at the bottom of the stairs and said as she wiped her cheeks, "No. It's okay. I'll be back in a few minutes. I'll be fine."

"Kiera, your face is not agreeing with your words. Are you sure?"

Kiera choked back another sob and sniffed as she replied, "Yes. I'll be fine. I'll be right back."

She started toward the front door and then stopped and looked at Josh. She said nothing but seemed to be considering several thoughts, none of which Josh thought he wanted to know. Josh offered a shy smile, to which Kiera shook her head and went out to her car.

Josh looked at Ethan and Tabby, trying to gauge the room and determine if he was in hot water or an icebox. Either way, his tension meter was running at ten.

"I didn't mean to upset her. I'm sorry, it's just, the heartbeat is so strong, I assumed she knew already, and I—"

"It's okay," Tabby told him, "That's just a pretty big bomb you dropped in the middle of the room. She's going to need a minute."

"I'm sorry, really."

"Where did she go?" Ethan asked.

Tabby looked at Ethan as if he should have guessed and said flatly, "The drugstore, where do you think?"

"Yeah, that would make sense."

"Ah, I'm gonna go outside for a minute," Josh said as he stood uncomfortably from the chair.

Josh went to sit on the front steps. He sat quietly for about five minutes, watching one of the Hensleys' neighbors playing with a puppy on their front lawn. The neighbor was trying to get the new puppy to sit. The commands must have sounded like jump and play because that's all the little dog was doing, much to the neighbor's frustration. Josh heard the door open behind him and turned to see Tabby coming out. She sat down beside him and began watching the puppy.

After a minute, she asked, "Have you ever had a dog?"

Josh shook his head and answered, "Nah. Animals aren't allowed at the home."

"That's no good. Every boy needs a dog."

"I always thought having a dog would be awesome. I think it's one of the first things I'm gonna do when the state releases me."

"Releases you? You make it sound as if you're getting released from prison."

"That's actually a big misconception that people who have not been in the system often make. Murders and drug dealers are a lot nicer than angry nuns most of the time." After a brief chuckle from both of them, he continued, "No, it's not like that. I just meant when I am no longer a ward of the state. It's not that bad. At least I'm not on the streets. I have seen those kids. That can get real ugly fast."

Tabby found herself speechless again. It was beyond her comprehension how Josh's only options were a boys' home or the streets. Growing up in a healthy family environment, she had difficulty seeing what it must be like to be that alone.

Josh saw Tabby was thinking about what he had said and offered Tabby a concentration breaker, "Hey, it's okay. It's not like I don't have plans. Being an orphan isn't a fatal disease, and as far as a family is concerned, I can make my own family later. Who knows, I might even be better at it than the ones that brought me into this world."

"Yeah, I guess. It just seems unfair."

"A fair is where you go to get corndogs and popcorn. It's not a unit of measure by which to gauge your status or position in life."

Tabby looked surprised to hear this bit of wisdom from a fourteen-year-old mouth. Her surprise must have been evident in her expression because Josh offered, "No, not an original. Sister Adeline always says it when one of the boys gets down or starts having a pity party." He chuckled. "Yep, Sister Adeline is going to kill me for this little field trip when she finds me."

"I imagine they have to deal with runaways a lot."

"Oh sure, but I've always followed the rules. The shock is probably just now wearing off so they can figure out what to do."

They both looked up as Kiera pulled back into the driveway. Kiera got out of her car and walked up the steps without saying anything. She stopped at the top of the landing and looked at Josh.

"Hey," she said, to which Josh did not dare respond. "I'm sorry. That was a pretty crappy thing to do before I left. To make you feel that way. It was just the shock. I mean, it's not like it's yours." She forced a smile at him, but her lips were still quivering as she went into the house.

Once inside, she went up to the guest bathroom. Josh and Tabby followed her inside but went to the living room to wait. Tabby sat down on the sofa and Josh the recliner. Ethan was busy in the kitchen making himself a snack.

"Hey kid," he called, "You want a snack?"

"No, sir, but thank you. I'm still full of the frittata."

"Okay, how about you, Tabs?"

"No," she replied, then added, "Geeze, how can you eat so much? You're like a bottomless pit."

"Good genes, baby, good genes. So, what is she doing anyway?" Ethan motioned to the upstairs.

"Just give her a few minutes," Tabby replied.

Tabby looked at the clock. Fifteen minutes had passed, so she got up and went to check on Kiera.

Tabby walked through the guest bedroom and gently knocked on the bathroom door. "Kiera, you good, sweetie?" She paused, got no reply, so she called again, "Kiera?"

A throaty, ragged voice replied to her, "Yes. I'm fine." Kiera's answer was soaked with uncertainty.

"Can I come in?"

"Yes," came the throaty voice again.

Tabby opened a narrow seam in the doorway, just enough to see Kiera sitting on the toilet looking at the floor. She was trembling from head to toe. At first, Tabby remembered how Kiera had thrown up earlier and decided that she must have gotten sick again.

Kiera looked up, and her face told the story. Tabby could read in Kiera's blood-colored eyes and swollen eyelids. She read it in the cherry red nose and her fiery, wet cheeks. In Kiera's blood-colored eyes, Tabby saw terror staring back at her. Tabby pushed the bathroom door open a little further, and something by the sink caught her eye. She saw three thin white narrow rectangular objects on the counter, each about six inches in length. The three objects had a discolored tab jutting from the narrow edge on each object's end. There were two small white indentions in the middle of each object that resembled tiny little windows, like the ones you would find on a miniature dollhouse. In each of the matching windows of the rectangle shapes were faint blue lines.

CHAPTER 28

"Are you okay?" Tabby asked.

"I don't know?" Kiera responded.

"Is it Nick's?"

"Yes, of course," Kiera replied, wiping another tear, "He's the only one I've been with since we became exclusive, and before him, it's not like I was playing the scene."

"You know we're here for you regardless of what you decide, don't you?"

"No," Kiera said, looking at Tabby, "I don't think I could do that. It would be like killing Nick."

Tabby tried to console her as Kiera started to cry again. "Come on, go downstairs."

"I don't understand what is happening. How did this kid find me? How can he see my dreams? Nick's dreams? He knew I was pregnant before I even knew. I'm scared, Tabby, and I don't know what this kid is or what any of this means."

"He's an orphan, honey. A kid. I am sure whatever is going on has him just a scared as you."

Once downstairs, Kiera asked Josh, "How did you know? You said the heartbeat?"

"Well, it was like I felt both heartbeats when you came to the door. When I focused on following you around the room, I was sure I heard a second heartbeat. It is a lot faster than yours and seemed to be strong. I guess there must be more than a compass needle in my head."

Josh scratched his head nervously.

Kiera opened her mouth to ask another question, and Josh blurted out, "No. I don't know how or why. My life was pretty normal until a few weeks ago, so I'm just as in the dark as you." He looked at her and pleaded, "Look, I didn't mean to add stress. Can I see if I can ease some of it for you?"

Kiera looked at Tabby as if silently asking her for advice. Kiera placed her hand on her stomach without realizing she had done so, but Tabby nodded encouragement. Tabby's eyes were smiling again. Seeing that Tabby's melancholy was gone, Kiera said reluctantly, without looking at Josh, "Okay. Let's try. What harm could it do?"

"Awesome. Let's move the table and sit on the floor."

"Why do we need to sit on the floor? Tabby just sat on the sofa."

"Tabby's pain was recent, shallow. Close to the surface. Her pain didn't have time to set in. You know, burrow. At least, that's the way I've come to understand how this works. You have been dealing with this for a longer time."

"And, of course, you know exactly when Nick went missing. Why am I not surprised at this point?"

"I know. Like I said, it's like I just know. Anyway, sometimes, if the pain is intense, I've seen some of the kids at the home pass out for a little while."

"Wait, pass out. Why?"

"I told you, I don't know how it all works. I just know that it works. When they wake up, they always feel better. One kid told me he felt more ordered. So, will you let me try to help? It's the least I can do." Josh waited for Kiera's answer.

"Yes, you can try."

"Great. Ethan, can you help me move this table out of the way?"

Ethan sighed but got up and helped Josh move the table to clear the area. Josh sat down first, folding his legs crisscrossed, and motioned for Kiera to sit. Kiera puffed a piece of hair out of her eyes, tucked it behind her ear, and sat down. She felt silly as she sat down in the same yoga pose, almost touching Josh's knees. Josh stretched his hands toward Kiera, palms up, as if he and Kiera were about to play a game of slap, and offered Kiera his best attempt at a warm smile. Kiera apprehensively reached for Josh's hands.

Once she had placed her hands on his, she began, "Alright, now what am I…."

She immediately stopped as she and Josh both flung their heads back, their faces straining as their bodies seemed to tremble and spasm, as if grasping at the air, unable to breathe. After a few seconds, they snapped their heads upright and faced one another. Their open eyes were the color of dirty snow.

Kiera repeated the phrase, "Lemesu fa slovate dashkwel," as Josh simultaneously repeated, in rhythm with Kiera's chant, "Dark will purge the seed."

After three cadences of this chant, they both fell silent. Ethan was about to pull Kiera away, but then Josh spoke, sounding more than ever like an amazed child, "Kiera, are you seeing this?"

"I see an interstate," Kiera replied, "There are cars piled everywhere. Jesus, there are bodies in the road."

Josh, in his mind, turned to see Kiera standing beside him and asked, "Do you see me?"

"Yes, I do."

Josh motioned with an ethereal hand and said, "Look past the wreckage. Do you see him?"

"I'm looking, wait. Yes. Oh god, it's Nick."

"Try to focus with me. Think about being in front of him, past the pileup. Focus."

"I am moving past the pileup."

"Me too," Josh informed.

"I am in front of Nick. Does he see us?"

"No, I don't think so. I think we are just outside his realm of sight."

"What? What does *that* mean?"

"I don't know. It just seems right. I don't think he can see us."

"I'm going to try to talk to him."

"No, Kiera, I don't think that is a—" but it was too late. Kiera was in front of Nick, calling his name.

"Nick! Can you hear me? Nick!"

"Kiera, I don't think that he can hear us."

Kiera focused her will and yelled, "Nick, stop!"

Nick stopped and looked around as if trying to spot a small bug in front of his face. He cocked his head and listened and then spread his lips into a grotesque smile. The sickening smile made him seem less himself and more something else.

Nick stopped listening and looked directly in front of him. Kiera thought he was looking at her but then saw his eyes looking through her. Kiera turned to see Josh standing behind her in the roadway.

Nick continued to smile his insane grin, showing his now inhuman teeth. Two fine white rows of pointed animal-like teeth as if someone had put dog's teeth into an almost human head. Nick strained his eyes into hard slits and said with an angry growl, "So, I see you are walking this world now, Nathalue. You will not be able to intervene this time. This is the fourth and final crucible."

Nick spread his hands then continued, "This is my divine destiny. The reason for which I was born." Nick screamed with insane rage, "You cannot stop the inevitable. I am the eternal, inevitable solution."

Nick softened as if bored, no, not bored but as if he were very weary. He waved his hands and said softly. "I am inevitable. I *am* the solution. I was born to reset the balance, to wipe the slate clean."

Nick began to walk forward. He took two steps and walked through Kiera. She shivered as a sensation of spiders dancing across her skin enveloped her. She let out a shuddering breath. Nick stopped, turned back to look where she was standing, and studied the empty air in front of him. He seemed not to see her but instead sense that the air where she stood was different. He reached out with fingernails that more resembled claws rather than fingernails and clutched at the air.

Kiera, thinking of the spiders on her flesh, took a step back in her mind. Nick grasped at the air and felt nothing, so he shook his head then turned back to where Josh was standing.

"You can try, Nathalue, but you will not succeed. I am the only truth in this world, in any of the worlds. This will be my final glory, my reason for being." Nick's toned turned mocking. "Ah yes, Nathalue, the light, the birth. The propagation of this mistake," Nick said as spit flew from his lips. "If you are here, Nathalue, just know, you will not suffer this journey to the end of my path. This will be *your* greatest failure."

Nick began to walk again as he took a deep breath. The air seemed fresher now that all the little ants were smashed behind him. All the ants smeared upon the long flat stone way with all their little chariots piled in heaps. No, again, that wasn't right. He searched the database that was Nick's mind then thought, "All the little ants' *automobiles* piled up along the *roadway*." He smiled his sick smile and walked onward.

Kiera and Josh pulled their hands away from one another. It felt like trying to separate two magnets. As their hands separated, a small spark, like miniature lightning, arced between their palms. Their eyes faded from the dirty white snow back to their regular colors as they sat on the floor, breathing heavily.

Ethan stood beside them with Tabby still grasping his arm. During Josh and Kiera's encounter, he had gotten up, intent on tearing them apart, when he saw Kiera look at Josh with pale, unnatural eyes, but Tabby had held onto his arm.

Ethan saw that Kiera's eyes were normal now, so he knelt, putting one hand on her shoulder, and asked, "Kiera, are you okay?"

"I'm fine," Kiera replied. She looked at Josh, "Josh, what was that? What the hell just happened?"

"I don't know. Nothing like that has ever happened to me before."

"Why did he call you, Nathalue?"

"I don't know." Josh made a hasty retreat from the floor. "I don't know. I just wanted to help. I'm sorry. I don't know what happened."

Ethan, seeing the panic in Josh's face, stood putting his hand on Josh's shoulder, trying to reassure him, "Hey, look," his tone was soft now, concerned, "Let's just figure this out. Clearly, something happened we all need to understand. Just sit back down, and let's talk about what happened."

Kiera was still seated on the floor, unknowingly rubbing her stomach again. She used the other hand to wipe sweat from her forehead and cheek.

She looked at Josh and asked, "Why could he see you and not me?"

Again, Josh had a lost look on his face. He was seated again in the recliner, deep in thought.

Josh looked at Kiera, his desperate face pleading, and said, "I am not sure he could see me. Maybe he, I don't know, sensed me maybe? We have to connect again. We need to know what this means."

"No. Absolutely not," Ethan said, pushing Josh away from Kiera. "We need to think about this. We don't know what just happened, and most importantly, we don't know if this is dangerous or not."

"It may be dangerous!" Josh yelled, seeming to almost grow in front of Ethan. "But how can we know anything unless we try again."

Seeing Josh's anger growing, Ethan attempted to calm him. "Josh, look, we don't want anyone to get hurt. This whole thing is strange, and it seems like there's a lot more going on here than any of us understand."

As Ethan spoke, Josh's anger swelled. He jumped up and roared at Ethan, "Lata vetulush slamalki divie! I don't know how I know; I just do."

Ethan stepped back, he didn't know if it was adrenaline or fear, but his throat went dry at Josh's words. He asked, "What the hell did you just say?"

"I said we have to stop this."

"No, you didn't," Tabby said. "You said something else. What language was that?"

"What are you talking about?" Josh asked, his confused eyes swelling. "I said that something is wrong, and we have to stop it."

"No, you spoke in another language. It sounded like the language Kiera spoke when you guys were holding hands. Josh, what the hell is going on here?"

Josh looked at Tabby but had no answer in this panic-stricken face. He was blinking back tears as his breathing began to hitch in his throat. He turned and ran out the front door. Ethan followed him to the front stoop, calling after him, but Josh did not stop running as he disappeared from sight.

Ethan walked back into the house. Kiera was seated on the sofa again, and Tabby held her hand, trying to offer comfort. "Well, what now?" she asked. "Our best chance of understanding any of this just ran away."

"Don't worry. I know teenage boys. Let him calm down, and he'll be back." Ethan motioned to the bag, still resting at the side of the recliner. "His whole life is in that bag. If I were in his shoes, I would eat my pride and come back for it."

CHAPTER 29

Around seven o'clock, the Hensley's doorbell rang. Ethan went to the door and peered through the peephole. On the other side of the door was a lost fourteen-year-old boy. Ethan turned back to Tabby and Kiera with a smug look on his face, nodded, and gave the two ladies a very satisfied smile that seemed to say, "I told you so," then opened the door. Standing on the stoop, looking like a whipped puppy, was Josh. He shuffled back and forth from foot to foot and took a moment to look up. Once he choked his pride back down in his stomach, he stared at them with uncertain eyes, not knowing if they would accept him back into their home after his childish display.

"So," Ethan said, "How long did it take for reason to set in?"

Josh swallowed the rest of his pride. "End of the next block. I couldn't exactly go anywhere anyway. My whole life is in my bag," he said, pointing to the bag still resting on the floor by the recliner.

Ethan returned Josh's sullen answer with a knowing smile, a hearty pat on the shoulder, and said, "I know. Come on in. It's getting late anyway. Unless you want to sleep in a ditch again, you'd better come inside."

Once inside, Josh looked at Tabby, cheeks ablaze, and said, "I want to apologize for my behavior, Mrs. Hensley." He then turned to Kiera, "I also want to apologize to you, Ms. Clayton. It was unacceptable."

Tabby took a step forward and put a hand on Josh's shoulder. "Josh, it's okay. We have all been fourteen," she winked at him and added, "and not as long ago as you may think. Let's just try to control ourselves from here on out."

Josh felt tears begin to sting his eyes. He knew Tabby didn't mean the words the way he had heard them, but he thought it might be words a new parent would say. "From here on out." It had a ring Josh figured he would never hear.

"Oh, yes, ma'am. I will," he assured, looking back down at the floor.

Seeing Josh's previously non-existent frailty, Tabby's heart swelled. She could imagine herself sitting down and having a family meal with this child, without all of this insanity and weight bearing down on all of them. Something tugged at her, better yet constrained her, to be a part of Josh's life. She didn't know how she and Ethan could be a lasting part of Josh's life, but she had a plan to make his life a little better for right now.

Josh started to speak again, but Tabby interrupted him, "Look, it's been a weird day for everyone. Let's just put all this on hold for now."

Ethan and Kiera agreed.

"Let's fix dinner and maybe watch a movie," Tabby offered. "Everyone is done in for now. I think that we've had enough weirdness for one day."

Josh opened his mouth, but Tabby would not have it, "No," she said, "That is enough for today. Let's settle down and have a normal family-style evening, or at least act like we're just a group of friends," she amended, "I think we could all use a little of that right now."

After the dinner and movie were over, Josh took the sofa. He thought it felt better than his bed back in the home. Before drifting off to sleep, he allowed himself a small dose of deathly hope as he took a few minutes to think about how they had all sat down together, had a homemade dinner with dessert, then had watched a movie. It almost seemed that he belonged. He thought to himself, *This must be what it feels like to be a part of a real family*, then he drifted off to sleep.

CHAPTER 30

Josh dreamt he heard a voice calling to him from the bottom of a pit. The voice echoed and bounced as it continued to call him. It seemed to draw closer until he thought he recognized the voice. He heard the voice again, only this time accompanied by something striking him on the arm this time. The voice filled his ears again then he realized it was Ethan's voice. Ethan softly poked Josh in the arm and said again, "Come on, kid. Josh. Time to get up. Come on."

Josh opened his eyes and blinked the morning smear that was Ethan into view. As his other senses swam into existence, Josh first smelled, then heard bacon cooking. He slowly sat up, feeling very heavy, and looked around to see Kiera and Tabby busily working away in the kitchen.

"What time is it?"

"It's eight o'clock," Ethan replied. "Get up. Breakfast is almost ready."

Ethan walked around the sofa to the kitchen. He asked Tabby and Kiera if there was anything he could do to help, to which he was informed to stay out of the way. He sat down at the kitchen table and scrolled through the morning news on his tablet. He looked up from the headlines long enough to motion for Josh to come over. Josh slipped on his shoes and joined Ethan at the table.

"So, are you a coffee or juice type of guy?" Ethan asked.

Josh offered Ethan a timid smile, then answered, "Juice, please."

Ethan retrieved a glass from the kitchen cabinet then pulled out a jug of orange juice from the fridge. He sat the glass down in front of Josh and filled it.

"Thanks," Josh said with widening eyes. He intended to take a small sip, but once the juice hit his tongue, he drank until the cup was empty. Once finished, he sat it down and looked at Ethan with a ping of shame that lit his cheeks again. Ethan gave Josh a slight smile and filled his glass again.

"Sorry," Josh said, "It's just we don't get the good stuff at the home. This stuff is awesome."

Josh stared at the glass of juice for another ten minutes. Tabby sat a plate down in front of him as his stomach roared its complaint about the wait once more. There was French toast, maple syrup, bacon, and a glass of orange juice, with pulp. Pulp orange juice was Josh's favorite. He loved how he could drink the juice, then chew the little bits of tangy-sweet orange with each mouthful.

Because he had run out of the house the day before, then crawled back with his tail between his legs like a whipped puppy, Josh didn't say much at breakfast. As the group finished their morning feast, Josh studied each face. He noticed Kiera stealing a glance at him as he ate. He swallowed then asked, "Okay, so what's next?"

Everyone stopped eating and exchanged glances with one another. Ethan slowly stopped chewing. Put his fork down, then said, "Yeah, so, the plan for today?"

"I mean," Josh started, a bit more defensively than he intended to sound, "Are we gonna try to…" then he stopped. "Well, it's just, I mean…."

Kiera looked at Josh over a fork full of French toast, "We have been talking this morning. We agree that you and I need to try the thing again. The hand thing we did yesterday. Specifically," she said, pointing her french toast filled fork at him, "we need to see if we can stick at it a little longer."

"Yes," Josh said, pumping his fist, "Awesome," then quickly finished off the last of his orange juice in three gulpy chugs. Twenty minutes later, Josh was seated beside Kiera on the sofa as Ethan and Tabby sat in chairs, each on opposite sides of the couch.

"Are you ready," Josh asked Kiera, holding out a hand.

Kiera puffed a strand of hair that had fallen out of her tight ponytail and shook her hands as if she were trying to get feeling back into them, then said, "Sure. Let's see what happens this time." Then she offered an unconvincing, "Should be fun."

Kiera closed her eyes and took Josh's hands. This time there was no sudden seizing or spasms. There was no gasping for air, nor was there any bizarre chanting. They both sat very still with their eyes closed. At first, Ethan and Tabby thought Josh and Kiera's special connection must have been a one-time thing when suddenly both Kiera and Josh snapped their nearly colorless eyes open.

Josh spoke first, "Kiera, I can see you. Do you see me?"

"Yes. Where are we? Do you recognize anything?"

"No, but it looks like a downtown main street in one of those old movies from the fifties."

Kiera turned her consciousness, scanning the area. She and Josh did seem to be standing on a small rural downtown's main road. Small mom-and-pop shops lined both sides of the street. Toward the end of the main row of businesses, Kiera saw a road sign that read "McCaversville High School 3 Miles" with an arrow pointing up along the road leading out of the small downtown area. Just to her right was a sign that read in big bold lettering "Eats" then under that "Home of the Fat Mouth Burger."

Josh turned to see another shop. There was no sign above it, but a business name was plastered on the large picture window in shiny silver lettering. It was an attorney's office. Beside the attorney's office sat an accountant's office.

"We are in the town we saw on the interstate sign yesterday," Josh said.

"What sign?"

"When we were at the accident site yesterday, there was a sign on the side of the highway that said there was a town up ahead named McCaversville. This must have been where Nick went after he left the accident on the interstate. But where is he now?"

"I don't know," then Josh thought for a moment, "I want to try something. Do you remember your dreams about the black place?"

"What do you think?"

"I have been thinking. I don't think the black was just a dream. I think we can go there now."

"How would we do that?"

Maybe we just need to think—" Before Josh could finish his thought, he was jolted off his feet and sent hurtling forward, away from McCaversville.

The moment he and Kiera thought about going to the black, a dark rip appeared in the air in front of them. They were lifted off the ground and sucked into the fissure. As they passed through the tear, Kiera heard a sound that reminded her of someone ripping apart a short Velcro strip. As suddenly as they had begun moving, they stopped and found they were standing beside Nick's suspended body.

"Oh God," Kiera gasped, her hand involuntarily covering her mouth.

Josh followed with an astonished, "Jesus."

"He's half gone," Kiera said, her eyes beginning to sting.

Josh and Kiera watched as the particles of Nick drifted away from his body in a slow, unimpeded flood. The particles were still moving slowly, but more of his body was simultaneously pulling itself apart. What remained was less than half his original form. Everything below Nick's chest seemed to have been erased, dissolved away like sand rising on a storm wind. There were particles of him beginning to dislodge from his face and chest as the tiny bits of sand joined the slow-moving stream, mobbing away from Nick's body.

"I know what this is, and it's not good." Josh said, "I think that this is called rending." He stepped forward and put a hand out toward Nick's head. The closer his hand moved toward Nick, the more intense the tingle on the inside of his palm became. When he was about twelve inches from Nick's head, there was a flash. Josh jumped and pulled his hand away. His palm felt as if someone had connected it to a small battery. The sensation reminded him of how his tongue felt when he tested the charge of a 9-volt battery. He reached again. At six inches from Nick's head, energy began to arch between Josh's palm and Nick's head. Josh yelled and pulled his hand away. The shock did not hurt, not really. It was more an instinctive survival mechanism than a reaction to pain.

Kiera grabbed Josh's hand. She turned it over and examined his palm, "Are you okay?" She did not see any burns or scorch marks on the palm.

"Yeah," he said with relief, "It didn't hurt. It just startled me. That was freaking awesome."

He looked at Kiera with curiosity that only fourteen-year-old boys could summon. Kiera shook her head in disagreement and said, "No, you don't know what will happen. I touched him, and it nearly knocked me on my ass."

"It didn't seem like that to me. I have to try. We are all linked somehow, and we need to know why. We didn't see Nick in McCaversville, but here he is, right now, with us, the real Nick. I have to try!"

Josh moved his hand toward Nick's head again and stopped when the lightning began to arc. Once he felt comfortable with the tingling sensation in his palm, he pressed his hand slowly forward. The lighting popped, crackled, and buzzed, singing out in the quiet blackness like a choir, as sparks jumped from Nick's head to Josh's palm. Josh pressed forward until he touched Nick's head. When he made contact, Josh's eyes shined with light so brilliant that Kiera had to close her eyes for a moment for fear of being blinded, as did the eyes of his physical body.

Tabby asked Ethan, "Do we stop it? What do we do?"

Ethan studied both Josh and Kiera. Neither seemed to be in distress. Josh had a confident look to him again, supported by the warm smile they had all seen after meeting him, so Ethan said, "They look fine. Let's leave them alone for now."

Tabby motioned to Josh and Kiera's entangled hands. He saw a glow emanating from between them. The light was growing into a bright white shine. Ethan tried to stand, but his knees were locked at the sight of this new unreality unfolding in front of him. In truth, he could not have moved to separate them if he had wanted to, and he knew it. He felt like his legs had been set in chains, and he stared, utterly mesmerized at the light emanating from between their hands, as well as the glow of Josh's fiery eyes.

From within the black, Kiera saw a white light glowing from beneath her. She lifted her hands to see that her palms were now brimming with a brilliant, white glow like soft ribbons of wisping light. The light seemed to dance away from her palms like smoke. She looked back to Josh. His eyes continued to shine like two flashlights, cutting through the darkness. He looked to be in some kind of trance. The lightning from his contact with Nick continued to crackle and sizzle as sparks fired and shot out from beneath his palm in hot bursts of ultra-bright sprays of plasma.

Kiera called his name, but he did not respond. She reached to shake him. As she touched his shoulder, her muscles seized as she was drawn into the trance. Her eyes flashed brilliant white as her mind filled with images she didn't understand.

Kiera saw a black sky with no stars. She watched as the black sky began to fill with tiny white dots. At first, it didn't make sense. Next, it seemed to make perfect sense. Although she did not understand why somehow she knew someone was filling the sky with stars.

She rose above the earth and saw it was on fire, the entire planet burning. Wind rushed past her like a cold breath, quenching the fires. The ground grew cool and dark as the current flowed around the planet, its torrent calming the raging heat.

She felt something approaching her right and turned to see what it was. Hurtling toward her, she saw a small orange dot among the stars. The color was different from the stars in the distant sky. To begin with, it wasn't white, and it didn't seem distant at all. It felt familiar some-how. The small dot pulsed and wobbled and grew like a melon in time-lapse. Kiera couldn't see anyone, but she felt hands pulling and tugging at the dot, increasing its size until, at last, she saw the dot grow into the sun. She gazed at it in wonder as it flared into all its radiant brilliance, sending its rays to warm the now cold dark earth.

She watched as millions of comets collided with the cold planet covering its surface with water as they exploded and melted in the at-mosphere. She saw the seas below her begin to swirl and grow angry as landmasses appeared, pushing the waters aside so the new sun could dry the lands. The land changed from hard grey, then to brown. Green began to appear. It spread like unquenchable fire until the planet's sur-face sang with every shade of green the spectrum could produce.

She could hear no sound, but Kiera's skin vibrated as a tsunami came toward her. She turned to look over her shoulder and saw billions of stars falling toward earth. She watched as they grew closer. In each tiny star, there was no white-hot death of burning meteors. Instead, in every small falling star was a creature streaking toward the earth. She did not know why, but she thought, "These were seeds. The new begin-ning, the birth of a celestial haven."

At the end of the streaming display, she saw two bright lights streaming from the heavens. These two seeds appeared different. Their light was more brilliant. Instead of the white-hot glare of all the other seeds, their light changed colors. It slipped from white-hot light to a brilliant blue, then into the color of the flaming sun, then back to the white-hot flare of the other seeds.

Without searching, Kiera knew this was the planting of man. The hope of a new, better, and perfect creation. She felt energy pass from her into the new seeds as they flashed by. She could see the pull of cosmic energy being sucked into the seeds, like thin ribbons of string, as they roared toward the planet and landed in a small donut of dust and haze on the earth's surface.

She continued to watch as cities rose and fell, wars raged, and man grew and prospered, then exerted their dominance over the entire surface of the earth. Soon Kiera saw men fly across the sky in shining aerial machines that evolved into capsules orbiting the earth. Then, to Kiera's amazement, she saw the seeds of man flying away from the world, hurtling toward the neighboring galaxies in crafts unlike she had ever seen.

Kiera gathered her strength and pulled her hand from Josh's shoulder. Kiera fell into the shallow water covering the black expanse, an energy bolt arching between them. She called Josh's name, but he did not respond. Just as her throat began to close at the urging of her surging heart, the light in Josh's eyes began to dim. Josh looked at Kiera with new calm. A calm that seemed misplaced considering what they were both experiencing.

"It's okay," he said, removing his hand from Nick's head. Again, the lightning arched and argued against the silence.

"Josh, my god, what was that?"

Without answering, he said, "Come on. There's nothing we can do here. We need to get out of this dimension. Think about Nick in your mind."

Before she could respond, Josh took one step, spoke Nick's name, then zipped away with the air around him, producing a ripping sound as his body shot from the black. Kiera hesitated for a moment, barely feeling the icy water soaking through her jeans. She looked at Nick again, sniffed, then said Nick's name. She snapped out of the black dimension with the same instantaneous rip as Josh. When she stopped moving, she found she was standing on Main Street in McCaversville again. Kiera blinked the black vision away, only to see Josh looking calmly in her direction. He was not looking at Kiera. His gaze was set on something just beyond her.

Kiera turned to see what had drawn Josh's attention. Nick was standing in the center of Main Street. His face was upturned, having the contented look of a lizard drawing warmth from the sun. Nick lowered his arms and turned his pale grey eyes in Josh and Kiera's direction, seeming to receive them with a twisted smile from his oversized mouth.

Nick bowed and said with a condescending tone, "Well, well, well. I see you have found me again Nathalue. I am glad you will see the precursor." Nick raised one hand to his face and tapped the side of his nose with his clawed finger as he began to pace back and forth in slow, lumbering strides from one lane of the road, then back to the other. Nick let out a soft chuckle and said, "Oh no, It's true that I cannot see you, but I do feel you watching. You, being the voyeur, from wherever your pitiful form reaches out to me. I feel your prying eyes crawling over me from a distance. You will like what you see."

He lifted his head to reveal the smile on his deformed face as he turned in Josh's direction and said, "Just be patient, old friend."

Nick outstretched his arms as he turned his face to the sky again. He began to speak in a tongue that Kiera did not recognize.

"Rafala me tuto vadala le mleck. Rasva da ladu metonshna peccoria." Kiera began to feel her ribs rattle as each word he spoke seemed to become more powerful. As he spoke, lines of blue energy began to surge between the palms of his hands. Nick continued, "Torbelusha meshala buloc mel far."

"You do not have to do this, Eulahtan. We are more than our nature," Josh yelled as the surging of the blue energy beams increased. The cracking, popping, and hissing coming from their twisting dance rose to a near-deafening spike at each surge.

Kiera looked at Josh with the soul-bled look of a battlefield soldier. She knew something had happened to Josh when he touched Nick. Josh now seemed to know more of what was happening. He seemed to *be* something more. Josh continued to watch. As his anger toward Nick seemed to grow, his eyes began to glow again, the physical manifestation of his rage increasing.

Eulahtan uttered another phrase in his bizarre language, "Bellada comdatho shaldoma compal rees," he said as the energy hummed with the sound of an industrial turbine.

Kiera turned to see a school bus full of middle school children round the corner onto Main Street. Nick straightened his head, looked in Josh's direction, and smiled with his wide mouth. He unfolded a long tongue from behind his inhuman teeth and licked his face as if to say, "This will be delicious," then he slammed his hands together. When his hands connected, a kinetic force radiated out in all directions like a bomb. Kiera saw the bus crumple like an empty beer can. All the buildings along Main Street were blown out in all directions, smashed flat, as the wave rushed out from Nick like a radiating plow blade. The force of the blast seemed to crush everything as its power churned, unstopping, out from the downtown square.

When the blast hit Kiera, the world spun and blurred away as Kiera felt herself tumbling through the air, spinning out of control. Her mind screamed, *Home. I want to go home.* She instantly snapped back into her body, gasping, nearly collapsing onto the floor. Ethan rushed forward and steadied her.

The blast did not, however, send Josh reeling. It seemed to have no effect on him. His heart broke as he realized why he was thrust into this world as a human child. He stepped over to Nick, making sure to stay well more than arm's length away. He didn't think Nick could touch him, but he didn't want to chance that now.

Nick stood with his hands on his hips, slowly turning in circles, watching as the blast rolled away from him like an invisible scraper, leveling everything it touched, leaving the landscape a flattened field of debris.

Nick gave a satisfied nod as he let out a deep-throated laugh. He then muttered to himself, "Not bad for a trial run. Not bad at all. I believe the well is tuning nicely."

He continued to circle, admiring the growing blast radius. He looked up and saw the few clouds hanging like loose vapors in the sky above him, being pushed along by the energy wave as it radiated up as well as outward. He said, "Ah yes. Mother would be so proud of me."

Nick lowered his head as his watery smile wilted. His face seemed to wrinkle and sag. Josh could see the creases around Nick's dead eyes telling about his loneliness and age. He then uttered in a low, mournful voice, "Oh, mother." He turned and walked down Main Street with heavy feet. Josh had a thought occur to him. He focused his will and thought, *Go back!*

No more had he finished the thought than the world stopped and began to move backward until Nick was standing with his smile removed and his eyes cast down. Josh studied his face. A lump rose in Josh's throat as his eyes began to burn. He reached a hand up and felt wet cheeks. He wanted to reach out and caress Nick's cheek. He reached up to touch him, then stopped. *This doesn't make sense*, he thought. He looked at Nick's face again. Was that genuine sorrow? But why? Looking at Nick's face, the almost entirely inhuman face with its pale eyes, brutal teeth, and blackened veins stretching from underneath the hairline, Josh was certain what he saw was sorrow. Josh's face twisted,

Sorrow for what? he asked.

Josh sighed and wiped at the corner of his eye with the palm of his hand. That was odd, also. He didn't feel sad, angry, or any other strong emotion right now. Josh closed his eyes and thought to himself, Home, and he was snapped back into his body.

There was no gasping for air, nor was there any slumping toward the floor. Josh's pale eyes simply faded to their usual bright emerald green, and he blinked. Ethan and Tabby were on their haunches in front of him. He drew back in surprise. Kiera had gotten up and was seated in the chair beside the sofa but still watching. Kiera saw Josh was upset and reached to comfort him but pulled back, remembering the destruction she had just witnessed. Making the bond again, even by accident, was not something she was ready for right now. Josh noticed her hesitation and gave her a look that told her, "It's alright. I'm okay."

"Josh," Tabby said, "Are you okay?"

Josh looked at Ethan and Tabby and replied with a simple nod.

"Can… Can we watch the news?" Josh asked.

The reality of the event Kiera had just witnessed seemed to grow as she asked Josh through trembling lips, her hand muffling her words, "Josh, was that… was that real? Did we just see Nick—"

"Yeah," Josh said, sounding somehow older and wearier now, "I think we did."

Kiera stood up, her chest heaving as tears began to wet her cheeks. "But that bus," she paused, then wiped her face with a trembling hand, "That bus was full. It flattened like someone stepping on a sandcastle. All of those children… I just… we…" then she stopped.

Josh said nothing. He simply looked at her and nodded, letting her know he had seen it too.

Kiera put her hand to her forehead, blew out another heavy breath, then snapped her hand over her mouth. He jumped up and ran to the nearest bathroom, flung open the door, and nearly dove into the toilet as her rising gorge overcame her.

Ethan turned the TV to a twenty-four-hour news channel and stood silently watching as Kiera walked back into the room. Everyone sat in silence as the talking heads droned on about politics, weather, the middle east, and a rise in crime in your neighborhood. Still, no one in the group spoke.

Kiera took a seat on the end of the sofa. She reached for a throw pillow and sat hugging it to her chest as she used a hand to wipe her cheek again.

Ethan looked over at Josh, who had started biting his thumbnail. "What did you guys see?"

Josh looked over, all the boyish humor gone from his face. "A preview."

CHAPTER 31

Nick…. Eulahtan continued walking down Main Street, his mind rolling. Why was Nathalue here, walking this earth? He thought he was the last one. There could not have been anyone else left, not after the previous crucible. Yet, he was sure he felt Nathalue's judging eyes molesting him from afar. No, no, no, this is not good at all. Nathalue was a meddler and Nick…. Eulahtan did *not* like meddlers. They were bothersome. Oh, Nick was not concerned that Nathalue could stop him from completing his task, but still, it was an aggravation. It was early in the transformation, and he was too tired to deal with agitators.

Why didn't Nathalue understand the bugs must be pressed, smashed, stomped until all the delicious smells come out. The squiggly innards spilling from their burst corpses? Eulahtan could see. Why couldn't Nathahlue? After all, both he and Nathalue were hewn from the same stone, so to speak? Nick… Eulahtan figured he would keep moving until he arrived at the center so the little shit stain would not be able to catch up to him until his duties were complete.

Suddenly, Nick smelled a scent he recognized. Its aroma dug deep within his mind and brought up a happy memory. Nick's heartbeat fluttered with excitement as the bad thoughts slipped out of focus, and he sniffed the air like a dog on the hunt for the beautiful aroma. He scanned the area, following the scent on the wind until he found its source. About half a block further down what used to be a neighborhood street, the remains of a home sat blasted off its foundation. The splintered remains were cluttered into piles like so much garbage in a refuse heap. At the end of the home's cracked driveway was a crushed accumulation of human debris among the crumpled house. Nick… Eulahtan assumed the bug must have been walking a pet in front of this house or perhaps checking the mail when the God wave hit. Nick guessed this because a smaller flattened splat of greasy flesh connected to the human remains by a thin leather strap about six feet in length. Eulahtan scanned the bloody patch of flesh and noted that harvesting the perfume would be easy. The man's body turned inside out when the blast hit him.

Nick smiled as he reached down with cupped hands. He dug inside the warm skin suit and scooped out some of the delicious juice he saw seeping out of the debris pile. Rubbing his hands together, then burying his face in the scent of happier times, he breathed in a deep breath. His face almost fell limp with delight. He breathed again, deeply while holding his mouth slightly open, as if sampling the aromatic bouquet of a priceless vintage. He breathed almost to the point of violence, all to savor the sweet smell of the pressed vermin. He rubbed his hands down his cheeks and across his neck as if applying aftershave. He bent and dug deeper into the pile, scooping up another handful of the sweet juice. He rubbed it over the front of his shirt and the back of his neck, then breathed deeply of the savory aroma of broken hope and desire.

He stood, breathed in the refreshing scent of the dead man and freshly scorched air, then continued to walk, eyes closed, thinking happy thoughts about the first time he pressed his first human bug. That was in an age before humans realized time could be measured. So long and weary a time ago was the first time he had smelled the flavorful aroma of that sweet perfume. He walked. He smiled. He swayed with almost sexual ecstasy, having returned his face to his hand. He held one darkly stained hand under his nose, fingers outstretched, breathing deeply of the sweet aroma of intoxicating death.

CHAPTER 32

"So, what scenario?" Rodney Todd asked with a mild look of disgust.

"I think the standard fed meet-and-greet should do," Marcus answered, then returned to studying his computer screen. After a moment, a sound smashed through Marcus's ear like a rock crusher. The sound reminded him of an old sloppy-mouthed yard dog eating a bone.

"Do you have to do that?" Marcus asked.

"Oh, you mean this?" Rodney turned the cup in his hands up and dumped another mouthful of crushed ice into his mouth, then worked his teeth like an auger while not breaking eye contact with Marcus.

"Yes, that. It is very distracting."

"Look, man, we have been sitting here for an hour. The surveil is over. I'm surprised that no one has called the cops on us yet. We need to get on this. Sitting here is getting us nowhere."

"I know," Marcus replied, "I just don't know what the hell type of bug Amanda got in her ass. I do not appreciate running lead on this."

"We finally share a mutual sentiment there, doc."

"Thanks. That's a huge help. Are you a motivational speaker on weekends? Also, might I remind you that your team requested me on this detail?"

Rodney chuckled, "Look, man, let's just go and see how the situation develops. We have the base scenario to start with so let's just move in and see where it leads. We can figure the rest out from there once we're inside."

Marcus sighed, then nodded. "Okay. Let's go then."

Rodney started the car, drove a block down the street, and parked in front of the Hensley's garage. As Marcus approached the front door, he reassured himself that he was an intelligent guy, knew the protocols, and could handle the task. After all, he had brought along a hammer to handle things if anything went sideways. Marcus took a deep breath and knocked on the front door. As they stood waiting for the door to open, Marcus nervously adjusted his suit coat. He knocked again, but no one came to the door. They could hear a TV playing loudly from the other side of the door.

"Damn, how could *anyone* hear a pussy knock like that with the TV so loud?" Rodney said.

Without answering, Marcus pressed the doorbell. After about ten seconds, the door opened. Marcus immediately recognized the greeter as the mid-twenties-something guy from the day Marcus discovered Nick had returned and had gotten past the whole team under his watch. The guy looked perturbed at their interruption but tried to apply his most polite smile.

"Mr. Hensley?" Marcus asked.

"Yes."

Marcus held up an ID badge that he had tucked into his wallet.

"Sorry for the intrusion. I am agent Thompson, and this is my partner agent Deveroe."

"Okay," Ethan said, looking slightly confused now, "How may I help you, Mr. Thompson."

"We're with the Department of Homeland Security. If you would allow us to come in, we'd like to ask you a few questions about Nick Mercer."

"I have already spoken to the Department of Homeland."

"Yes, sir, we would like to follow up. It seems that Mr. Mercer has been spotted in the area, and we are retracing all case details. You know, crossing our Ts, so to speak."

"Ah, sure, absolutely. Come in."

Marcus and Rodney walked into the house and greeted everyone. Marcus could see subjects one and two, but there was a new subject now. Some kid Marcus had never seen. He was curious about this new subject.

After being introduced by Ethan, Marcus, under the guise of agent Thompson, looked over to the new subject and said, "Hello, son. How's it going?"

"Fine," Josh responded.

"May we sit?" Marcus asked, looking at Ethan.

Josh got up and moved to the sofa with Tabby and Kiera as Ethan motioned for the two agents to sit. Marcus and Rodney sat down in the two chairs beside each end of the sofa and began their act.

Kiera started to ask what the two agents hoped to discover, which was not already known, but Ethan jumped in before Kiera could start, "We've all already been interviewed by multiple law agencies since Nick went missing. I don't know what else we could possibly tell you."

"I don't believe that anyone has interviewed him yet," Marcus replied as he shifted his gaze over to Josh.

Tabby said, "He is my cousin from DC, " before Josh could respond. He's here visiting and has never even met Nick, so you will constrain your condescending tongue and eyes to the three of us. You will direct your questions to the three of us and the three of us alone. Do I make myself clear agent Thompson? Otherwise, you are more than welcome to leave."

"Okay," Marcus said, slowly shaking his head, "Well, to begin, we understand that Nick was planning his vacation to Tikal for some time now." Marcus flipped through his notepad. "I cannot find any case details as to why you elected to forego joining him on this little trip. After all, weren't the two of you supposed to be getting engaged?"

Kiera tensed in her seat. She had told no one about her and Nick's possible engagement other than Tabby. The only way homeland could have known was if these government goons had watched them since Nick's disappearance.

A flash of anger sparked as she asked, "What exactly are you guys looking for? I get that you can easily gather he and I did not go on the trip together. The paper trail is easy to follow. So, what exactly are you asking? I was never really good at charades agent Thompson. If you have questions, just ask them, don't waste my or my friends' time. I've answered that question repeatedly, so what else do you need to know."

Rodney looked at Marcus and gave him a smile that said, "I like this one. She has fire," then thought to himself, "It's ashamed I'm probably going to have to put her down."

"Okay," Marcus said, closing his notepad and sliding it into the inside pocket of his jacket. "I'll be less delicate. Homeland is interested in your boyfriend and, therefore, the three of you by proxy. We have a United States citizen who left this country, disappeared for over two months, and reappeared without warning or reason. I think that smells a lot like homegrown terrorism in its purest form."

Marcus stopped speaking and measured the faces of each of the three, then turned to Josh, "And you, who are you and why are you here?"

Josh responded by saying, "Ah, I just got here, Tabby told you. I've got nothing for you."

Rodney shot a look at Ethan as if asking him to keep his woman in check. Ethan responded, "I second Kiera's comment and will reiterate my wife's statement. We've already answered all of you guys' questions more than once. As for Josh, you can leave her cousin out of this. Ask us what you've come to ask. So far, you have come into my home and presented a statement of fact regarding Kiera's pending engagement, followed by an accusatory statement. You haven't really asked us anything we haven't already answered for the D O H, so if you don't have any further legitimate questions to ask about Nick's disappearance, then you are welcome, as my beautiful wife put it, to leave."

"Hey, look, folks, we're just trying to solidify the timeline and event channel," Rodney said, leaning forward and holding his hand up. "We just need to get a few more questions answered, then we're out of your hair." Ethan did not fail to note the handle of the 45 caliber pistol protruding from the top of Rodney's shoulder rig tucked underneath his sport coat.

"Then ask your questions and lay off on the bullshit," Kiera said, looking at Agent Devaroe. She was unsure if it was the smug mouth or the cold eyes, but something in Rodney's, agent Deveroe's demeanor, was beginning to move the needle on her alert meter.

Josh saw Kiera shift in her seat. She began to pull at the seam of her jeans. Noticing this as her unease, he said to the room, "I am going to get a drink. Does anyone else want anything? Agents?"

Everyone shook their heads, so Josh walked into the kitchen. He rummaged through the fridge until he found a half drank soda. He searched around in the cabinet until he found the thick-walled beer mug and filled it from the half-full soda bottle. Josh took a small sip from the glass, pulled a chair from the dining room table, and walked back over to the sitting area, and sat down behind the sofa in the chair. Marcus, agent Thompson, was in mid-explanation as to why he needed to get more details from Nick's travels in proper order so he could decide whether or not Nick was a threat to national security.

"So, you see," Marcus continued, "it is imperative that we know where he was and what he was doing at each moment of his trip. Wouldn't you agree, Ms. Clayton, that it could be viewed as somewhat odd how he disappeared then just showed up again out of nowhere? I, for one, would say that is very strange indeed."

Josh asked, from behind the sofa, "So what do *you* guys think Nick was up to? I mean, you are asking a lot of questions but not offering much information about what *you* think he is up to or where he's been."

Josh tried to think of a reason to justify his asking the question and decided to play the innocent little kid, so he added, "I mean, are we in any danger?"

Suddenly Ethan lurched forward and reached for the TV remote. Marcus quickly sat back in his chair. Rodney instinctively reached across his chest and gripped his pistol.

"Kiera," Ethan almost shouted as he turned the volume up on the muted TV.

Marcus and Rodney turned as the volume rose on the TV. The entire room stared at the chyron along the bottom of the screen as the news anchor stared at them with deep eyes and tensed shoulders. She looked down at the tablet on her desk, touched it, then looked back to the camera.

"We do not have a great deal of information on the event at the moment, but it looks as if there has been some type of detonation of an explosive device in the downtown area of McCaversville, Alabama. Reports from the scene are that there is a blast area roughly twenty miles in diameter. We have had no word from authorities about the source of the detonation. Still, some experts have already speculated that only a tactical nuclear device could have produced such devastation over such a vast area. Wait…"

The reporter at the news desk put a finger up to the earpiece plugged into her right ear. She looked away from the camera in distant concentration for a moment as she listened. She lowered her hand and continued, "We are hearing that the Alabama National Guard was mobilized and are now rolling into the area. So far, they are reporting no survivors have been found within the twenty-mile blast zone. The guard is confirming that there is no indication the area is emitting any radioactive debris, or fallout, of any kind, nor have any other explosive compounds been detected at this time."

"Rebecca," a man off-screen could be heard calling to the anchor.

"Yes, John, you have more info?"

The image switched to a young man in a dark suit accented by his blue tie as he answered, "Yes, Rebecca. I am hearing that McCaversville, Alabama is a town of around ten thousand residents. According to aircraft now entering the area, the blast seems to be centered around the downtown area of McCaversville. We are hearing that the blast indicators are inconclusive as to the source and type of device that may have been used. It looks as if the blast rolled out in a radiating pattern, again from the downtown area. This blast's indicative pattern seems to be very similar to a large nuclear blast. However, there have been no reports of any measurable radiation in the area. Nor is there the typical scorching of the area that is normally associated with nuclear-related events."

"So, John," the anchor interjected, "What are you seeing or hearing about the type of damage so far?"

"Rebecca, what I am seeing is just total devastation. It looks as if anything within the blast area was simply blown apart. Unfortunately, as I said before, Rebecca, so far, no survivors have been recovered. Again, there is no scorching that you would normally see with a nuclear-type event or an explosion of any kind. It's like everything in the area was just blasted to splinters. The field commander referred to the damage as having been produced by a significant concussive event."

"John," the news anchor interrupted, "we are now getting reports that the Pentagon and the White House are set to make an announcement about this incident within the next hour."

The news anchor's eyes flicked to something off-camera, then she looked back into the camera. "So, to recap, there has been a detonation of some type that appears centered around downtown McCaversville, Alabama. There are almost no words to describe the devastation. Again, the blast appears to be centered around the downtown area. Authorities are stating that there is no sign this was a nuclear event at this time. We are staying with you as this story develops to keep you updated. For now, we are going to step away from coverage for a short break."

Josh studied the group as they sat frozen to the news coverage. Josh didn't need to see the coverage. After all, he and Kiera had been at ground zero when the blast occurred. Josh watched the two agents closely. Agent Thompson, Marcus, was glued to the coverage as intently as Ethan and Tabby. Agent Deveroe, on the other hand, had begun to sweat. Josh saw Rodney's hand moving from under his coat, closed around something. Rodney looked over to Marcus, who was still fixed on the TV screen, and said, "Agent." Marcus turned as Rodney said, "Lukurra."

What happened next took only seconds but seemed to play out in slow motion in Josh's mind. Marcus shook his head in disagreement as Rodney ripped his weapon from its holster. Rodney was already standing up as he wheeled his weapon around toward Ethan. Marcus pushed himself up from the seat using the arms of the chair and kicked Ethan as Rodney squeezed the trigger. Ethan jolted to one side, causing the shot to pass to Ethan's left, striking the wall behind him.

"Marcus," Rodney screamed as he tried to sight Ethan within the gaze of his unsheathed Colt. Suddenly Rodney let out a guttural growl as a cold explosion shattered in his face, as the mug Josh was drinking from smashed into Rodney's forehead and shattered. The glass shards cutting his head above the left eye as soda poured into his eyes and the newly open wounds on his forehead. Rodney stumbled and pawed at his face to flush the soda blindness from his eyes. As he spat, stumbled, and cursed, he waved the gun around frantically. He tripped over the coffee table and nearly lost his footing. The sudden jolt caused Rodney to squeeze the trigger again, firing a wild shot blindly into the room.

Kiera and Tabby managed to dive behind the sofa and lay on the floor, covering their heads with their arms. After Rodney sent his second shot blindly into the wind, the loud crack of a whiskey barrel breaking exploded as Ethan slammed the dining room chair that Josh had been sitting in across the back of Rodney's head and shoulders. Rodney fell to one knee, still holding the gun. His head bobbled at the floor like a half-dead zombie. He tried to speak, but the only sounds that came out were the gibbering sounds of an adult baby rather than a hardened killer. Ethan hit Rodney over the top of his head with what was left of the chair's back, which he still held in his hands after the chair shattered. Rodney's body went limp, and he fell forward. Rodney's unconscious body used the coffee table to break his fall via his face and then came to rest on his side on the living room floor.

Marcus sprang from the chair and fumbled at the gun in his belt holster, but Ethan hit him across the face with a broken leg from the chair he had picked up from the floor. Ethan grabbed the gun still in Rodney's limp hand and pointed the Colt at Marcus. Marcus froze, his hand around his still holstered weapon.

"Now, remove your gun from the holster with two fingers and hold it out."

Marcus thought for a moment. His mind filled with the tiny bit of training he had in field operations and the thoughts of how Amanda would tear him a new ass for this fiasco. He looked at Ethan and forced a smile that he hoped would make him look hardened and asked, "Do you even know how to use that?"

Ethan quickly checked the safety, verified a chambered round, then pointed the gun away from everyone and fired a shot into the wall. He quickly turned the gun back toward Marcus, saying, "I hunt and go to the range a bit. I know guns. Now, let me have yours, or you will be my next big game kill, buddy."

Marcus slowly reached under his coat, pulled out his gun with his thumb and forefinger, and then asked, "Okay, what now?" as Ethan took the pistol from him.

Ethan almost turned as Tabby cried out from behind the sofa. The sound of her alarm building pressure in Ethan's chest, "Oh Jesus! Ethan, Josh has been hit!"

Ethan took a couple of steps back and peered around the back of the sofa to see that Rodney's blind shot had struck Josh in the chest. Ethan took a quick glance at the floor behind the couch then turned to look at Rodney as a groan crept up from the sleeping man. He didn't want that insane giant to wake back up.

"Okay," Ethan said, as he turned his attention back to Marcus, "Kiera, call 911. Tabby, you're a doctor. Try to see if you can tell how badly he's hurt."

Both Tabby and Kiera were crying, more from concern for Josh than from fear of the two fake agents.

"Tabby!" Ethan called again, "Did you hear me?"

"I don't know," she said between sobs, "I'm not that kind of doctor."

"Baby, I know. Just try," Ethan prodded in a softer tone, trying to calm her, "You're the closest thing we have right now to that type of doctor. Just try."

"Kiera, have you called 911 yet?"

"No," Kiera replied, "I don't have my phone. It's upstairs."

"Go and get it. You're okay now. I have them."

"Okay," she said as she got up and ran upstairs to the guest bedroom.

Kiera ran back downstairs, trying to unlock her phone with fumbling fingers. As she dialed 911, Ethan sat down in front of Marcus with the gun still trained on him.

"Look," Marcus said, "you people do not know what you are dealing with here. You must let me go."

"No," Ethan replied, "I can tell you're not from the Department of Homeland. I also believe that you aren't really in any position, given your current status," Ethan said, motioning to him with the gun, "to make any demands. I do appreciate you knocking me clear of shitstain's shot," Ethan motioned to Rodney, "that's why you still have your teeth and are not all sleepy time with your partner there. But I think you will do more answering than you will, asking right now."

"I'm not telling you anything. I've trained for these scenarios. My lips will not budge."

"Funny thing," Ethan scoffed, "I think the guys who are really trained to keep their lips closed wouldn't have to announce that fact to anyone. At this point, I can do anything I want to you, buddy. You came into my home and tried to shoot my friends, me, my wife. Have you ever heard of castle laws? I can put a bullet in you right now if I want, and I wouldn't even be late for supper."

Ethan's talk with Marcus was interrupted by Kiera's voice saying, "Hello? Yes. I need an ambulance; my friend's been shot." Tabby paused a moment to listen to the 911 operator, then gave the operator Ethan's address. After another pause, she said, "Two men came to the house and said they were homeland agents. One of them took out a gun and shot Josh."

"Shit, shit, shit," Marcus said, hanging his head and wagging it in disbelief. This whole situation only reaffirmed what he had told Amanda. He should not have been put in charge of this op.

"Now," Ethan began again, "Let's begin with your real name."

"I told you, my name is agent Thompson, and I work for—" black blooms swirled in front of Marcus as Ethan landed a stone slap to his face.

Tabby looked up from behind the sofa at the sound and screamed, "Ethan! What are you doing? The police are on the way." Ethan looked at Tabby and shrugged.

Ethan looked back at Marcus, "Now," he began slowly, "Let's try again. What is your name?"

"I told you, my name is agent—" Again, black blossoms of pain exploded as a hand landed on the other side of Marcus's face. Marcus felt someone press against him and dig through his pants pockets as well as the pockets of his jacket. "Son of a bitch," Marcus moaned, trying to shake off the blow, "You're going to pay for that."

"Nah, I don't think so, sweet cheeks," Ethan said as he sat back down with Marcus's wallet now in hand. He opened it and took out an ID. He saw it was a New York driver's license. Ethan looked at Marcus and smiled.

"Wow," Ethan mocked again, "Not a bad picture. You must be a top-notch secret agent. You have your real ID with you, dipshit? Okay. Let's try one more time. What is your name, Marcus Garvey?"

Why the hell did I bring my license? Marcus asked himself.

"Fine. My name is Marcus Garvey. I am an agent—" Ethan drew his hand back to land another blow when Marcus yelled. "Wait, wait, wait!" Ethan stopped, "I am an agent with an organization called Nasaru."

"Nasaru. There is no government agency name Nasaru."

"We're not with the US government."

"Okay, so what government?"

"No government. We are a private organization."

"That's interesting. So, what is the Nasaru, and what do you want with us?"

"It's not you we are looking for."

Ethan slapped Marcus on his already red cheek. Marcus stomped his feet, almost as if tap-dancing, as he groaned, "What the hell is it with you and slapping all the time?"

Ethan leaned over so that his nose almost touched Marcus's nose and pressed the barrel of the gun against his knee, and said, "I don't hear any sirens yet. You know, I don't have to slap you. So, tell me, Marcus, are you a fan of physical therapy?" Ethan pulled back and smiled, "Now, I need to know what the Nasaru is and what you do."

Marcus seemed to be having a little trouble catching his breath.

"What's wrong," Ethan sneered, "I thought you were *trained* for this."

"Well, I'm not, okay. He is," Marcus tilted his head toward the heap of flesh still sleeping soundly on Ethan's floor, "I'm a data analyst. That's all. I just sit all day and analyze data streams."

"Okay, good. What data?" Ethan asked.

Marcus turned away and pressed his quivering lips together. Another moan came from Rodney. Marcus looked down, hoping he was waking to find he was just groaning in his sleep, accompanied by an occasional jerk from his right leg.

"Fucking idiot?" Marcus thought. "Why did Amanda send me with a hammer when I needed a scalpel?" He turned back to Ethan and said through trembling lips, "You need to let me go now."

"Again, Marcus, I repeat, I do not think you are in the position to make demands. I suggest you answer my questions."

"It's not a demand. It's a request."

"Well, I'm not a D J, so I don't do requests, Marcus."

"Look, I can't answer your questions. I'm not cleared to tell you anything. Ask all you want. Hit me all you want. You won't get any answers, so give it your best shot, chief."

Ethan glared at Marcus. His eyes had grown cold and unflinching. The room's silence was broken only by the ticking clock overhanging the dining table and Tabby's soft crying. The clock rang out its repetitive click, tick, click like a gong. Ethan stood and stepped in front of the chair where Marcus was seated.

He cocked the hammer back on the pistol and put the end of the barrel on Marcus's knee again. Slowly he began, "This is the last time—"

He was interrupted by the sound of a breaking windowpane followed by the breath of an enormous snake's hissing. Ethan looked around the room frantically to find the source. He tried to run around the sofa to shield Tabby from what he thought was more gunfire but found his legs were too heavy to move. The room began to waver as if Ethan was looking at Tabby through the surface of a wavering pool. His last thought as he hit the floor and the room faded to black was how strange it was to have his mouth filled with the taste of peppermint.

CHAPTER 33

Josh's eyes fluttered as flashes of light turned into images in his mind. His heavy chest moved with ragged fluid-filled breaths. The sound seemed to fill his ears like the rush of storm winds. He concentrated on the images, at first uncertain what they meant or what he expected to see.

The first thing he saw was a large crowd gathered at the foot of a stone temple. A priest adorned in a brightly colored headdress wearing a golden chest plate stood with his hands upraised to the sky, a knife in his right hand. Below the posturing priest was another man laid upon a stone altar with his hands and feet bound. The man's face was staring up at the priest's upraised hand bearing the gore-covered knife. Two other men dressed in ceremonial costumes stepped up to the bound figure and grasped him, one by his arms and the other by his feet. The priest continued to pray, face toward the heavens. The two men held the sacrifice as the priest's knife plunged from the prayer-filled air into the man's abdomen, striking him just below his chest.

Josh shook his head to clear the images away. The room swam slightly, then solidified. Josh took in a few more heavy breaths and began to think about time, as measured by man. How long had it been since he had last seen this world? He remembered now that he had once walked among the mortals. Another flash slammed through his mind with the force of a comet colliding with a dense atmosphere. This image was of an angry crowd screaming something in a tribal tongue as two armies clashed on a battlefield with wooden clubs, stones, and sharpened sticks.

Most of the soldiers wore only simple leather wrappings on their feet. Their clothing was of animal hides and thin ashen cloth. None of these soldiers wore armor, or any other heavy protection, to guard against their opponents' attacks. Josh could see the armies did not ride horses, carry swords, nor bows and arrows. The men crashed into one another in a bloody throng of colliding bodies wrapped in dust, blood, and noise.

Josh turned as a dull thud sounded beside him that reminded him of a board striking a rock. He turned to see a man who had just taken a blow to his unprotected head from a thick, wooden club. The man first fell to his knees, then to the ground. The man wielding the club raised the weapon again for another hit. As he towered over his fallen adversary, the club fell once, then twice, then a third time as the clubbed man's head opened like a bursting melon, spilling the remains of its contents onto the ground. The man with the club bent over the body. He screamed in rage at the twitching body lying on the ground beneath him. He spat on the corpse, then whirled around to join the fight once more.

Again, Josh shook his head to banish the images. He shivered from a chill as a bright sheen of sweat stood out on his forehead.

"Someone hold him down! We're going to lose—"

"Doctor, do you see the wound?"

"What the hell?"

Josh felt someone wipe something across his forehead. He felt the muscles in his right forearm tense as his hand began to tremble. He could feel his hand was lying on soft linen. He gripped at the fabric to steady his hand that was now twitching like a nervous squirrel.

Stop it, he thought to his hand. The hand twitched again then stopped.

Josh felt himself slip, being pulled deeper into the visions. This time he saw two men arguing. One man was irate, screaming at another man as he pointed at a large monitor where a cluster of people was gathered around a fire. The people displayed on the monitor gathered around a fire and shared the large leg of an animal that was roasting over a spit. The other man, who was not yelling, seemed to be attempting to calm the angry man. The more the first man tried to calm the angry man, the angrier he became. Josh saw the angry man say something, then hold up an arm as a burst of orange energy shot from the angry man's hand and disappeared through an observation window. The first man grabbed at his heart as if he were witnessing the death of a child. Next, he seemed to be asking the angry man what he had just done, but Josh could not be sure because their language was one he had never heard before. As the angry man answered with an arrogant smile on his face, Josh clearly made out the name Eulahtan. After a moment, the angry man seemed to calm. His face changed from angry to concerned, then fearful as the first man looked at him and roared something in the unknown language. The angry man, who was now the fearful man, turned to flee the first man. He changed into a cloud of blue and white energy as he did so. Before he could escape, the first man yelled something as he reached out toward the energy cloud. The energy cloud fluttered and changed shapes almost too quickly to see as it began to pull apart. The first man seemed to be stopping the cloud of energy, absorbing it. After the angry man's energy cloud disappeared into the first man's hands, he changed into a blue and white cloud of disconnected energy and shot from the room with a sound like a light-ning strike.

Josh lay as image after image, scene after scene, seemed to sear his mind, burning a path for the next series of memories. The images, no, the memories he now understood, were of a world in chaos that seemed to be constantly filled with blood, murder, disease, famine, heartache, death, and desperation. Josh felt pressure inside his head as if his brain may begin to melt if the bombardment did not stop, or at least slow. He somehow knew the memories were his but did not understand how. As Josh slipped further into darkness, he heard a man's muffled yelling for someone to get a medic as battlefield explosions, machine-gun fire, and heavy artillery mixed with the man's muffled voice.

Josh slipped deeper still, the memories continuing to flood his mind. Each vision seeming to come from a more primal place than the preceding image. Suddenly, they began to slow. He saw a darkened landscape, not like the black realm that held Nick captive, but it was not somewhere he recognized. He saw he was standing on the ground, which instinctively caused him to look up. What he saw were constel-lations he did not recognize through the clear night sky as the stars of a vast universe winked at him from above. He sensed a presence beside him and turned. Standing beside him was the first man from his earlier vision. Josh now remembered that the first man's name was Yartrua. Yartrua laid his hand on Josh's shoulder gently, then looked up at the wink of untold galaxy's suns with eyes that seemed to show the millions of years they had beheld, eyes that had looked upon the wonders of the universe and seen the sufferings of its peoples.

"I am sorry, Nathalue." Yartrua said, "You are the only one who can complete this task." Yartrua hung his head as a tear spilled from his face and splashed onto the ground between his feet. Through heaving breaths of grief, Yartrua continued, "It should not be this way. I would give all the essence that I am that you should not have to bear this."

Yartrua returned his eyes again to the blinking heavens. Josh could see by the starlight that Yartrua's cheeks were wet as the starlight reflected off his glistening skin.

"I do not know of any other way," he continued. "All of this beauty. All of this life." Yartrua looked at Josh. "This corruption must be cleansed, and I cannot. I have another path. Once the binding is complete, I must be put away, so *you* must bear this task."

Yartrua paused, then gave Josh a gentle squeeze with the hand still resting on his shoulder and said, "I did not want to see the darkness, the blight, in Parzeus. I could have prevented it, but I was a fool. My love for my brother blinded me. I am sorry."

With his hand still on Josh's shoulder, Yartrua turned to him and said, "You will be the honor of which none of us were strong enough to become. With the vastness of our knowledge and power, we could not defeat envy and greed in the end. But you alone have the will to evolve as we never could, Eulahtan. You will be the legacy of our birth, rise, and fall. The purpose for which we built and seeded."

Josh opened his mouth to ask Yartrua a question, but before he could say anything, Yartrua placed his hand on Josh's chest. As he did, Josh was blinded by a brilliant white light. Then the images were gone.

CHAPTER 34

Josh sat up and looked around only to find the four white walls of a room that contained no furnishings other than the thin mattress upon which he was now seated. The white of Josh's surrounding panorama was broken only by a single wooden door. Josh got up and walked over to the door. He reached for the doorknob and found it locked.

Josh hung his head and walked back over to the mattress, collapsing down like a brooding teenager. He questioned silently whether his new friends were in whitewashed rooms like his and whether they were nearby. Josh looked at the door again and noticed a single, black spec on the wall above the doorframe. This single spec was the only hint of color in this sea of white, other than the door. Josh turned around, placed his back to the spec, and then lowered his head to complete the picture of a sulking teen. He cleared his mind then reached for Kiera.

Kiera, he called without moving his lips. He waited a moment and received no answer. He tried to reinforce his concentration by picturing her face, the color of her hair, her smile, the shirt she was wearing, anything he could remember before he blacked out back at the house. After a minute, he felt her. Another moment he heard two heartbeats just to the left of him. The beats were weak, but he was sure it was Kiera.

He imagined himself prodding her by the arm, then from somewhere that felt deeper than his mind, he called more forcefully, "Kiera, wake up!"

Kiera's left leg jerked as she laid in the room beside Josh as his mind connected with her unconscious form. Josh pushed at her even harder with his next thought, "Kiera, don't move. Let them think that you are asleep."

"Josh?" she asked aloud.

"No, don't speak. Just talk inside your head. Think to me."

Josh could feel something filling Kiera's drug-filled mind. It felt like he was wading through knee-deep mud. Josh envisioned a thick morning fog filling Kiera's mind. Fog so thick you can't see your hand in front of your face. He blew on the mist with his mind and watched as it dissipated, giving birth to a clear sunrise.

"Does that help?" he asked, still without uttering a word.

"Yes. What did you do?" she thought back at him.

"Never mind. That's not important. Listen, we need to get out of here."

"Where are we? What happened. The last thing that I remember was tasting candy canes. Then I heard your voice in my head."

"Those two guys, the ones—"

"Oh my god. Josh, are you okay? They shot you." Kiera asked, suddenly remembering seeing Josh lying on the floor bleeding.

"What? I'm fine. I didn't—"

"That doesn't make sense. I saw you. I called—"

Feeling Kiera's growing panic, he interrupted her, "I don't know, but I'm fine. Listen, those guys that came to the house must have had a backup team. I think they gassed us or something. I guess it didn't have as much of an effect on me because of my age."

Thinking how Josh had just inadvertently called her old, she thought, "Gee, thanks."

"You know that's not what I meant."

"You heard that?"

"Yeah. You know what I meant. Anyway, we need to figure out where we are. These guys were clearly prepared. We need to find out who they are."

"It has to be some government agency. An off-the-books type."

"I don't think so. Kiera, remember back to your meetings with Nick, your meetings in the black."

Kiera noted how Josh did not refer to her travels as dreams any longer but as meetings.

"Nick told you to seek out the Nasaru. The Guardians. These guys are the Guardians. They just don't know they need our help. It's the only thing that could explain why they kept tabs on you guys or why they would have brought us here. I don't think they know we are on the same side."

"I remember. If these guys are the guys Nick told me to find, then why did they try to kill us?"

"I think the meathead jumped the gun. I saw the other guy try to stop him. I mean, he did push Ethan out of the way of the guy's shot. Meathead was already lining up another shot when I hit him with the glass, but the other dude never pulled his gun. I think these guys may have something we need; we just need to figure out what. Nick was directly connected with," then Josh paused for a moment, trying to sculpt his phrase carefully, "the *thing* inside him when he told you to find these guys. He must have had some information from the other thing's head that he was trying to tell you."

"I guess that seems to make sense."

"Kiera, let's go to where Nick is and talk there. I want to check something."

"No. I hate that place," Kiera sent to him, remembering the emptiness that filled her each time she went there. "That place makes me feel dead."

"Just trust me. Think about being at that place."

Kiera opened her mind's eye, and as soon as she formed the thought, she heard the sound of tearing then found herself standing beside Josh. He was staring down at what she now knew was Nick's corpse.

"Oh god!" Kiera exclaimed.

Nick's body, what was left of it, was still floating in its suspended state. Now all that remained of him were his head and half of his chest. The rest of his body had dissolved into oblivion. The dust of his essence still streaming out in a widening cloud, drifting away from his pale remains.

"Kiera?" Josh could see that pain on Kiera's face. "I think Nick is gone. I think what replaced him," he looked at Kiera grimly, "is bad. Something that wants to do a bad thing."

"What exactly is he becoming? How—" but Josh interrupted.

"We don't have time for me to explain. Just listen. These people are members of an organization that has existed for millennia. They are not our enemy, Kiera; they are just misguided and misinformed. We can help them help us."

"But how, and more importantly, will they listen?"

"Again, no time. We need to act now if we are going to stop him. Let's go back. Once we get there, I will get you out of your room. Think home."

With that single word, a rip tore through the air as Josh's body instantaneously dissolved, streaming through the fissure within a blink. Kiera stood for a few seconds more, studying Nick's body. A single tear fell into the cold, shallow water as she pushed the thought of her body lying on the mattress in the white room into the foreground of her mind. As she did, she too passed through a fissure and plunged back to reality.

Once back in his body, Josh turned around, then looked up at the black spec above the doorway and demanded, "Come let me out of this room. We need to talk."

Amanda Dalling looked up from the bank of computer monitors displaying the four rooms where the captives were being held within the Nasaru facility and found Marcus looking as if asking her what her next move was.

Josh got up from the mattress and walked toward the black spec. He looked directly into its cold, unblinking eye and said, "We need to talk. Please open the door. I want to talk to Marcus."

After about a minute of waiting, the lock clicked, then Josh's door swung open. As it did, it revealed a middle-aged woman of slim build with long dark hair pulled around to one side so that it hung over the shoulder of her business suit. Amanda's smoke-colored eyes met Josh's, and she said, "Hello, I am Amanda Dalling. I run this facility. To whom do I have the pleasure of speaking?"

"Is this a Nasaru facility?" The look on Amanda's face reminded Josh of how lions would stare at antelopes just before they pounced in nature shows.

"Young man, I am not certain who this Nasaru agency is, but we are the Department of Homeland Security."

"No. No, you're not. Homeland doesn't come into private citizens' homes and try to shoot them unprovoked."

"That agent made an error and is now on leave."

"Ethan sent him on leave back at the house. *Medical* leave for trying to murder him."

"Young man, I believe that you will—"

Amanda's words were abruptly cut short by an unseen force slamming into her chest, causing her to step back, as Josh shouted, "No!" Amanda's confident façade dropped as she stood blinking with her mouth open, clutching her chest. Josh continued, "Time is short. We do not have time to play games. Friends now. Talk afterward."

Amanda swallowed to open her choked airway, then straightened and pulled at the hem of her suit coat. After a few seconds, she stepped away from the door and muttered something to the guard beside her. Afterward, Josh heard a series of clicks as doors to the left and right of his room unlocked. Josh stepped out of the cell and saw Marcus standing on the other side of the door beside a burly man in a dark blue uniform. The man in the uniform was holding a radio in his hand.

Josh looked over to see Kiera exiting her room. The other two doors were open, but no one was coming out. Josh walked to the first room and saw Ethan lying asleep on a mattress. Josh heard someone else come into the room and turned to see a man in a white lab coat. The man walked took a hypodermic needle from his lab coat as he walked toward Ethan.

"What is that?" Josh asked.

The man didn't look up as he answered, "It will wake him up. It kills off the effects of the candy cane."

"Candy cane?"

Amanda answered from the hallway, "Yes. The gas is Glysofisto-cene, but everyone calls it candy cane because it leaves a peppermint taste in your mouth just before you succumb."

Ethan moaned and groggily sat up, scanning the faces in the room. Josh had already turned and left the room before Ethan realized what was going on. With the help of the man in the white coat, Ethan drunkenly stood and followed Josh into Tabby's room. The man in the white coat followed Ethan into the room and gave Tabby an injection. Ethan wanted to make sure he was the first face Tabby saw when she awoke, so he knelt beside her and began rubbing her arm as he repeat-ed, "Come on Tabs. Wake up."

She slowly opened her eyes and asked, "Ethan? Ah," she said, plac-ing a palm to the side of her head, "Why do I feel like I have a hang-over?"

Ethan and the man in the white lab coat carefully helped her to her feet.

Tabby saw Josh and smiled, "Josh," she said in a half-drunken slur, "You're okay. I thought they killed you." Her expression changed as she remembered the gas bursting through the window, then hugged Ethan and whispered into his ear, "What is this?"

"I'm not sure, but I think we're about to find out."

Josh turned to Amanda as she asked, "May we talk now?"

Amanda held her arm out, signaling Josh and the others to follow, then walked toward the end of the hall with Marcus in tow. Josh mo-tioned for his friends as he followed Amanda. At the end of the dimly lit hallway was a bright meeting room. There was a long, polished table with a marble top located in the center of the room with twelve padded leather chairs arranged neatly around it. Light spilled into the room from one of the room's walls from large floor-to-ceiling windows that opened onto a skyline that Josh did not recognize.

"Where are we?" Josh asked.

"This is our Atlanta hub," Amanda answered, her eyes studying Josh. "It is one of many operational hubs that we maintain."

"What *operations*, exactly, do you people run?" Ethan asked, stepping through the doorway.

Amanda looked at him with a cautious eye and decided to respond, "Various."

"Really? You come into my home, illegally posing as federal agents, one of your goons tries to kill me, he shoots Josh, and your answer is 'sorted.' Well, that's not good enough, lady. I expect—"

"That was an operational error?" Amanda said firmly.

"Operational error? That's great. Well, your operational error was almost the last error any of us would have ever taken part in if I wouldn't have put your dog back into its pen."

"I apologize for that, but I can assure you that the proper measures have been taken to ensure the agent in question will not make this mistake again."

"Big fucking reassurance that would have been if he would have pegged me."

"Please, Mr. Hensley, I understand your rage, but please take a seat so that we might start over."

"Start over? That is another thing. How do you know our names? We don't know you. We've never met. How long have you people been watching us?" Tabby asked. The stimulant in her blood had now given her a somewhat amped and wild look.

Amanda began slowly, "While it is undeniable that my people have been watching you, it is defensible. We need to locate Nick Mercer."

"Then why didn't you just come talk to us like all the other agencies?" Ethan asked.

"We are not affiliated with any government organization. We tend to work less in the open."

"So, you are the Nasaru?" Kiera asked.

"Yes, that is our current name, but publicly we are a multinational conglomerate working in nearly every industry around the globe, from food production to military weapons."

"Jesus," Ethan said, "How long have you been in operation, and why are you looking for Nick?"

"Because they are the guardians," Josh said. "They keep watch for the entity Nick is becoming."

"Yes," Amanda said, nodding and looking at Josh through a narrowed gaze.

"The entity? So, you fucking people hunt ghosts?"

Amanda turned, "No, Mr. Mercer. We, this organization, have existed in one of various forms since around three thousand B.C."

"Bullshit."

"I know that in this digital age of blink and forget, it is difficult to conceive of an organization that has persisted for that amount of time, but I assure you I am a direct descendant of the original founders."

"Lady, there is no way you could prove a five thousand-year lineage—"

"Actually, I can," Amanda interrupted with a cold glare, "but there would be no point in exploring my ancestry."

"Fine. So, your organization has been around thousands of years before Christianity, and you hunt spooky things." Ethan said, waving his hands in front of him.

"That is an oversimplification, Mr. Hensley. And we do not hunt."

"Oh, that's awesome. So, you spy on people, run a global power-house, hunt for some entity, then act like you are some sort of neighborhood watch?" Ethan sniffed the air, taking in a deep breath as if he had just stepped through a bakery door, then said, "Lady, that smells of so much horseshit that I can almost taste ass in my mouth."

"Well, we know our rights, and here is what is going to happen. We are leaving," Ethan said as he stood up.

"Please sit," Amanda said, as a big man in a blue uniform grabbed Ethan by the shoulder and urged him back into his seat. "Josh is correct. We do need to talk."

"Ethan, just sit for a minute," Tabby said, grabbing his arm.

He turned to her, sighed then sat back down.

Tabby looked at Amanda and said, "I want to hear what she has to say about the laws she has broken. We need to get the full story for the lawsuit."

Amanda looked at Tabby, amused but did not take the bait. Instead, she said, "Josh, please tell me what you meant about how you were told to seek out our organization." But before Josh could begin his answer, Amanda turned to Ethan and said, "And while we may be the neighborhood watch, Mr. Hensley, we are firmly prepared to deal with this threat."

"So, you've secured the key?" Josh asked.

Amanda took in a deep breath. "In the past, the records indicate that our ancestors were able to recover the key and hold it until the next iteration. However, it has not been discovered since the last recorded appearance of the entity."

"That's it then. Without the key, there is nothing you can do to stop him." Josh said.

"Wait a minute. Are we talking about an actual key? A key to what?" Ethan asked, looking at Josh.

"I'm not sure. I just know he needs a key of some kind to finish."

"So, you're both saying that you know there is this key but do not know where or what this key is?"

"Unfortunately, no," Amanda answered. "The key has been lost to time since the last iteration of the entity's appearance."

"Well, you need to go find him," Josh said.

Realizing the group knew less than she did about Nick, she sighed and said, "The three of you are free to go at any time," Amanda motioned to Ethan, Tabby, and Kiera, "however you will need to stay."

"What?" Josh asked.

"Oh, no. No. No. No." Ethan said, pounding the table, "We're all leaving together."

"Unfortunately, that will not be the case. You, Josh, have presented an interesting set of properties that our organization needs to understand better."

"He's a fourteen-year-old kid," Ethan said. "I don't give a damn about any properties you need to understand. He is leaving with us."

"Is that your final stand on this issue, Mr. Hensley?"

"I'm the only one who can find him," Josh said. "How am I supposed to do that locked up in here?"

"That is part of the equation. How can you find him?" Amanda asked, placing her elbows on the table and leaning forward with a smug look on her face. "How did your body reject a forty-five caliber slug as if it were a splinter?"

"What are you talking about?"

"I intend to answer that question. Also, do not think it has passed me that you walk onto our organization's radar just when the entity reveals itself. That, to me, is very interesting indeed."

"Look, lady," Ethan said, "we are all leaving together, and we're leaving now."

"This is ridiculous," Josh said with an aggravated tone, throwing his arms up in exasperation. "I thought you people were supposed to help us. We were *told* to find you."

"What, exactly, are you?" Amanda asked.

"I am an orphan from South Carolina," Josh replied.

"Oh," Amanda responded, "okay. Well, how then did an orphan from South Carolina make his way to these three in Georgia?"

"We don't have time for this."

"Okay, let's try this one. Where is Nick Mercer?"

Amanda could feel the heat rising as red crept up her neck and cheeks. The cleavage between her breasts was now splotched with red patches as her temperature rose at Josh's refusal to answer her questions.

Amanda stood from her seat with fury and asked, "What happened in McCaversville. Was it the entity?"

Josh looked at her coldly and calmly, "It was Nick. Kiera and I were there. Nick destroyed that town."

Amanda sat back down, her chest heaving as her mind worked. She recalled a cluster of files in the archives that spoke of a dawning day that would begin with the brightness of the sun and end with blackest night.

"Then how? Let's say Nick did cause the episode in McCaversville. How did he do?"

"He did it by performing the Gathering Ritual because he knew I was watching. He knows I can't stop him, alone anyway, and he wanted me to see what was coming. Call it a dry run."

Josh's eyes slipped between their normal color to white, then back again.

"A dry run for what?" Amanda asked.

"You know," Josh replied, "For the fourth crucible."

Amanda stood and walked over to the window. She looked out to see crowds of people below her milling about on the streets like scuttering ants. She could feel the weight of the responsibility slung around her neck like an anchor, and it felt as if it were about to break her spine.

"How do we stop him?" Amanda asked.

"I don't know. I need some more time—"

"That seems to be a commodity that is in short supply," Amanda shot back as she turned to Josh.

"I understand." Josh replied, "but what else is there?"

"So, we just sit and wait for him to do whatever he wants? Where is he going?"

"He is going to the Center."

"What is that? We have no reference for a Center."

"I don't know yet. All I know is that he is headed somewhere he thinks of as the Center. The center of alignment."

"Alignment of what?" Ethan asked.

"I'm not sure," Josh answered. "Maybe it's somewhere that holds some significance to him. Maybe a cross-section of power or something."

"Okay," Amanda said, remembering the force that had thudded into her chest when Josh yelled at her, "Do you know his capabilities?"

"I'm not sure. My memories are still fuzzy."

"Yes," Amanda agreed, looking more interested than intimidating now, "We have marked repeated references to a key in the Wisdoms and other tablet lore. So, he cannot complete whatever he hopes to accomplish without the key?"

"That's the way I understand it," Josh replied.

Amanda looked at Marcus and nodded. Marcus left the room as four armed guards stepped in.

Amanda looked at Josh and said, "Thank you, Joshua. I believe that we can take it from here."

"No," Josh pleaded, "You can't face him alone. You need me."

"I believe we have all we need." She motioned to the armed men stationed around the room, who began to herd the group up and out into the hallway like a cluster of bleating sheep.

Ethan tried to resist but fell to his knees after one of the guards clubbed him. Tabby screamed and tried to reach for him. When she lurched forward, the man turned and raised what Josh now saw was a riot baton held in a white-knuckled grip. Tabby yelled, "No," but it was too late. As the club struck, Tabby was sure her forearm had broken.

"Wait, I can tell you more," Josh yelled to Amanda. Amanda appeared to have lost her interest. "Wait!" Josh yelled again as something rushed through the room.

Amanda called after the guard, "You there, hold." The guard that had been busy herding Josh stopped and turned to Amanda.

Josh began, "You need a key to stop him." Amanda stood, looking as if she were waiting for him to continue, "I don't know how it works, I mean, I don't remember yet, but I know if we don't find the key, there is no way you can stop him. He is paired with a perfect host. Without the key, no one can stop him."

"What do you mean a perfect host?"

Josh scanned the room to make sure none of his friends had been hustled down the hall, then he continued, "Nick is a man, but his bloodline spilt from its natural order after Cecily seeded his ancestral lineage."

Amanda motioned to the guards, who had stopped to watch her, to start herding their human cattle again.

"This is a mistake," Josh yelled. He struggled to hold his ground as one of the uniformed guards pushed against him with his club. Amanda heard a glass tip over on the conference room table, so she turned to look.

Josh continued to plead, "You have to listen to me. I can help." A loud thump came from the conference table as one end of it jumped about six inches off the floor then slammed back down as a seam appeared across the table's top.

"Come on, kid," the guard urged and continued to shove Josh out the doorway.

"Amanda! Ms. Dalling, you have to stop this! You are making a—"

"Shut that damn kid up now before I—"

The guard raised his club over above Josh's head. Before the club could hit its mark, Josh closed his eyes and screamed, "No!"

As the word came out, an unseen pulse blasted through the conference room, knocking the guard across the room. The exterior wall windows turned into glass rain as they burst from their encasements and rained onto the streets below. The conference table lifted into the air then came crashing back down onto its side, striking Amanda and knocking her unconscious in the process. She came to rest lying with one arm hanging out one of the open portals into the city skyscape.

Marcus had returned to the room during the bustle of the guards ushering the group out. Josh saw him leaning against a wall to his left with his chin on his chest. He appeared to be breathing, but Josh didn't care whether he was or not, in truth. Two of the four guards were also unconscious on the conference room floor, one bleeding from his nose. The other guard was lying beside Marcus with his head twisted at an angle that didn't look possible. The guard's eyes were open, but it was clear he wasn't looking at anything.

Josh heard a commotion behind him and turned just in time to see Ethan introducing one of the guards to a day nap with a club he had wrestled away from the man. As the guard dropped into a jiggling heap onto the floor at Ethan's feet, Tabby yelled as Josh saw her and Kiera assaulting the other guard. Tabby was on the man's back, biting his ear as Kiera was trying to kick him in the groin. The man yelped each time Kiera kicked and hit his shins in her attempts to crack the man in his apple bag. The guard managed to free his neck from Tabby's grasp and flung her off his back, causing her to stumble and fall, hitting the wall as she fell. As the man turned to look at Tabby, Kiera squared off behind him and kicked. The swing ended in a muffled thud as her foot struck squarely in the man's crotch. He immediately stopped defending himself and let out a wheezing breath that sounded like a cross between a fart and a vomit. As the guard fell to his knees, still holding his exploding testicles, Ethan rushed over and hit the man with a club, sending him off to nappy time along with his friend.

The three of them did not have time to catch their breath. Ethan bent and took the sleeping guard's access card. Josh saw what Ethan was doing and did the same with the other unconscious guard. Tabby removed a set of keys from the man's belt. Ethan scanned for the nearest exit sign.

"Come on," he said, motioning the sign above a door a few feet away. Kiera grabbed the other guard's club and hurried to the doorway. The exit door opened onto a set of stairs. They began to move down the stairs as fast as possible without tripping. After four floors, Ethan stopped.

"What are you doing?" Tabby puffed in a breathless whisper.

"Listen," Ethan said, trying to catch his breath, "We need to slow up a bit."

"No, Ethan," Tabby protested, "We need to get out of here."

"I agree, but we also need to make sure they don't catch us again. We also don't need to fall down the stairs and break a leg. For that reason, we need to slow down, calm down, and listen. We don't even know how to get out of this place."

Kiera nodded in agreement.

"We also don't know what we're up against here. We don't know what kind of firepower these guys have. It's clear they have chemical weapons, so there is no telling what else they may have. We don't want to get hit by that shit again, or we're done. And we damn sure don't want to get our asses shot off. I don't know about you, but I'm pretty attached to mine."

"So, what do we do if we meet any more of them?" Josh asked.

"I don't know. Just try to get them before they get us if we can't outrun them. Josh, what the hell was that back there? What did you do?"

"I'm not sure. She just made me mad, and it just sort of happened."

"Do you think you could do that again? I mean, on command if we needed you to?"

"I don't know. I don't even know how I did it."

Ethan shook his head, "Alright, well, come on. Let's see if we can get out of this building."

The four of them started down the stairwell again at a more cautious pace. Ethan pointed out a sign by the door at the bottom of the stairs that read, 'Three.'

"Looks like we're on the third floor," Ethan said, "We need to be careful when we get to the first floor.

"Sh, I think I hear someone," Ethan whispered. He began to move slower. Ethan heard a small yelp behind him and turned to see Kiera covering her mouth with both hands, her eyes the size of small saucers.

"Really?" Ethan asked.

Keira moved her hands from her mouth to say something, but all that came out was a sound like a puppy yelping as she hiccupped again. "I get hiccups when I'm nervous," she managed to get out, then covered her mouth again.

Ethan took another delicate step down then saw a sign indicating that they had reached the first floor.

Ethan slowly pushed the door's crash bar until he heard a click and saw the door move slightly, then he stopped to listen. Hearing nothing, he opened the door enough to see a sliver of the lobby on the other side.

"I don't see anyone," he said, "I can see the front door from here. Once we get through the door, try to act normal. I don't think they own the entire building. Otherwise, this place should have been crawling with guys looking for us by now. But we don't know where their guys are at."

Ethan looked at the club in his hand. After a moment of consideration, he pulled the waistband of his pants out and slid the stick down his pants, then held it in place by grabbing the side of his leg with his now free hand. Seeing Ethan do this, Kiera did the same with her club. Tabby put the keys she had taken in her pocket.

"Okay, ready?" Ethan asked.

As Ethan pushed the crash bar, he heard a door open a couple of floors above him, followed by the sound of heavy footfalls descending rapidly down the stairs. Ethan gave the door a hard push as the group hurriedly rushed into the lobby of the ground floor and began to walk toward the exit. They tried to be as casual as possible while moving at a fast-paced speed walk. Kiera walked a bit stiff-legged because her club was stuffed too far down her pants leg, interfering with her bending her knee. As they got within reach of the door, they heard the stairwell door crash open as two men, not in blue uniforms, stood looking at them.

"Run," Ethan said as he pushed through the lobby doors. Once outside, Ethan turned to look as he and Kiera pulled the clubs from their pants. In the process of doing so, Kiera tripped on a crack in the sidewalk and nearly fell.

"Ethan, where the hell are we?" asked Tabby as they broke into a run.

"I'm not exactly sure, somewhere on the south side, I think."

Tabby saw a group of men ahead on the sidewalk. After a glance, she said, "Everyone, follow my lead."

Tabby stopped, put on her best victim face, and said between breaths as they approached the men. "Guys, please. Help. Two feds behind us in suits."

Tabby's plea was returned from the big burly man as if she were an escaped mental patient. Seeing they were not going to lend any assistance, she started to run again.

"This way," Ethan said, ducking into an alleyway.

As Ethan rounded the corner, he saw a dumpster and instructed the others to climb in and hide.

"No, Ethan, I'm not going to—"

"Tabby, there's no time, damn it. I will get them to follow me." He bent down, laced his fingers together so the others could step into his hands so he could hoist them into the container. He first hoisted Kiera, then Josh. As Tabby placed her feet into Ethan's hands, their pursuers ran past the alley.

Tabby stopped. "Ethan, they ran past us."

Ethan turned to see no one running down the alley toward them. He turned to Josh and Kiera, standing in the trash bin. He motioned for them to climb out. "Come on." As Ethan started to help Kiera over the edge of the container, he heard a ping as pieces of brick exploded from the wall beside the dumpster and hit him in the face. Tabby screamed as Ethan pushed her around the side of the bin and dove behind her for protection. Kiera and Josh ducked down into the trash for safety.

"Over here!" A man called out.

Some other indiscernible talking followed up the first man's call before she heard another voice yell, "Hey man. What's going on up here?"

There were some more indiscernible voices, then Kiera peeked over the edge of the bin and saw the two men that had been pursuing them were now talking to the group that Tabby had asked for help from earlier.

One of the two men said something to which the apparent leader of the other group promptly replied, "Y'all motherfuckers best be on your way before shit gets weird up in here, man."

One man, sporting a large tattoo of a dragon on the left side of his face, looked at Tabby and yelled, "Don't you worry, mama. We got this."

Ethan moved back around and began to help Kiera and Josh out of the trash container.

"Thank you," Tabby mouthed just before she turned to run down the alley with the rest of the group following.

As the two men tried to renew their pursuit, they realized the group of gang members had encircled them.

The first pursuer looked around to find himself encased in a wall of bandannas and leather jackets. "Move!" One of the pursuers yelled as he motioned for the gang to clear a path. A man in the middle of the alleyway turned as if he were going to move out of the way, but as the men tried to run through their line, one of the gang members put his foot out and tripped him, leading the man to fall, face first, onto the pavement. The other man close behind got his feet tangled up as the first man fell, so he followed him down onto the sidewalk. The six men circled the two men and began to taunt them.

"Yeah, little bitches. You can't run if you don't have legs, now can you?" said one of the gang members.

Then another said, "I think we need to send these bitches to school," which brought several grunts of approval from the other members.

"Yeah," said another member, "I fuckin hate feds."

One of the men tried to get up from the sidewalk. He made it to his knees and hands before a gang member kicked the man in the gut, which sent him back down to the ground with a gasp. The other man, whose attempt to get off the sidewalk was met with a broad fist to his face, was lying on the ground holding his broken nose.

"Yo, Roach, looks like these bitches like to shoot at women. Let's show 'em what we think about that."

Ethan saw the two men getting jumped by the six saviors as he, Tabby, Kiera, and Josh rounded the corner at the end of the alley.

"Where are we going?" Kiera panted.

"It doesn't matter. We just need to get out of the area." Ethan realized they were perhaps two blocks away from their beaten pursuers now, so he stopped and looked around. "Look he said," pointing ahead to a subway sign. "Come on. That should work.

They ran to the subway entrance and hoped the turnstiles as an overweight security guard yelled at them.

"Sorry," Josh called back. "Emergency."

As they ran into the terminal, they saw the train doors begin to close. Ethan ran faster, yelling, "Hold the door!" A man in an expensive-looking business suit saw Ethan and thrust his briefcase between the closing doors. Ethan almost slammed into the doors as he came to a stop at the train. Grabbing both doors, he pulled as the bespectacled briefcase man assisted. Once the doors gave way, Ethan ushered Tabby, Keira, and Josh onto the train then stepped inside the doorway. As the doors closed and the train lurched forward, Ethan turned to see two scraped, bloodied, and beaten men coming across the terminal toward the train.

Ethan breathed a sigh of relief, thanked the bespectacled man, and then sat down beside Tabby.

As he sat catching his breath, he couldn't stop himself from laughing.

"What are you laughing about?" Tabby asked.

"I can't believe you sicked a group of bikers on those guys." He continued to laugh, "They're lucky they weren't killed." He chuckled again and said, "I bet they didn't see that one when they got up this morning."

After a few more seconds of letting Ethan get control of his composure, Kiera asked again, "Where are we going."

Ethan looked up at a sign attached to a wall of the train's interior and said, "It looks like this line runs through downtown. Let's just get off at any stop."

"Do we just take a cab home from there?" Tabby asked.

"No," Ethan almost snapped at her, "I guarantee that if they are not still watching the house, they will be able to get there before us, and they'll be waiting."

Ethan felt something in his right back pocket and reached around to feel what it was. He smiled. "Well," he said, "They didn't pat us down or take any of our stuff."

Ethan pulled something from his back pocket and held it up, and then the group understood his meaning.

"I still have my wallet, which means we are going to rent a car, make a withdrawal and then figure the rest out." He thought for a moment, then looked over and asked, "Josh, you said you could feel Nick. Do you know where he is?"

"Not exactly. I can feel what direction he is in. That gives me an idea, but I don't know where he's going or exactly where he is."

"So, can you find him?"

"I have to. If I don't, it's going to get bad."

"Alright, then. I guess we follow the kid's nose from here on out," Ethan said, then leaned his head back against the wall of the train.

CHAPTER 35

Nick sat on the roadside, looking up at the stars spilling across an endless night sky. He was tired but getting stronger. The merge was almost complete, but Eulahtan was forced to reveal himself too soon. His early revealing to that nosy shrink had slowed the merging of the two consciousnesses. The day had been long, and the trip was harder on his new body than he expected. His choice to walk the remainder of the distance to the center may have been premature as well. Nathalue was nothing to him. Eulahtan could harness the power of the rift, one final gift from his creator, Parzeus. Yartrua had consumed so much power from the others during the decimation that he did not dare free himself from his self-imposed prison. Neither could all of his power be contained within the prison cell sitting at the crux of creation. Even now, Nick could feel the power flowing all around him, through him, filling him from the breach in the cage that Parzeus had manufactured before his fall.

Eulahtan heard a noise in the trees and turned to see a small doe creep from the treeline to the edge of the roadway. The dear bent to nibble at the tall green grass along the verge. Nick sat still, so the dear didn't notice him. He studied it. It was a beautiful creature. So, frail-looking, yet so powerful. Her lustrous brown coat's natural sheen reflected the moon's light, making the small dear look like a forest spirit.

In her own way, the dear seemed to be happy and content. Nick sneered at the thought of contentment. It was a disease. How could this presumptive creature believe it had any right to be satisfied when Nick was always struggling with the weight of the duty placed on his shoulders. Everyone was against him, yet he was only trying to do his job, to fulfill the destiny for which he was created, just as Parzeus had told him.

Nick's stomach growled loud enough for the deer to hear, causing it to look up from eating and glare at him with distrusting eyes. It was then he remembered this host was not yet fully merged and must therefore be fueled. Nick scanned the area. He found what he was looking for and concentrated on a large pine tree near the road's edge. As he focused on the tree, it began first to shudder, then to whine, giving off an otherworldly mule as the wood fibers at the base of its trunk strained. Suddenly, there was a loud crack as the base of the tree snapped into splitters. The tree fell across the road. Then Nick returned to resting.

Nick waited, switching his attention between the grazing doe and the stars, when he heard a distant sound. He realized it was the sound for which he had been listening. The big game had arrived. First, the sound started as a low hum, then grew until it sounded like a rushing wind as the game rushed along the roadway. As the game carriage crested the hill, its two glowing eyes, like a savage giant, glared hate toward the space that lay before him.

The game carriage was a light-colored minivan. Nick didn't know models. He just knew it was a vehicle. He smiled and watched, waiting for his trap to be sprung. The car sped along the straightaway at seventy miles per hour through the night. Just as it approached the fallen pine tree which Nick had felled across the road, the wheels began to scream in agony as the driver turned sharply, ran off the roadway into the ditch, then began to pirouette through the air.

The car danced, performing several turns for Nick to enjoy, flashing its pretty lights as if they were winking to him like the distant stars. Once the car finished its dance and its metal shell had stopped crumpling, Nick got up and walked over to the wreckage.

Ah, he thought as he looked through the window. *This will do nicely.*

Nick grabbed the handle on the side door of the car. The metal hinges of the door let out a sharp pinging sound as he ripped it from the wreckage and flung it toward the tree line. Nick scanned the inside of the wreck. He was pleased his trap had given him such a bountiful harvest. Nick always thought since people were made of people meat, it only made sense to eat each other instead of plants and other animals. Besides, people were *much* easier to hunt.

He surveyed his catch again and saw four people in the car. *My, that one is far too much food for just this one host,* he thought as he scanned the driver. He thought he would take just one. Someone else could eat the other three. Nick reached into the car, removed one of the occupants, and slung him over his shoulder. This one was smaller than the others in the vehicle, not quite as large as the two in the front, but it should suffice for a meal. It seemed to be healthy, had lots of muscle, and was more than enough for one meal.

Nick walked away from the wreck and moved to the tree line to find a nice grassy spot for his super. Nick dropped his prey on the ground and heard it give a low moan along with an outrushing breath. As Nick knelt and began to eat his supper, the soft parts first, he thought he heard one of the other injured prey in the car screaming.

As he dined, Eulahtan thought that if Nick were still able to think, he would appreciate how well he was taking such good care of this host body. After all, they were almost one person now.

CHAPTER 36

"What if these people *are* a government agency, one that is not publicly known?" asked Kiera.

"What do you mean?" Ethan asked.

"Well, what if they can track your credit cards? Won't they see as soon as you rent this car?"

"Oh, that's right." Tabby agreed.

"Yeah, I've thought about that. I think we get the car, get to the closest bank and get all the money we can from our account. Enough to carry us for a few days or weeks. After that, we can move around on cash only. If we run on cash, I think they should lose track of us in a day or two." Ethan smiled, wanting to reassure them his plan would work. He reached up and gave the back of his neck a nervous scratch.

"Oh, oh, oh! There's a branch about three blocks that way," Tabby said, pointing down the street, "we can get there in no time."

"How much do you think we need to get?" Ethan asked, looking at Tabby.

"We should get as much as they will allow us to withdraw. We don't know how long we'll be on the road."

"Alright," he replied, then leaned over a gave Tabby a quick kiss on the cheek. "I'll be right back."

After a minute, Tabby offered a suggestion, "We can probably walk to that branch and be back before he can complete the paperwork for a car." Tabby turned and began to make her way up the sidewalk, with Kiera in tow. She turned to look at Josh and called, "Go inside with Ethan. We'll be right back."

Josh stood for a moment and watched Tabby and Keira walk up the street, scratching their necks until Tabby turned around and motioned for him to go into the rental car office.

"What's up?" Ethan asked as Josh stopped at the counter beside him.

"I a…" then Josh paused a moment and started again, "I was told to come wait with you."

"Why?" Ethan asked, looking over to Josh, then over his shoulder out the rental office window.

"They said they'd be back before you can get the paperwork done."

Ethan stopped writing. "What?"

"They walked to the branch down the street and said they'd be right back."

Ethan scowled and pressed his lips together as he scribbled his signature on the rental agreement.

Josh shrugged and said, "I couldn't stop them. You know your wife better than me, and even I can see that telling her to stop would be like talking to a road sign." Josh paused and examined Ethan's face to determine whether he had crossed the line, then added, "I'm just saying."

"Yeah, I know?" Ethan confirmed, "There's no stopping her when she has her mind set on something."

Just then, the attendant stepped back over to Ethan and asked, "You have any questions, hon?"

"No," Ethan replied. "Here you go," he replied as he handed her the paperwork.

"Awesome. Now did ya'll want the insurance on this?" the attendant asked as she scanned the application.

"Nope. We're good." Josh replied. "We just want to get on the road. The beach is calling."

"Alright. Ya'll just sit here, and I'll be right back," She turned and walked outside carrying the keys to the rental.

Ethan turned to Josh and asked, "What the hell are those two thinking? We should be together at all times."

"I don't know," Josh answered, "I just know there is no way that I could stop her."

"I know how Tabby and Kiera are. I just wish she would stop a minute to consider our circumstances."

"I agree, but still," Josh persisted, "it *will* save us some time if they are making withdrawals while you are renting the car. If both things happen at the same time, it may make it harder to track, too."

"No, not harder to track," Ethan argued, "but it will save us time."

Ethan heard a chime and looked up to see the attendant, Megan, bouncing through the doorway.

"Okay, ya'll. She's all gassed up and ready for liftoff. Ya'll gonna need anything else before you shove off to golden shores?"

"I think we're good," Ethan answered, smiling unnecessarily wide, "All we need are the keys and the open road."

"Well, here are your keys," Megan said, holding the keys out to

Ethan. "But," she paused before offering them to him, "Are ya'll sure you don't want the insurance? Miami is a long drive, and a lot can happen between here and there."

"Nah," Ethan said, "I have never had an accident, and I don't plan on having one on this little adventure." He offered Megan a wink and a friendly smile.

Ethan took the keys and grabbed Josh's arm, and began pulling him out the door. They saw Tabby and Kiera walking quickly down the sidewalk toward them as they stepped outside. Both ladies were still scratching at the back of their necks. Josh and Ethan walked over to the parking lot's edge to meet them.

"What the hell were you thinking?" Ethan asked in his best fatherly tone.

"I was thinking of efficiency."

"Well," Ethan began, then stopped, remembering the reasons that he had first pursued, then had married Tabby in the first place. Tabby was strong-willed and determined. He reached out, grabbed her, and squeezed her tightly. After kissing her on her cheek, he said, "Well, good job, I guess, but please," then he paused for a moment to craft his words, "Please promise to stay with Josh and me from here on out, please?"

Tabby looked at Ethan and saw the concern behind his pleading, so she replied, "I'm sorry, I just wanted to help. We both did. We'll make sure the group stays together from here on out."

Ethan sighed and looked at both Tabby and Kiera, "Okay, let's get this show on the road. I have the keys, so let's eat up some miles."

After they were all in the car Ethan adjusted his rearview mirror to have a clear view of Josh, then asked, "Okay, kid," he corrected himself, "Josh. Where are we going?"

Josh looked at him and smiled. "I think we need to head west. For some reason, Arizona keeps popping into my head. I believe that's where he is going."

"You believe, or you know?"

"Know," Josh replied, "Definitely Arizona."

"Alright," Ethan replied, dropping the car into drive, "I hope you know what to do when we get there."

I hope so too, Josh thought.

CHAPTER 37

Nick moved slowly from his spot in the leaves beyond the tree line, where he had allowed his host to rest for a few hours after his unfulfilling supper of bug in a box. After he'd finished his meal, he went to the trees to find a dark place to lay. Just as he was beginning to drift off, he heard wailing fading into earshot from a distance.

Nick rolled over onto his stomach and looked in the direction of the roadway where he could see more automobiles. These had bright flashing lights and produced ear-splitting wails as they approached. He lay and watched, curious about what these new arrivals were doing. As he watched, he saw the new arrivals empty of their passengers. The large vehicle contained two occupants in matching clothing. The two occupants got out and retrieved a bed on wheels from the automobile's rear. They rushed over to the wreckage of the family car. They began to climb all over the vehicle, poking their heads in through broken windows, yelling at the remaining car dwellers, and then yelling to one another. Nick found this activity fascinating.

He continued to watch as another wailing vehicle drove up, this one with bright flashing blue lights. Another blue light adorned car arrived directly behind it. Both cars produced more men in matching clothing, but not like the clothing the red cross car men wore.

"What are they doing?" Nick thought. He closed his eyes and searched what remained of Nick's memories for an answer. After a minute, he said to himself, "Ah, these are human doctors and security personnel." Nick continued to watch from his hiding place. He became bored with the ambulance men's attempts to hack and chop on the wrecked car with their noisy tools. Suddenly a delicious thought popped into his head that caused him to smile. He remembered back to the bar, where everyone had fought in a grand melee after sending his thought to them. This was a new trick that he had never been able to do before finding Nick. He wondered if he could practice here with these little mice. He focused on one of the men from the car labeled state trooper and burrowed himself into the man's mind. He watched as the man scratched the back of his head, then stood up and looked around as if someone was speaking to them. Nick thought harder, depositing a seed, a thought in the man's mind, then waited.

The officer looked around, becoming more frantic as his head scanned the area at a quickening pace. The other officer, in the matching uniform, spoke to the distraught officer. Nick could not make out the man's words, but his body language seemed to convey fear. The target of Nick's mental assault put his hand on his gun and put his arm up as if telling the other officer to stay back. Just then, another man pulled up in a car with flashing blue lights, but his clothing was different. This new officer stepped out of his car and yelled to the man in the state trooper uniform, "Dave, what the hell is wrong with you, man?"

"Stay back!" The target yelled at everyone. "Just stay back. I know what the fuck you are doing."

Nick clapped his hands like a giddy child as he heard the men's voices raise, their stances growing more aggressive. He thought the show was playing out too slowly. He sent another wave that caused the other men to put their hands on their guns. The paramedics ran to their truck. His thought was of impending death, a threat.

The officers continued to yell at one another.

"Dude, calm down," one trooper called to the panicking trooper.

"It's you too, you little fucker," the trooper called back.

The security officer dressed in different clothing yelled, "Dave! Jesus, put the damn gun down."

The officer had not realized he had unholstered his weapon and was now pointing it at the trooper. The trooper swung his gun toward the third officer and yelled, "Are you in on this too, Jimmy?" as he began to back away from the second and third officer.

"Look, man, I don't even know what's going on. I just got here," Jimmy replied.

A motion to the right of the officer caught his attention. He turned to see one of the paramedics rushing toward him with a syringe in his hand.

"No stop!" the second officer yelled, but the paramedic was already on top of the trooper. The two men rolled around on the ground, wrestling as the paramedic tried to jab the needle into the officer's neck. The paramedic finally got the upper hand and pinned the trooper to the ground by sitting on his chest. The trooper continued to struggle with his free hand, grabbing at the paramedic's hand that contained the syringe. As the other two officers ran to break up the brawl, a loud pop suddenly rang out as the pinned trooper squeezed a shot into the paramedic's chest. The paramedic immediately stopped struggling with the officer. He slumped to one side and fell to the ground, still clutching the needle. The other two officers stopped and looked at the trooper lying on the ground.

"Oh, dear god, Dave," the second officer said, "What the hell did you—" but his words were cut short by a blast from the officer's weapon that landed squarely in his chest.

The third officer tried to grab the trooper's weapon, but before he could retrieve it, he fell to the ground after a hole opened in his face to the right of his nose. Dave, the officer on the ground, frantically looked around and saw the other paramedic running for one of the slain officers' guns, his belly bouncing side to side as he tried to cover the distance. Dave raised his service weapon, took careful aim at the ambling man, and pulled the trigger. The paramedic fell to the ground clutching the middle of his belly as his shirt began to change from white to bright red. Afterward, Dave got up and looked around. He began to murmur something to himself that was inaudible. He let out a scream and began to cry. Then, he pressed the barrel of his service weapon to his right temple and pulled the trigger without another sound.

The entire time, Nick sat silently watching. He began to see the blink of another light. This light was orange and was not accompanied by the wail of a dying animal. Nick looked back over to the center of the festivities as a tow truck driver exited his vehicle. The tow truck driver stood in stunned silence as he saw the bodies lying strewn about the highway's verge. A voice broke over the wind to Nick as he saw a second passenger in the tow truck. It was a female screaming at the man.

"Robby! Come on! Let's get the hell out of here!"

Robby turned and shook his head. He stumbled as he ran back to the truck. Nick heard him telling the other passenger, "Call it in. We'll come back when the other deputies get here."

Nick watched as the tow truck driver got into the cab and maneuvered the growling beast back in a direction that faced down the road away from the scene. It belched giant clouds of black smoke as it accelerated away from the scene. Nick sat, listening to the woods around him as he let his eyes slowly began to close. He awakened to the sounds of several big cats dying as the night around him lit up. He turned to look in the sounds' direction and saw more security personnel and ambulance vehicles coming into view.

"This host will never get any rest," he thought, "with all that noise and scuttering about of the emergency ants."

Nick got up and walked deeper into the woods until he could no longer hear the sounds of the scuttering men or their noisy sirens and fell asleep on a soft pile of fallen leaves.

CHAPTER 38

"Why the hell did you take all of it out. Hell, never mind that. How did you convince the bank to *let* you pull three thousand over the max daily?" Ethan asked.

Tabby smiled, fanned herself with their life savings, and replied, "I told him that it was a surprise birthday present for my hubby. I told the manager that I planned on surprising you with a classic cart you had always wanted and that if I didn't get back with the money in an hour, the car would be gone because the seller already had someone coming over in two hours who claimed to have money in hand."

"Wow. Remind me never to divorce you. You'd leave me destitute in the streets."

Tabby popped him on the arm playfully and stashed the money into her pants pocket.

Ethan started the car and pulled out the rental company's parking lot, then said, "We need to take a detour before we *actually* get on the road."

"Detour to where?" Kiera asked.

"I know a guy that can get us some new IDs."

Ethan cut his eyes toward Tabby and saw the gaped-mouthed expression on her face.

"There was a guy that worked with Nick and me about five years ago. He got busted for making fake licenses and social security cards for people. I kept in touch, so if he's at home, he may be able to help."

He paused a moment to check Tabby's disapproving stare, "Look, just trust me. Unless you want to sleep in the car for the next three or four days, we need to pay this guy a visit."

Tabby considered, then shook her head. She looked to the other two passengers in the back seat as if asking their opinions. Kiera realized Ethan was concerned an organization that could easily create and manufacture chemical weapons may have the ability to track their movements by using their IDs.

"So, you think they may be tracking us?"

Ethan nodded to Kiera in the rearview mirror.

"Then I say yes."

Josh looked at Tabby, then added, "I'm already a runaway. What's another mark on my record at his point?"

Twenty minutes later, Ethan walked up to the doorway of a house on the west side and rang the bell. He followed thirty seconds later with a knock then waited. As he swung his fist to knock again, the door opened.

"Jesus," a man said, "Ethan, what are you doing here?" as the door opened.

Ethan smiled in return. "Jacob, it's nice to see you, man." Then he paused, scanned Jacob's face, and peered over his shoulder into the room. "Hey, listen, I know this may come out of left field," Ethan scratched at the ich on the back of his neck, "but my friends and I require some special services."

"Special services, huh?" Jacob asked.

"Yeah, you know. I have an *I Dea* that you may be able to help," Ethan said, giving Jacob a wink.

"Okay. How does that, ah, little situation bring you to *my* door?"

Ethan's heart sank. "I remember why you got caught…."

Jacob started closing the door as he was saying, "Look, man, I don't know what you're into, but I am clean now. I can't help you."

"Jacob," Ethan said, inserting his foot into the closing doorway. "Look, man, I know you are clean now. I wouldn't have come if it were not a matter of life and death."

Jacob considered for a moment. After a brief inner confrontation with himself, he said, "Come in. Let's see if we can talk about the services you need."

Ethan followed Jacob into his house, and the door closed behind him. Around ten minutes later, the front door opened, and Ethan jogged toward the rental car. Tabby, who had moved over to the driver's seat at Ethan's suggestion when he exited the vehicle, let the window down.

"Hey, babe," Ethan said, "you guys get out and come into the house."

"Is he going to give you what we need?" Kiera asked.

"Yes. He is going to set us up."

"Oh, do we get to pick our names?" Josh asked excitedly.

"I don't think it works that way."

"Come on. We need to get this done as fast as we can." Ethan said as he opened the driver-side door.

Once inside, Jacob walked the group into a room at the back of the house. The room was packed from wall to wall with clothing. It reminded Tabby of a wardrobe room from some low-budget play. A table was set up along the room's front wall with makeup lighting beside a large mirror. A double rainbow of makeup lay strewn across the table's surface. After all, you wanted to be wearing your best darling mask to have a photo taken of you that required you to look at it for the next five years. Tabby and Kiera used an adjoining bathroom to wash their faces, then sat down and took turns painting one another like excited ten-year-old girls. Ethan and Josh plowed the racks of clothing as the ladies worked.

"What do you think?" Ethan asked, holding up a black pair of jeans that looked like they would surely cut the blood flow from every vital organ below the waist, a wide grin spread across his face like butter.

Josh looked at the pants, then to Ethan's face, then back to the pants. "Ah, well, I guess if you…." Josh's sentence was cut short by a quick flapping sound in his ears and a soft crumple into his face as Ethan whipped the pants at his face. The pants landed squarely then crumpled onto the floor. Josh stepped back, a wide-eyed look of question on his face.

"Dude. For real? I wouldn't be caught dead in a pair of girly breeches like that."

Whether from Ethan's laughter or the reference to girly jeans, Josh got the joke and started laughing as he bent to pick up the clothing from the floor.

"Yeah. You didn't strike me as a skinny jeans type of guy."

"Nope," Ethan said, looking off to the side, "I'm more a boot cut with shit kickers type."

As the two continued to sort through the clothing, Jacob came over to Ethan, "Look, man, I haven't done this in a few years. I was not even allowed near a computer for five years after I got out."

"I get it," Ethan offered, "We don't need to pass a CIA audit. We just need to be able to safely rent a hotel room, so we don't have to sleep in the car for the next couple of days."

Jacob looked at Ethan side-long, his right eye nearly squeezed shut, then asked, "What's this about, Ethan? This is all a little out of character for you. You and Nick were always straight."

"What do you mean?"

"Look, man, you and Nick are about the straightest two guys I've ever met, but now you show up at my doorstep and ask me for new identities and tell me that you are going to need to use them for a couple of days and I…" then Jacob trailed off, his confusion snatching the words from his mouth.

"Look," Ethan said, placing a hand on Jacob's shoulder, "No one will ever connect us to you. All I can say is that Nick got himself into something, and we are just trying to help him out of it. That's all I can say about it."

"Well," Jacob began, with a stammer in his voice, "Just make sure. I cleaned up, man. I sure as hell don't want to go back to jail for five hundred dollars or any other amount."

"Five hundred dollars? When you were doing this on the regular, it was—"

"Yeah. I know, but I'm not going to take advantage of a friend, dude. Even after I was busted, you stayed in touch, which meant a lot to me. When I got out, I had nothing. Even my wife divorced me while I was in the pen. Divorced me for some shithead that she went to high school with after they reconnected on Facebook. So yeah, I could use the extra cash, but I'm not gonna bend you over for it."

"Hitting a hard patch doesn't make you a bad person. At least I always try to think that about people." Ethan thought back to his uncle getting busted for trying to hold up a community bank branch after being unemployed for eight months. "I've seen good people make the wrong choice before. That's not always a reason to throw them away." Ethan shrugged. "That's how I see it, anyway. As far as the papers go, I promise, a couple of days and they're burnt. I give you my word. I just didn't know where else to turn." He smiled and added, "Besides, you are the only guy I've ever met who could even come close to doing work of this quality for someone."

At this, Jacob looked up, his face not revealing that Ethan had, in fact, insulted him without knowing it, "Come close?" He asked, "Man, this shit don't come close. It's real papers. You're new people now. You could take these IDs to the TSA and get cleared to fly to Russia."

"Hey man, don't get me wrong. I would come to you even if I knew other people who could do this work. It helps that I know you. That's why this was our first stop after," Ethan stopped.

"After what?"

"Never mind. Just believe me, you could save a life with the work you do here tonight. This is not just some kid needing to get lit on a Friday night. This may be the most important job you have ever done."

"Fine then. Don't tell—"

"I would if I could, but it wouldn't help."

"Okay. Fine." Jacob said as he threw up his hands and turned to walk away. "Let's get your photos. Then it should take about twenty minutes."

"Alright, let's get it on and get it done then, dude."

"Yeah, let's get it done."

After an hour and a half, Jacob came up from his basement and handed Ethan an envelope. "Here you go, Mr. Adkinson."

"Adkinson, huh?"

"Yep. That seems about as far away from Hensley as you're going to get on short notice."

Ethan opened the envelope, took out the newly minted IDs, and read them silently. He reached a grateful hand toward Jacob, which Jacob shook.

"Look, I know you want to stay clear of all this," Ethan said, holding up the envelope, then lowering it to his side, "But I can't tell you how grateful we are that you were willing to come out of retirement for this little project."

Jacob smiled, squinted at Ethan, and replied, "Yeah, retirement." His smile broadened just before he took on a more serious expression. "Look, Ethan, any time I can still take a hot shit on the system, I'm game. I just hope Nick is okay. He was always a friend to me, you know, before. I don't mind at all. Glad I was able to lend the assist." He pulled Ethan by the hand and asked, "Still can't tell me anything, I guess?"

"Better you don't know," Ethan replied, patting Jacob on the shoulder.

Ethan handed Jacob five crisp bills and said, "Again, thanks for this. At least now we can move around a little easier."

After leaving, Ethan drove to an adjoining neighborhood and pulled into a gas station parking lot before distributing the new IDs, as Jacob had advised. After putting the car in park, he retrieved the envelope from the glove compartment where Tabby had stowed it, opened it, and began distributing its contents to everyone.

"Okay," he began, "It looks like we're all family now. I am Nathan

Adkinson. Tabby, you are Lucy Adkinson,"

Tabby rolled her eyes. "Oh good god, why do I have to be a Lucy?"

Ethan ignored her disgust and continued, "Kiera, it looks like you are Rebecca Adkinson and Josh," Ethan thought for a brief moment, then said, "I guess you are my little brother."

Josh took the new driver's license and looked at it.

"I still don't think you look old enough, but hey, you have a license now."

Ethan could see Josh rubbing his thumb over the name printed on the new ID. Josh read the name, saying it silently to himself. A heavy wet droplet appeared in the corner of Josh's right eye as he thought, knowing he was foolish to feel this way. Still, he was finally part of a real family, even if the family only existed on the laminated paper in his hand. He was no longer Josh, the weird loner in a Catholic home. He was now Thomas Adkinson, someone's little brother. His shoulders shuddered as he fought to hold back the flood of emotions. A family. He had a brother, a sister, and a sister-in-law. He unknowingly reached and wiped the tear from his eye. He felt a light tap on his knee and turned to see Kiera, who was staring at him.

"What?" Josh asked, blinking Kiera into frame.

"Earth to Josh," Kiera said, "I asked what's your name."

Josh looked back down at his new license and social security card in his hand, "It says that I'm Thomas Adkinson." He looked back over to Kiera and gave her a smile brimming with a tinge of the murderous hope he had managed to push down so long ago. "I guess you guys are my older sisters now."

"Hey, watch that," Tabby jeered, "I'm not old."

Josh looked to see Tabby put on her seatbelt as she smiled at him from the front passenger seat, then reach up and absently scratch the back of her neck.

Amanda Dalling walked into the control room of the Atlanta hub and quickly scanned the computer displays to see if the little red dots were still bounding across the screen. Marcus was bent over a table in the middle of the room, sliding his finger across it as if he were tracing a line. The table's surface, a large computer display, was lit up with a satellite image. Marcus was tracing a path for the three blinking dots.

"Do we know their trajectory yet, Marcus?" Amanda asked.

Marcus looked up from the flattened image of the world and gave an uncertain nod as he pointed to the three blinking dots.

"Good. Do we know where they are going yet?"

"No. Their cone of probability is narrowing, but they do not seem to be stopping yet. All we know right now is it seems like they are headed west. They're in Shreveport right now."

"We had one tracker fail."

"No. Only three of the targets were tagged."

"Why are only three of them tagged?"

"The surgeon said when he tagged the boy, his body rejected the tracker, quite literally."

"Rejected how. We've never had this tech fail."

"It was similar to how the boy's wound responded to Rodney's slug. Five minutes after implanting, the surgeon says the implant fell out onto the table after which the insertion point closed."

"We need to start the cleardown protocols for this hub and transfer everything to the Albuquerque hub immediately. If they are headed west, we must do the same."

"I have the pilots filing their flight plans, the files are transferring to Prometheus as we speak, and I have two teams designated for cleardown here once we leave. One team will direct cleardown, and another will stay behind to manage the conference room repairs. We're good to leave whenever you are ready."

Amanda smiled. "Excellent. I knew you would find your footing, Marcus. Gather your things and ride with me to the airport. There are some items of import which we must to discuss."

CHAPTER 39

Ethan walked from the bathroom of the room he had rented for the evening in the Shreveport Anthem Hotel, still toweling off his hair. He stopped rubbing his hair and saw Josh seated on the hotel room sofa watching television. Ethan sat down in a chair beside the sofa and slung the towel around his neck. He looked at Josh, who was laughing at a game show where the contestants were currently dangling above a pool from cables as the host asked them questions.

Ethan heard the host ask the second contestant, in the group of three adult spiders, "What is the capital of Maine?" After the contestant answered incorrectly, a loud buzzer sounded as smoke cannons fired clouds of billowing white smoke into the air from the pool below. The thin thread of cable holding the woman plunged her into the pool. Josh laughed again as the woman swam to the surface gasping, and wiping her face.

Kiera came over and sat alongside Josh. She looked over and said,

"I've got a couple of questions."

Josh turned to see Kiera's furrowed expression and pressed lips. In truth, she looked like a woman wearing the weight of a gravestone around her neck.

"I want to know how much *you* know about this whole process. Whatever is happening to Nick, I mean."

Josh nodded as Ethan lifted his towel and abused his hair some more.

"I mean, *do* you know what is happening to Nick? Is there a way to stop this thing from," she stopped short of finishing the question.

Josh thought about how to answer, carefully measuring his response. He wanted to be as delicate as possible but not give false hope. The wrong response here could send Kiera and their little band in the wrong direction. If he was going to have a chance of doing what he now thought of as his duty, he needed them, Kiera most of all.

"It's a ritual, a process, called the rending," Josh finally offered. "It's a process of erasing, or more like absorbing, a person's essence. What you call a soul."

"Can it be stopped?"

"I think it's gone past that point now for Nick. I don't think it's ever been stopped once the process has gone this far."

Kiera leaned back in the chair, propped her head on her hand, and forced herself to steady her trembling lips. Her silence continued for a moment as one crystal stream of hopelessness ran down Kiera's cheek.

"So," Ethan began, "If we can't stop this process from killing Nick, then why are we driving halfway across the country? What are we doing?"

"This is bigger than Nick or *you*," Josh said, looking back to Kiera, "and it's bigger than me. I think it may be bigger than any of us."

"Why, Josh. Why is this happening? What is this job he was talking about when we went to McCaversville?" Kiera asked, wiping her nose with a tissue.

"I'm not sure. Well, I can't remember. I just know it's bad. He's done bad things in the past, and I think that this time he wants to do something bigger than anything he's ever done before."

"But how do you know? How can you be so certain?" Tabby asked after taking a seat in the other chair.

"I don't know. It's like I can't remember much, but then at the same time, it's like I remember a lot of stuff, but it's all jumbled up. Have you guys ever put together a puzzle? I mean, like the really big ones, a thousand pieces or more?"

Keira and Tabby nodded as Ethan shook his head, "No," and followed by saying, "I still know what puzzles are."

Josh thought for a moment, his face drifting into distant thought as if trying to fit an ambiguous clue into an otherwise concrete thought process. He and the other kids at the home would often spend rainy days working on large puzzles as a group exercise. The sisters thought the task of using one's mind to assemble such large works required a practice in patience and cognitive perception to determine the pattern of how the shapes and colors would all bind together. Add to that, the act of working in a group was thought to teach the boys, some of which were lone isolationists, about working in a team. To achieve a particular goal, thus serving to build in these abandoned youths a sense of trusting another person again, if only to a small degree, meaning the sisters always had plenty of puzzles around the house.

Josh removed himself from his memories of rainy days and puzzles then continued, "It's like a giant puzzle. You know how when you work on a puzzle and get to a point where it's about half done? You can see the image starting to look like the picture on the box cover. It's like that. There's like, big chunks of this image I can see clearly." Josh hung his head a picked at his thumbnail with his fingers. But then, I don't know. It's like, at the same time, the big chunks aren't helpful because I can't see how they fit into the whole picture. Then there are the little pieces that are always scattered. You can see shapes and colors on them, but you can't seem to find where they fit. It's like that."

"Is the process of assembling this mental puzzle improving at all," asked Tabby.

"I think so. Maybe. I'm not sure." Josh thought a moment. "Okay, an example of one chunk is I remember a man named Cecily. I can clearly remember him for some reason and that he is extremely import-ant. I also remember he is connected to Nick somehow, like a relative."

"Okay, that's good," Ethan said, leaning forward on the edge of his chair, "Maybe that is something that we can use. Do we know where this Cecily is now or how to find him?"

"Well, we can't exactly find him. Cecily is dead. I guess he's been dead for at least. I don't know, like twenty thousand years maybe. The important part is Cecily was one of Nick's ancestors. Nick's bloodline descends directly from Cecily. Cecily's last living child, actually."

"Whoa, whoa, whoa. So, you are telling us you know Nick's bloodline back as far as twenty thousand years? How?"

Josh looked at Ethan and immediately saw the doubt, "Well, not all of it. I just know that Cecily is Nick's ancestor. Yartrua told me before…" then he stopped and said, "Well, I don't know, a long time ago."

"Who is Yartrua? Can he help?" Kiera asked.

"I don't know. That's the problem. I mean, I don't remember a lot about him yet other than Yartrua was someone I knew. He wanted to save Cecily's children from something, of what I don't know. I think it was a ritual like the rending that is happening to Nick. He can't help because he's in prison."

"So, he was some sort of criminal?" Tabby asked.

"No," Josh shot back, "Absolutely not. He was a hero. He ended the war then locked himself away in a prison that he created."

"What war?" Ethan asked.

Josh bounced his closed fist on the sofa's arm. His eyes darted from side to side as he searched the broken collage in his mind. He slammed his clenched fists into his thighs, almost as a reflex, and said, "I don't know. I'm trying. The pieces are just all floating around. I know he stopped a war that threatened to end his entire race. Then for some reason, he had to lock himself into a prison to protect everyone. All I know is that what he did was a good thing, not for his race, but for the universe. He's the reason I'm here."

"So, and I can't believe I'm asking this question," Ethan said, leaning back with a sigh, "Are you saying that you are an alien?"

Josh thought for a moment, then slowly looked over to Ethan, "I think yes, and no. I know that we, they were not human, not like you and me anyway. Their existence would more closely resemble gods, as people understand gods, but they weren't gods."

Josh now found himself staring into opposing thought groups as Kiera sat, looking slightly horrified as if she expected lightning to explode into the room at any moment. Tabby looked numbly at him as if she were trying to dissect his answer like a frog in high school biology. Ethan sat with his head propped on his palm.

"Here's the crazy thing," Josh said when no one spoke, "These people, beings, are the reason people seek religion. I remember that part. It was like an intentional design flaw or something when they made us. I mean you." He quickly corrected.

"What does that mean?" Ethan asked with a sudden burst of interest. He was so far out on the edge of his chair that Josh thought he would slip into the floor on his butt at any moment.

"I think they called it echoes, and people were designed to be kind of pulled toward these echoes." He looked away for a moment, then said, "Yes. They called it echoes."

"Echoes of what?"

Josh turned to Ethan again and frowned a little, "I don't remember. I just remember they called it echoes. It had something to do with their existence as pure energy, as pure essence."

"Made of energy? You mean they had no physical bodies?"

"No. Not really." The searching look appeared on Josh's face again, then he said, "I just can't remember everything clearly. I seem to remember they were known as the Shaqwelldashnis. The Architects in English."

"Oh man, this is too much. I mean, we've dropped right off the damn planet now." Ethan said, shaking his head and rubbing his hair some more, this time as if he was trying to massage away a lump. When he stopped rubbing his hair, his face twisted into a scowl, then he said. "So, let's recap. You are an alien, but you're not. You descend from a race that we would think of as gods, but they're not. These guys are still alive, and this thing is taking over Nick—"

"Eulahtan."

"Okay, this Eulahtan thing that is taking over Nick's body wants to finish some final bad something and what, only you can stop him? Does that pretty much bring us up to speed?"

Josh nodded. "I know. It sounds kind of stupid when you say it out loud."

"Stupid? It sounds bat shit crazy. I don't know if I can fully wrap my head around this, and now you're telling me these guys were walking around, on earth, over twenty thousand years ago, and now they're all gone, but they're not."

"No, not gone. Just locked up." Josh closed his eyes and strained against the clutter inside his mind, then said, "Think of our universe. We, people, know relatively nothing about it. I mean, really, we don't. But imagine you were a race advanced enough to develop some technology that allowed you to unlock all the secrets. Not only did you unlock all the secrets, but you learned how to use that knowledge to do amazing things. Access features in our reality that scientists only have theoretical models for right now. Flawed models. Knowledge that would allow you to do things humans couldn't even dream up at their current level of evolution."

"Things like what?" Ethan asked.

"Things like build human beings or slip from one universe to another."

"That's science fiction, not real life."

"Maybe to you, but to these beings, it was just another piece of knowledge they took advantage of to further increase their understanding of creation as a whole. I mean, think about it. All of those crazy science fiction stories and movies have to come from somewhere. Maybe it is the echoes."

Josh could see in Ethan's emotionless expression that he had not yet convinced him, so he continued, "I said they were in a sort of prison, right?" Ethan nodded in acknowledgment. "Well, that prison is not here, in this reality. I remember this clearly. When Yartrua created the prison, he placed it *between* the spaces."

Josh surveyed the group expecting to see clarity, only to find blank stares mixed with slack jaws. He tried to think of the model he had in his head and then a way to describe it.

"Okay," he began, "Think about plastic wrap, you know, like you would use to cover a bowl. Well, if you took the whole roll of plastic wrap, unrolled it, then folded it over and over again until the whole roll was one giant folded, uh, stack, I guess. Then imagine you took that stack and formed it into a ball, no more like crumpled it up so that the folded layers were more disorganized but still stacked on one another. That is how the universes interact. They're folded alongside each other in this tangled quantum state. But, there is a space between each layer of the universes, a separation of the layers. The prison is in one of those spaces. Those spaces are the hardest to access and the hardest to leave if you stop in them."

When Josh stopped speaking, he looked to see Tabby rubbing her head as if she were swearing off a fledgling migraine and Ethan sitting slack-faced, overwhelmed with the mental image Josh had created.

Josh met Kiera's astonished gaze, "So is that where you and I were? Inbetween? You said, 'Let's leave this dimension,' and we left through that tear. And that sound—"

"The ripping sound," Josh remembered, "That was energy transference as we passed through the barriers."

The thought of Kiera having shot her soul not just through space but outside of known reality into a fissure between realms turned her stomach to water.

"Oh god," she said, through trembling lips, "So, we were physically there, our souls, I mean?"

Josh nodded slowly

"I think I'm going to be sick again." She got up and rushed into the bathroom with her hand over her mouth. Tabby followed.

"So, you took Kiera to another reality when you two went to wherever this thing took Nick?"

Josh nodded. "Yeah, but I didn't know that at the time. I mean, not until we left."

"You never left the room."

"We did. Your body is just a vessel, like your car. You, the real you, exists in another state inside of that vessel. Think about it. When you leave your car to come into the hotel room, you don't have to drive your car up here. You just need to leave your car and walk away. Your essence, the you inside of you, is the real you. The energy that makes up your consciousness. Living here, in our bodies, is a temporary state that the Architects found a way of shedding."

Ethan thought for a moment, not believing he was having this conversation with a teenage kid, then asked, "So, what happens when we die if the real us is this essence. What happens to our soul?"

"I'm not sure. I guess, unless you learn how to exist without physical form like the others did, it just eventually dissipates like an uncaged electrical charge."

"Well, that's bleak."

The bathroom door clacked, and Ethan turned to see Tabby and Kiera returning.

"False alarm," Kiera said, picking up the pillow from the seat cushion, then holding onto it like a protective barrier as she sat back down. "Just knowing what happened to me, how far we went, and where we went, that was just a lot to take in." She gave a small, weak smile and said with a sigh, "I guess that makes me the only human to travel across our galaxy, out of our solar system for that matter." The tiny smile wilted from Kiera's face. " I want to know something. All the dreams I had of that place. If this Eulahtan is as powerful as he seems, has the ability to," she paused, swallowed, and seemed to choke on the next words, "erase someone from existence, why would he need to torment his victims? Does he get off on it or something?"

"No, not really. He likes to see people die, but that's not why he does it. I think it takes a lot of effort on his part to manipulate a healthy mind like Nick's. I think it helps the changing process. If he can break down the host's mind, I mean. I think it must weaken the host mentally and make them more pliable if their minds are breaking. You and I got the benefit of that treatment as well because we're all linked somehow. I get how Nick and I are linked. I just can't figure how you and I are, you know, connected." He shuffled in his seat under Kiera's glare and began to pull at the seam on his pants, then added, "Yeah, I can't figure that part out. It's almost like I can sense you more than I can sense Nick."

"How are we supposed to stop something with this kind of power? We barely got away from that basket full of flakes and nuts back in Atlanta. How are we supposed to basically stop a god? You have got to give us *something*, Josh. There has to be more." Ethan's tone was not harsh, but there was a seriousness in it that clearly conveyed their little quartet's inadequacies.

"I'm trying. It's like all this stuff is just mixed up. It kind of feels like I am looking into a bowl of spaghetti."

"Well, you need to concentrate and clear away the sauce. We're lost here. Unless you come up with something we can use, we may as well head home and wait for him to finish his plan. I've never been one to lie down on a job, but you've gotta see, we're walking on pretty thin ice here."

"I know. Look, if I knew how to force this stuff out, I would. I just haven't found a…" then Josh paused, shrugged, and said, "I don't know."

"Josh, is there anything that seems to help these thoughts come together?" Tabby asked.

"No, like I said—"

"No, calm down and think." Tabby interrupted in her clinical tone. "Think back to times when these memories seemed to become more vivid or seemed to have more of the puzzle assemble itself."

A spark of recognition appeared on Josh's face as if he had found a key. Almost as suddenly as the key appeared, Josh's eyes flashed to white, and he was gone once more to the space between spaces, gone again to Nick's bleak, hopeless prison.

"Ah, shit!" Ethan said, throwing up his arms and leaning back in the chair, "Why in the hell did he do that?"

"Just wait, Ethan," Tabby said. "He did say that touching Nick was like throwing a switch in his mind. That must be where he went. Maybe it is a switch for him. Let's just see what happens."

They sat and watched Josh as if he were the new family puppy, and everyone was trying to make sure it didn't hurt itself as it played.

CHAPTER 40

Josh tore into what he now understood was Eulahtan's rending chamber and stopped beside Nick's essence. He stared for a moment, partly in disbelief and partly in pity of what was happening to Nick. This process, the process of wasting away someone's soul into particle after particle of timeless oblivion, was the cruelest thing Josh had ever seen. Yet, there was a dark, sad beauty in the process. The rent particles looked like colored sands against the black backdrop. If one stood and watched the dancing flow of energy as it streamed away into the open seam between time, it was almost mesmerizing, beautiful. The colors moved in a slow upward river, changing as they flowed from the pale greyish-brown of dead skin, red blood, and white bone. Each color representing a marked characteristic of the human body and the parts of which it is composed. Josh studied the flows of Nick's life for a moment more until he realized he was standing mouth agape, considering how a man being torn apart, essentially atom by atom, was beautiful.

On his realization of this, he closed his mouth as a ping of shame shot through him.

There remained only the left shoulder, a portion of the chest, and Nick's head. Josh stepped toward it. He stretched his hand out, then thought a more aggressive turn might better serve his needs. Stepping around to where the lower portion of Nick's body should have been, he walked through the streaming grains of Nick's soul. Goosebumps rose on his skin as the particles seemed to send an electrical charge through him. He bent over the remains and opened his arms. In a single, lightning-fast move, he closed his arms around the remains. There was the expected spark of lightning Josh was expecting, as well as the tingling of energy transference, but this time the sound rang out like a bolt released from Zeus's hand. The leaping spark of his energy felt like a punch to his gut. His body began to tremble, no, not tremble but to quake, bordering on the rigorous spasms of a seizure. He tried to open his mouth, but his jaws were locked closed. His body instantly blazed, consumed with what appeared to be a white-hot flame, yet his flesh did not burn.

Josh's physical body began to tremble as well, mimicking his body in the black. His legs bounced, his shoulders jumped, and his mouth hung open, letting out the wheezing cry of a small dying animal.

"He's seizing?" Ethan said, looking at Tabby with huge eyes.

"I don't know. It doesn't look like a seizure, but—"

Tabby was cut off as Kiera said, "I'll get him," Then, before anyone could stop her, she moved to the cushion beside Josh and put her hand on his shoulder. As soon as they touched, Kiera's eyes blinked to pale haunting grey as her consciousness departed. As suspected, she found herself standing in the black, watching Josh burn with white fire.

Kiera screamed his name to be heard over the crackle and zap of energy bursts. She took a step forward then stopped, remembering when she had touched Nick in her dream. Although she felt no heat, she worried the fire would burn. Bolts of energy flashed and sparked from Josh and Nick, striking the water at her feet. Kiera took a deep breath, took a step, and thrust her hand forward. There was no heat as her hand moved into the blazing aura. The brilliant light nearly obscured Josh from view. Josh clung to Nick's remains, holding him as if he were a life raft in the open ocean. Between Nick and Josh, a blaze of blue electricity burned. Arcs of jutting energy exploded loudly enough to reverberate across the entirety of all the universes. Kiera pressed an ear against an upraised shoulder to dampen the overpowering volume of sizzling and popping blue bolts. She stepped closer, groping for Josh in the blinding light. Still feeling no heat, she called his name again. Josh did not reply or acknowledge her presence, so Kiera grabbed onto Josh's shoulder. She intended to shake him loose from Nick's remains but instead disappeared as the white blaze wrapped around her.

Kiera's physical body began to tremble. Her lips muttered something that Ethan and Tabby could not make out. Tears flowed from her eyes, wetting her face as Kiera saw the images Josh was absorbing. Kiera fell into Josh's visions as their minds synced, became one. Her consciousness flashed through scenes that were never meant for human minds to view. Images that threatened to shatter her reason. She saw Cecily by the water's edge, reaching out to seek the hand of a young maid washing her garments in a river. Cecily laughed and cried as his human wife gave birth to their four children. Then there was a flash as the images changed, and Kiera saw Parzeus's rage at discovering no one would be allowed to rule over humanity, only work as a group to care for and guide them. She saw the rending of Cecily's three children. One by one, they were harvested from their physical bodies as the ritual was performed to erase their souls. Their essence scattering endlessly across the universe as the agony of their pain caused Cecily's mourning to shake the heavens.

Kiera saw as Cecily turned to Yartrua and begged him to intervene. She saw the War of the Last Child as Yartrua summoned what seemed like the energy of the cosmos itself and set upon the remainder of his kind, ending the war, saving the last child, then sealing himself into the great prison that sits at the crux of creation. Kiera not only saw all this but also felt the pain, the agony, the death, and betrayal. A billion souls in hell, defeat, and despair. She cried out as pressure built inside her head as if it were filling with an ocean.

Tabby gasped as she grabbed onto Kiera's arm. Two fine beads of blood began to seep from Kiera's nose. Kiera's pale greyish eyes began to fade to a greyish pink as the blood vessels in both eyes began to burst from the bombardment of having all of human history poured into her mind.

Suddenly the images stopped as Josh's mind within the black turned its attention to his right. He saw what he first thought was the darkness of a black hole. A scar of space where no light had ever touched stood out above the wet ground. Josh's consciousness began to stream toward the blackened absence of light and Kiera's mind along with it. As the consciousnesses mingled, Josh and Kiera understood that this was the bleak, corrupted mind of Eulahtan. Eulahtan's mind was such a cancer of hate from Parzues's manipulation that it seemed to give off an odor that reminded Kiera of corpses left to bake under a hot sun mingled with hot piss.

"Oh god," she uttered, not knowing if she would be able to throw up in this space between spaces but wanting desperately to get away, to move. Somewhere, deep in the back of her mind, her survival instincts told her that to venture too deeply into that mind would be a journey through something far worse than hell. As Kiera drew closer to the black aura of Eulahtan's mind, pressure tightened her chest as the hurricane-battered sea of hate, sadness, isolation, pity, and rage closed in around her and Josh. In the center of the storm, an eye of sick, twisted love and longing. Kiera didn't feel, more sensed a separation, an even darker void, of what Kiera could not exactly nail down. She thought the hunger in this dark void was the final blow that ruptured this devil's heart if there had ever been a heart there. Still, Josh pressed deeper, the white light and the black tendrils of despair twisting and knotting themselves around one another as a blue fire blazed brighter and louder until it almost overtook the white energy of the original aura.

"Pull back, Josh!" Kiera screamed, "Pull back!" She felt her grip on him slipping as she tried to pull Josh out of the mass.

She didn't know if Josh heard her through all the electric fire of the disparate life forces contending with one another here in this corrupted space. She tugged harder on Josh's shoulder, but his arms seemed bound to Nick instead of simply holding him. Moving them was like trying to open the clamped jaws of a workman's vice. Kiera opened her eyes once she realized she could not break the embrace of the two consciousnesses and noticed something else had begun swirling around, no not around but from Josh's head.

"Oh god! Josh, you have to let go!" She forced her will into his mind. "Josh, you are starting to break."

At this, Josh seemed to blink his eyes.

"Don't be afraid, Kiera. This is right where I need to be."

"What are you doing?"

"I'm cheating," was his reply, "tipping the scales."

She sensed his smile. Once Josh seemed to be content with what he had glimpsed in Eulahtan's mind, he pulled himself and Keira's minds free of the black entanglement and released Nick's remains with the thunderous explosion of a canon. The blue fire and the white-hot aura quickly fizzled into calm nothingness. Josh turned to Kiera. She had released his shoulder and fallen to her knees once the bond broke. He nodded at her as if in agreement that it was time to return to their bodies.

Once back, Josh sat, sweat beading on his forehead as Kiera sat slumped back against the sofa wiping pink tears from her bloodshot eyes. She sucked in a half sobbing, half relieved, chuff of a breath as if gulping life itself, then asked in a hoarse voice, "Josh, what was that?"

Josh looked over and said through a grin that would have been at home on a used car salesman's face, "That was advantage home team, I think."

"Kiera, are you okay?" Tabby asked as she wiped around Kiera's eyes and forehead with a warm, damp cloth. "You scared the hell out of us." She wiped the blood from under Kiera's nose and from her lips.

"What did you guys do," Ethan asked.

"I don't know," Kiera said, looking over to Josh, "I just saw all this stuff. It was like watching a video montage."

"A montage of what?"

Josh looked at Ethan and calmly said, "Of the life and death of civilizations and the birth of mankind."

"Did you see anything we can use?"

"I did. I found where the key is hidden."

"What key?"

"The key to stopping him. To prevent him from arming his weapon."

"Okay, where is it?"

"Not in this realm. Eulahtan hid the key after his last attempt, but I saw where he put it."

"Can we get to it?"

"I don't know. It's further than either of us have traveled, but I think that it is doable."

"Think?" Ethan asked, "Does that translate into an actual percentage or just a gut feeling?"

"No percentage, but I can tell you I'm going to try."

CHAPTER 41

After seeing the key's location, Josh realized there was no way to reach it without help from a stronger link. He needed a bridge between Eulahtan and himself. That link, as it turned out, was a reluctant Kiera. There needed to be a more substantial connection than just clasping hands. Simple contact would not do. To create a bond that would carry them both across the barriers to the place where the key was waiting would require blood. The only way to ensure the bond would bring them to where they needed to go was to amplify the blood bond between the two of them.

"We need some copper," Josh said. "Do you have a penny?"

"Yeah, but a penny is not made of copper. Pennies haven't been made of copper in decades. The mint only plates them with copper." Ethan thought a moment, "I know where I can get pure copper. The question is, how much do you need."

"I'm not sure."

"How about a whole hand full?"

"Considering I was going to try with just a few pennies, that should do it."

Before they stopped for the night, Ethan had insisted they stop and purchase a laptop. He thought it would be useful for checking news headlines or for any more signs of Nick. He also expected the Nasaru to plaster their faces on all the news outlets. Ethan spotted a local discount electronics store as soon as he crossed the Mississippi state line. He stopped and purchased a refurbished laptop, picked up a couple of data cables, and grabbed a cheap bag in which to stow everything.

After a moment of rummaging, he pulled one of the new cables from the bag. He studied it for a moment, then reached back into the bag and pulled out a small knife he purchased during a snack stop sometime after they had passed through Birmingham.

Ethan sat down and looked across the table at Josh, "Give me a hand?"

"Sure," Josh replied.

As Josh approached, he saw Ethan begin dissecting the cable, then understood what Ethan was doing.

"Here, hold this end," Ethan said, handing Josh the decapitated end of the cable.

Josh grabbed the exposed inner wiring of the cable and began to pull. As he did, Ethan ran the knife's edge along the length of the wire's outer cladding. Once the wire's cladding had been peeled away, Ethan began to strip the inner wiring of its coverings to expose the delicate tendrils of copper hair that composed the cable's core.

"Will this be enough, or will we need the other cable too?"

Josh looked up from trying to skin the limp copper strands, "I think this should be plenty. We just need an extra bit of conduction."

Ethan continued to work as he moved his gaze between Josh's skinning of his cable strands and his own. "Are you sure you can get to where you need to go and then back?"

Ethan reached up and gave the back of his neck an agitated scratch. "Should."

"Babe, let me look at that for you," Tabby said, walking over and pushing Ethan's head forward, "you've been scratching at that spot all day."

"It's fine. It's probably some reaction to the shit they dosed us with at the house."

"I don't see anything, but you need to try not to scratch anymore. The skin is getting irritated from where you've been clawing at it all day."

"Yes, mother," Ethan said with a smile. "I'm telling you, it's probably some type of allergic reaction to that gas. There's no telling what kind of unregulated chemicals they use in that little cocktail. I'll be fine."

Tabby laid her hand on his cheek, nodded, then bent and kissed him on his forehead. She looked at Josh and smiled when she saw the red bloom of adolescent embarrassment on him.

"So, are you guys about done with this little project?"

"Yes, this is the last strand," Josh said, turning to his wire and pulling the last few inches from its sheath. "That's it."

Ethan looked at the delicate threads of copper hair that had made up the strands of the computer cable and asked, "Okay, copper, now what are we supposed to do with it?"

Josh studied the strands briefly, took two metal hairs from the bundle, and laid them aside. He smoothed the remaining strands into a single, long metal cord. Josh wrapped the strands around two fingers, forming them into an oblong ringlet. Before winding the cable, he twisted one end of the bundle to bind the fibers together, then finished by twisting the other end of the copper ring into another tightly twisted mesh of cords. He laid the ringlet on the table and then grabbed one of the two wires that he had separated from the bundle and began to wrap it around one of the twisted ends until only two inches of the fine copper wire was left protruding from the ringlet's end. He did the same with the other end.

"There," Josh said, sitting back and smiling, "I think this should do the trick."

Seeing the puzzled look on Ethan's face, Josh said, "It's like an alternator.

"What?"

"An alternator." Josh said, emphasizing the words this time, "You know how an alternator has brushes inside it. The brushes inside the copper coils create an electric charge. Then the electrical excess is passed into the battery, so the alternator charges the battery and runs the car at that same time. This is the same concept. It helps enhance electrical conductivity."

Ethan looked at Josh, still not fully getting the concept.

"Okay, think of what links Kiera and me as just plain old electricity. That is not really far off from what it is. So, think of us as batteries, and this," Josh pointed to the coiled cable on the tabletop, "This is like the coils of copper wire wrapped around an alternator's core. Once our connection is linked, our energy should build as it circulates through this coil, which will act like an amplifier. Hopefully, it will build a stronger bond between us. At least, I think that is how it works in my mind," he added.

"How are we supposed to use that to get where we're going," asked Kiera as she walked over, picked up the ringlet, and began to turn it over in her hands to inspect it.

Josh looked up, "I think we need to use it to connect us."

"Ah. I get it. We just need to plug you guys together. Then you'll be connected. Like connecting a DVR." Josh looked at Ethan, and his smile melted in confusion.

The smirk on Ethan's face slipped into a disapproving grimace. "You're shitting me. How in the hell are you supposed to plug yourself into another person, Josh? That's not reality, dude." Realizing that none of the experiences of the past few days agreed with Ethan's statement on the state of reality, he slunk back into his chair. Trying to determine how they were supposed to wire two living human beings, well, one human being and one something else, together like they were two pieces of household electronics.

"Well," Josh began slowly, "We need to insert the wire into Kiera's hand here."

Josh held up his hand and pointed to the middle of his palm. Ethan saw the line that ran from the outside edge of Josh's palm, across the hand, curving upward toward the middle finger.

"This is the line that palm readers call the heart line. He moved his finger to another area of the upraised palm. He traced a line that ran from the bottom center of the hand, curving upward and outward toward the outer edge of the index finger. Josh wiggled his thumb in and out to exaggerate where the flesh of the palm folded.

"You have to insert the other end into my palm here. This is called the lifeline."

"Josh, that wire is stranded, not data core wire. It's not thick enough to puncture the skin. How do you propose we get you, two guys," Ethan held up air quotes, "hooked up?"

"The knife," Kiera suggested.

Ethan looked at Kiera with surprise.

"You're serious?"

Kiera nodded without saying a word.

"So, I'm supposed to just what, cut open your hand and install a network cable into your palm like some sort of fucked up Dr. Frankenstein computer network? Do you realize what that sounds like when I say it out loud?"

"Ethan, we have to try. If this crazy idea helps the two of us supercharge our connection, we have to try. It's not like you would need to amputate our hands right here in the room. It's a tiny wire. It would be like a finger prick, like when someone checks their blood sugar levels."

"Yeah, all we need to do is break the skin enough to get the wire into the tissue and blood below. From there, we'll lock our fingers together to hold it in place and maintain the connection."

"Guy's, this is insane. The body doesn't work like that. Kiera, look at what happened to you the last time you went under with him. Tabs and I thought that you were—"

"That's the point," Josh said, "When I was in there by myself, with Nick, I saw the past, the lifetimes. It was like falling backward through time. But once Kiera touched me, it was like we fused or something. When she touched me, I could see things in Nick's mind and Eulahtan's mind. I was able to see the dark, unguarded part of Eulahtan's thoughts. Having Kiera there seems to double my ability to travel and see what I need to see. This amplifier," he said, pointing to the table where the wire lay, "should give us an even bigger advantage."

After reluctantly agreeing to assist with the connection, Ethan found himself on his knees in front of Josh.

"Are you sure this will help? It still seems like nonsense."

Josh nodded.

"Will your body even accept the wire? I mean, those suits said you took a bullet back at the house, then…."

Josh shrugged, then looked nervously over to Keira.

"Yeah. Okay. Give me your hand."

After a moment of uncertain deliberation, Josh and Keira sat on the sofa awaiting Ethan's knife. Ethan took Josh's hand, laid the knife tip at the base of the thumb where Josh had instructed, and then pressed the blade into his skin. Josh closed his eyes tightly. The more force Ethan applied to the knife. The harder Josh pressed his other hand into his thigh. Ethan felt Josh's arm tense as blood began to bead around the knife tip. Josh's shoulders relaxed as Ethan drew back the blade and looked at Kiera.

"That wasn't that bad," Josh said with a sigh. "Not as bad as a bee sting anyway."

Ethan took Kiera's hand the pressed the blade against her palm.

"You know, I tried to pierce my ears once with a sewing needle. So that you know, I didn't make it through my earlobe. As soon as I saw the first drop of blood, I threw up."

"You're not going to barf on me, are you?"

"Blood hasn't made me barf since I was a kid. I just felt like I should warn you."

"Great."

After a short period of sucking in deep breaths and biting lower lips, both participants sat on the sofa with small beads of blood weeping from the tiny wounds in their hands.

Kiera and Josh turned as a rip came from the sitting table. Tabby smiled and tore another strip of fabric for the hotel pillowcase.

"What are you doing?" Ethan asked.

"You are poking holes in people and inserting foreign objects into their bodies. I am making sure that we only have to do this once. The last thing we need is for them to separate from one another before they are ready. I am making some binding strips. Once they are set, we can tie their hands together, so they don't slip apart."

"I didn't think about that. I suppose that makes as much sense as any of this other stuff does."

"Kiera, we will need to concentrate. Once we touch, keep your mind focused on staying here in this room. Hold yourself here until Tabby gets our hands tied. When she is done, we'll go together."

Kiera nodded, still biting her lower lip, whether from nervousness or the knife, Josh could not tell.

"Are you guys ready? No matter how I do this, it will be uncomfortable, to say the least."

Josh placed his arm over Kiera's and laid his hand palm up on the cushion between them. Kiera rolled her palm to face up on the cushion as well. Kneeling in front of them, Ethan took a paper towel and wiped away the bead of blood so he could see to thread the wire into the incision in Josh's hand. As the wire pierced the wound, Josh turned his head and squeezed his knees together. As Ethan pushed the wire further into the raw tissue, the small bead of blood returned and formed into a small puddle in Josh's palm.

"Josh, hold this in place. If it comes out, we'll have to do it again."

Josh pressed a finger against the wire to hold it in place.

"Ready, Kiera?"

Kiera nodded, still biting her lower lip. As soon as Ethan began to insert the wire into Kiera's wound, she could feel the connection start to pull at her mind.

"Kiera, stay here," Josh urged.

"I am, but we need to hurry."

"Done! Tabby, give me the bindings."

Tabby handed Ethan the cloth strips as Josh and Kiera clasped their hands together, securing the coil of wire. Ethan quickly wrapped the strips of torn pillowcase around their hands.

Ethan tied a knot then leaned back on his haunches.

"Ready?" Josh asked, looking at Kiera. He could see that her eyes were already beginning to fade.

"Think about me. Try to see my mind. Do you see what I see?"

"It's dark. I see an old ruin in the distance," she replied, as her gaze ceased staring at the wall on the far side of the room and appeared to now be looking through it.

"Does it look like an old castle?"

"Yeah, sort of. I guess."

"Good, now stay focused on that castle as you push yourself toward it."

No sooner had Josh finished his instructions than both he and Kiera's bodies seemed to empty of themselves. Their clasped hands began to exude an orange glow from between their interlocked palms. Kiera's body gave a slight twitch as if having been pinched, and her grasp on Josh's hand tightened.

Kiera felt her breath freeze in her chest as her body seemed not to move as before but rather to fall. She felt the barriers between realms wrap around her and tear as if she were running through spider webs. Her already pulsing heart almost stopped when she lost sight of the ruins for a moment, then seeming to fall toward empty nothingness, her consciousness beginning to slip its boundary of control.

See the walls. See the towers, she thought.

She focused, trying to imagine the tall spires jutting up from the darkness into a sky as black as sorrow. The ruined outline of the castle walls, shadowing the distant horizon like the jagged teeth of a broken mouth, where loosened stones had fallen to the ground. A distant flash of lightning illuminated the ruins for a moment. Kiera almost thought she saw movement at the foot of the ramparts, only to have the black swallow the cold stones again into silent silhouette.

They seemed to move faster with each heartbeat until the tearing sound of their essence punching through the barrier walls was the constant roar of tearing fabrics of the realities as they rushed toward some monolithic gravitational force.

See the walls.

Kiera didn't know how far, or how fast, they were moving through the realms, but she felt like home was now a thousand universes away.

Tabby squeezed Ethan's hand as they sat vigil over Josh and Kiera's near lifeless bodies, their cold, pale eyes staring into distant nothing.

"What are we doing, Tabs?"

Tabby looked at Ethan then back to Kiera.

"I mean, this is insane."

"Ethan," Tabby suddenly said, motioning to Kiera.

Kiera's body seemed to be growing dim. No, not dim. She was fading. She appeared as though she were beginning to fade away.

"Oh god, Ethan, what's happening?"

"I don't know."

"Should we stop it? Can we break them apart?"

"Josh said there was nothing we could do. I think that means not to interfere."

"Ethan, she's disappearing. I can almost see through her."

"I know, but what if we break them apart and she gets stuck?"

"But Ethan," Tabby said, reaching.

"Tabby, just wait," Ethan said, squeezing Tabby's hand. He looked into her eyes. "We have to believe she's ok."

"Josh, something doesn't feel right this time. I feel different," Kiera said as they fell.

"What?"

"I feel thin. And I'm having trouble staying focused."

"Hang on, Kiera. We're almost there."

Just as Josh finished speaking, they stopped falling with such force that their physical bodies rebounded from the sudden stop and would have fallen face forward off the sofa if Ethan had not caught them.

"What the hell was that?" Ethan asked with wide eyes.

"Josh, are we here? I don't feel so good."

"Hang on, Kiera. It should be right over here."

The two of them had come to a stop in front of the broken doorway of what appeared to have once been the largest castle Kiera had ever seen. Josh made his way to an entrance partially blocked by the large stones that once made up a gatehouse wall. Josh began working to clear the debris. The large ones were too heavy to move, but fortunately, most of the large stones had broken up upon impact with the ground, so they were small enough for Josh to push out of the way.

"Kiera, come with me," Josh said, grabbing Kiera by the hand and dragging her up and over the mound of rocks and through the broken doorway.

They wove around a debris-littered bailey and into the castle keep.

"Come on. This way." Josh said, motioning across the great hall to a door on the other side of the chamber. Josh pushed open the door and stepped into another room that appeared to be some type of chapel or worship hall. Josh did not recognize the specific scenes depicted on the faded murals inside the room, but the story they conveyed felt familiar. Behind the broken alter was another door, large stones blocking piled on the floor in front of it. Josh ran across the chapel and began to excavate an opening through the doorway.

"Kiera, come with me."

"I can't move, Josh."

"What?"

"I can't move," Kiera replied in an almost dreamy voice devoid of fear, nervousness, or any other emotion other than listless melancholy.

Josh turned and froze.

"Kiera?"

Kiera's eyes, the eyes of her consciousness, were beginning to cover over with a film that resembled the black marble floor.

"Stay there, Kiera. I'll be right back."

Josh hurried over the remaining rocks, pushed through the narrowly excavated entrance, and rushed to a chest located on the floor near the base of the room's rear wall. There was a hole in the wall beside where the chest was sitting. Josh looked out and saw a world of nothingness. He could see the ruins of villages, other distant, collapsed castles, and the pale light of a dying sun holding this world in eternal twilight. There were no sounds of animals or people, no living vegetation, no crying of livestock from a distance. From what Josh could see through the dim glow of the dying sun, this world, which appeared to have once teemed with life, was now a graveyard, floating through endless space, guided only by the wane of a dying sun.

Josh heard Kiera calling him from beyond the doorway like a distant ghost.

"Almost done. Hang on," he called back.

Josh opened the chest and reached in to remove the key, which he had seen in Eulahtan's mind had been hidden there ages ago but found the box to be empty.

"No," Josh said, banging his fist on the rim of the box.

He stood and hurried back to the doorway. As he squeezed through the small hole he had excavated at the top of the rock pile, he froze.

"Kiera," he said. "I need you to walk over to me?"

"I can't move. I want to, but I can't move my feet." Her voice sounded like that of someone on the verge of deep sleep.

The wet slap of moist flesh on stone, followed by something dragging along the stone floor, came from a hallway behind Kiera.

"Kiera, I need you to listen to me," Josh said, trying to sound calm.

Another wet slap upon the floor. This time slightly closer.

"Kiera, please. Walk to me."

Josh struggled to get out of the tiny hole. He pushed at the crumbling wall, kicked at the stones in the pile to gain purchase, and worked to move forward and reach Kiera. The hair on Josh's neck raised when he heard a series of garbled clicks, followed by an answering set of clicks, coming from the direction of wet dragging flesh. Josh thought he felt the wall shift, and the hole seemed to tighten. He looked up and saw two figures approaching Kiera from the dark hall. One figure was tall and slender, with a curve in its spine that caused it to stand as if swaying to one side. The creature was difficult to see in the low light of the room. It was almost as if Josh felt the entity rather than saw it with his eyes. The second form was squat in appearance. It appeared to walk on six thick legs as it eyed Kiera from its head, perched atop a stalk of jiggly neck meat. As the second entity moved forward, it slowly crawled, making its way up the wall until it was on the ceiling. It continued toward Kiera, its feet letting out sloppy wet kisses on the stones with each forward movement.

"Kiera, please focus, please. I need you to concentrate on going home, okay? We both need to go home."

Josh gave one last push at the tiny hole and freed himself from the doorway. He rolled down the stone pile, landing hard on his side on the floor. He lay, panting to catch his breath after the hard thud to his ribs. The tall creature continued to advance until it stood beside Kiera, who seemed oblivious to its presence. The creature lifted the hand it dragged along the stones and placed it on Kiera's shoulder, grasping her with three long fingers. It sniffed her from the holes in its face where Josh thought a nose should have been. The creature's skin hung as if melted by fire but refused to sluff from its body. It ran a thin tongue from its small mouth and seemed to taste Kiera's right cheek as its saliva dripped around its feet like sewage from a leaky pipe. When the creature touched Kiera, her eyes grew darker, slipping deeper into the black marble haze that Josh saw when they arrived.

"Kiera, please listen." Josh pleaded. "Don't move. Let's go home, okay." He lifted a pleading hand toward her as if willing her to move. "We need to get back. I don't think we need to stay here any longer. Are you ready?"

"I don't know if I can, Josh. I feel like I need to lay down a minute."

"No, no, no. Just think about home, Kiera."

The creature sniffed her again and seemed to tremble with delight. The insect man was now perched directly over Kiera. The creature released three legs, swung them around, and attached itself to the ceiling again to face Kiera. Josh saw the flesh of the creature's belly quiver as a hole that reminded Josh of an anus appeared in the center of the creature's weeping flesh. The creature extended a set of thick tentacles from the hole within the folds of its stomach. The gelatinous tendrils stretched toward Kiera as if they had no end. Dark, foul-smelling fluid dripped from the tendrils as they stretched toward her. The creature's body gave a sloshing shudder as it produced a chattering series of gargling sounds. As the tendrils stretched closer to Kiera, the sound emanating from the creature changed from the sloppy guttural slosh to a deep-throated clicking. The sound caused Josh's knees to weaken at what must have been the sick sound of this creature's excited lust for its prey. With its arm around Kiera, the tall creature licked her face again with what looked like more excitement and aggression.

"Kiera, please. Snap out of this. Let's go now. Home Kiera, home!"

The creatures seemed to be ignoring Josh, so he tried more forcefully.

"Home, Kiera! Home now!" He thought to her.

Kiera's eyes seemed to lighten, and she said in a hushed breath, "Home, Josh."

Josh saw her essence disappear almost instantly as a tear of breaching barriers filled the black hall. Josh heard the two creatures' agonized screams as they saw their new visitor tear away into nothingness. Josh felt his bones vibrate at their ear-piercing screams. He shut his eyes and thought of home, then the creature's tormented cries were replaced by the sound of the fabric of space ripping around him. Josh focused on Kiera and felt her presence accelerate forward but not toward home.

"Kiera!"

He reached for her with his mind, felt her fingertips, then she was gone as he felt her essence slip beyond his grasp.

Ethan was pacing in front of the sofa, wringing his hands like a new father awaiting the first-born child of a troubled delivery. Tabby was standing, not realizing she was half holding her breath as she stared at the fabric covering the back of the sofa through a ghostly imprint of where Kiera's body should be sitting. As Kiera's mind pulled away, her body had faded. Tabby and Ethan could see the impression of her body's weight still imprinted on the seat cushion and back of the sofa. They could also see the binding that secured her arm to Josh's remained taut and seemed to be secured around an invisible mass. They also saw that the orange glow emanating from Josh and Kiera's bound hands was the amplifier ring Josh had made from the copper wiring. Through Kiera's transparent hand, they could see that the light was generated from the energy flowing through the coil between them. The energy first caused the coil to heat up, melt, then flow within their clenched hands in what seemed like a molten ribbon of metal and electricity. They saw when the wire fragment inserted into Kiera's palm came alive. It burrowed itself deeper, making its way up her arm, across her chest, and into her heart. It followed her veins into the inner portions of her heart and seemed to pulse brighter with every beat of her heart. Now it looked like a suspended tendril of glowing fire, running through her body and pulsing with a heart that was no longer there.

"Ethan," Tabby said, taking a step forward and beginning to breathe again.

Ethan turned and stopped pacing. The golden strand of molten energy began to shrink back from Kiera's heart, slowly unwinding from her chest and twisting its way down her arm, marking the path of her unseen veins. Her transparent form began to fade as her body began to replace the invisible girl. As Kiera's body solidified, her eyes slowly regained their color.

Josh moaned, then rolled toward Kiera and began to cry. "No, no, no, no, no. Kiera, please wake up. Please. No, no, no, no. Oh god, Kiera, please wake up."

Josh's body lurched as something pushed him. He felt the bindings drop from his arm as Ethan quickly sawed them loose with his knife. Ethan pushed Josh back against the sofa again and used the knife to cut away the remaining bindings that tethered Kiera to Josh. Once Josh's hand was free, he covered his face and continued to cry as he muttered, "No, no, no, no."

"Dear God, Ethan, what is this?" Tabby asked, roughly wiping the viscous fluid off Kiera's face and out of her hair with a damp towel she had retrieved from the bathroom.

Ethan checked Kiera's pulse. He placed his ear by her mouth to listen for breath. He scooped Kiera from the sofa and laid her on the coffee table. After two puffs of air into Kiera's mouth, Ethan began to press on Kiera's chest with interlaced hands, counting aloud with each thrust.

"One. Two. Three. Four. Five. Six. Seven."

He blew another two breaths into her lungs.

"One. Two. Three. Four. Five. Six. Seven."

He continued seven pushes, then two breaths. Josh continued to cover his face and cry, repeating the word "No," over and over as Tabby sobbed while frantically wiping the foul-smelling fluid out of Kiera's hair.

"Breath goddamn you. Breath." Ethan said just above the sound of a whisper through clenched teeth.

Ethan's senses seemed to close off to reality around him. He continued to pump Kiera's chest and offer her life from his lungs. Ethan heard Tabby crying distantly, saying, "Oh god no, baby. Please wake up. I need you. Please wake up," as she continued to wipe the putrid fluid on Kiera's face.

Behind her cries of agony were the sounds of Josh still covering his face as his cries rose to a silent, near breathless gasp of, "No, no, no, no. It's all my fault. Why? Please no, come back, come back," the last uttered in not much more than a whisper.

CHAPTER 42

"What do we do?"

Tabby and Josh looked at Ethan as if not fully understanding the question.

"So, what do we do now?" Ethan asked, wiping his face as he turned to look, once again, at Kiera's body still lying on the table. Tabby and Josh looked everywhere in the room except at Kiera's body as she lay, mouth agape, arms splayed, chest unmoving, with clouded eyes. Ethan sat staring at Kiera as memories of her smile bloomed in his mind. Ethan chuckled as he wiped his face again at the memory of her laughing at one of Tabby's stupid jokes. He remembered seeing the last time she Nick and Tabby were happy together and breathed deeply, expanding his chest to make room for his breaking heart. The pressure of losing this child of creativity and creation caused him to momentarily lose control as he struggled to keep himself from weeping openly. He averted his gaze from the now immobile angel.

Ethan turned back to Tabby and Josh, wiping away more tears, and said, "Josh, what happened?"

Josh refused to meet Ethan's eyes. He sat with his head facing the table as he sniffed and let out long, open-mouthed breaths. He wiped his face with a washcloth from the bathroom, then grabbed at a passing breath and said through quivering lips, "I am not entirely sure. I mean, I have an idea, but I can't be sure. I mean, if I would have known, I wou…." Josh stopped and began to cry again.

"Just try, Josh. We know what you and Kiera were doing was trying to help everyone, not just the four of us. I know it hurts. We're angry, yes. But not at you. I'm as much to blame as anyone." Ethan stopped and turned back to Kiera. His face warping into pain. He took another breath and looked up as if asking an unseen God why. Tabby reached across the table and squeezed Ethan's hand. Ethan recalled Tabby explaining to him about patients dealing with loss and abandonment, the emotions, pain, resentment, and ever-present loss. Ethan reached across the table and gave Josh's hand a fatherly squeeze. Josh broke and began sob in a low mournful wail that seemed to Ethan came from a place of deep anguish. Anguish that an ordinary teenage boy should not know or understand. Josh opened his mouth then closed it. He wiped at his face with the washcloth again. He looked back down at the table, wiped his tears from the table's surface, then sat pulling at the rag with his fingers.

"I killed her," Josh said, looking up.

"What?" Tabby asked, wide-eyed.

Josh looked up. "I killed her." He folded his arms on the tabletop and collapsed into them, hiding his face as his tears returned.

Tabby reached a mothering hand out and rubbed Josh's shoulder. "Josh, you did not kill—"

"I may as well have," Josh said, looking into Tabby's eyes. "I may as well have. I should not have taken her that far away. I shouldn't have done it."

"Josh, we need to know what happened. Can you please explain?"

Josh sat back in his chair and studied the rag in his hand. He picked at a frayed string on one corner of the cloth. "I just don't know why…" then he stopped. He wiped a tear away from his cheek with an angry hand, then adjusted, "I do know. That son of a bitch moved the key. He left that image for Kiera and me to find so we would follow his clue." He looked at Ethan with red eyes. "He set us up."

Ethan squeezed the hand of the lost child again and offered encouragement by saying, as delicately as he could, "Josh, just tell us what happened."

Josh looked at Ethan, drew in a couple more heavy breaths, trying to blow the pain from his chest, then began, "It was the inbetweeners."

"What? What is an inbetweener?"

Josh looked up, "The inbetweeners." Josh said as anger flashed across his face. "I didn't remember them until it was all happening, but I know now." He laughed, shrugged, and began to cry again, his face warping into shame.

"What, Josh?" Tabby asked. "What did they do to her?"

Josh seemed to gather his breath and summon something from deep within himself to offer a steady explanation.

"The inbetweeners are the ones who live in the layers between of our physical realities. They are always trying to access our realities so that they can benefit," then he amended with the truth, "no, not benefit, *feed* on us, our energies. There was never a way for the inbetweeners to breach the barriers of the multiverse until Eulahtan destroyed the core verse. Once it was compromised, it set off a ripple effect. The wave left tears everywhere."

"What is the core verse," Tabby asked as she dabbed her eye again with her towel.

"The core verse was the blueprint, the foundation." Josh looked at Ethan and Tabby, not seeing true understanding on their faces. He continued, "The core verse is the blueprint for all the other universes."

"My God, the Architects created all the universes?" she asked.

"No. They didn't create any of the universes. Someone else did that."

"Wait, wait, wait. What about the big bang?"

Josh turned to Ethan, "There was a big bang. We just didn't cause it. That was someone we have never met and never *hoped* to meet. We always suspected it was an inbetweener race of people but never found any evidence of them. Some people even theorized that at some point, we were the antiverse races and the inbetweeners the original Architects."

"So, what did they do to Kiera?"

"So, these inbetweeners are the ones that live, no not live, exist, in the space between the physical realms. They have always wanted nothing more than to feed on the light energies, like how a negative and positive charge attracts one another. There is no way for these beings to move across a barrier and interact with the living realities until the rips happened."

"So, if there is no way for them to interact with us, how did they get to you guys?"

"I think," Josh began, "It is because Eulahtan killed that universe, too. Maybe if there is no life in a reality, then maybe they are free to take over because a dead reality is nothing more than another lifeless space."

"Wait a minute," Tabby interjected, "Hold on. I thought you said that these creatures could not cross over and that Eulahtan would die if he destroyed a universe."

"He will. There's a catch, though. You see, Eulahtan was not from the core verse. He has a different resonance. He could destroy it without suffering from its demise. I think Parzeus corrupted Eulahtan's mind so badly that he doesn't even know causing the death of this universe will cause his own death. He used the core universe's destruction as a trial run. Once that verse was dead, nothing was stopping the inbetweeners from invading and scavenging the leftover life from anything that survived. There was just not enough resonance to keep them locked in their own dimension. I think Eulahtan uses the inbetweeners as a failsafe for a verse's destruction. Once the verse is dead, the inbetweeners claim it as another level of their realm since there is no intervening power to stop them. I didn't remember until I saw them...." Josh began to cry again, "I didn't remember any of this until I saw them, then another puzzle piece fell into place." Josh began to strike the side of his head with the palm of his hand.

Tabby grabbed his hand and said, "Josh, stop. That will not help." Josh stopped and looked at Tabby, his lips trembling. He used the rag to wipe the snot from his lips.

Josh wiped his eyes and looked at Ethan, "Life. Each layer of the multiverse has, like, a frequency. Each space between resonates on the same frequency as the others. What we know as living realities vibrate at different quantum frequencies. The life in each universe creates a harmonic resonance that repels the incursion of anything from the in-between spaces."

"Until a rip appears," Ethan said.

Josh nodded. "Sometimes things leak through, but for the most part, the frequencies of the opposing dimensions repel one another. Once the frequency gets weak enough, the amount of life that exists cannot create a large enough signal, then the barriers meld and essentially become the same region of space and time. The negative space."

"I thought you said nothing lives in these spaces," Tabby said.

"There is nothing alive in those spaces. Not life how we define it anyway. Those things don't know mercy, love, hate or family, or any of the concepts we consider necessary to constitute life or society. They don't have hearts that beat. They don't seem to form families. They don't need food, water, or air, as far as we can tell. They just exist. No one ever figured out where they came from or why they are in those spaces. It's almost like they are an underverse, a negative charge to the living universes' positive charge. It's like they are there just to keep the living verses in balance somehow. The one thing we do know is that they will kill anything in the living verses if left unchecked. I don't mean they will tear us apart or eat us. They feed on us by draining our essences. They feed on the energy of our souls."

"Oh god. Is that what happened to Kiera?" Tabby asked as she wiped her cheeks with a fresh tissue.

"I don't know. I guess. I didn't see them do anything other than touch her, but I don't know how they feed or how long it takes to," Josh swallowed back another burst of tears, "eat someone's soul."

"Is there any way to get her energy back, to replenish it?"

"No. Even if there was, I can't get back to that verse without Kiera. Somehow," Josh looked over to Kiera's body, "somehow, she was a beacon that guided me to that spot. I mean, I saw it in Eulahtan's mind, but Kiera somehow knew where we were going, and I don't even think she knew that I was following her."

After a moment of quiet, Ethan asked, "What do these inbetweeners look like?"

"They're almost like snowflakes. Each one is different. You never want to see one of these things. Think of any nightmare you have ever had or heard someone describe, then multiply it by a thousand."

Tabby got up and walked to Kiera's body. She sat down on the floor and began to rub Kiera's cheek and clean her hair again. Ethan walked over, took her by the shoulders, and urged her up into his arms. After a moment, she turned to Josh. When her gaze fell on him, there was rage in her eyes. The like Josh had never seen directed at him, then Tabby spat through clenched teeth, "You better make this count, Josh. You better make sure that Kiera didn't die for no reason. I don't give a damn what it costs any of us. Do you understand me?" Josh nodded, then Tabby quickly went into the bathroom and closed the door behind her to cry until her reservoir emptied.

Ethan walked back over to stand beside Josh, laying a gentle hand on his shoulder. Josh was sitting, eyes closed, sobbing into his hands. Ethan gave him a gentle squeeze, and Josh wiped his face and looked up.

"She wasn't angry with you. She just wants Kiera back. I do too." Ethan sniffed and ran a hand over his cheek. "We just need to make this count, all of us. We can't dishonor Kiera by failing to stop whatever it is that Eulahtan is trying to do." Ethan sat down in the chair beside Josh. "Look, I was raised to believe that there could be no quit in me. I have never let myself be labeled a quitter. Figure out what you need to figure out because I assure you, this is going to end, one way or another."

Josh nodded.

"Look, tell Tabby I will be back in a few minutes if she comes out of the bathroom before I get back."

"Where are you going?"

"I need to take a walk and check on a couple of things. I'll be right back," Ethan got up, grabbed the keys to the rental car from the nightstand, and left the room.

After twenty minutes, the bathroom door opened, and Tabby came out with red but dry eyes. Her face was steel. She looked at Josh, although this time there was no longer the flash of rage in her eyes, she looked again at Kiera. Josh had taken the top sheet off one of the beds and covered Kiera so that no one could see her open, cloudy eyes that had once reflected her deep love of life. Tabby walked over to the table where Josh was still seated.

"Where is Ethan?" Tabby asked, taking a seat.

"He said to tell you he would be back in a minute. He went for a walk."

"Did he say where?"

"No, just that he wanted to check a couple of things."

"Look, Josh," Tabby said, reaching across the table and lightly touching one of Josh's hands, "I know that it's not your fault."

"It is my fault," Josh argued. "If I didn't take her there, to that place, she would still be sitting here with us. And the worst part is that it was for no reason." Josh added as he began to cry again.

"Listen. You couldn't have known. No one could have known. I believe Kiera wouldn't blame you. She was one of the most incredible people I have ever known. She couldn't walk into a room without the sun shining a little brighter. She had a choice, and she was always the one making strong decisions about her life. Yeah, that was Kiera," Tabby said, leaning back in her chair. "She was was like a sun surrounded by candles."

"Maybe so, but I still took her there. Me. She would have never known anything about that place if I had not told her about it."

"I get it, but now, what we need to focus on is making sure that her sacrifice mattered, that her death was a price worth paying."

To this, Josh had no reply. He sat in stone silence, looking once again at the table's surface in front of him. He wanted to tell Tabby what he believed was the real reason for Kiera's death but was afraid Tabby would hate him. Tabby started to get up from the chair but stopped when Josh said, "I've been thinking more about it." Tabby looked at him and sat back down. "I thought about it some more, and I remember something called Rendell's Principle of Subversive Separation.

Tabby wobbled her head and raised her eyebrows. "Okay, what is subversive separation?"

Josh looked up, his lips still trembling, "The best way to understand it is to think of a rubber band."

Tabby tilted her head and furrowed her brow, not understanding the reference.

"You know how when you stretch a rubber band. It gets thinner? If you keep stretching it, it gets thinner and thinner until it snaps, then flies off somewhere. There was an observed phenomenon when we were first learning this shifting of our essence," Josh paused, seemed to rethink his explanation, and began again. "If you are a physical being, when you move your consciousness to another realm, you are essentially using a tether. Imagine your essence is a rubber band that stretches between your body and wherever you send your consciousness. Imagine the further away your consciousness goes from its body, the thinner the tether is stretched until, just like a rubber band, if you stretch it too far, it snaps and flies off. I think that could also be what happened to Kiera. She was so far away that her tether snapped. I didn't know we were going to the core verse, or I would have never tried to amplify our connection," Josh rolled his hand over and looked at the spot of dried blood on his palm, then rubbed at it with the thumb of his other hand. "She was amazing. She should not have been able to extend herself half the distance to the core verse, much less all the way. I don't even know how she did it."

"Yep, that was my girl," hearing herself refer to Kiera in the past tense. Tabby placed her hand on her stomach as if to hold her insides together. She swallowed, then said, "She was one of the most amazing people, amazing heart, I have ever known. God, I loved her. It was like we were sisters from the first time we ever met. Did I tell you how she and I met?"

Josh shook his head, but before Tabby could say anything, they both turned as the door clicked open. They turned to see Ethan entering the room, pushing a large square cart with cloth sides. Josh could see the word 'Linen' printed on the cart's side as Ethan wheeled it up beside the sitting area coffee table.

"What are you doing?" Tabby asked.

"I'm not leaving her," Ethan said. As he turned to Tabby, she could see the pain lining every inch of Ethan's face. Even though he held his lips pressed into a tight, straight line, they still trembled against the pain he was fighting to keep under control.

"I am not leaving her here like a murdered whore in some shitty movie. We're leaving now, and we're taking Kiera with us. Josh, give me a hand."

Josh hurried over and grabbed Kiera's legs as Ethan grabbed her under the arms. Together they gently lifted her and laid her in the bottom of the linen cart.

"Ethan, I don't want to leave her here either, but how are we supposed to get a body out of a hotel? We'll get arrested before we get out of the lobby."

Ethan glanced at Tabby, then said, "It's not a problem. Get your stuff."

Tabby quickly grabbed her belongings which now only consisted of her new identity cards and stuffed them into her pants pocket.

"Let's go." Ethan began to wheel the cart out of the room.

"I don't think anyone is up yet, but if they are, just follow me and don't talk to anyone."

"But we're parked right in front of the main entrance to the hotel."

"Nope, where do you think I went. I found a spot with no cameras around the side of the hotel and moved the car. I also found the service elevator and a side exit. I moved the car over by that exit. It should be a blind spot in their security configuration."

Ethan turned left, away from the guest elevator, and stopped in front of an elevator marked 'Staff.' He reached into his pocket and pulled a keycard out, swiped it through the slot of the service elevator card scanner, then waited as the elevator doors slowly opened. They got into the elevator and watched the empty hallway as the doors closed behind them. Once the elevator reached the ground level, Ethan pushed the cart out as Josh and Tabby followed. He turned to his right and used his butt to depress the crash bar of a door with the word 'Exit' displayed on a sign above it, then pulled the cart through the doorway into the parking lot at the side of the hotel. Tabby looked around the parking lot, saw their rental car two spaces away, and moved in that direction.

"Josh, help me get her in the back," Ethan said, bringing the cart to a stop at the rear of the car.

Once Kiera was safely laid in the back of the rented Tahoe, Ethan,

Tabby, and Josh got into the car.

"Okay, Josh, where to now?" asked Ethan, looking at Josh in the rearview mirror.

"Just west, keep heading west. I think he is headed for Arizona."

Ethan sniffed, gave a deep-chested sigh, then guided the car onto the highway heading away from the brimming morning sun.

CHAPTER 43

Tabby and Ethan stood at the open rear hatch of the Tahoe, looking at the sheet covering Kiera's body. One of her hands had shifted and was now exposed, neatly manicured nails visible. Tabby gave her cheek an angry wipe and took a deep breath, forcing her emotions to run dry. Her lips pressed together in anger, not sadness, at the loss of her sister in spirit. If there were truly *any* justice anywhere in this universe, she would kill Eulahtan for creating the circumstances that had led to Kiera's death, leaving a pain inside her that felt like hammer blows deep within her gut. Tabby felt a weight on her chest again as a deep pain in her belly swelled once more. She turned red, weary eyes to Ethan and saw him frozen in a dead glare at the sheet. The true tragedy was that no one would ever know how Kiera always saw the world in the light of every color and shade. She had flung herself a thousand universes away in a selfless attempt to save a world that would never know her name or her sacrifice. There would be no editorials, no parades, no presidential medals for this angel of Tabby's heart. Still, Tabby vowed to remember and playback her life in memories until Tabby's mind failed. She wiped her cheek again, then turned to see Ethan standing with clenched fists, refusing to give up his swollen tears to the thirsty earth.

Tabby reached over and took his hand. Ethan turned to her, pain marking every weary line on his face. Ethan swallowed his pain down in one large gulp as if choking on a stone. The tremor Tabby felt in his hand was not from fear. Tabby knew Ethan was past fear now. She saw the truth in his eyes. Ethan pushed his loss down deep to make way for his rage and his anger. He was weaponizing his pain, giving it had time to blossom into a breaking wave against the creature that had once been his best friend.

"Come on," Tabby said softly, wiping her cheek again, "We need to move. Josh says he's close, but he still has a giant head start on us."

Ethan did not answer, only nodded as a single tear overcame Ethan's struggle and fell from his eye to feed the thirsty earth. Ethan leaned over Kiera's body and produced a bow and arrow set, as well as the wilderness survival machete collection he had picked up after they had crossed the state line. He took one final look at Kiera, wiped his nose with the back of one hand, then closed the vehicle's rear hatch. Ethan imagined the closing door was like the closing of what may well be Kiera's casket. If they failed, no one would come back from the canyon to give Kiera the proper care and respect that only their small group knew she deserved. The rear hatch made a soft click as it latched, followed by a barely audible hum of an electric motor as the latch tightened its hold and sealed.

Ethan turned to Tabby and gave her a large knife, the edge of which felt like it could cut through a tree and whose serrated top looked as if it could saw through rock. The outfitter who ran the store told Ethan, "This one's made for hacking. It'll make short work of any-thing you might run into in this area." Well, hacking through a few things, like perhaps limbs and neckbones, was Ethan's intention, so he had gotten three, one for each of them. He stopped himself when he realized he was reaching for a fourth blade for someone who was no longer there. He closed his eyes and shuddered at the memory of the hotel room.

He turned and gave Josh a knife and a machete that was identical to Tabby's and told them both, "Look, we are going to have to run as much of this as we can. Josh, how are you at distance running?" Ethan knew Tabby's routine of a three-mile morning run three days a week, and he usually ran a good two miles after a long cross-fit session.

Josh returned Ethan's question with a wide-eyed stare at first, then answered, "Well, I never ran track in school or anything like that, but I play a lot of pickup basketball, and I've mowed a lot of lawns in the summer for the past two years. Push mower mowing," he added for extra clout.

"Okay. Well, this is going to be for distance, not for speed. Let's set a pace so everyone can stay steady and together. I will start, then let's adjust from there. There's also going to be a lot of areas where we won't be able to run. We still need to move as fast as possible in those areas, but safety will be the priority. Are we ready?"

Tabby and Josh nodded but said nothing.

"Alright, let's get it," and with that, Ethan turned and headed to the trailhead at a brisk pace, with Tabby and Josh following on his heels. After three hours of descending, in an almost uneventful passage marked with periods of running, walking, and climbing, the trio came to a small opening in the cavern wall.

"Here," Josh said, stopping to wipe his brow with his shirttail while trying to catch his breath. "I can feel him in this direction."

"Are you sure?" Ethan panted. "I don't want to get stuck in a crack in the earth on some hunch."

"Yes, I can feel him. And look," he said, pointing to a debris field in front of the opening, "These rocks have clean breaks on them like they were just busted or something. I can't explain. I can just feel him in this direction, and well, this hole is the only thing here."

"Alright, it's all we've got. Let's get moving." The group walked into the cave's opening and vanished into the bowels of the earth.

"I don't like this," Ethan said, shining a flashlight around the tunnel. "I feel like we're walking into a," What Ethan wanted to say was a tomb but instead opted for, "well, I don't know, but I don't like it."

"I don't either, but I know he came this way. Look, here." Josh said, motioning to an apparent end to the tunnel.

"Yeah, but where did he go? It's a dead end." Tabby asked.

Josh looked up, "I think he is on the surface again."

"How? How the hell are we supposed to get up there now? We probably made a mile in this cave by now?" Ethan flicked his bow around in his hand. "Jesus, Josh, we have to be under a mile of rock by now. If he's over us, how did he climb out? Does anyone see any openings or cracks in the ceiling?"

Everyone strafed the cave ceiling with their flashlights.

"Hey, look at this," Josh said, pointing to an outcrop of rock on the cave wall's face. "What do you guys see when you look at that area there?" Josh motioned for the others to look at the rock protuberance in the craggy wall's surface. "Does this rock kind of look like a face to you guys?"

After looking at the rock more closely, Tabby pointed then said, "Yeah, it does. Look, this could be eyes, and here could be a mouth."

The face had deep-set eyes with curly hair that blended into the wall and wrapped around the forehead. In the area where the mouth should have been was a roughly chipped hole with what resembled a tongue pressed out in a maniacal laugh that matched the high raised cheekbones of the bust. Josh felt along the surface of the bust. "Yeah, this could even be a nose," he said. He felt the image's nose with his finger, then quickly jerked his hand away as the nose sunk into the rocky face. The empty eye sockets began to glow pale blue.

"Whoa," Ethan said in a low voice, "What the hell did you do?"

Josh looked at Ethan, eyes wide, and shrugged, "It just seemed right to me. I think it's a transport control system. He must have come down here to get something before he could get started with his ritual. Look at that spot." Josh pointed to a set of drag marks on the floor. "It looks like something was recently moved around down here.

"Okay, but still, what does that do for us? How do we get up there?" Tabby asked no one in particular. "There's no way we could get out of this damn cave and make it back up the trail before daybreak, much less back across the canyon to wherever Nick's gone in time to stop him." She wiped the sweat from her forehead, causing a muddy smear to appear above her eyes.

Josh responded, "I don't know, but if this thing is—"

He was interrupted by Ethan grabbing his arm and saying, "Sh, listen. Do you guys hear that?

"Yeah." Tabby tilted her head to one side and furrowed her brow. "It sounds mechanical."

Ethan looked at Tabby as if agreeing with her.

"Josh, Ethan asked, "is this a good or bad thing?"

"I don't—"

"Yeah yeah, you don't know. Well, do you know if we need to run?

It sounds like whatever it is, it's winding up to something. It's gone from clanking to humming."

Before anyone could say another word, a cloud of dust and small pebbles pelted them from above as a cluster of lighted rings descended from the roof of the cavern. The rings dropped so fast it took a moment to realize they were trapped within the wall of glowing rings. The lowest ring was resting on the cavern floor, and each subsequent ring hovered about six inches above the ring below.

"It's is at least twenty feet to the top," Ethan said, scanning the cylinder. "Josh, do you know what this is? Can we climb it?"

"I think, but I'm not sure."

"Is it safe to touch?" Ethan asked, slinging his bow across his chest. As Ethan reached out to touch one of the rings, a bright light filled the cylinder beginning from the bottom ring and continuing up the structure until the light vanished into the bedrock above. The flash lasted less than half a second.

Before anyone could register what had happened, they found themselves standing under the stars of a cloudless night sky.

"Jesus," Ethan said slowly. "Did we just—"

"Yeah, I think we did," Tabby said in between pants.

"Oh, God. I may be sick." Ethan said, bending over and propping his hands on his knees. He closed his eyes and breathed deep heavy breaths to calm his churning stomach.

Josh was scanning the area around them. "Where is Eulahtan? I don't see him."

Ethan stood back up and began checking the area as well.

"Yeah, I don't see anything either."

"There," Josh said, pointing to an area roughly two hundred yards away.

Ethan and Tabby saw a faint glow coming through the trees.

"Is it him?" asked Tabby.

"Yes, that's definitely the direction, but my sense of him is weaker now." Josh shook his head. He didn't understand why his connection with Eulahtan seemed to be no more than a thin whisper now that he was this close to him.

"Well, what do you guys say we get over there, find out what he's doing, then see if we can ruin his night," Ethan suggested with a grin.

As they crept toward the glowing light through the trees, they could see a clearing with a large rock in the center of it. Eulahtan seemed to be sitting quietly in front of the rock, appearing to meditate.

"Did he moved that rock by himself? That thing is the size of a car."

"I guess. I don't see any equipment."

Ethan dropped to his hands and knees and began to crawl toward the treeline.

"Ethan," Tabby said, grabbing his pant leg. "What are you doing? There is nowhere to hide out there."

"I know, but why is he just sitting there? We need to try to get closer."

"He is performing the Ritual of Right," Josh said.

"The ritual of what? Right? What is that?" Ethan asked as he stole a brief glance in Josh's direction, then back toward Eulahtan.

"It is a ritual where you gather power, kind of like charging up before you perform a very demanding task."

"Is all the stuff he's doing, with the words, the clapping, and now this meditating... Is it like magic?" Ethan shook his head in disbelief at hearing a question like this fall from his mouth.

"No. There is no magic. Magic, the *real* magic, is only science that humans haven't figured out yet."

"Then why the rituals, the words, the specific places?" Ethan asked, motioning to Eulahtan as he continued to sit calmly in front of the rock.

Josh seemed to search his thoughts. "I think, once you learn to exist in an ascended space, many of the objects, the power sources in the universe," he amended, "are accessible to you. Different areas, words, actions. They all have peaks and valleys in their component energy that can be manipulated differently, like adjusting frequencies on a radio."

"Okay, that almost makes sense, I guess."

"Well, we don't have time for me to explain it any better than that. Just understand that all energy and matter can be manipulated using harmonic resonance. And the rituals, they are kind of like tuning a guitar."

Ethan looked at Josh with a confused look again, so Josh added, "You know, like when you tighten or loosen a guitar string to get it to vibrate at the correct pitch. On an ascended plane, words carry weight. They have meanings other than just the value of their space on a page."

"So, how long will this ritual take?"

Josh looked at Tabby. He closed his eyes and seemed to be trying to dig up another buried memory. After a moment, he opened his eyes and said, "It seems like this takes just over an hour. Maybe an hour and ten."

"Great, and we don't know how long he's been here."

"No," Josh said, "He hasn't even begun the final ritual yet. I can feel him getting stronger. I think when he blew up McCaversville, he drained himself. He also had to charge the portal to bring that rock from the cave. I think his batteries are low. I can feel him recharging, though. He's not meditating. He's powering up."

"So, once he's powered up, it will take about an hour to complete the ritual?"

Josh nodded.

"So, what we need to do is somehow put a stop to this."

"Yeah, but I haven't figured that part out yet."

"If I shoot him, will it distract him enough to slow him down?"

"Not likely, probably won't even affect him."

Ethan looked down at the bow in his hand, then back to Josh, "Then why the hell did I run across this canyon carrying this damn thing?" He held the bow up to Josh.

"I thought you brought that along for snakes and stuff."

"Snakes." Ethan rolled his eyes. "So, then how can we stop him?"

Josh dug again, shifting the puzzle pieces around in his mind until he had what he thought was a plan. "Okay, the last twenty or so minutes of the ritual will take all of his concentration and power. He won't even know that we are here, not even if we are standing right beside him. That is our window."

"So, your whole plan is for us to sit here with our thumbs in our asses until the final minutes before what we think is the end of the world?"

"I think it's our best shot."

"Oh my god," Ethan said, sitting down and looking up at the sky. "We have to try something." Ethan looked at his bow. He removed an arrow from the quiver attached to the bow's side. He nocked the arrow.

Josh looked at Ethan and held his hand up. "No. Don't." Josh pleaded in a low breath as he crawled toward Ethan on his belly.

"I can't just sit here. I have to try something."

Ethan raised himself from the ground to a kneeling position and aimed the arrow toward the still sitting Eulahtan. He steadied his breathing, remembering back to the last time he had hunted big game. In his mind, he could almost smell the falling leaves on the crisp November air. The rustle of the dried foliage dancing in a weak fall breeze filled his mind. He could smell the wet earth and almost felt the cool autumn breeze brush his face as he drew the arrow back and held it steady. Ethan adjusted his bow's elevation for what he knew at this range was a kill shot into his best friend's back. He closed his eyes, took in a deep, steadying breath, and held it. Clearing the image of Nick from his head and replacing it with the image of a deer, he opened his eyes and loosed the arrow. The bowstring twanged as the arrow left its nest and bolted across the clearing on its course toward Eulahtan's heart. As the arrow met its target, an explosion shook the ground. Nick/Eulahtan was flung back and rolled across the ground. The night lit up for an instant as the sound of a rotor-wing aircraft, beating the air, cane into earshot from a distance, spewing a barrage of tracer bullets into the earth around Eulahtan's body. Ethan could see by the motion of Eulahtan's body that many of the rounds hit their mark, causing him to lurch under the force of each thundering strike.

When the firing stopped, Eulahtan slowly got to his feet and stood heaving, black blood oozing from his wounds, as a second helicopter sped out of the night toward him, firing another barrage. Eulahtan clawed his way up the side of the rock then limped around behind it. The pilot saw the movement, so he yanked on the stick. The aircraft turned in a steep bank to swing around for a pass at Eulahtan from another angle. As the chopper passed over the rock, Eulahtan looked up and sent a thought to the pilot. The lumbering vehicle slowed and came to a hover about two hundred feet above the ground. It began to rotate as the first helicopter came beating back toward the area. Once the first helicopter had flown to within a few hundred feet of the second helicopter, the second helicopter pilot opened fire. The rounds from the hovering demon tore through the opposing pilot's chest, causing his limp hands to fall from the controls. The helicopter listed then quickly spun into the desert floor in a burst of flames. After the crash, the second helicopter nosed down and accelerated over the rock and into the night. Once it reached the area where the first helicopter had crashed, the pilot banked his helicopter steeply, rolling belly up like a dying whale until it fell out of the air and crumpled into a flaming heap not far from the site of the other crash.

Eulahtan stepped around the rock and stood staring at the wreckage in the distance. Ethan could see a spider's web of white energy shining from the wounds where the rounds had struck him. He watched as the wounds glowed brightly at first and then dimmed into nothing as the tiny energy flashes wove Eulahtan's flesh back together.

Ethan, Tabby, and Josh ducked back into the trees. Ethan wasn't sure if they had been seen or not. While Eulahtan confronted the helicopters, so he stole a cautious glance around the tree he was hiding behind.

"Who the hell was that?" Ethan asked.

"It must have been the Nasaru," Tabby replied.

"How did they find us?" Ethan asked, nervously scratching at his neck.

"Ethan, hold on," Josh said, then reached up and put his hand on Ethan's neck and closed his eyes.

"What are you doing?"

"Sh. Hold on a minute. Yeah, I can feel it."

"Feel what?"

"I feel an electrical pulse coming from where you have been scratching on your next since we left Atlanta."

"What does—" Ethan began as he tried to push Josh's hand from his neck.

"Hold still." Josh closed his eyes again. The hair on the back of Ethan's head felt as if it were beginning to stand on ends as a warm tingle began to grow from the spot on Ethan's neck where Josh held his hand.

"Josh, what are—"

"Hold on."

Ethan felt something under his skin begin to move like a parasite, an invader from within his body. It wasn't a painful sensation, but it was uncomfortable. The warmth grew, the tingling sensation increased then it suddenly stopped.

Josh removed his hand from Ethan's neck. Ethan reached up and began to rub the spot where Josh laid his hand.

"What did you do?"

Josh held out his hand showed Ethan a capsule-shaped object about half the size of a grain of white rice.

"This," Josh said. "They let us escape. They have been tracking us the entire time using these." He pushed the little tracker around in his hand with his finger. "They couldn't find him. They didn't have the key. They didn't know how their ancestors stopped him, so they needed us. They needed us to escape and lead them to him. We were rats in their little maze the entire time."

"Those fucking bastards. All this time. They could have helped us all this time, but instead, they just used us. We did the work, we ran across this fucking canyon, we found him, and they didn't do a damn thing." Ethan turned to Josh and grabbed the back of his head, and pulled him in close, "Kiera may not have died if they would have helped."

Tears swelled in Josh's eyes. When Ethan saw, he pulled Josh closer until their foreheads touched. "No. No. Not you, Josh. This is not on you." Ethan's tears mixed on the dry ground with Josh's, and he said again, "No. You will not carry this on your shoulders. You tried to do the only thing you knew. It's not you." Ethan pulled back, his hand still clasped on the back of Josh's head. He looked into Josh's eyes. "This is not on you. Do you understand? We did what we could. Those bastards are the ones that will carry her blood. Do you understand?"

Josh nodded, tears still welling. He wiped his nose with a dirty hand and nodded again. Tabby sniffed, wiped her eyes, then said, "He's right, Josh. You did the only thing we knew to do."

Ethan smiled, patted Josh's shoulder, looked at Tabby, and said, "That could not be all the Nasaru had in their arsenal. Surely they have more than two stupid helicopters as the Nasaru's full-frontal assault plan."

Ethan peeked around the tree he was tucked behind to see what he was doing. He didn't see Eulahtan moving around within the pale shifting orange glow of the burning wreckage. Where in the hell did he go? Ethan turned back to the others and used two fingers to point first at his eyes, then to the distance.

"No," Tabby whispered as she grabbed his arm.

"It's okay," he whispered, then gently but firmly removed her hand from his arm.

Ethan slowly rose and began to ease along in the direction of the rock like a stalking cat, his head on a swivel. He scanned the area for any sign of movement or activity as he stalked. About thirty feet beyond the perceived safety of his tree, he stopped at the sound of a snap. Turning his head in the direction of the sound, he strained at the shadows trying to glimpse whatever had broken the twig. Crack. Ethan strained harder, his eyes nearly pulsing orbs of pain, only to find dim movement of black ghosts cast in a soulless dance from the firelight of the burning wreckage. He took a deep breath and wiped the sweat from his brow as the sound of his billowing lungs roared in his ears.

The twigs stayed silent. The shadows remained still. Ethan began to breathe again. As he started to turn back toward the rock, he felt the ground beneath his feet vibrate from the weight of a heavy mass thudding beside him. Before Ethan could register what was happening, a hand was around his throat. He managed a wheezing cry of, "Run!" to the others before his throat completely closed from the vice around his neck. Tabby screamed as she saw Eulahtan lift Ethan off the ground with one hand and drew back a clenched fist to strike him in his chest. Eulahtan turned when he heard Tabby's screams.

"Run, Tabby!" Josh yelled, "Run!"

Tabby looked one more time at Ethan and saw his fear, fear not for himself, but her, in his eyes, and she found her feet. Tabby did run, but not toward the darkening forest. She ran toward Eulahtan, her long knife raised in the air, with a primal yell of rage echoing across the canyon's rim. Rushing toward Eulahtan, she brought the machete down. Her strike aimed to remove Eulahtan's arm from his body. The blow missed as Tabby's sight changed from the dim of night to black. Eulahtan's free hand swung out, striking her along the side of her head. Tabby's body flew up and back, smashing headfirst into a tree then spinning down onto the ground. Tabby's jaw exploded with radiating pain through the top of her head as it shifted just before the world disappeared into nothing.

Hot tears flowed down Ethan's face. He beat and clawed at Eulahtan's arm. He used the last of his might to hit Eulahtan in the face with his bow. The strike caused Ethan's hand to sear in white-hot pain.

The blow seemed to do nothing more than divert Eulahtan's attention away from Tabby's motionless body and back fully to Ethan.

Eulahtan's grip slowly tightened around Ethan's neck. The pressure behind Ethan's eyes felt as if his head would explode. He pulled at the hand and kicked like a man in a hangman's noose. Ethan kicked Eulahtan in the groin with his dangling feet, which he seemed to barely noticed. The darkening circle of black overtaking Ethan's vision thickened. Ethan used his free hand to claw at the side of his bow, trying to grab onto one of the arrows from the quiver attached to the weapon's side. His fingers found a broad-tipped arrow and pulled it free. He raised the arrow and drove it down toward Eulahtan's neck with all his failing strength. Before the arrow struck its mark, Ethan felt as if an ape had seized his arm. He struggled against the ape-like grip as Eulahtan used his overwhelming strength to pull Ethan's hand away from his neck with the arrow still clenched in it. Once Eulahtan had pulled the arrow away from his neck, he began to pull on Ethan's arm. Eulahtan loosened his grip on Ethan's neck just enough so Ethan would remain awake for this part of his penance for the transgression of daring to attempt to stab him. Eulahtan pulled on Ethan's arm, stretching it until Ethan was sure his arm was about to rip from his shoulder. With a quick jerk, Ethan's arm bent into an unnatural angle with a crack like a twenty-two caliber rifle shot. He screamed as the bones in his lower forearm snapped, sending white-hot fire up his arm and into his chest. The arrow dropped from his hand. Ethan tried to scream, but the sound came out in more of a muted wheeze because of the pressure wrapped around his neck.

Eulahtan pulled Ethan close and sniffed.

"Do you smell it, bug?"

Ethan looked at him through failing eyes.

Eulahtan smelled Ethan again, then said, "Do you smell the fear? The dwindling? I smell the past overtaking you, bug."

Ethan heard Eulahtan let out a deep-throated laugh.

Josh sat behind a tree with his arms wrapped around his knees, rocking back and forth in an almost animalistic panic. Burning tears flowed down his face. He chattered to himself as he listened to his two friends suffering at Eulahtan's hands. He covered his ears and began to whimper. "No, no, no," he cried out into the night, "No, no, no." His mind whirled back to Kiera, lying dead in the back of the rental car. His fault. Kiera would be alive if he would have never taken her to that place. He remembered their journey to the black, the pocket between the spaces. He thought back to their shared bond. He, an orphan, and she a stranger slammed together by a fate they did not fully understand. He thought of Ethan playing his tough-guy routine. The persona he used to try to make the world see him as a hard man, yet knowing, Josh thought, that the hard façade only wrapped around one of the kindest hearts he had ever met. Then there was Tabby, the woman Josh had realized had a fatal weakness, her greatest strength, in her character. Tabby's fatal flaw was that she cared too much for the humanity she dealt with every day. Tabby's heart was too big to effectively be kept behind the walls of a single person's chest. Where the world looked out and saw a seething crawl of the infestation of humanity upon a perfect planet, Tabby only saw the hurt, loss, worry, and hope of individuals that, to her, counted in the grand plan of mankind's existence. Tabby's flaw was perfect love of her fellow man and of this useless orphan whose only apparent success so far in life was to kill the first true friends he had ever known. At that moment, something in Josh broke, his tears falling like rain from a tropical storm, streaking his dirty face, shirt, and the ground beneath him. Just as Josh thought he was breaking, something broke loose inside him then something began to rise. Something new.

Josh stood up, wiped his face, and stepped from the cover of the tree. He turned to Eulahtan, and with clenched fists, Josh screamed from the bellows of his lowest reach, "No!" As he did, a wave of energy went out with his voice like he had never felt before and seemed to strike Eulahtan in a concentrated punch. Eulahtan stumbled, nearly losing his footing. Eulahtan looked at Josh, rage flashing in his empty eyes. He let go of Ethan's limp arm and then, with the ease of a child tossing a ball, flung Ethan away like yesterday's garbage. Ethan, too hit a tree as he flew. He felt a pop in his back as he fell to the ground a short distance from where Tabby's still motionless body had come to rest. He lay moaning as he gasped for air, trying to push away the black circle of sleep that had almost overtaken him over.

Eulahtan turned to Josh, a sick smile dripping with hate and disdain. He bowed to Josh in fake honor then began to walk toward him. "It is so nice to see you, Nathalue. I have missed you so these many eons." Every word pouring from Eulahtan's mouth like poison. "Here we are," Eulahtan said, holding out both hands like an offering. "This will be our last meeting. This will be the last dance of which you and I will ever partake." The mocking smile and courteous tones all slipped away as Eulahtan bellowed, "And I, I intend to be the last one standing." Eulahtan charged toward Josh/Nathalue as he let out an unearthly cry like a wounded animal trying to defend what remained of his life.

Josh concentrated, knowing now that his power came from deep within, from the place where his emotions lived. He dug deep and screamed at Eulahtan, "No!" Nothing happened. But before Josh could try to center himself again, Eulahtan had him by the throat. Josh felt his feet leaving the ground. Josh clawed, kicked, and punched. Josh raised his fist to strike again when a blinding flash filled his mind as Eulahtan brought his hand across Josh's face in an open-handed slap that nearly knocked Josh out of his mind. Then Josh's head whipped back and forth as repeated blows fell on him. Josh felt something run across his lips. He could taste salty iron in his mouth.

The world went black as Josh's head rocked back as far as the choking grip would allow after what felt like a rock thumped his forehead. Eulahtan drew back and struck again, rocking Josh's head and sending him into near oblivion again. The blow sent Josh into a senseless stupor for a moment. Once he recovered enough of his senses to realize that he was no longer in the strangling grip of Eulahtan's iron hands, he looked up to see a clear night sky. Stars, not of pain, but the stars of the open universe filled his eyes. Eulahtan held Josh over his head as he growled, something barely understandable. As soon as Josh realized what was happening, he felt the world shift. His body descended, not like a sensation of falling, but rather a feeling of being forced to the ground until he felt his back come to a stop on Eulahtan's knee. His upper and lower torso continued their descent past Eulahtan's knee until Josh felt, and heard, a crack from somewhere in the middle of his back. He then felt his body rolling across the ground, his legs flopping like dead weight. Josh knew what he felt was his back-breaking. He noted that he no longer felt the weary pangs of aching muscles in his legs. He felt someone pull his shoulder as his crumpled body was rolled over to face the stars again. In the starfield, a dark silhouette appeared as it straddled Josh's body. Josh felt a weight push the air from his stomach as his diaphragm struggled to move against the force that had settled on him.

Josh opened his eyes and saw the silhouette disturb the starfield above him, this time just before a blast hit him in the face, driving his head back against the immovable ground. Josh no longer felt the blows as they came at him one after another until Josh's thin hold on life seemed to be slipping. Eulahtan continued to beat Josh until all that was left seemed to be a mat of battered blood and mishappen angles. After a few more blows, Eulahtan stopped, used his bloodied hands to wipe away the sweat from his brow, leaving his face red with swathes of Josh's blood. Eulahtan got up from Josh's failing body. He slowly turned and walked over to the rock in the clearing, sat down, then seemed to resume his peaceful meditation.

Ethan came around enough to see Eulahtan finish pummeling Josh and walk back over to the rock. He tried to stand but found his legs wouldn't respond. He looked over and saw Josh lying on his back, his bloodied and disfigured face shifting in the firelight. He strained for air from what sounded like water-filled lungs. Ethan couldn't make out the rise and fall of his chest, so he assumed Eulahtan had beaten Josh to death, or at least close enough that it was only a matter of time. Ethan turned to find Tabby lying lifeless. Gathering his failing strength, he used his unbroken arm to drag himself over to her body. At the sight of her, his lungs began to pump. His thin grasp of control slipping as if his breath was being perpetually pressed from him as effectively as Eulahtan's grip had choked the air from his throat. It took a few painful pulls with his only working limb until he was lying beside Tabby's body. He pulled and pawed at her with his working arm, ignoring the burning pain in his other arm with each movement until he had rolled her over to face him. He could barely see her through the watery blur of the darkened world.

He touched Tabby's face as he asked, "Why didn't you run? Baby, you should've run. Why didn't you run?" As his tears devolved into a sobbing mass of whimpering nonsense, Ethan let go of consciousness and slipped into a world of nothing, his last thought being that of he and Tabby's wedding day.

CHAPTER 44

"Sir, did you see anyone come back to the vehicle at any point during the day?" the officer asked the young man holding a bicycle.

"No, man. It was just like I said. I saw two dudes and a chick get out of the car, and when they came around to the back, they got out a bunch of weapons from the back here. When they stepped back to close the hatch, I saw a body under a sheet in the back of the car. I kind of mingled around the area instead of going on my usual rim ride, and no one ever came back. I'm telling you, I saw a woman's hand sticking out from under a sheet when they closed the hatch. They left a dead woman in the back of this car and ran off into the canyon."

"Sir, I told you, my supervisor is on the way. Once he arrives, he'll decide how we proceed. I can't just bust the windows out of a car."

As the officer finished his statement, a blue light flashed from within the car, and the sheet that had been covering Kiera's body settled gently down onto the car's floor as if riding a puff of wind. In the forest by the clearing where Eulahtan was biding his time by the rock, a fourth body seemed to materialize on the ground among the three other shapes of human wreckage. Kiera opened her eyes, drew in a deep breath, and blinked away long sleep. She looked up to see the sky above her, the stars seeming to wink down at her return. She slowly turned her head and saw two broken bodies that she did not immediately recognize. Kiera's first thought was that they were dead. Neither moved, and if they were breathing, their breaths were shallow. Kiera struggled for a moment to sit up then finally raised her head and upper body from the ground. She braced herself with her hands. She lifted one hand and studied it as if it were the hand of another. She used the strange hand to feel her chest and stomach like an alien beginning a symbiotic relationship with a new host. She struggled to her feet, grasping at the air for balance. She took one testing step to see if her strength was returning. She took another step, an adult toddler waddling for the first time. She looked around at the bodies on the ground until she saw Josh's bloodied and beaten body lying twenty feet away from Ethan and Tabby's remains.

Kiera began to move toward Josh, almost falling, then steadying herself, her body slowly syncing back within her control. In truth, she thought she must have looked like a drunken toddler as she walked over and knelt beside Josh's body. Kneeling over Josh's broken face, she could hear a labored, wet rattle moving in and out as his body clung to life. Kiera's vision blurred, but she ate the pain forcing it back down. There was no time for useless emotional tantrums. She knew if Eulahtan was going to be stopped, it was up to her to give Josh, Nathalue, the gift.

Kiera lowered her head to Josh's ear, not knowing if he was able to hear her, and softly said, "Yartrua sends you this gift, this hope, and wishes you wellness, Nathalue."

Kiera placed her hands on Josh's chest and closed her eyes.

"Lemeca yasut comdalla yatolda. I give this gift on behalf of the one who made you."

White fire bloomed from under Kiera's palms then spread over Josh's body until it covered him like a cocoon. Josh spat blood, twisted, and bent violently. He shook as if being electrified. The unnatural movement made him look like a boy possessed. Josh's face, still bloodied, began to remold itself into the face that Kiera recognized from the front door in what now seemed a time forever ago. Once the reshaping had stopped and Josh lay breathing normally, Kiera wiped the blood from his face with her shirt and sat down beside him, feeling as if she had given him most of her life essence, and waited.

Josh's eyes began to move rapidly back and forth under his closed eyelids, his mind pumping with images of his past and of who he was, reminding him of his purpose. Something had happened to Josh when he touched Nick's body in the space between, which was, in essence, touching a part of Eulahtan, but the gift that Kiera brought back to him from the cage at the crux of creation was everything. All his dreams, nightmares, memories, and most of all, all of him. Nathalue, the order, and balance against chaos. The order to balance the disorder, Eulahtan was corrupted to sow into the hearts and minds of man.

Josh saw how Cecily was set upon this planet in a time before time was measured to monitor the life-giving waterways of the earth for early man. Josh saw Cecily being given the title of Principality by Yartrua. He saw Cecily watching a human woman through the waters as he dangled his hand into a lake over the side of his boat. He saw how Cecily watched the woman almost daily as she washed her garments by a stream, and the moment Cecily decided he would go to this woman in a physical form. Knowing this behavior was forbidden by the Architects, Cecily kept his marriage and the birth of his four children a secret. Josh saw again how Parzeus became jealous because, although humanity was his design, Yartrua would not allow Parzeus to rule over them as a king. So Parzeus set lose other creations from his workshop to pollute the hearts of man. In doing so, he created and let loose Eulahtan to sow discord and disorder, to define chaos. In his jealousy, a moment of prideful hope he would still be chosen to rule over man, he also created a counterbalance for man in Nathalue. Nathalue, the balance meant to keep chaos from committing the world to destruction before it had an opportunity to blossom into what Yartrua hoped mankind would grow to become, a companion race to the Architects.

Josh saw the war between Yartrua and Parzeus over the slaughter of Cecily's children. He watched as Yartura devised a method to drain the others' essence and then lock himself away into a prison for all eternity.

The images shifted as Josh saw Parzeus in his workshop, drawing prototypes for a new race. He saw Parzeus's corruption as Yartrua confronted him over a flaw in man's design. Yartrua raged about the component in man's design that Parzeus argued would make men more pliable and easier to control.

"They are not pets, Parzeus. The Gignesthai Committee did not commission another design for subjects. This will not stand."

"The project is already under production. The commission will stand as selected, Yartrua."

"You hid this design aspect. You committed fraud before the committee."

Yartrua realized this betrayal only after the seeding had begun, so he wept for the lifetime of discontent that the new organisms were going to face in the light of this illogical construct within them.

Josh's eye movement slowed until they stopped altogether. He opened them, the light of cold fire still blazing within them. He sat up and turned to Kiera but said nothing. He stood, and Kiera stood along with him but backed away a couple of steps. Josh quickly covered the two paces between them without saying a word and hugged Kiera.

"I thought you were dead," Josh said, squeezing Kiera tighter.

"No. Not dead. Invited. When you went home, Yartrua felt us and pulled me deeper."

Josh released his embrace and took a step back, eyes wide. "You mean—"

"Yes, I've been to the prison at the crux. Yartrua showed me everything, told me everything then sent me back with his gift. He knew unless you could remember everything, there was no way to stop this. He found the rupture in the box that Parzeus created that allows Eulahtan to siphon off his power to perform these crucibles. He is going to seal it once this is complete."

"Why is he waiting? Why doesn't he do it now?"

"Because it has already begun, and *you* will need his power to stop the cycle. He said—"

Before Kiera could finish, a volley of hell was unleashed against Eulahtan. Josh turned to see a rocket blast hit the ground where Eulahtan was seated, followed by rapid-fire machine-gun bursts. Desert brown Humvees equipped with heavy machine guns roared out of the darkness spitting a curtain of high caliber rounds in Eulahtan's direction. Another rocket struck the rock Eulahtan had been seated by and erupted into a blast that turned the clearing into day and sent a warm shockwave across Kiera and Joshs's faces. The vehicles sped in and out of the area, turning the area into a battlefield. The soldiers inside the vehicles continually shot into the burning smoke where Eulahtan had been sitting. Several gunners tossed grenades. Explosions and ammunition ricochets rang out as the sound rolled across the canyon rim and disappeared into the valley. Kiera and Josh dove behind a large tree for cover.

"My God," Kiera said, "Did they get him?"

"No," Josh said, shaking his head. "You cannot stop him will bullets. You need the key."

The entire battle seemed to roll on in slow motion for an eternity, but in truth, it was over in about a minute as a third helicopter landed just outside the radius of the blast area. The Humvees circled the area again then stopped in an orderly row, facing the attack area. Men piled out of the vehicles with their weapons drawn. Kiera and Josh could see the mark of the Nasaru painted on one of the vehicles. The soldiers began to move in on the rock at a cautious pace, weapons drawn. Once they had come to within fifty yards of the rock, a figure crawled from the smoldering and scarred earth and began to walk toward them. The line of men opened fire. Eulahtan screamed at the men in animalistic rage, gathered his will, and sent a thought toward the soldiers. The thought he sent was one of rage, anger, hopelessness, and black chaos. His thought hit the men and infected them like a drug. The men threw down their weapons and turned on one another. They tore at one another's clothes, gouged out eyes, and bit into the flesh of arms, legs, and throats. They beat, kicked, and choked one another until the last two men lay upon the ground, each locked in a bitter struggle to tear the face off the other one.

"Can't you stop this?"

Josh peeked around the tree. "No. I cannot do anything until the Fabric Engine is unlocked, and only Eulahtan can do that. He is the one who created it."

Once the last man had killed his opponent, then lay dying on the ground beside his comrade, one eye hanging from its socket and blood streaming from a knife wound to his abdomen, Eulahtan got to his feet and walked back to the rock. Josh and Kiera could see Eulahtan's body repairing itself, the tendrils of electricity weaving his body back together, closing open wounds and repairing burned skin. Eulahtan stood in front of the rock and studied it as if trying to decide the next move on a chessboard. He then reached out and put his hand on the stone's dry surface. At first, nothing happened, then he closed his eyes. Markings began to appear on the stone, first glowing dimly, then increasing their brilliance until the light shining from the carved runes blotted out their shapes. The rock stone began to crack and pop in a series of tiny bursts of dust and debris.

"What is he doing?"

"He's unlocking the Fabric Engine."

Eulahtan held his hand on the rock, the energy within it rising until it vibrated the ground. Kiera and Josh looked at one another, then at the ground as the hum from the rock reverberated beneath them. Eulahtan stepped back and waited. The rock gave one last loud crack as it split into multiple fragments and fell to the ground. Hidden within the rock was a large ring sitting on top of a polished silver pedestal. On each side of the pedestal were two long appendages resembling giant corkscrews. There was a small silver dish on top of the ring that began to glow. The glow brightened into something Kiera recognized, the white-hot blaze of the fire that burned but did not consume, the same fire that she had brought back to Josh from Yartrua's cage. Suddenly, the two screws on the pedestal's sides plunged into the earth and began to burrow, drilling down until the machine sat firmly secured to the ground. Once the screws stopped, what appeared to be a small carriage attached to the ring began to rotate around the ring's circumference. It moved slowly at first. Each time it passed under the dish at the top of the ring, it seemed to gather some of the light the dish seemed to be collecting, causing the light to pulse brighter momentarily.

"What do we do?"

"We wait," Josh said, offering Kiera a sympathetic glance. "He must have the key. If we reveal that I am recovered before he uses the key, there is a chance he may be able to stop me before I can access the fabric."

Kiera heard Eulahtan mutter something and turned to him. All she could make out was that he was using a combination of words in that strange language and humming, almost as if he were singing.

"He's beginning to tune to the engine."

"So, what does that mean?"

"It means we have about twenty minutes before he has enough charge to arm the device."

Eulahtan finished tuning the machine, then raised his face toward the sky and opened his arms as he tore the tattered and charred shirt from his body. He bent one arm and ran a long fingernail up and down the center of his chest. Suddenly, he stopped and plunged the claw into the top of his chest, just at the base of his throat, and began to tear his flesh. He cried out but continued to saw and rip with his nails until Kiera saw bone. He then took both hands, grabbing one hand to each side of the open wound, and pulled the flesh away from his chest until he had exposed a three-inch wide tear. Spittle flew from his mouth, his head shook, and his eyes fluttered as he flayed himself. He reached into the wound and pulled out a silver object, covered in pieces of flesh and black blood, held it up, and examined it. The wound on his chest began to knit itself together again slowly, the tiny white threads of energy pulling and sowing his flesh until his chest healed.

"Jesus, is that part of the ritual?"

"No, but it explains why the key remained hidden during this cycle. He found a way to cleave the key within his chest."

The object Josh called a key more closely resembled the handle of a small dagger. From what Kiera could make out of the thing in the glow of the burning vehicles. It looked to be a smooth silver handle with intricately carved symbols that she assumed were writing. Eulahtan placed the blunt end against the pedestal base. A slit opened in the pedestal's seamless metal. A small, flat blade with a blunt tip slid from within the handle. The edges seemed to change from smooth to jagged in alternating patterns along the blade.

As the key slide up the handle, the runes and etchings that marked the handle's entirety began to glow with deep blue pulses of light. Eulahtan removed his hand after sliding the key into its slot, seemed to examine the glowing patterns a moment, then retook the handle in a tight grip and turned it until the pedestal produced a slight click. When the handle clicked to a stop, two additional disks extended from each side of the pedestal. The energy collecting in these disks appeared to be a black cloud.

Josh gasped, and Kiera turned around to see him wide-eyed with his mouth hanging open. Seeing Josh shocked made Kiera's stomach turn. "Josh, what's wrong?" she asked.

The hum from the little device spinning within the ring on top of the pedestal increased.

"He's modified the machine since the last time he used it."

Kiera looked back toward the device and watched the little sled slide along the rails of the circle. The sled seemed to be mixing, Kiera thought, the two energy types that the three dishes were pulling into the machine.

"Modified? How?"

"The two collectors on the sides were not present the last time I saw the machine. They seem to be…." Josh stopped speaking and put his fist to his mouth, and studied the machine as Kiera watched concern grow on his face. "It looks like he is pulling energy from the inbetween. He's not just charging the machine; he's going to try to collapse as many layers as possible when he releases the pulse this time."

"Look," Kiera said, pointing in the direction of one of the black energy collectors. At the spot where the black energy from the inbetween became visible, a tear appeared and then widened.

"As long as that tear in the fabric remains open, the inbetweeners can come through," Josh said.

"I thought they could only do that once a universe was almost dead."

"Normally, but if Eulahtan has found a way to adjust the resonance of the other layers to draw them into this plane, then that leaves it open to cross freely. With the quantity of power as he is pulling from the light disk, it will be like pouring chum in the ocean from a container ship."

Josh turned to place his back against the tree as he sat on the ground. He looked back over his shoulder then turned back around. Kiera knelt beside him and put her hand on his shoulder.

"What do we need to do? How do we turn that damn thing off?"

"We just need to turn the key back around and pull it out of the machine. It will shut down on its own."

"Okay, any thoughts?"

"I am going to distract him. I need you to do one thing."

"What?"

"I have to tell you something that I think you already know. Still, I must tell you out loud so that you hear it and understand."

"Go ahead."

Josh looked at her with pity and understanding, lining his young face that seemed to come from a heart as old as time itself, and said, "The reason Eulahtan is able to manipulate the box, the reason he has grown so powerful is because Nick is gone. His essence is depleted."

Even knowing what Josh was going to tell her did not lessen the blow. As soon as the words leaped from his mouth, making the thought real, it felt as if they hit her in the chest like a fist. Kiera involuntarily put her hand on her belly as tears began to flow in rivers from a pain that seemed to come from the bottom of her chest, up over her head and cry out for the loss of a life that she had been robbed of building with Nick and their unborn child. She leaned back against the tree and covered her mouth with her hand to stop a moan that wanted to escape from somewhere deep within her. She felt a hand on her shoulder and let her hands fall to her lap as she turned to see Josh. He had blazing red water dancing on the rims of his eyes as his standing tears reflected the fires through the shadow of the trees.

Suddenly, Josh and Kiera were both startled by a loud metallic ping. They turned to see Eulahtan pulling the handle away from the pedestal, the broken key being sealed as the keyhole vanished into a seamless surface again. Josh and Kiera looked at one another.

"Can you still get the key out?"

Josh looked down, appearing to be searching his memory.

"I don't know. Maybe there is another key, or maybe an access panel on the back. Listen," Josh said as he looked over to Kiera, "I am going to try to stop this."

"How, Josh. He nearly killed you last time?"

"I know, but I have to do something. Please do not interfere. There's nothing you can do. Believe me. If I can't figure this out, it will be better to die quickly when he sends the pulse than it will be to die anyway he," he motioned to Eulahtan, "can dream up to kill you before the blast."

Before Kiera could say anything, Josh moved away from the tree and began making his way to the spot where Eulahtan had been sitting. Josh darted from tree to tree as if he were playing a game of commando. He moved from one tree, peaked around, then darted to another, always trying to maintain a line of sight on Eulahtan. Just as Josh drew within thirty feet of the clearing, he felt a tingling sensation in his stomach. He thought it must have been nerves and started to continue, then suddenly fell, his knees giving way beneath him. He managed to fall into a kneeling position and was so able to avoid cracking his newly repaired face on the hard earth. His body trembled uncontrollably. He wrapped his arms around his stomach as if trying to hold his insides together. He screamed, but the agony racking his body was so intense it robbed him of sound. What came out of his mouth was a dry whisper of breath as spital flew from his twitching lips. He heard his bones begin to crack as if they were popcorn in a microwave. It felt like his limbs, his ribs, his spine, and even his head were ripping themselves apart. Finally, he fell to the ground writhing in agony, struggling to catch his breath.

Kiera saw Josh writhing on the ground and ran over to where he had fallen, disregarding the need for stealth. By the time she got to him, he had stopped rolling, the pain apparently gone, and he lay breathing heavily as if having run up several flights of stairs. Kiera gasped, covering her mouth to mask the sound. The strength left her knees, and she wobbled down to a sitting position, like a toddler just learning to walk, and sat trembling.

Josh sat up, looked calmly at Kiera, and said, "You were right, Yartrua did indeed have a gift, but it was more than a gift of life. It was equality, Kiera."

Josh stood. Kiera followed him with her eyes, her hand still clutching her mouth as her body continued to tremble. Josh looked down with an outstretched hand, offering to help her to her feet. Kiera removed her hand from her mouth and slowly stretched it toward Josh's hand. She stopped and said through lips that were trembling so badly the words barely came out understandable, "J-J-Josh? Is this you?"

Josh looked down at her with eyes that now seemed benevolent, gave her a smile so filled with warmth that she thought it might actually warm you on a cold day, and said, "It is. Please." Then he motioned for her to get up with his outstretched hand, continuing to coax her up with his loving smile.

Kiera stretched the remainder of the distance to grab hold of Josh's hand. As Kiera reached her feet, Josh said, "No, Kiera, I am no longer the child Joshua Roland. I am who I have always been. I am Nathalue. I am the last remnant of Pandora's box, the cruel trick of a jealous man. I am the one who is here to offer you the hope that I was never able to offer in previous crucibles. I know now what I must do, and I promise that I will try not to fail you." He smiled a smile that seemed to show a lifetime of regret mixed with a tinge of hope from a well that ran eternity deep within his soul.

Kiera took a small step back to get a better look. She looked into his aged face and saw the wisdom his eyes had seen. She saw the rugged face under the dark beard that showed lines of learning she could never know or understand. She saw sadness hidden just behind the warm smile that oozed with love and affection for Kiera, this human of ordinary means that had been to the crux of creation, and had returned him home, just when he needed it most. The man carried the more mature face of Josh but was rugged and strong in his shoulders and chest. His arms were of a man that had worked at hard labor for many years of his life. His deep amber eyes spoke of things humanity had never seen or could ever understand at their current development and evolution level. He stood about six and a half feet tall, and his broad form looked as if he had earned every day of his long life. Kiera looked again at his face and placed a hand on his cheek. She leaned into him and gave him a motherly kiss on his cheek, then quickly drew away.

"You may call yourself Nathalue," she said, "but what I see is the face of a boy that my friends and I have grown to love."

Nathalue let the shock of Kiera's motherly kiss to his cheek pass as a single tear moved down his cheek, disappearing into his dark beard. He wiped tear, then looked at his wet hand in awe. He looked back to Kiera. "I must try and stop this. We can doddle no longer, dear Kiera. But know this Kiera Clayton, I have never known a more honorable trio than the three of you, whom I have come to think of as friends and family."

As he turned, Kiera asked, "Josh…." Then corrected, "Nathalue. What will we do since the key is broken? Josh, I mean, oh damn it, this is weird." She said, placing the back of her hand against her forehead, "What can we do without the key?"

"I know one way to put a stop to the crucibles." His eyes filled with sorrow as he said, "I will do the one thing I know will stop this and all other crucibles to come, or I will commit to breathe my last as I try to thwart this fatuity." He placed the closed fist of his right hand over his left breast in salute of promise, then turned to face Eulahtan.

"Wait, is there not anything I can do to help?"

He turned and offered another warm smile, "Yes. Stay here, and if I succeed, love your life, and live it well, Kiera. But, if I should fail, remember a quick death will be better than the alternative of which you will have left to choose." He turned and continued walking into the clearing, and Kiera could think of nothing else to say to the boy that Yartrua had determined would be a man.

Josh moved into the clearing, bathed in the light of the battlefield debris. The Fabric Engine was humming at a higher frequency as the pulses from the spinning sled blurred into a constant drone. The ring grew brighter and brighter in its sick, gray glow from the mixing energies of Yartura's weeping power from the cage and the black corruption of the inbetween spaces mingled in the ring's center. Nathalue heard what sounded like a garbled yell and turned to see gray tentacles feeling along the edge of one of the rips like a prom date testing the waters of his date's limits. The drowning scream of the creature, followed by the sounds of many other creatures close to the tear poured from the wound in the universe. Snorts, gagging, and the sloshy sound of liquid in a flesh container filled the air at the edge of the clearing. The wet slap of moist flesh, like a body hitting the wet pavement, began to vibrate the ground above the hum of the engine. The creatures from the inbetween began clawing their way toward and through the tear in the dimensional fabric.

"Eulahtan!" Nathalue called, "It is time to put a stop to this!"

Eulahtan jumped as if he had been stabbed in the back, then rose using the strength of only one of his crossed legs as if dancing. He whirled in Nathalue's direction and glared at him.

"I ended you. I should have known there would be one last trick the charlatan would seek to play. He is always playing at his games, trying to manipulate the story's outcome." Eulahtan spat on the ground. "Well, not this time. This time, I have the true key. I have the key of Odisyis, and it is locked in my engine. You cannot retrieve it. I will end this infestation and cleanse this realm from the vermin of man, along with all the other realms."

Nathalue heard the machine's hum whirl to a slightly higher frequency as if responding to Eulahtan's anger. Nathalue heard the sound and turned to see the stream of light pouring into the top of the machine and the stream of dark being pulled in from the sides harden, seeming almost to solidify.

"You have become unhinged, brother! You need to stop this madness!" Nathalue yelled.

"You cannot stop me. Three times you have tried and failed. The only difference this time is that I know now how to prevent you from interfering!" Eulahtan held up the handle of the key. "You know there is no other way to stop the mechanism other than turning the key. You come before me a failure, even before you stood on the ground you occupy." Eulahtan turned his face skyward and laughed. The sound, both a mocking of Nathalue and a confirmation of his insanity.

"There will be no tomorrow for this world, brother," Eulahtan said, pointing a twisted finger at Nathalue.

"You know that I cannot let this stand. The Prime Covenant has been broken, and this creation has been interfered with for the last time. This course must be ceased. Together you and I will—" But Nathalue was silenced by a shriek of madness from Eulahtan as he rushed forward, his arms raised.

"You will not stop me," he screamed as he charged, swinging his fist at Nathalue's face.

Nathalue turned, dodging his blow, and yelled, "Stop this, brother! We are the last. This is not the way."

Eulahtan whirled from his missed blow, planted his foot, then spun, sailing another blow that met its target as it landed on Nathalue's chin. A field of stars exploded in Nathalue's vision. He stumbled, almost fell to the ground, then caught himself with his hand and pushed himself back to his feet. Now understanding the violence required to stay Eulahtan's advance, he countered with a hooking fist to Eulahtan's left cheek. Eulahtan stumbled backward and shook his head to clear the stars from his mind. He raised his hand to his cheek and rubbed while gifting Nathalue and sickly grin, the smile matching the insanity in his eyes, together forming a complete portrait of his corruption.

"You have learned of the violence that must sometimes occur to meet one's goal Nathalue."

"Violence begets violence Eulahtan. There is no reasonable end to this course. Please, stop this before it is too late."

Eulahtan's eyes narrowed, his rage rising, boiling on the surface. He charged again at Nathalue. Kiera felt kinetic waves crashing through her body as they exchanged blows, fists crashing into one another like waves on the shore from a tempest. Each resounding impact shook the ground. The machine's hum whined more as Nathalue ran to it and began to beat at the casing enclosing the pedestal. Eulahtan screamed as he picked himself up from the ground. The ground beneath Kiera's feet reverberated, matching the Fabric Engine's growing hum. Kiera saw movement to her left and turned to see a creature from the inbetween crawl out of the rip in the fabric between the realms.

The beast pushed its grey, swollen head along the ground as it clawed its way out with its gelatinous arms. Its skin was the pale rot of a wasted corpse. The creature inched toward the Fabric Engine, drawn by the energy buildup. Behind that creature was another, also covered in moist grey skin, stepping through the fissure, its hands nearly dragging the ground as they dangled limply from the ends of its long spindly arms. It turned its charred face toward Kiera. Skin covered half the face, the underlying bone of the skull shining a dark grey in the firelight. It licked at the air, tasting it, clicking deep within its throat. The creature's head fell back, mouth open, and it seemed to let out a long hollow breath. The creature stumbled forward as another misshapen beast pressed its way from the hole. The hole began to fill with creatures clawing, pushing, and pressing out from both rips located at the side of the machine. Kiera's breath caught as another creature turned, seemed to find Kiera's eyes, then turned away and began crawling toward the fight.

Eulahtan sat astride Nathalue, beating him in the face as he hurled curses at him. Nathalue tried to raise his hands to block the blows, but Eulahtan continued to hammer him. After Eulahtan landed a blow that rocked Nathalue's head to one side, he saw a rock, a fragment of the stone that had fallen away from the engine's encasement. He stretched one hand toward the rock. His fingers struggled toward the stone as Eulahtan stopped beating him and wrapped his clawed hands around Nathalue's neck, and began to squeeze. Just as the glowing fires of the burning vehicles grew to a dim glow, his vision failing, the stone moved toward him. He pulled it closer, wrapped his hand around it, and swung. A hollow thud sounded as the rock struck the side of Eulahtan's head.

Eulahtan's grey-white eyes seemed to roll back in their sockets as his twisted mouth twitched. He chewed at the air as he fell from Nathalue's chest. Nathalue rolled to his side, clutching his throat, his lungs grabbing at the air. The dark shade closing in one his sight began to fade, the colors of burning wreckage blurring into clarity. He tried to stand, but something struck his forehead. His eyes blinked to images of endless dark. Nathalue thought this would be his failing, that his loss of consciousness would allow Eulahtan to put an end to him and complete his plans. Nathalue felt his body being raised, being stood up. He opened his eyes to see Eulahtan staring hate into his face. His mouth was a hard line as Eulahtan grasped Nathalue by the throat again, lifting him off the ground. He squeezed. Nathalue beat at Eulahtan's arm, trying to kick him in the chest with his dangling feet, but Eulahtan's focus was set. His present task, he intended to complete. His insanity was now complete. He would not stop until Nathalue was lying lifeless on the ground or as close to lifeless as was possible.

Nathalue's strength began to weep from his body as he felt his throat close under the crushing pressure. Every reach for air was a struggle in sipping through a straw. His vision was nearly dark when he began to chuckle in a weak, wheezing whisper.

Eulahtan loosened his grip just enough for Nathalue to draw air and asked, "What is there for you to laugh about, you fool? You are lost!"

At that moment, Nathalue realized he had been wrong to tell Kiera to stay away. He then saw the wisdom of Kiera in her intent. While it was true Nick was gone, a portion of Nick's essence still existed, growing inside her womb. Kiera approached Eulahtan from behind, her hands raised, her face determined, her eyes fearless. She no longer wore the mask of fearful, red-eyed innocence. She was the woman who had been to the crux, communed with Yartura, then returned Nathalue home. If Nick was in her, then he was with her. He had fought against Eulahtan's power in the black. She would fight here. She crept up behind Eulahtan and grabbed the sides of his head. His concentration broke as he began to scream, the agony of a million souls. Kiera felt power surge from her. It seemed to come from the earth itself and course through her body. Eulahtan dropped Nathalue and fell to his knees, Kiera maintaining her grasp on his head. Eulahtan looked skyward and let out another moan, as did Kiera. Both Eulahtan and Kiera's eyes glowed brilliant white, pulsing in unison. Light bloomed from under Kiera's hands as Eulahtan let out another scream in unison with Kiera.

Nathalue gained his breath and frantically looked around for the key's handle. The machine whined like a turbine as the carriage glided around the ring at blinding speed. The grey mix of the two energies began to stretch, to search for a master like a ghostly arm. Nathalue found the broken handle, ran to grab the device, and placed it against the surface where the keyhole had been located on the pedestal's front casing. Nothing happened. He began to hit and kick the machine as he hurled curses in another language. He turned to look at Kiera, who was still holding Eulahtan in her grip. She seemed to have slipped into a trance, locking Eulahtan in place in his agony. Eulahtan continued to scream at the night sky as Kiera's womb began to glow from beneath her shirt.

Nathalue turned to run to her, to pull her free from Eulahtan's head. As he turned, the surging machine shot a blast of energy that struck him in the back, freezing him in his tracks. More images flooded his mind. He saw the jealousy of Parzeus as the council, led by Yartrua, would not allow him to rule their newest creation of man. He saw jealously grow like black mold in Parzeus's heart until it led to the corruption of a young maid named Pandora. He saw Parzeus's gifted a locked box given to Pandora. Because the box called to her day and night, she opened the box at the peak of her madness, releasing the suffering of man onto the earth and into their hearts. Nathalue saw the council condemn Cecily for his relationship with the human woman and how they bound together to rend the children. He saw how Yartrua wanted to end the rending of the last child out of pity for Cecily, his brother, and how the council disagreed. Parzeus worked against him to sow descent and disharmony against Yartrua within the council. He saw how the echoes of the ascender's lives left echoes, longings, on humankind's hearts. He saw too the binding of the other's within Yartrua as he devised a way to drain their essences into himself, then lock himself away in a cage at the crux of creation. Nathalue opened his blinded eyes and saw a child, the last child of Cecily. The child looked up at Nathalue and smiled, showing innocence eternity deep. The boy, Nicalos, grew, become and man, and created descendants, of which Nick was the last. Nathalue, the hope of mankind, and Josh, the orphan, knew there were no more choices in his moment. He would need to do something he had never before been willing to do.

Nathalue came to himself as the beam continued to drill its power into his back, filling him with the life force of multiple universes. He reached for Kiera with his mind, "Kiera, listen to me. Your work is done. You carry a bloodline that must survive within your womb. Tuck deep your mourning and leave. Leave as fast as you are able from this place."

Kiera blinked her glowing eyes in understanding. She removed her hands from Eulahtan's head and ran toward the trees, toward the motionless bodies of Tabby and Ethan.

Eulahtan remained kneeling on the ground, slowly beginning to recover his wits. Nathalue looked at the markings on the key's handle as they started to glow again. He looked down, examined the blade as the blue glow of the runes shifted, then he understood. He and Eulathan were cut from the same tapestry, opposite sides of the same coin. The machine knew him. It responded to its will just as it had done for Eulahtan. He held up the handle and read the words "Life from Pain" on the hilt, then complete understanding flooded him. He held the handle to his mouth and said, "Laplora." A twelve-inch blade of blue energy shot from the handle's end. Nathalue looked up at Eulahtan, then rushed toward him. Eulahtan grabbed for Nathalue's wrists as he thrust the energy blade toward him. Eulahtan opened his mouth to cry out, but all he produced was a gasp as the blade entered his heart, searing flesh and spitting bone. Nathalue pulled his brother in close and caressed him as Eulahtan began to slump to the ground.

Nathalue soothed his brother as he lowered him softly to the ground. "Do you not see, brother? I am no longer an orphan. We have found one another again. We are family. This I do because we are all that remains of a clan that is no more. We die here together as kindred again, just as we were born. You are not the dark brother, and I am not the light. We are us, brother, and we must pass."

Eulahtan let out another faint wheeze as the last breath of life left his body. Nathalue lowered his head and began to weep, squeezing Eulahtan as his tears wet his brother's hair. The loss of his home and the loss of all the lives that had been taken in pursuit of Parzeus's envy overwhelmed him. He suddenly felt weary, as if the whole earth pressed down upon him. The symbiotic relationship that had paired Nathalue to Eulahtan, the bond that brokered the balance of their existence with equal resonance, was now offset, out of balance. The scale had indeed been reset as Nathalue felt his essence breaking, drifting away. His form now seeming to seep out from the unseen, severed tether that connected him to his brother. He determined his last act would be to balance the scale of death and decay that Eulahtan had left in his wake, the untold truth of knowledge without wisdom. He stood, then watched as Eulahtan's body began to turn, first to stone, then to dust, then to dissolve away like the whispering vapors of Nick's last remains. Nathalue held up a tired hand in front of his face and watched as tiny grains of himself began to separate and join Eulahtan's dust as it rose skyward. He turned and looked at the machine, the twisted vision of a madman's promise. It continued to draw energy from the dark and light universes. The carriage was moving so fast that it seemed to be a solid object within the ring. The whine had heightened and mixed with an energetic buzz as the unit continued to charge itself. Nathalue took a weak, stumbling step toward the device and spread his arms to his side as if in submission. The machine had stopped pouring into him when he ran to plunge the knife into Eulahtan's heart, and the ghostly arm hung, poised awaiting its connection, seeking its command.

Nathalue spoke one word, "Transitum."

The grey ghost of energy shot from the ring and blasted Nathalue's chest. His body jolted as if a tidal wave had hit him. He struggled to stand against the beam's power, pressing against its force as his feet began to lose hold, and he slid backward as energy poured into him. He felt every atom of his being quake. He saw not just this world, this earth, but all worlds pass through his mind as if he were tethered to every realm by a string of infinite length. He opened his fiery eyes and saw the machine continuing to pull and tear the fabric breaches just beyond the beam that was filling him. Nathalue drew in his outstretched arms and raised his hands, palms toward the Fabric Engine. He focused, his body feeling as if it would come apart molecule by molecule at any moment. He summoned his will as his mind carried him back through time, back through space, and across worlds not seen in a billion years to the spot where a tiny spark bloomed in a darkened void.

Nathalue heard a voice echo across the void. "This spark, this one tiny spark, will grow into an infinite legacy, a great mystery. Oh, there will be pain, to be sure. But there will also be life, and there will be love. I should think it shall be grand."

Nathalue sent a thought to the device. Instantly beams of grey energy shot from the palms of his hands and into the engine's pedestal. The machine, having not been designed to have its immense energy turned back onto itself, erupted in a bright blue blast, exploding outward like a ball of lightning as it disintegrated into pieces, none being larger than the size of a pen's tip.

The force of the blast lifted Nathalue off his feet, then vaporized his body as he flew backward through the air on the shockwave, a restful smile upon his face. As the energy rolled toward them, Kiera heard the blast and tried to lay over Tabby and Ethan's motionless bodies. A tree not ten yards away snapped in half. Kiera screamed, feeling the ground beneath her quake. Suddenly, she felt the energy wave roll over her, thinking for a moment the pressure would crush her. Then as abruptly as it hit her, it dissipated. She lay with her face toward the ground, arms around Ethan and Tabby as she slowly began to feel unconsciousness take her. She laid on the ground for an unknown amount of time, telling herself to get up and go for help, hoping Tabby and Ethan were still alive but still not able to hear their breathing. Her legs wouldn't obey, and she continued to drift deeper and deeper into darkness. As her surroundings slipped away, she thought she heard the sound of a machine beating the wind and what may have been shouting.

As the last of Kiera's strength faded, she heard men in the distance, "Over here! We have something over here!" Then there was black as Kiera gave in to the overwhelming heaviness of darkness.

EPILOGUE

"How are you doing, baby? You look a little heavy today."

"No, I'm good, really," Kiera replied with an unconvincing smile.

"Oh, sweetie, I know you better than that. Do we need to talk?"

"Not really, it's just one of those kinds of gloomy days. I had another dream last night. Not a bad dream, just another one."

"Nick again?"

Kiera looked at Tabby and nodded, biting her lip. Her eyes told Tabby what her mouth did not.

"Tell me about it. It's the good memories that we need to focus on when things happen in life. I see them as the glue that binds life's meaning together."

"It was nothing. I just dreamed about the time Nick took me to the zoo. We walked around, held hands. Acted like two teenagers while we sweated our asses off."

Both women giggled.

"Yeah, Nick thought it was a good idea to go to the zoo in July and walk down into that giant bowl of hot air and prowl around the animal cages all day. The weird thing was that Josh was with us. In my dream, he was the kid Josh, you know, with that big goofy smile."

"You know if Josh had not done what he did, his sacrifice, we wouldn't be here having this conversation. No one would have *any* conversations."

"I know, it's just…."

Tabby took a sip of her coffee as Kiera twisted a strand of hair around her finger and seemed to drift off to somewhere where she and Nick were back at the zoo, holding hands and watching the apes lounge around or the lions roar.

"So hey, how's Ethan doing in his new gig? Didn't he start this past Monday?"

"He hasn't said much about it, but he seems to be settling in. You know Ethan. Nose down and grinding away. It's all he seems to know how to do. You know, Gerald is lucky he only got fired instead of prison."

"Well, serves him right. That's what you get when you overbill your clients so you can pocket the money. I can't believe he thought he could get away with it."

"How's his back?"

"He has not had to go to the chiropractor in over a month now. I think he's finally getting everything lined back up. Yeah, nothing like getting tossed into a tree to give you a reason to become best friends with a chiropractor."

As the two women giggled, a wide-eyed toddler came wobbling over. He reached a chubby-fingered hand up and gifted Tabby his pacifier and a smile. He then went around to Kiera's side of the table and worked at pulling a chair from underneath the table beside his mother.

"Hey, baby," Kiera said, turning to assist the little guy with the chair. The little boy climbed into the chair as she rubbed his dark hair and said, "You still momma's little man?" She wiggled his nose with her thumb and forefinger, which made the toddler laugh.

"How has *he* been?" Tabby asked, motioning to the toddler with her cup.

"You know Nicholas. He seems to always have a smile on his face and a giggle in his mouth."

"Still hasn't said anything yet?"

"No, but the doctor says his hearing is fine, and there should be no reason, physically, why he doesn't speak. They said his motor development doesn't seem to be impeded either. They keep telling me there is no reason he won't speak, so just keep working with him."

Just then, the toddler looked up at his mother and asked, "Cookie?" then followed the request up with an ear-to-ear smile.

"Oh my god," Kiera exclaimed. "Nick, say that again."

To which the child responded, "Cookie?"

Tabby looked at Kiera, who was wiping tears from her cheeks as she laughed and smothered the toddler in kisses.

"Oh damn, straight," Tabby said. "This little boy gonna get all the cookies he wants today," then she got up and walked over to the pantry.

Kiera rubbed the sides of Nick's dark hair and leaned in to kiss him on his forehead as Tabby sat back down at the table with a pack of chocolate chip cookies.

At the sight of the cookies, Nick began to bounce up and down in the chair as he reached for the package.

"Hold on, baby, let me get you a couple," but as Kiera reached for the package of cookies, it slid across the table as if someone had slung it at the toddler, stopping when it reached his tiny hands. He looked at his mother, gave her a giant smile, and said, "Cookie."

Tabby and Kiera looked at one another. Neither woman breathed for a moment.

Then Tabby slowly asked, "Did he just…."

Kiera nodded.

Connect with the author

Twitter
OfficialLuthi

Instagram
officialjamesluthi

Facebook
James Luthi